J, Jolo

To Geraint, Maria & Jorge

I, Jolo

Gareth Thomas

First impression: 2018
© Gareth Thomas & Y Lolfa Cyf., 2018

Cover design: Tanwen Haf
Cover picture / illustration: Robert Cruickshank

ISBN: 978 1 78461 451 5

The publishers wish to acknowledge the support of
Cyngor Llyfrau Cymru

Published and printed in Wales
on paper from well-maintained forests by
Y Lolfa Cyf., Talybont, Ceredigion SY24 5HE
e-mail ylolfa@ylolfa.com
website www.ylolfa.com
tel 01970 832 304
fax 832 782

This book

THIS BOOK IS a creative dramatisation of the life of Iolo Morganwg from his adolescence until the Glynogwr *Gorsedd* in 1798. The events in the story are true. Information has been drawn from his letters and from the scholarly research of others.

However, this is not a history book, nor an academic biography. In the interests of establishing a readable narrative, the order of some events has been altered, a number of imaginary characters have been introduced and some historical characters have had their roles extended. The words and the details of scenes are for the most part imaginative conjecture although the publication of his letters has enabled me to use Iolo's own language on many occasions.

If the book excites your interest in the work of this unique man, then I would urge you to explore the riches offered by the professional historians listed in the bibliography.

GT

Gorsedd Glynogwr 1798

'WHATEVER THEY DO, do not retaliate. No violence of any sort. That's exactly what they want. Stay calm.'

I put my hand on Ifor Bardd Glas' shoulder. He is a young poet, able, deeply passionate and currently furious. I repeat myself:

'If one of us was to offer violence or was seen to threaten violence of any sort, even a gesture, then they will use it as an excuse to start arresting people.'

I make him look in my eyes.

'Ifor, do you understand?'

He mumbles reluctant agreement. I do not know if I can trust his temper. He is due to be made a full bard in today's ceremony. I tell him to concentrate on the ode he will have to recite and ignore the officers.

I look up over his shoulder at the place where we are gathered. I have prepared a *Gorsedd* circle on the side of a mountain to the south of the river. A group of twenty of us stand ready to process up the rough ground for the start of the ceremony. Surrounding the circle stand a ring of special constables in uniform, bearing truncheons. Alongside them stands a large delegation of the Cowbridge Volunteers carrying muskets and pikes. In front of both and closest to us I see important-looking men in tall hats, the magistrates. I recognise several. I count nine, ten... maybe more. All in all, constables, volunteers and magistrates, they outnumber us by about three to one. They stand between us and the circle of stones ensuring a confrontation if we continue forward as planned. I do not want confrontation. This place is remote. Were one of them to strike to maim or even kill, who would believe our version of the story? I ask Ceithiog, who carries the symbolic sword, to sheath it before we process, against our usual practice.

I look at Gwilym Glynogwr who is an old man – older than I. He looks small and frail in his worn jacket with a blue ribbon fluttering on his arm. Is it fair to expect him to do this? Is it selfish of me? Before the mass intimidation of the authorities fuels any more doubts in the minds of my fellow bards, I give the order to walk.

As we progress up the mountain two of the magistrates move down to meet us. They place themselves directly in our path. One of them I know as Walter Lloyd, a local farmer full of his own self-importance. He holds up a hand and we halt. He and I have had dealings before.

'Edward Williams. As a Justice of the Peace I am here to ensure that the law of the land is being upheld. I would remind you of the restrictions imposed on all His Majesty's loyal subjects by the Seditious Meetings Act 1795.'

I am prepared for this.

'I am aware of the legislation and do not believe we are offending against it. It restricts the size of any gathering to fifty or less. As you can see we are well below that number. If anybody offends against the Act it would be your gathering of constables which I suspect numbers more than the Act allows.'

He looks at me as if at a louse.

'You have no licence. A licence is required from the magistrates.'

If pomposity won wars, this man would be an emperor.

I answer calmly, 'Yes of course, for meetings in halls where a charge is made or policy discussed. We are meeting on the open hillside free to the view of any man. We meet to pray, to praise God, to initiate new members of our order and to recite poetry. None of these acts require a licence.'

'I have reason to suspect you of treasonous practices.'

'In which case, you should present your evidence. I have been examined on this subject by better men than you Mr Lloyd, including the Prime Minister himself. If you believe you can do better than he, then arrest me. Otherwise, step aside and allow us to proceed peacefully.'

Walter Lloyd hesitates, then steps aside cursing me under his breath. As we pass he shouts, 'We know you of old, Edward Williams; son of an honest tradesman and a mother of good family. How did you end up staging these… pantomimes?'

It had been a gloomy day but the sun comes out from behind a cloud as we continue up the mountain. The magistrate asks a good question.

Part One:
1760 to 1773

1

Good with words

I AM KISSING Peggy Roberts in the lane by the church. She kisses passionately, better than Gwen Rees. Gwen lets me kiss her but she remains stiff and unresponsive, whereas there's a sensuality to Peggy. She responds with fervour. I squeeze her breast and pull her tighter against me. She wraps her arms round my neck. I can feel her body wanting more but instead she looks to her right and pushes me away protesting,

'Stop Ned, what if someone was to see us?'

I tell her that, hidden behind this yew tree, we are well away from the crowd, but she is not convinced.

'My Mam and Tada are just round the corner talking to the rector outside the church. If they were to come down this lane...'

'Why would they?'

'Looking for me, that's what!'

I pull her to me and kiss her again, holding her firmly in my arms whilst she pretends to struggle. We kiss more passionately than the last time before she pulls away again, laughing and smiling and giggling with pleasure.

'Ned, I mean it. My Mam already thinks that you're a wild one.'

'Why? What does she say?'

Peggy pauses, looking up at me, playing the personification of maidenly virtue.

'That you're too full of words, and too ready with the charm as can turn a young girl's head – here today, gone tomorrow. The sort who will take advantage of a poor girl's innocence. Promise the world, but off like a hare when you're asked to live up to your promises.'

'Do you believe that?'

She pretends to think hard. 'Not sure.' This answer is coy and coquettish at the same time.

'She doesn't like the poems you write me.'

'You showed them to her?!'

'Of course! I tell my Mam everything, like a good girl should. Well nearly everything.' Her eyes flame with naughtiness, teasing with every word and every look.

'And what did she find wrong with my poem?'

'Well, we all had problems finding out who Aphrodite was.'

'Greek goddess of beauty.'

'I know that now. Felicity told me. Then there was the line '*Agorid y wawr ar ei grudd*'.[1] What does that mean? That I'm red and blotchy like a rough farm girl?'

I try to kiss her again but she ducks away and starts to walk down the lane. I follow as if on a lead.

'My Mam's biggest complaint wasn't what was *in* the poem. She thinks that writing poetry to a girl is a sure sign that the boy's not to be trusted… of a young man with sin on his mind.'

'How does she know what's on my mind?'

'Oh, I think she was a girl once and I have my suspicions she wasn't always as good a girl as she would have me believe. Or else why would she keep warning me against the dangers of wild young men?'

'I didn't write that poem to your mother!'

'I should hope not.'

She thinks for a moment and with a mischievous grin adds, 'but who did you write it for – originally?'

---

1   The dawn rises on her blush.

I panic slightly. It's important to remember that girls do talk to each other. I act outraged.

'Peggy. How could you? That's cruel.'

'What about Gwen Rees? She carried a love poem of yours around for ages. We all had to listen to it over and over.'

'A piece of doggerel. Nothing like the poem I wrote to you.'

She stops, slips her arms round my neck and looks me in the eyes. 'Well I don't know if I'm making a big mistake having anything to do with you, Edward Williams.'

I whisper to her, 'Why ever not? I'm a good catch I'd say – a skilled tradesman – and…

Doubt thou the stars are fire,

Doubt that the sun doth move,

Doubt truth to be a liar,

But never doubt I love.'

She looks impressed. 'Did you write that?'

'No, that's Shakespeare. *Hamlet.*'

She shakes her head in disbelief. 'That's typical. No one ever knows if you are being you or someone else half the time. Who are you now? Do *you* know yourself?'

'Probably not.'

2

Carving the letters

I AM CAREFULLY inspecting the 'B' I've just carved on the tombstone in front of me. 'Bs' can be tricky but this one is as good as any my father has carved. I move my chisel along to start the next letter – an 'O' – I like doing 'Os'. They are quite perfect. There is something profound in their simplicity. They leave no room for error.

I am aware of my father's steps behind me. He is walking across the small yard to inspect my work. Once, this would have caused apprehension or even fear. He is quick to anger. If my work or any of my brothers' work is below standard or if one of us has ruined a valuable piece of finished stone by mistake, he is liable to launch into a torrent of abuse and a rain of blows. Not any longer. I'm seventeen, and I know that my cut letters are as good as my father's – and my 'Os' are probably better. I wonder, for the umpteenth time, why he, a farmer's son, ever chose to become a stonemason. It is no occupation for anyone lacking patience. It is slow work which cannot be rushed. The mallet has to strike the chisel squarely and with just the right amount of force each and every time. To become impatient and to strike too hard can destroy a day's work in a second.

He is standing behind me, silent. That means that he is satisfied with the emerging memorial. Displeasure would be quickly expressed. Sometimes I enjoy this reversal of roles. As a boy I spent many hours standing just behind my father's shoulder watching his chisel as he inscribed each letter. Now he watches me. I've always been fascinated by the letters and how to form them. Father taught all of us, John, Miles, Thomas and I how to cut, shape and dress stone. Every day we visit the large houses of the Vale replacing crumbling masonry with good new stone, plastering, lime washing or whatever building work is needed. It keeps bread on the table. But I was the only one to really master the advanced skills of the mason's craft: the shaping of stone. I can take a block of limestone and chamfer the edges or work detailed mouldings and decoration. For me, the summit of the craft is this cutting of fine letters. It's important work for us as a family. It pays well. Only wealthy landowners or prosperous merchants can afford to have their graves marked in this way, so the work is not commonplace.

When we were younger, the price to be paid in father's fury – if a mistake occurred – made lettering a task best avoided. When I chose to make letter carving my specialism, my brothers were all very content for me to put myself at risk. I was the eldest. That status came with privileges and certain penalties. I take first place in most things. They accept but still resent the fact.

I adjust the low stool I use as I inscribe the name and dates of a George Bowen Esq. of Eglwys Brewis who has died aged fifty-five. I have no idea who the man was apart from the fact that he was sufficiently moneyed and important for his existence to be memorialised in the best Glamorgan limestone. This monument in the churchyard will preserve his memory longer than that of common souls whose immortality is limited to the failing memories of their contemporaries. If common people are remembered at all it is because their memorable act or kind deed has earned a place in another's memory. Does George Bowen Esq. deserve to be remembered beyond living memory? If so, for what? How futile to believe that one can cheat death by inscribing names and dates on cold stone. If a man wants immortality then surely it is necessary to carve the memory of your actions into the face of the world of which you are part.

'Good work,' remarks a voice from behind me. I am astonished. Praise is not usually in my father's lexicon.

'Who was he?' I ask.

'Does it matter? Think of him as three guineas' worth of monument.'

'What did he do?'

'Fell off his horse whilst hunting. Probably drank too much before setting out and broke his neck as a result.'

'No. What did he do to be worth a proper monument like this?'

By now Thomas and Miles have drifted over from their side of the yard to inspect my work and take advantage of an opportunity for a break.

'Very fine, Ned,' agrees Thomas, approving with the eye of a fellow mason the chamfering of the edges and the simple carved leaves surrounding the name and dates.

'No verses though,' objects Miles. 'The *crach*[2] usually like to have a few lines of verse on a monument. Sort of finishes it off, I think.'

'The family did not mention a verse,' observes father dryly.

I look at the space below the name and suggest, 'I can always write one for them.'

'Go on,' urges Thomas with a note of anticipation in his voice. This is my cue. They like me to delight and entertain with rhymes. I know I can always win popularity amongst the boys by composing bawdy songs and disrespectful verses. I clear my throat.

'There was in heaven but little remorse
When George the fat fell off his horse.'

_____

2 Posh.

18

The boys laugh in delight, expecting and awaiting more. Father shifts uncomfortably but I ignore him. Words are searching for rhyming partners in my head. I turn to my small audience. I stand.

'Immortalised in stone the name
Of one unworthy of such fame.'
There is more laughter from my brothers.

'That's enough,' says my father quietly. I hear him but the noise of the rhyming machinery in my skull means I take no notice of a warning I should heed.

'With stone we mark this hallowed spot
Where a tub of lard was placed to rot.'

'I said, that's enough!' This time father is shouting. I turn to face him and there is real anger in his eyes. No laughter. We all stand silent as he rages, 'Your quick tongue will be the ruin of all of us one day. So clever of you to spread silly rhymes about the very people who give the work that puts bread in our mouths. What if word was to get about that when you pay good money to Edward Williams for a monument you get the added bonus of having your dear departed ridiculed and mocked by the very people you have paid to honour their memory! We would be ruined.'

I try to speak. I want to point out that it was father who had speculated that the late George Bowen had fallen off his horse whilst drunk. I think it fair to add that this was only a private joke amongst family, but I do not. Father is shaking with rage and his flow of angry words shows no sign of faltering. I know the signs well. To argue or reason with him now would only be to incite even greater anger. I feel sick with the injustice of it.

In the coldness of defeat I despise myself for succumbing to the temptation to seek cheap and easy applause. My mother taught me how to versify – how to write sonnets; how to create verse in the traditions of the greatest Welsh and English poets.

What do I do with the skill? Like a cheap balladmonger shout whatever doggerel will win the applause of whatever audience is available.

3

Ann Matthew

'BETTER TO REIGN in Hell, than serve in Heaven.'
I am Satan, the grandest of the angels, a fallen God,
my arms outstretched defying the authority of Heaven. I see my
shadow projected by the fire flames on the cottage wall. Milton's
verse causes sparks to flash in the grate, the wind to howl louder
and the oil lamp to burn brighter. I feel the blood throbbing
in my veins. I feel my chest swell with passion as I lead the
rebellious cohorts of fallen angels.

I end. My arms drop to my sides and I move back to my stool
beside my mother. My younger brothers, John and Thomas,
applaud. They are always attentive and receptive, partly I think
because they are so much younger than I. Miles, the brother
closest to me in age, does not. He resents what he sometimes
complains of as 'Ned showing off'. He also resents that I am
Mother's favourite although he never says that out loud.

My father tries to dampen the excitement by tediously
pointing out that the poem describes the fall of Satan and that
we should all be on our guard against the mortal sins of pride
and disobedience. He forgets that charismatic Satan has all the
best lines. The rebellion of fallen angels is far more exciting
than heavenly accord, however righteous. I had no thought of
moral improvement as I declaimed demonically. I'm certain
my father disapproves of these recitations but cannot say so
as they are requested by my mother and selected by her from
her small library. It is thanks to Mother that we can all read,

at least to some degree but, as with carving letters, I came to it first and am the best. I understand more than my brothers and enjoy performing more than them. My favourite, on dark winter nights such as this, is the rebellion of Satan from *Paradise Lost*.

My mother is of noble blood and, as a girl, was taught to read and write and acquired the skills appropriate to a woman of privilege. I watch her as she smiles with pleasure and praises my efforts. Now she is looking into the fire. I watch the line of her jaw and neck as she talks. Her skin is so pale and her neck so thin and fine. Her eyebrows arch and move as two fine black songbirds. Her hair falls in fine tresses tinted orange by the firelight. There is refinement and sensitivity in everything she does.

There is silence now. I think there is nothing I can say that would not annoy Miles. Winter forces our confinement in each other's company and the tensions in the family intensify. John and Thomas are bored, trying to play a game they have devised with small stones. My father snoozes. My mother turns the pages of her book. I would love to talk to her now about poetry, about her upbringing, about her father, Edward, after whom I am named. I want her to talk of their house and farm with its servants and gardens and horses. I want her to talk of her family's houses in Llandaff and Radyr and the noble pedigree of the Matthew line back to the golden age of Welsh princes. I do not prompt her and she does not venture. She and I both understand that our closeness is resented by Miles and more so by my father. He does not like to be reminded that he has been fortunate to marry so refined a gentlewoman. Further, he does not share or understand our passion for literature. My mother catches my eye and smiles at me only. It is a smile of conspiracy. We will not let others intrude on our secret garden of thoughts and sentiments. That will have to wait for warmer seasons.

Miles annoyingly is distancing himself from his family by

whittling wood with a sharp penknife. He carves the pieces into the form of boats; small, large and fantastic. By the time spring arrives he will have assembled an armada.

**

As the seasons turn, the evenings lengthen and the earth warms. Then we cease to be bound to the cottage but are free to explore the lanes, fields and woods around Flemingston. I believe I know every inch of the countryside around.

Even so, I frequently let the others wander off by themselves, or make some excuse so that I may be alone with my mother around the now-cold hearth. These are special occasions for us both. She teaches me everything she knows and she knows a great deal. This is when she can tell me of her family. I have heard her story many times before but never tire. She tells of her mother's death from consumption when she herself was only a child of nine, of her father's emotional collapse and financial ruin... of how she had been rescued from destitution by her dead mother's sister and taken to live in the manor house at Boverton Place where she had been raised as a gentlewoman and taught the skills appropriate to such refinement. She tells of her grandfather's love of poetry and the family sponsorship of itinerant bards who would call at their house, Ty'n Caeau in Coychurch, to be feasted and housed with honour in the old Welsh style in return for a composition in praise of the master of the house. These noble poets, she insists, had been taught their ancient craft not from books, but by listening and learning from older skilled poets in the Welsh oral tradition. She tells me that I will learn this craft, that I will join this elite.

Today she is coughing again. In between her excursions back to a greater past she coughs so violently that her thin body is shaken as if by invisible demonic forces. Her frailty makes her all the more precious in my eyes. She is a fine and delicate thing, too sensitive for the cruel trials of this world. I try all I can to make her stronger. Together we pour over books of ancient cures: the *Prescriptions of the Physicians of Myddfai* and *The Vanities of Philosophy & Physick*. As a result of the knowledge gained she has confined herself to a special diet of baked apples and goat's milk. I collect herbs and prepare infusions according to her instructions. Now that they are in flower she has asked me to collect hyssop and red fennel, an ancient remedy of the Physicians of Myddfai, guaranteed to strengthen the lungs. I watch as she drinks with care and solemnity, as if at Communion. Sometimes I play my flute to her. It was a present she gave and taught me to play. Now I can repay her with music to still her pain.

If there is enough I drink the remaining infusion myself. I have inherited my mother's sensibility and, with it, some of her frailty. On mornings when the damp mist hangs over the Vale I am troubled by asthma which causes me to wheeze and gasp for air. My brothers do not suffer the same ailment nor do they understand. They observe with mute hostility whilst I boil thistles with nettles and marchalan or grind the roots of marrow to a fine powder. They think this to be a mere affectation.

4

Mabsant[3]

I AM CROUCHED like a greyhound waiting for the start. Four of us are poised in the middle of the floor of the public room of the Bush Inn, balanced and alert, every sinew tense and ready. Alongside me three other dancers, Dafydd Tŷ Canol, Gwilym Village Farm, and the young parson, similarly tensed, similarly waiting for Tom Lewis the fiddler to strike up the first chord and begin the dancing. We are the first of the night, the young steppers waiting to demonstrate that we are the fastest, fittest, most skilful dancers of this or any village.

Around the edges of the room, villagers of St Hilary, young and old, peer out of the gloom. There's a cluster of new arrivals looking noisily for seats. There is a delay whilst more candles are lit. I am aching to start but Tom Lewis is in no hurry. He leans over to William Morgan, his harpist, and they agree something. Another delay whilst the landlord brings beer for the players. William Morgan raises his tankard in thanks, places it on the bench beside him and, at last, Tom Lewis gives the nod.

Tom plays a short intro before they both plunge into a fast and insistent jig to which we step as fast as our feet can move. The tune repeats. I repeat the sequence but this time with flourishes of my own devising. Out of the corner of my eye I glimpse

---

3   These were village festivals set aside to celebrate whatever saint had given their
     name to whatever village or church. The local vicar would give a fine sermon at
     Sunday morning service before the sports, entertainment and feasting began. The
     dancing would follow in the tavern or the barn of an accommodating farmer and
     last long into the night.

Gwilym jumping high, his arms easily touching the ceiling. The young parson goes one better, clasping his hands behind each leg on each step which earns applause from the watchers. Still dancing, I lower myself almost to the floor and rest on one hand whilst still performing the jig, kicking up towards the ceiling. The watchers clap and cheer. I am back on my feet and enjoying the applause. Now the musicians are quickening the pace, each repetition forcing us to speed up till our legs move by themselves, driven by demons. The noise of our clogs on the floor fills the room. Blood is pumping and pulsing in my temples. My lungs ache. I am fighting for breath but I cannot stop. The audience are cheering. I see nothing but a blur. Surely the music cannot be played faster without scorching the strings. It doubles in speed, now it trebles, now it quadruples whilst the cries, claps, sobs, wails, howls, cheers and tears of excitement and pleasure break over us in waves.

At last, with a final grand set of chords, Tom and William announce a very definite end. I collapse in triumphant exhaustion, sweating like a young stallion. Miles comes over and helps me up. His face is flushed and happy. He slaps me on the back and puts a pot of ale in my hand.

'That was great Ned, just great!'

I embrace him in gratitude. There are so few occasions when I feel at one with my brothers but dancing is one of them. Tensions with Miles and the others are eased when there are entertainments we can all enjoy, but there are few amusements for us in Flemingston and a high proportion of what is available is forbidden as corrupting or ungodly.

Top of the list of prohibited activities is the horse racing on Bryn Owain. Just as forbidden is the cock-fighting at St Donats and the bull baiting held at Llantrisant. Unsurprisingly, public executions are not viewed by my mother as 'entertainment', despite their popularity. Neither does she allow gambling with cards or dice. *Bando*[4] *is* permitted if not actually encouraged, as my father was a keen player in his youth. But there is one entertainment of which both our parents approve. Dancing they view as a recreation everyone can enjoy, and in which few, except the Calvinists, see harm. Dancing is exciting, enjoyable, cheap, and I am a champion.

I receive much praise. Admiration is unbounded for the skills of the musicians, particularly Tom Lewis.

'The finest fiddler in Glamorgan – bar none,' asserts the young parson.

One of the other dancers agrees. 'To my mind, it's not enough for a fiddler just to play well and know all the old tunes. What's rare about Tom is the way he "plays" the mood of the gathering.' Tom can change the mood of a *mabsant* dance in a second from a sad air to jaunty jig, from sweet tune to a frenzied caper.

Next comes the 'reel', danced by four couples. Their skill is exceptional and much applauded, but in truth this is only an appetiser. The couples are married. Joyful though their dancing might be, it lacks the spice of the main course to follow, the 'country dances'. Here, single maids and eligible boys are brought together, without accusation of forwardness, into the close partnership of the dance.

There is a murmur of excitement from the doorway. The girls appear. Peggy looks wonderful, shapely and elegant. She has a new dress which I know she has been making for weeks, although it's meant to be a secret. It's a blue cotton print with small white flowers, trimmed with lace. Her hair is in ringlets and decorated with ribbon. Millicent is alongside her and behind them come several other maidens from surrounding

---

4   A traditional game not unlike hockey but played by teams of twenty or thirty players representing villages. The *bando* sticks were made of ash or elm. Rules were flexible and games frequently violent.

villages. I wonder how long they have been loitering in the dark of the churchyard waiting their moment.

They try to look unconcerned, unaware of admiring eyes following them. Tom plays a sliding glissando in lieu of a fanfare. Peggy acknowledges the tribute with a nod. Two of the other girls giggle, which spoils the moment a little. We form up in lines, boys facing girls for the first 'country dance'. The steps are second nature, practised since childhood. We follow the patterns, rapidly exchanging partners, the girls whirl just beyond our grasp. There is much stamping, more clapping, many cries and mighty laughter.

The dancing gathers pace, the heat of the room increases, the cries and shrieks multiply and the supply of beer to the musicians flows. I step and prance and clap like a man possessed. I glimpse Peggy swirling gracefully somewhere across the room. Now, Tom starts to use his most devilishly manipulative device, the salute! In the middle of a dance, for no reason other than a whim, he nods to William. The music stops. Thomas plays a chord of astonishing resonance whilst William runs his fingers rapidly across the strings of his harp. The boys salute their partners and the girls respond with deep curtseys, demure smiles or a flirtatious flash of eyelids.

If only this could last for eternity.

5

Hendre Ifan Goch

I AM WALKING. This is unremarkable. My brothers and I walk long distances most days. As father often reminds us, stonemasonry is an itinerant profession. Whereas a smith or a miller may prosper by serving only those who live within a few miles of the smithy or mill, a stonemason has to serve a larger area. Unless he lives in a city of large monuments and noble houses such as Bristol or London, a mason has to travel to his clients. Robert Jones of Fonmon and the Edwins of Llanmihangel are the families of the Vale who were currently making significant alterations to their country houses and neither is particularly close to Flemingston. Robert Jones has for some years been improving his inherited estate by remodelling the exterior with crenulated walls and adding a folly watchtower. My father's handiwork features prominently. We own two small ponies but these are seldom ridden. Their purpose is to transport stone and memorial tablets in panniers. We walk alongside.

Even though we all think little of walking distances, I walk the furthest. It gives me great pleasure. I feel more alive, more alert and at one with the miracle of the world about me. I often cover thirty miles or more in a day without feeling tired. This morning I must already have walked ten miles but not, this time, in the direction of Fonmon. I am walking north of Cowbridge through Pontyclun and up into Y Blaenau, the uplands of Glamorgan. These areas are harsher, less fertile lands, but breathtakingly magnificent. I feel a thrill as the verdant slopes give way to steeper climbs and rocky outcrops, as the gentle streams turn into singing mountain torrents and tinkling waterfalls. Walking energises me.

I am on a poetic mission at my mother's suggestion. She was cross with me after yet another row with Father. Her annoyance is less to do with family cohesion and more to do with disapproval of my composing doggerel verses. These she perceived to be an abasement of my talent. She is, of course, right. She has given me a poetic gift which deserves respect.

I am heading towards Llandyfodwg where I will spend most of the day being instructed by one of her old acquaintances, Lewis Hopkin. As I approach the whitewashed cottage, Lewis is standing on the doorstep enjoying the sun. His ample frame fills the doorway and his broad red cheeked smile radiates welcome. '*Dere 'ngwas i*. Come in my boy, and welcome.'

He gestures me to a chair at the oak table he has made. Lewis has made almost everything in sight. He built his house, glazed the windows, thatched the roof, made the furniture and stacked the shelves with his own books. He is the master of many crafts. Now he makes and pours tea with a similar meticulous pride in technique.

I place before him the poems I have brought. Lewis reads them aloud because, as he explains to me, the sound is all important. He uses his skill as a bard of the old tradition to analyse my work. He had already taught me how to construct lines of *cynghanedd*[5] in the manner of the traditional bards; how to create the 'chime' effect by the repetition of consonants, how to 'balance' a line, where the stress must lie and what is permitted within the rules of the old tradition. When he has finished with my pages, Lewis goes over to his surprisingly large library of old books, mostly handwritten, and manuscripts. He

---

5   Traditional Welsh-language strict-metre poetic form.

chooses one of his favourite poets for us to read and analyse, often a copy of a poem by Dafydd ap Gwilym, the greatest master of the tradition.

'Remember my boy, poetry is a great craft – but a craft it is! Never believe those modern writers who talk of muse and inspiration. *Barddas*, the creation of great strict-metre poetry, has to be taught and has to be learned in the same way that you would learn any craft. When you learnt to cut letters in stone did you do it through impulse or inspiration? Did you just get up one morning when the sun was shining, take a chisel and carve because of the beauty of the morning? Or did you learn the skill from your father by watching and imitating and copying until you mastered the craft? Then and only then do you have the right to let your own feelings and emotions guide your composition. Only then can you let your own verve and ingenuity shape your lines.'

More tea is poured. The brew has strengthened.

'Your mother came from a highborn family but she understands better than most that it's not wealth and idleness that makes for nobility. It is not the landowner who builds his great house but the mason. It is not the nobleman who furnishes his castle but the joiner. It is not the fat English bishops who save souls, but the Lord who sent his son to be a carpenter, a craftsman. Craft has to be taught and passed on from person to person. It cannot just be taken from a book. It requires the intense joining of minds it has been my privilege to experience today.'

Lewis explains that his son, whilst a good man and a hard worker, has never been able to master the poetic craft. He tells me that I could be an heir to the tradition if I work hard at it. 'Come here as often as you want, *fy ngwas i*. I'm an old man now and I don't have much longer to live. The more I can teach you before I go, the more restful will be my eternity.'

I walk home with a sense of privilege. I have in my bag, not just my own work but two very old and fragile manuscripts presented to me as gifts. I am instructed to read, study, analyse and copy the techniques used. These are priceless. They are so much more than a means of improving my own skills. They are a small part of a heritage of literature that, scattered as it is amongst cottages and private collections throughout Wales, could so easily be lost forever without anyone even knowing. I will copy them twice. If there were two copies they will be at least twice as safe. I ponder on the new printing shop that has opened in Cowbridge. I have stood outside that shop, marvelling at the sight of the big black machine, all rollers and wheels and iron levers. That is the way to make ancient manuscripts safe: to print tens, maybe hundreds of copies so that every man might have their own collection.

Walking makes for good thinking time. I turn over in my head Lewis' antagonism towards the Established Church and the overweight, pompous ungodly English bishops who run it. Lewis' idea of the truer nobility of craftsmen over those with mere wealth appeals greatly to me. In my mother I can behold the dignity of thought and nobility of expression which transcends poverty. I also see how the bardic tradition is not just about how to write poetry. It has implicit within it the values of an older, wiser, more Welsh and more just civilisation. My head spins. My blood boils.

6

An apparition

COWBRIDGE IS BOTH entertaining and exciting. Its inns provide good beer and high spirits. But there is more. From the taproom of the Bear I sometimes watch the coaches arriving with mail and visitors from Bristol, Cardiff, and London, then changing horses before whisking travellers onwards to the west or north. My curiosity and wanderlust are stimulated by the idea that there is a new world beyond the Vale available to any with the courage and energy to explore it.

Cowbridge is our window on a wider world. I prefer to go to town on a fair or market day when the world's window opens a little wider. Ordinary market days are on Tuesdays when the shops in the high street have to battle with livestock sales for customers. More interesting are the big fairs which happen two or three times a year. Then the whole world seems to visit. Miles and I are in Cowbridge for the March fair which is the biggest of all. The streets between Westgate and Eastgate are crowded with farmers buying and selling animals, farmers' wives and girls selling produce such as eggs, cheeses, butter, hams and fine stockings knitted from the wool of Glamorgan sheep. We also have entertainers, jugglers, hurdy-gurdy players, traders, dealers of every sort and preachers. A Calvinist has set up a stand near the Cross from where he rails against drink, loose women, cockfighting, horse racing, dancing – all things that will be available somewhere close by this week.

We are struggling with the load of *bando* sticks we have made to sell. Fairs are great fun – provided you have money to spend on beer. The plan is simple: to sell the sticks as soon as possible and spend the proceeds on enjoying ourselves through the rest of the day and evening with Peggy and Millicent. There will be dancing in the Assembly Rooms at the Spread Eagle, providing we can earn enough money for the entrance. We have problems finding a spot to sell from as all the best places have already been occupied, but eventually we squeeze ourselves in between a seller of inferior quality lace and a purveyor of a tonic which promises to restore health, hair or virility – whichever is most needed by the buyer.

Our sticks are of good quality but we will have to work hard to be noticed amongst the hubbub of competing hawkers. I stand on a box to give myself more height before announcing the availability of the 'finest *bando* sticks, shaped by craftsmen from the best ash in the Vale'. No one takes any notice. I need to turn on a performance which cannot be ignored – and I do! Something seems to click inside when I have an audience. I don't plan it but I can't help wanting to entertain, to command my spectators. I love the feeling when I draw and hold attention. I know how to use voice, gesticulations, energy and wit to do so. I feel as if a different Ned has taken over. Without an audience I am a serious sober person, but here I am – not for the first time – playing the extrovert jester who craves attention and applause.

I compose couplets in praise of our sticks and attribute magical powers to anyone who wields one. As faces turn towards me I see the crowd as a preacher might – from a high vantage point with faces pointed upwards, seemingly unaware of how their expressions reveal so much of their inner character. It is as if their attention puts them in my power. I recognise people in the crowd and compose doggerel verses in their honour to encourage them to buy. People laugh. Miles takes money for the sticks. One man turns away. A less flattering verse follows him and more laughter. I can see Peggy and Millicent at the back of the crowd, watching and giggling. Both are dressed in their finest frocks with straw bonnets trimmed with ribbon. I perform for them. I wave to them and they wave back. The crowd are demanding more verse, preferably scurrilous. I see that William Richards, big bellied landlord of the Horse and Groom, has come out onto his doorstep to listen. He is soon honoured.

There's Richard of the Horse and Groom
(Remember what I tell ye),
You'll hardly in his house find room
So monstrous is his belly.

The crowd laugh and Richard shouts, 'Someone buy that boy's blessed sticks so as we can all have a bit of peace.'

'How about you buying one first?' shouts a voice.

'Don't mind if I do,' roars the landlord. 'Not that I play any more but it might be useful in keeping order on a day like this.'

Miles is doing a fine trade. Eventually the last stick is sold. I am on the point of jumping down from my box when I am struck dumb by a glimpse of angelic perfection! I am transfixed, awed and inspired by the vision. Across the road there has appeared out of the doorway of the Horse and Groom the most exquisite of young female forms, dressed in a light blue tailored gown and bustle with a fine silk covered bonnet. But it is her face which captivates me, alive and alert eyes set either side of a small snub nose in a delicately sculptured face; self-evidently the face of a creature of sensitivity, beauty and intelligence. The apparition is being shepherded by a prosperous well-dressed middle-aged man, perhaps her father, closely followed by some nondescript man of the cloth.

'Who's she?' I demand of Miles who dutifully jumps onto the box to see. 'There, by the doorway to the tavern.'

'I'm pretty sure that's Mathew Deere, a businessman – owns several taverns and a number of shops.'

The girl is presumably his daughter? By now the crowd is moving away looking for fresh entertainment. Peggy and Millicent are edging towards us. I must have time. 'Quick,' I urge my brother, 'you talk to the girls. I've got to find out who that is.' I run to the door of the tavern. The Horse and Groom is the meeting place of the well-to-do men of the town who hire upstairs rooms for their own meetings and private dinners.

The landlord, Richard of the big belly, tells me, 'That's Kitty Deere, my boy. Mr Deere's niece and the apple of his eye. Not for the likes of you, I should think. High Sheriff of Glamorgan he is, and a fine gentleman. He'll be someone of standing who gets that girl to bed. Now buy a beer or get out of my way.'

If the landlord had wanted to inflame my passion or strengthen my determination to win the heart and hand of that high-class beauty, he could not have done more. I dart down the street following the direction the apparition and her uncle have taken. I glance in each shop and put my head round the doors of the coffee houses. No sign. They would not visit one of the low taverns such as the White Hart or the Three Tuns and it's far too early for them to be leaving the fair. They have to be on their way to some other amusement. The only other tavern – that would be acceptable to people of status – would be the Bear. I run down the street weaving around sellers, cattle, hawkers and vagrants. Then, to my joy and pity, I see her, Kitty Deere, as she steps, or rather glides, up the stairs and into the entrance hall of one of the fine mansions at the west end of the street. Her guardian and the accompanying minister of religion follow. The door closes firmly on my hopes.

I am still standing desolate in the middle of the street staring at the closed door of Caecady House when Miles and the two girls find me. They drag me away, with Peggy hanging onto my arm asking if I feel unwell. I say nothing. Whenever he thinks the girls will not notice, Miles makes imploring or threateningly furious faces at me. Miles was hoping to spend the afternoon and evening with Millicent and does not relish the prospect of having Peggy along as a chaperone. I wander round the fair with them, as I must. I dutifully go with them to the dancing in the Assembly Rooms but I cannot hide my distraction and lack of enthusiasm for the proceedings. Even the fact that Tom Lewis the fiddler will again lead the dance does not fire my interest.

As we walk home there is a bitter row. Miles calls me 'a pig-headed ass' for thinking that I was ever going to be able to introduce myself to the niece of Mathew Deere. He calls me 'selfish and self-centred' for spoiling what had promised to be a day and a night of high spirits and romance. He is right but I cannot help myself. I say nothing, for there is nothing to say. Eventually Miles runs out of words, but not out of anger.

The bad feeling continues the next day whilst we work. I try not to offend but Miles needs no additional provocation for a further explosion of temper. A small disagreement over who had failed to sharpen the bow saw leads to a fierce war of words. The only difference is this time I do not stay dumb but respond eloquently. Not for the first time Miles does not understand my meaning and assumes that I am using long words to make him look ignorant. His face is red. He clenches his fists and shouts at me.

'*Diawst!*[6] You may be the eldest of us but that doesn't make you some sort of prince! *Esu!*[7] You speak so much *rwtch*[8] out of your arse, but because you can do it in posh language everybody thinks you're so clever.'

---

6   Devil.
7   Esu is a short form of Iesu – Jesus.
8   Rubbish.

I can only laugh at him for being so feeble.

'You'd understand if you'd only spend a bit more time studying and a little less chasing girls who don't even like you. You've been trying to court Millicent for months now and I don't suppose you've even kissed her yet.'

The row grows. The floodgates open and torrents of pent-up feelings and resentments flow freely. Soon Miles is squaring up to me, feet planted, fists clenched and slightly raised as if working out where to hit first.

I warn, 'And don't think of fighting me. That would just show how pathetic are your arguments.'

'Just 'cos you're the eldest does not make you the cleverest.'

'No, but I am.'

'No you're not. You're just the bloody favourite. The spoilt *twpsyn*.[9] Mam's favourite who always gets the best of everything and thinks he's so bloody clever. Well, I've had enough.'

He swings at me but I'm too quick and he misses. I grab his arm and we fall onto the dusty ground wrestling and punching. Words have given way to blows and punches. My two younger brothers scream and shout. If they take sides it will be to back Miles. Father runs out of the house to restore order.

The damage is done.

---

9   Thickhead.

7

High designs

I SIT IN the same pew in the parish church as my brothers, but all my senses, my sensitivities, my bristling resentment place me in another world. In front of me and the congregation is displayed my Ark of the Covenant: the coffin containing my adored, sweet, noble, beautiful mother. I refuse the insinuation that my brothers and I are as one in being her sons. The produce of the same womb, the flesh of her flesh we may be, but the bonds between my mother and I transcend the mere physical, the animalistic, the crude carnal realities. My mother inspired me in so many ways to rise above the brutish and the everyday. She led me into a wondrous garden of fine perceptions and great literature, of noble expression and high resolve – and now she has abandoned me. She weaned me away from the simple delights of ordinary young men to appreciate and emulate those of aesthetic sensibility. She made me her dependant disciple – only to abandon me – now – so suddenly and so cruelly.

I feel rising panic as I look at the atrocity of the coffin. Whilst she had lived there was another to whom I could talk with in the language of sensitivity; we would read, write and think together. It is as if I have learnt a great classical language only to find that no one is left alive who can, or will, speak the words and glory in the thoughts it enshrines. My devastation and loneliness is now complete.

She died of consumption. In my eyes she had always been a beautiful frail creature, too pure for this world. When consumption took hold I had been forced to watch her form wither and the enchanting light of her soul dim. I sat at her bedside for days on end, afraid to sleep lest the absence of my childish urging should allow her to weaken further – or even depart. Others had tried to tear me away but without success. They had obscenely accused me of excessive or showy grief. How could they know the devastation I felt?

Even if I had not stayed at her side I would not have slept. My head echoed and still echoes with the majesty of the things she had taught me. I feel I may explode with the power and knowledge she has given me. How could I possibly forsake one second of the short time we still had together? At her bedside I read from our favourite books. In Welsh, I read the Bible and the poetry of Dafydd ap Gwilym. In English, Shakespeare's *Hamlet*, some Pope but particularly Milton. Our favourite was *Paradise Lost* where blood is stirred by the struggle for liberty. On our last night together she had asked me to read from *Paradise Regained*, and Satan's temptation of Christ in the wilderness. Even now the words of the sermon are drowned out by the words still hammering in my head.

All thy heart is set on high designs,
High actions, But wherewith to be achieved?
Great acts require great means of enterprise.

She means me to honour her, to fulfil her intentions for me, to set my heart on the highest of 'high designs'. But how?

Above us the Reverend John Walters looks down on our tribulations. His face is kindly. His voice is deep and comforting, but I do not hear his words. I remember he visited the deathbed several times during Mother's final days. He sought to comfort my father and my brothers after the death. I did not want to be comforted. I did not want any man to try to lessen the intensity of my grief. When the rector tried to do so, desperation forced me to choke, then to laugh, to laugh in a strangulated wild and uncontrolled screech which made birds fly from the trees.

8

The Reverend
John Walters

I HAVE RECEIVED a note from the Reverend John Walters. He 'would be pleased if I were to visit him at the rectory to take tea and discuss my future education'. What is this? I show it to my father who shifts awkwardly before confessing his part in this turn of events. He explains that the rector had spent time with him following the loss of his wife, my mother. The conversations had ranged widely.

'I told him that I was worried about you, my eldest son, being as how you were so very close to your mother and how she had taught you to read and write and understand poetry and the like. He offered to help, suggested that he might have a word with you and perhaps give you some direction in your studies now that your mother is no longer here.'

It is meant kindly, particularly as I know how father sees my studies as a waste of time and Mother's instruction of no help in putting food on our table. I do not reply to the invitation for some days. I do not want to do anything that might dishonour my mother's memory or cut across the proper period of grief. But, in my case, the grief will last a lifetime. I think of Milton's words she put in my head as she was dying:

All thy heart is set on high designs,
High actions, But wherewith to be achieved?
Great acts require great means of enterprise.

How indeed, without the 'great means of enterprise'? Mother would have wanted me to seize any opportunity that presented itself. Perhaps this is one.

***

'Do come in. Edward, isn't it?'

I nod in answer to the tall woman before me. I remember Mrs Walters from the day of the funeral service. Her height makes her easily recognisable. Her voice is quiet and gentle but infused with a natural authority. She wears a sober grey dress. A chatelaine hangs from her waist displaying the tools of domestic management: scissors, needle case, notepad. She exudes efficiency.

'The Reverend Walters is expecting you.' She opens the front door wider to reinforce the invitation. I step into the hallway blinking whilst my eyes become accustomed to the gloom.

'As I said, he is expecting you but I'm afraid he had an unexpected call from one of his churchwardens – about the readers for next Sunday. I hope you won't mind waiting a few minutes. Come into the kitchen and you can meet my boys. This way.'

I follow Mrs Walters into the cavernous kitchen. You could fit our cottage inside this single whitewashed hall and still have room to spare. A large black cooking range with a giant chimney breast dominates. Cupboards and dressers line the walls whilst pots and pans dangle from the ceiling. At one end of the long refectory table a short squat woman is kneading dough. Around the other end sit five boys. All faces turn to inspect the visitor.

Mrs Walters makes the introductions.

'This is Mrs Owens who helps me in the kitchen.'

The 'help' nods.

'And these are my boys. Stand up to greet a visitor!'

They do so obediently, making me appear a great deal more important than I feel. She points at them in turn:

'John, Daniel, William, Henry and little Lewis.'

The five are ranged in perfect height and age order, reflecting the good organisation of the household.

'We've all just eaten I'm afraid, but I'm sure we can offer you something. Mrs Owens, have we any of the soup available?'

I join the boys on the benches. They smile politely at me whilst I sip the soup and praise Mrs Owens' cooking. Mrs Walters retreats to take care of other business. The boys are obviously used to visitors and appear in no way intimidated. She had not given their ages but I guess that the tallest, John, is about ten years of age with the others spaced at regular intervals down to 'little Lewis'. They talk easily and eagerly about themselves, about school, about the two ponies the family keep. They want to know about me.

'Do you play *bando*?' asks Henry.

'Sometimes.'

'We're not allowed,' explains Daniel. 'Mother thinks it's too dangerous.'

'She's probably right,' I agree.

'What else do you do?' asks Daniel with unsettling directness.

'I'm a stonemason.'

'Is that why you're here? Are you going to mend the rectory stone?'

'No.'

'Are you clever?' asks the inquisitive Henry.

'Yes,' I reply. 'Are you?'

'Yes, but not as clever as Daniel. What can you do that's clever? Can you read Latin?'

'No, but I can write poetry in Welsh and English.'

'Can you?' chorus two or perhaps three of the boys together. 'Recite one for us.'

'Please!' insists the voice of Mrs Owens from the far end of the table.

'Recite one for us – please!'

'But in English, we don't speak much Welsh,' adds John.

'I'll do better than that,' I reply. 'I'll compose a poem just for you.'

I'm thinking of rhymes, puns and limericks I can work on the boys' names. Lewis is difficult so I use his surname. 'Walters' rhymes with lots of silly and sensible words like acres, cobblers, dodgers, warblers and so on. The performance mechanism in my brain takes over. I gesticulate, my voice soars and soon I have the five boys and Mrs Owens laughing with delight and demanding more.

The noise brings Mrs Walters back into the kitchen to investigate. She restores order. 'If my boys are prepared to let you alone Mr Williams, the rector will see you now in the study.' Gratifyingly, the boys groan with disappointment. John suddenly assumes the duties of an eldest son. He stands and, in a manner older than his years, formally declares,

'It's been a real pleasure to have you here, Mr Williams, and we do hope you will come again soon.'

I shake their hands one at a time and thank them for their company – and thank Mrs Owens for the soup. As I follow Mrs Walters, she remarks, 'I hope the boys weren't too troublesome to you. You are a novelty you see, younger by far than the rather aged canons, vicars and churchwardens they normally have to suffer.'

The door opens. The rector stands to greet me and gestures

me to a seat. Tea has plainly been dispensed to the rector's earlier visitor. A maid appears to clear away the cups. The rector waits patiently whilst she fumbles with the expensive china. I catch her eye. She nearly drops the tray. I know her. Gwen from Howe's Mill. I once wrote her a silly poem which earned me a kiss. This is not the occasion for either of us to recall such adventures. She retreats in confusion, the china on the tray rattling.

I am questioned as ruthlessly by the father as I was by the sons, but with more politeness and in Welsh. Why is he speaking to me in Welsh when English is clearly the language of the home? Is it because he doubts my understanding of English? Should I feel affronted? He asks why I never attended school.

'Because my father could not afford to lose me from the work.'

What have I learnt from my mother?

'To read and write in Welsh and English and to love good poetry and learning.'

What have I read?

'Dafydd ap Gwilym, Shakespeare, Milton, Pope. Copies of the *Tatler* and *The Spectator*. Also Bacon's *Advancement of Learning* and Purshall's essay *Mechanical Fabrick of the Universe*.'

'No Latin?'

'No, sir.'

'French?'

'No French either, sir.'

'You have had lessons from Thomas Richards the curate of Coychurch, I believe?'

'Yes, sir. As a favour to my mother. He taught me grammar and encouraged me to widen my vocabulary – particularly in Welsh.'

'He speaks highly of you. He tells me that you were a diligent and intelligent student with an interest in his studies of Welsh lexicography.'

'Yes, sir. He let me spend some time in his own library and we discussed the derivation of Welsh words.'

The rector of Llandough stands, walks over to his bookcase and removes a volume which he places on the study table with theatrical deliberation. He looks hard at me as if trying to read my mind. He moves to another shelf and removes another book which he places alongside the first. There is a long pause before the rector speaks.

'Let me be clear, Edward. I am willing to help you further your education if you are prepared to discipline yourself to the work.'

I want to protest that no one ever had cause to doubt my determination to learn but I am plainly not meant to interrupt.

'You have read widely but the absence of Latin and French is a handicap. I will help you with that.'

He picks up a book on the table and offers it. 'Take this.'

I reach for the battered volume and read the fading embossed letters. *An Introduction to Latin Syntax.*

'Look through the first two chapters and we'll agree a regular time when you can come here for an hour to tackle some Ovid.'

The rector picks up the second volume, new and gleaming. He weighs it in his hand with care.

'If you wish, you can do something for me in return. Something for which curate Thomas Richards suggests you are well suited. You read and use Welsh well. You have a love of the language and its words. You can help me in what is an endeavour so large that I fear I may not live to see it completed.'

He hands me the second volume.

'You hold in your hand the first volume of my English-Welsh Dictionary. It contains entries from 'A' down to the word 'Breach'. I plan thirteen other volumes, perhaps more, before the work is complete. To do this I must collect Welsh words, test their meaning, provide variants and classify them. I would like you to help me.'

The rector does not wait for a response. He stands and starts to pace the room as if thinking through a complex theorem. He speaks as if to a congregation.

'Edward! This is vital work. Welsh is one of the oldest and most beautiful languages in the world but we, as a people, have no university, no great library, no academy to charter its past, protect its existence or enrich its future. We speak it, but carelessly.'

He turns to look out of the window.

'I have had to argue its cause against men of learning who believe that the Welsh language is a poor creature with far fewer words than English or French and a poverty of expression. I am pained not to be able to prove them wrong.'

He turns to face me.

'Even worse, there is no easy way for a man who cannot find the word he wants in Welsh to consult a dictionary that will supply his need. There have been dictionaries of varying quality available in English since 1600. Samuel Johnson's new dictionary has imposed order on the chaos of an ever-changing vocabulary. We must have the same facility in Welsh.'

The rector walks across the room towards me and sits in the chair opposite. His tone is urgent, almost imploring.

'Edward, I prefer this language we speak now, our Welsh, to any of the languages ancient or modern with which I have acquaintance. I wish with all my heart to disprove those who deride the Welsh tongue, to shame them for their servility.'

He pauses. This time the rector appears to expect a response.

'What do you want me to do?'

'Thank you, Edward. Quite simple really, but the very crux of this matter. I want you to collect words for me. From manuscripts, from old verse, from the everyday conversations of people you meet. Your work as a mason takes you all over Glamorgan I understand.'

'And further, sir.'

'Collect words and their shades of meaning. If you hear a word in English for which you cannot find a Welsh equivalent, then ask. If you still can't find one then construct one. Knowing Latin will be a help with that, Greek would be even better.'

'Make it up?'

'Construct one, I said, from existing words joined together with Latin or Greek prefixes or suffixes.' The rector moves to sit alongside me. He takes a pencil and paper and gives me my first lesson on the history of words. He lists examples of Welsh and English words that derive from Latin or Greek or French.

'Look, that's how language grows. Words can also be formed by the alchemy of joining two existing words to create a third. I believe that Welsh has a richness that will allow new words to be developed with a minimum of borrowings. Understand?'

I nod, dumb with excitement.

'I will set you a task. Are you aware of Rousseau? From the writings of Rousseau the philosophy of our time has become suffused with the idea of *humanité*. The English word is merely a borrowing from the French and there is no Welsh word that I am aware of. We have need for such a word. By the time I see you next week I expect you to have devised a serviceable Welsh word that encompasses the concept that all men have their nature in common, that we are all the children of one God. A challenge! Do you accept?'

'Of course, sir.'

The rector sits back and smiles as if relieved of a burden. I am finding it difficult to know how to react. I started this conversation as a supplicant pupil and inside twenty minutes I've grown to become an apprentice in a great enterprise. Suddenly, as if to restore the relationship between us to that of pupil and master, the rector's tone hardens and his voice becomes cold.

'One last thing, Edward. I have had good reports of your abilities. I have also heard less complimentary observations suggesting you are prone to wild and disorderly behaviour. It has been reported that you misuse your poetic talents, coining cheap ale house ballads or turning the heads of innocent maidens for immoral purposes. I have to tell you that such behaviour is not appropriate in a pupil of mine. Do I make myself clear?'

I do not know how to respond. He pays me the compliment of requesting my participation in his great enterprise. He talks to me as a partner – then he treats me as an unruly child! First his tone is engaging and friendly, then harsh and overbearing! It is as if he wants to praise me, then belittle me to ensure that I know that he is being beneficent in dealing with me at all!

I smart from the accusation that my harmless ballads and love songs are somehow reproachable 'immoral' activities. Indignation swells in my chest. I am not a child! At the same time I know that this man is offering me not one but two pearls of great worth: the chance to learn Latin and French and an opportunity to be part of a prestigious literary project to which I could bring much.

I swallow my indignation. I mumble something vague, signifying assent. I have learnt much today. The trick of being an obedient rather than a rebellious angel is the hardest lesson by far.

9

Kitty Deere

L EARNING LATIN IS a welcome challenge. I can lose myself for hours in its elegant phrases and precise vocabulary. It numbs the pain of Mother's death and, at the same time, is a means of paying homage to her memory. She would have been so pleased. I am also writing more. It is a way of expressing the anguish from my tortured brain. More of what I write, I write in the traditional strict metre Welsh forms I had been taught by Lewis Hopkin and others. When I am not writing or studying I read books borrowed from the Reverend John Walters.

I am careful to pull my weight at home. I do all the work Father bids me and go with my brothers to work on the Fonman crenulations. Without Mother to insist that we behave towards each other, rows keep breaking out. They have always resented my position as her favoured son but now see little reason not to say so. I try to talk with them as little as possible, either at work or in the cottage. I have even taken to hiding my books and papers for fear they may be the target of vindictiveness. I study as far away from the cottage as is possible. If the weather is good I work under a tree. If it is raining I look for a corner in the outhouse or even sit in a rear pew of St Michael's Church.

I walk. How I walk! I have always enjoyed walking. Now with a book in my hand, my mason's tools, my flute and a pen and paper in a bag across my shoulder, I find great solace just walking and walking for tens of miles each day along the narrow lanes of Glamorgan. I feel at one with the gentle fruitfulness of the Vale.

Here is my perfect environment for study or composition. In the months following my mother's death I watch and observe as I have never done so before. I see the summer turn into an autumn of great beauty and sadness. I try to capture in my verse the exquisite qualities of ripeness, decay, death and the hidden promise of rebirth. It is a sad love song I write to my mother.

Sometimes I take the opportunity to get away from the cottage and my quarrelsome brothers by looking for work in the west or the east, often staying away from Flemingston for days or weeks on end. Nobody appears to object.

The rector is pleased with my progress. He is never lavish in his praise but he admits that I am mastering Latin grammar faster than he had thought possible. I am entranced to find that French, Latin and Welsh have words that are related but distinct, like cousins in a far-flung family. As he requested, I have also become one of his chief collectors of Welsh words and dialectal alternatives. I have suggested new coined words which the rector has noted. His challenge of finding a word for 'humanity' met with my suggestion of '*dynoliaeth*' which I believe is both elegant and expressive. He noted it but has not promised to include it. I made the mistake of trying to interest him in my original poetry. He confessed that the composition of *cywyddau*[10] was not a skill he had ever found time to develop. I find it impossible to comprehend how a man – who professes to love the language so much – can be so uninterested in its finest flowerings.

I am trying to avoid Peggy. I think that she will soon be fed up with me. I brood too much for the taste of a girl who likes to be happy all the time. We walk across the meadows in the weeks following Mother's death. She is trying her best to comfort me. I have no wish to be cruel but in truth I do not want her company. She hangs on my arm radiating sympathy when I want to be

---

10   A poem written in *cynghanedd*.

alone. Worse, she offers her lips to be kissed and her body to be caressed as if passion can somehow obscure the pain of my loss. I do not respond in the way she wants. I cannot. When I feel the silken smoothness of her kiss or the press of her firm breasts or full feminine hips I feel disgusted by the lust so induced and the baseness of my feelings. I do not respond as she thinks I should. Instead of withdrawing modestly she tries to encourage me, undoing her blouse too far or squeezing herself against me lasciviously like some loose wanton. I feel dirty and see her as a caricature of femininity, all swelling breasts, lecherous thighs and voluptuous haunches. The carnal lust she tries to invoke offends against the memory of my mother, against the feminine purity and serenity she had represented and which I am duty-bound to honour. I extract myself from Peggy's all-consuming embrace as gently as I know how and walk away. I regret that I leave her crying, but everything tells me that the best thing I can do for us both is to see her as seldom as possible.

Yet I do seek comfort. For me the female form must be pure, chaste, refined and a natural home of sensibility and dignity of mind. My mother apart, I have glimpsed only one such, on Cowbridge High Street on the day of the March fair: the sublime Miss Kitty Deere. Her high forehead, delicate face, gentle features and elegance of stature are in all ways an echo of my mother. I have never spoken with her but I know just how sweet her voice will sound. I have never walked with her but I know the delicacy of her step and the intelligence of her discourse. I have never kissed her but I know her lips would be as fine, as insubstantial as gossamer and as sincere as a holy vow. I have no way of meeting her, but I can write to her. I am convinced that if only we may have a face-to-face meeting then she would recognise at once our natural affinity. We would be instantly united.

I write several letters to her, including verses praising her beauty, her mind and her refinement and requesting an opportunity to visit. These I will deliver myself to her home, Ash Hall in Ystradowen.

***

Walking up the main drive of Ash Hall might intimidate a lesser man but I march confidently across the crunching gravel, up the steep steps and pull the front door bell boldly. A tinkling sound from inside the house is followed by the scurrying of feet as a housekeeper of great girth and unsmiling aspect answers the door. Before I can draw breath she looks me up and down and snaps, 'Tradesmen at the back door if you please.'

I start to explain but the door closes with a firm slam and a clicking of latches. I am justly furious at this insult to my self-respect and the seriousness of my mission. I swallow my pride and head to the back of the house where I am answered by the same housekeeper. She in no way acknowledges our previous encounter.

'I'm calling to see Miss Kitty Deere.'

'Is she expecting you?'

'No, but…'

'Well, she's not at home and even if she was I doubt very much if she would wish to meet the likes of you. Now clear off and let me get on with my work.'

'Would you make sure she receives this?' I offer a neatly sealed letter which the housekeeper looks at is if it might be contagious. She inspects it for a few moments before taking it from my hand declaring,

'I'll see she gets it. Now off with you.'

I have no idea whether Kitty will receive the letter but suspect she might not. I fear her guardian may intercept her mail or that the housekeeper might make her own judgement whether to pass the letter on. It might even now be in the kitchen fire.

No matter. I will send other letters and other poems. I will keep copies of everything I write so I can bombard Ash Hall with my messages.

I persuade a young gardener at the Hall to act as go-between and, for a shilling, to pass my letters to Kitty Deere when she walks in the gardens. After an anxious week the young gardener reports success. He tells me that the beautiful Kitty sat in the shade of the old yew tree and read my note and love poem on a glorious day. I am overjoyed.

'*Haul yr awen a seren fy serch*'[11] I had addressed her. The gardener reports that she had folded the letter and placed it in her catch bag with a smile of joy and contentment. But he then demands two shillings for the next delivery. I sense extortion. There is no reply.

My only certain way to see her is in church. Her uncle and guardian is a churchwarden of the Church of St Owain, Ystradowen. He has contributed large sums to the improvement of the building and has strong views on the catechism. His family parade to church on Sundays mornings, settling like a nest of preened doves into the foremost pews. Behind them, observing the graceful movements of the finest dove, sit I, intent on capturing every nod and movement of the rear of her silk bonnet with its graceful blue dyed ostrich plume.

My poetry soars in beauty the more contact with the apparition is denied. Love will find a way.

---

11 Sun of the muse and star of love.

1 0

Print shop

COWBRIDGE HAS LOST some of its magic for me. I no longer want to dance and I have no reason to visit the markets. I do visit the Bear occasionally, where there is conversation and good ale. Here I amuse myself by performing verse of low quality for an audience of no discernment. I should confess that there is one new establishment in the town that arouses my interest. At 70 Eastgate stands the printing shop of Rhys Thomas. Several times now have I stood on the pavement outside, admiring the elegance of the large press and the technical sophistication of the processes involved: the rollers, the massive castings, the trays of print. It has a romance and the promise of a future of knowledge, enlightenment and commercial success. Today I venture inside, although I have no direct business there, apart from my involvement in gathering words for the great Walters Welsh-English dictionary – the first volume of which was printed on this very press. This alone, I feel, makes me a qualified member of the brotherhood of those who would make the world a more literate place.

Rhys Thomas turns out to be a temperamental argumentative proprietor, a charming host one day and a fearsome bulldog the next. I suspect that the bottles of brandy stored in the shop are not part of the printing process, unless lubrication of the operator is essential to its smooth working.

Rhys is welcoming on my first visit. He greets my curiosity as a missionary might greet a potential convert. He demonstrates the workings of his machines with pride and skill. I am captivated by the process of compositing typeface; the manipulation of those thousands of small blocks of lead to form a page. I am thrilled when Rhys performs for me the miracle of turning the base metal of the plate into the gold of a page of fine print through the operation of the press. He permits me to turn the handle and print a page advertisement for a local wholesaler of grain.

I do have a reason for being here apart from the thrill of being in contact with a technology which will certainly change our world. How, I venture tentatively, does one get one's own work printed?

'What kind of work?'

'Poetry.'

'What sort of poetry?'

I produce a sheaf of paper which I offer to Rhys. He throws his hands up in surrender.

'I don't want to read it! Look I'll print anything that anyone can pay me to print – apart from blasphemy of course. But someone has to pay for my time, the paper and ink, for the use of the press. Then there's the binding, the sewing and the pressing, the trimming and the bookending. It all takes time and all costs money. I'm not interested in the quality of what I print, only the depth of the pockets of whoever asks me to print it! Are you a wealthy young man?'

'No.'

'Then have you a patron?'

'What?'

'Someone who does have money who will pay the cost?'

'No.'

'If it's in Welsh you'll be hard-pressed to find a sponsor amongst the gentry. They're all becoming pretty indifferent to anything in Welsh.'

I feel I have been corrected, reminded of my proper low station in the order of things. I say nothing but prepare to leave the shop in some embarrassment. Rhys calls me back. He appears anxious to repair the impression of disinterest. He talks expansively whilst walking about the print shop – the master of his domain. He has an easy persuasive manner and the swagger of a highwayman. He announces,

'There is a way.'

I look up in expectation.

'Subscribers. It's how many books get published. Basically, you sell the book *before* it's printed.'

I do not understand and it shows. Rhys tries again.

'You put together a list of people with a few guineas to spare and a liking for your poetry. Show them a prospectus – a single sheet saying what will be in the book. In return for cash upfront they are guaranteed a copy when it's eventually printed. You also print a list of their names in the front of the book so they look important. So when you have, say, fifty subscribers who have all put in, say four shillings each, you come here with your ten pounds and I'll print sixty copies for you. The first fifty you present to your subscribers and the ten you have left you can sell at a profit. Simple! That, by the way, is how Mr Walters is finding the money for his dictionary.'

Rhys does make it sound simple. I nod and then ask quietly, 'How do I find fifty such people?'

'Ah, you detected the snag! Well, if you're famous, of course, there's no problem because you will already have a readership who hopefully will want to read more. If, like you, no one knows your poetry, then you might be better off broadening the appeal by including the names of people they have heard of.'

'Like?'

'Anyone famous and preferably dead so they can't sue you for stealing their words.'

I start to think. What of the manuscripts I brought back from Y Blaenau? There are others I could easily locate.

'But that doesn't get my work read.'

'I'm sure you can give yourself a section in your own book. Anyway, that's the best I can do for you.'

Rhys appears to have lost interest in our conversation and starts doing very noisy things to the press. I assume the conversation is at an end. I back thoughtfully out of the shop.

On the road

I AM SPENDING less and less time working with my brothers and father and more and more travelling across Glamorgan, into west and north Wales and even down to the West Country. I am pleased to discover that being an itinerant stonecutter can provide a decent if unsteady source of income. I carry only my mallet and chisel, a notepad, a few books and, if I'm fortunate, some bread and cheese. I am enjoying a life of chance encounters as I journey between the large houses looking for work. Whether I am successful depends on the needs of different houses for repair, and the ability of their owners to pay.

My travels have awakened my urge to see and know more of the world. I enjoy journeying for its own sake, to see the moving landscapes and relish the changing seasons. Travelling also allows me to pursue other interests. I continue to collect words for the Reverend Walters. I visit the great houses where I beg access to their libraries and their collections of books and manuscripts. I transcribe as much as I can into my notebooks. Very occasionally the owner lets me take papers away, convinced that 'those dusty old things' are of no real value. More often they refuse me access, suspicious of my motives and jealous of their possessions.

I am also following Rhys Thomas' advice by selling subscriptions to what, I hope, will be my first publication. *Diddanwch y Cymry*[12] will be a collection of the ancient and

---

12 Entertainment of the Welsh.

modern poetry of Glamorgan. To my delight, I have persuaded some ten individuals to subscribe four shillings each. I have a pocketful of money to jingle.

Travelling allows me to visit scholars and bards in other parts of Wales. After three days' work on the gates of a big house in Machynlleth, I am heading towards Towyn and my first meeting with Ieuan Fardd. I do not want to arrive unannounced and have already sent a letter forewarning him. Ieuan Fardd is a hero to me for his knowledge and his writings. He has already published *Some Specimens of the Poetry of the Antient Welsh Bards. Translated into English, with Explanatory Notes on the Historical Passages, and a short Account of Men and Places mentioned by the Bards.* This remarkable book deals with Welsh poetry from the earliest times to the Age of the Princes. I have read it several times and dream of building on the great man's work.

I am unprepared for what I find. I regard Ieuan Fardd as an intellectual giant but had not thought it might also be physically true. The man towers to six-and-a-half feet. The slenderness of his body enhances the impression of height. This is further reinforced by the low ceilings and doorways of his small, disorganised cottage which cause him to walk with a permanent stoop inside the house. His head brushes the whitewash of the ceiling and deposits small flecks on his shoulders. He has prepared some refreshment for us both, the thinnest gruel that I have ever tasted. It is little more than water in which a bone and peelings have been boiled. It is obvious from his clothing and the scant comforts of the cottage that this literary giant is impoverished below the level of the poorest farm servant. Only pride gives him dignity.

He shares with me his own experiences of collecting and discovering ancient manuscripts. He advises me where next I should look, which houses to visit and which libraries to search in pursuit of more and older papers. He reads to me from his own *magnum opus* to be published soon. *The Love of our Country* is an epic poem celebrating the heroes and the history of the Welsh. As he declaims the valour of the princes, the wisdom of Hywel Dda and the mysticism of the druids, his thin voice resonates round the walls of the small cottage. I am moved with patriotic ardour. When he finishes, the audience of one stands at the table and applauds.

We talk long into the night. I wonder how a man who had achieved such eminence and served the literature of his country so well can be so little valued by the society of which he is part. He had studied divinity at Oxford and served as a curate in five or six churches in England and Wales before coming to Towyn, but never rose above the level of humble curate. The English bishops who run the church in Wales have no understanding of Welsh and are blind to his achievements. Ieuan's speech is punctuated by fits of coughing which tear at his body. I finger the shillings in my pocket, itching to lay them on the table to support the great scholar, but I know that they would be refused, not for lack of need, but excess of pride.

As we pour over some of the ancient manuscripts in his collection, my excitement grows at the importance and significance of the papers. Would Ieuan mind were I to spend the next day transcribing?

Of course he agrees. He might even be able to spare some other manuscripts which he was certain would aid me in my work. I see an opportunity.

'I can't just take them away. Let me pay you for them.' I lie that I had just had six days of well-paid work in Barmouth and could well afford to pay a proper price for such valuable manuscripts. Would Ieuan Fardd accept a guinea? The old man agrees eagerly and gives several other manuscripts without further charge.

So we part. Ieuan tells me he is proud to meet someone who will carry on his work after his days are ended. He also thanks me for the twenty-one shillings with which to buy bread, cheese and beer.

I have made a friend of one of the greatest scholars of my day, an ally I can trust in our quest of collecting and ordering the work of the great bards. I leave with a bag bursting with priceless manuscripts from which, I promise, I will never be separated. I also leave without the money that would have enabled Rhys Thomas to print the volumes I have promised to my subscribers.

1 2

Kitty Deere again

AFTER MONTHS OF sending my love messages to the sweetest of doves without response or acknowledgement, I receive a reply. It arrives by the hand of the same young gardener whom I have been paying as a dependable postman. The grin on his face is as wide as the road as he hands over the vellum package.

'Go on, open it. I'm dying to know what she said.'

I refuse to share my moment of triumph with him or any other. I pay him and walk with the precious envelope to the top of Bryn Owain so as to sit in a place of great panorama but with total isolation and privacy. I weigh it in my hand. It is no trivial note. The envelope plainly contains many pages of writing. Breaking the seal feels like an act of destiny.

Inside I find a note in Kitty's careful rounded schoolroom script. She thanks me for my verses and wonders if I might be interested to read hers and, if I can spare the time, pass an opinion on their quality. With this all-too-short letter are enclosed a dozen or more single sheets, each with a poem written in praise or appreciation of an animal, insect, or unique moment. There is 'On observing a butterfly', 'On regarding a cat asleep' and 'On being startled by a slug'. There are two sonnets, 'On choosing a bonnet' and 'On a beautiful morning'. I search in vain for any response to my messages of love and offers of eternal soulful partnership. The disappointment is bitter but I console myself with the knowledge that a dialogue has been opened. Given our mutual sensibility, a marriage of true minds is the only possible outcome.

I write a reply as lengthy as Kitty's original message was short. I praise her sensibility and the refinement of her poems. I applaud the delicacy of her observations and the clarity of her perceptions. I tell her that I find the purity of her thought inspirational and profess myself her eternal debtor for the profound effect of her words on my own poetic creations. I also include a new love poem in her praise which has been some weeks in its composition. I end by urging a meeting – soon – so that we may reflect on her muse and together look to create sublime poetry.

My return package is in the hands of the gardener within a day and, so I hope, delivered with promptness to her favourite garden bench in the cultivated settings of Ash Hall.

Daily I check with my go-between, hoping for a reply and a time and place for assignation. It is a week before I receive a response and it does not come from the direction I was hoping. A letter arrives from John Charles, solicitor, warning me that my approaches to Mistress Deere are unwanted and unreciprocated, that I am to cease all attempts to contact Mistress Deere forthwith on pain of a lawsuit for trespass, defamation of character and causing a nuisance.

This insulting letter spurs me to greater action. I write her a long message comparing our situation to the 'Maid of Cefn Ydfa'[13], the girl of fine sensibility who was forbidden to marry her sweetheart because he was of lower social status. I plead with her to elope, to free herself from the bonds of social convention and devote herself to the search for higher poetic values. When I try to deliver this message, my gardener go-between is nowhere

---

13   Traditional Welsh folk tale set in the Vale of Glamorgan and the basis of the song *'Bugeilio'r Gwenith Gwyn'* [Watching the White Wheat].

to be found. It soon emerges that he has lost his position, dismissed for betraying the confidence of his employer.

My fury knows no bounds. I respond with passion and words. John Charles becomes the subject of a satirical poem in which the solicitor is described as a 'cowardly wretch'. I point out how I am the innocent victim of 'rascalities' perpetrated by 'persons of no conscience'. These ballads I declaim to great applause in the taproom of the Bear in Cowbridge and the public room of the Old Globe in Cardiff.

The next response is a formal court summons from John Charles for defamation. It is served on me at the cottage in Flemingston, which only makes matters worse. When Father hears that his eldest son is upsetting gentry and people of substance, he threatens to disown me. He complains, not for the first time, that I will ruin the family business by giving the name of Williams a bad reputation throughout Glamorgan.

I write once more to Kitty explaining my pitiable circumstances and imploring her to intervene with her guardian on my behalf. I tell her to warn him that she will end up unable to eat or sleep and might decline into an early grave in the manner of the 'Maid of Cefn Ydfa' as a consequence of being barred from seeing her true love. I advise tears and tantrums. The envelope is ready but I have lost my postman and am certain that the housekeeper would immediately destroy any message I send. I determine to deliver it myself by climbing unseen over the wall into the gardens of Ash Hall and wait in the bower, for as long as I have to, until my Kitty appears.

I clamber up the wall in the early morning convinced that the garden will be empty and hoping that Kitty will be tempted into an early walk. I scrape my knees and shins reaching the top of the wall but am then able to jump lightly down into the soft earth of a flowerbed beneath. The garden is quiet. I move silently and discreetly to a bush behind the bower and hide. I sit unmoving for several hours, observing the movements in and out of the house. No one comes into the garden. The sunshine is warm, the flowers perfume the bower and I drift into a delightful dream in which Kitty and I are laughing and rhyming as we walk through fields of wild flowers.

I am awoken by the sound of snarling. When I open my eyes two large dogs block out the light above me, slavering and growling threateningly as if contemplating their breakfast. Behind the two dogs stand two rough-looking men, bailiffs I suppose, holding the dogs back on thick rope collars. Their faces suggest they may change their minds and release the brutes at any moment. I am manhandled out of my hiding place, then dragged roughly along the ground with the two dogs yelping and nipping at my heels. Where the path meets the driveway, the two bailiffs put me up on my feet facing the main gate out of the Hall gardens.

One shouts coarsely, 'You have thirty seconds to be out of these gates before I let these dogs go. And in case you're in any doubt, they like their meat raw.'

I am scarcely more popular elsewhere. The Reverend Walters has heard of my carousing in the Old Globe public room and the taproom of the Bear. How, he demands, could he, as the rector of Llandough, afford to be associated with a pupil who keeps such bad company, offends the gentry, falls into debt, makes promises he cannot keep and is the subject of a court summons? I try to pacify the rector with a notebook full of words I collected on my travels through north Wales. I spoil the good work by recounting the story of my visit to Ieuan Fardd whom the rector dismisses as 'academically unsound and unsteady of character'. There is, he insists, a reason why the curate has never been promoted to a higher position in the Church, 'He dreams too much and drinks too much.'

In Cowbridge Rhys Thomas the printer refuses to set the

type for *Diddanwch y Cymry* until he receives the full fee he had quoted for printing. I explain that I have 'invested' part of the subscription money in rare Welsh manuscripts which will be of mutual benefit in years to come. Rhys is unimpressed. So are several subscribers when they learn that the book for which they have already paid for looks increasingly unlikely to appear.

Rhys tells me bluntly that I have to find new sponsors or subscribers or the work on my book is over.

'Where?' I ask.

'London?' suggests Rhys. 'There are lots of Welsh in London who have made enough money to give something back to the old country. Something about living in London too that makes the Welsh exiles soft-hearted about all things Welsh.'

The idea of London appeals greatly but cannot even be considered whilst I am engaged in wooing Kitty and freeing her from the tyranny of her family. I tell Rhys that this is the single most important cause in my life. Our love for each other is unshakable, despite the behaviour of her family and their heartless retainers. Rhys sniggers unkindly.

13

The Marriage
of True Minds

THE ENGAGEMENT IS announced in *The Glamorgan Gazette* of Miss Kitty Deere, niece of Mr Mathew Deere of Ash Hall, to the Reverend William Church, rector of Flemingston, Llanmihangel and Llanilid. The wedding is to take place one month hence on 14 October in Llandough church. Great celebrations are planned, with much free beer expected to flow at Mr Deere's expense.

When I recover the power of thought, I convince myself that this is not possible; that the marriage has been arranged against Kitty's will; that the poor child is being forced into a loveless marriage just as in the story of the 'Maid of Cefn Ydfa'. That is it! History repeating itself as history does. If this is so obvious to me, then why not to everyone else? Rhys the printer laughs again as he destroys my last tenuous hopes.

'They've been courting for a few years now. His aunt has a house in the main street in Cowbridge where she visits with her guardian. I can't say that she looks anything but a happy bride-to-be when I've seen them about.'

I recall the first time I watched her disappear into that very house. I now recall seeing her with a young cleric who I assumed was some part of her guardian's official party – never my rival! I am unmercifully teased and tormented by my brothers, my drinking companions, the population of Flemingston and, to be honest, most of the population of Glamorgan. The only person who shows me kindness in my grief is the person who had most right to be vindictive. Peggy tells me that I've made a fool of myself for love. She adds that I am not the first and will not be the last. I tell her that I will be leaving for London within days, just as soon as I have settled my affairs. I have new business to attend to.

'That sounds very grand, Edward Williams. It will take more than a few days to clear up the mess you've made. You're running away, if truth be told.'

She's right. She knows me far too well for me to deceive her, so I say nothing more. She continues, 'Just remember that there are some who forgive you and will be thinking about you, so write when you have the time – promise?'

I promise and am pleased to do so. She kisses me lightly on the cheek, squeezes my hand and walks away.

Part Two: London 1773 to 1776

1

Westminster bridge

I BLOW AWAY the dust from the stone and run my hand down the smooth rounded edge I've created. I look back to the foreman. The large red-faced man nods and grudgingly admits, 'Very good. All right, you can cut a true edge, I'll give you that. If you want to work here, you can use that bench over there. You'll be paid ten pence for every block you finish, or fined five pence for every block you spoil.'

The foreman looks approvingly at my test piece.

'We get lots of country masons coming along, but most of them just don't have the skills. They'd be all right patching up a barn but not up to the standard I need on the bridge.'

I look behind the foreman, beyond the flapping canvas door of the temporary workshop to the elegant magnificence of Westminster Bridge. Its stretch of fourteen symmetrical arches reaches across the wide river to Lambeth and the palace of the archbishop.

'It's very beautiful,' I venture.

The foreman snorts with derision. 'That's as maybe, but it would have been a sight better if they'd built it twice as strong and half as pretty.'

'What's wrong with it?'

'Won't stand up!' responds the foreman as if delivering a well-practised punch line. He warms to the telling of a tale he has clearly told many times before.

'They built it on mud. Got in some architect from Switzerland where rivers, we are told, have stone beds. If we'd only employed an English mason anyone could have told him that the Thames is different. But did he ask? Did he listen? No, he plonked the whole blessed thing on London mud. Now can you credit it? So, bit by bit, it keeps sinking. Mind you, it provides steady employment for the likes of you and me. I've rebuilt two of the piers already and I'll probably have to work my way through the other twelve before it's safe. Just as long as the masters keep paying, I'll keep repairing. Mind you, I half expect to turn up here one morning to find it's collapsed overnight.'

He does not wait to find out if I find the saga believable.

'Right, enough gabbling. Do you want the work or not?'

'Yes, please. Yes, I do.'

'What's your name?'

I hesitate and reply, 'Iorwerth.'

I decided during the long journey to London that I needed to escape my childish nickname. I hope to build up my reputation in Welsh literary circles and need a name with more maturity and character than 'Ned'. I like the sound of Iorwerth, and Iorwerth is said to be the Welsh version of Edward. Coming to London is a chance to start again, to escape the silly things I did as a youth and those people who always wanted to remind me of them. A fresh name is like a clean page. I also hope a new name will place me well outside the reach of any legal summons that may follow me down the road from Cowbridge. Yes, I have thought it through, but not until this moment had I considered how my new name might be received by a master mason working on the banks of the Thames.

'Luv us an' all – Welsh! I'm not going to start getting my tongue round your impossible bloody language. I'll do myself a mischief. Taffy you'll be. I've no other Taffs in the workshop, so that will do me fine.'

I do not like the word 'Taffy'. It has insulting associations,

'Taffy was a thief' and so on, but I say nothing. Firstly, I need the work. I've arranged lodgings, but don't have the money to pay for them. Secondly, the foreman is using the word in a casual, almost friendly manner. Perhaps I should not take offence when none is intended? I let it pass.

It is harder to be so forgiving of my fellow journeymen masons. Some ten of them work in the temporary workshop, producing dressed sandstone to exact dimensions for the piece-by-piece replacement of one of the piers. My father always taught me that there is a bond of fellowship between itinerant masons by which we support each other and welcome strangers into our company. That was true in Wales and again in the English towns I passed through, but here the bonds of fellowship have apparently dissolved in the Thames. My fellow masons appear to harbour resentment against me, for, in their opinion, taking work which might have gone to an English mason. They say so openly to each other in my hearing and the atmosphere around me bristles with subdued aggression. If any worker mislays a chisel the cry goes up, 'It's probably that thieving Taff.' If I protest, they jeer. If I turn my back to ignore them, they cry 'toasted cheese' and laugh as if they had made the cleverest and wittiest joke ever heard.[14]

I try to ignore it, to concentrate and block out the abuse. It shocks me but I persevere for two weeks hoping the situation will improve. It doesn't. I leave my bag unattended, only to find that someone has deposited something foul inside. On the first occasion I am greeted by a decaying rat; on the second by excrement. I boil with fury. I tell them all that they are uncivilised, uncultivated morons who disgrace the trade of masons. They

---

14 Anti-Welsh prints and cartoons of the eighteenth century often depict a witless Taffy carrying leeks, cheese and ale, and leading a donkey. Toasted cheese was supposedly Taffy's greatest passion.

stand together enjoying my anguish. I shout. They laugh. I shout louder. They jeer and ridicule. One starts singing:

'Taffy was a Welshman

Taffy was a thief.'

The others join in:

'Taffy came to my house

And stole a piece of beef.'

Eventually I can take no more and tell the foreman so. The round florid face nods. The chin wobbles a little and the eyes grimace in recognition of a bad situation.

'They've been a right bunch of little shits to you. I'm sorry. Really, I am.'

I look at his eyes set in his broad honest face and am pleased to perceive that he means what he says. The foreman continues, 'I've put in a word for you with John Bacon at Hyde Park Corner. He's a friend of mine. Runs a statuary workshop there – all classy stuff. Told him you're a cut above the usual and he's happy to give you a trial. I can't guarantee his workmen will be any more civilized than this shower but at least you'll enjoy the work rather more. Listen to John. You'll learn something. He's one of the best, worked in Italy.'

We shake hands. I walk off into the London evening.

2

The streets of London

I HAVE LODGINGS in a house in the tangle of dwellings, workshops, factories and warehouses to the north of High Holborn. It is a confusion of narrow lanes and dirty alleyways. My room is small, damp and smells of overcooked cabbage and cats' wee. But it is very cheap and is also well placed for me to reach the places that make London famous. The owner is a rope merchant with a shop in the next street, but my landlady is a wretched-looking woman who occupies the ground floor. She appears to spend her days boiling the cabbage and tending the cats that give the building its characteristic aroma.

From this base I explore London. During the first seven days I wander at will through every square and avenue from Grosvenor Square to the duck pond in Mile End Road. I drink in the sounds, sights and smells of elegant squares, green parks and filthy backstreets. I wander as if invisible, not wanting to engage with any of the beings I observe, but rather enjoying the anonymity that comes from being one of so large a multitude. In this city of bright silken ladies and gorgeously brocaded gentlemen, it would take a great display to attract attention. My dowdy, country clothes guarantee obscurity.

In St James' Park I marvel at the splendour of the gilded and brightly painted coaches in which travel elegant ladies, their hair piled into impossible haystacks and surmounted with bonnets of great ostentation. These coaches have liveried footmen riding on the rear or sometimes astride the leading horses. Some carriages display the fortunes their owners have built from Indian trade, by the presence of black, ornately turbaned and jewelled footmen. The carriage occupants incline their heads to acknowledge the greetings of their peers. I watch couples walking with measured pace, like peacocks displaying their fine plumage. The ladies' skirts stand out from their bodies, supported by structures I can only guess at. Their bodices are of every bright colour you can imagine: ochre, florescent yellows, deep reds and delicate blues trimmed and decorated with cascades of lace and ruffles. Some carry miniature dogs, who are themselves decorated with ribbons of silk and tiny bells tied into their fur or round their necks.

The coaches are, I suppose, a recognisable if distant relative of the mail coaches of the Bear. The private sedan chairs, on the other hand, are a revelation – a triumph of silliness. These ornately decorated boxes are carried by yet more footmen weaving about the pathways at speed. Their carriers cry 'By your leave' as they thunder forwards compelling dawdlers to get out of the way or face a dangerous collision. I move nimbly aside.

With a mason's eye I inspect and admire the rows of fine terraced buildings and the symmetrical perfection of Cavendish Square. Soho Square, with its statue of Charles II at the centre, is my favourite. I stand in wonder under the dome of St Paul's, at once awed by the glory of God and thrilled by the exquisite craft that has shaped his house.

I want to see the theatres of London. I stand outside the Theatre Royal, Drury Lane, watching the larger-than-life actors come and go, acknowledging the adulation of their admirers. I read the playbills of the Haymarket Theatre where *The Nabob* is doing good business. I learn from the doorkeeper that the play makes riotous fun of gentry who have returned from India with enlarged livers and greatly expanded bank balances. How splendid! I wonder if there is a place for my own satirical verse somewhere in this city. My only disappointment is that I cannot afford to observe the play for myself.

It is in the Haymarket that my ordinariness momentarily fails to protect me from reality. I feel my arm being held in the grip of a talon. A harsh female voice rasps in my ear, 'From the country are we, my fine man? Wager they didn't have as fine ladies as me where you come from. Got enough money for a good time, dearie?'

I look and see with alarm a parody of the elegance I had observed in St James' Park. The whore wears a full gown of similar brilliance but made of cheaper shinier material. Her cleavage leers at me as if trying to consume me whole. Her face is only inches from mine, caked with powder and paint but betraying what might once have been beauty. I prise the woman's hand off my arm. She is stronger than I think and it is like removing a leech. I have encountered prostitutes before. There are women in Cowbridge who earn additional moneys on fair days by selling their services to farmers flush with cash from a good livestock sale. But the whores of Cowbridge are not in the same league as these elaborately painted and costumed Jezebels.

'No need to hurt, young sir,' protests the whore. She rubs her wrist where I had held it. Had I hurt her? That was not my intention. She looks into my eyes as one pleading for a favour. Her voice becomes gentler, softer, beseeching.

'Strong young man new in town could do with a girl who knows her way about. Just to help him find his way. Would you like that, mister?'

I am astounded by the way her face and whole aspect has softened. I am confused. How old is this woman? Probably not much older than myself but so much, so very much more worldly. She smiles winsomely and I am charmed. I shake myself out of the spell. I am angry. I am allowing myself to be beguiled by her. I am enjoying her courtesy. I am angry at the way she so easily insinuates her way into my emotions. I take a step back and ask, 'Why do you do this?'

She roars with laughter, revealing decaying teeth.

'Why? You could lead an honest life.'

'Oh, could I now?'

Her manner and tone alters once more to become as rough and mocking as any fishwife.

'Tell you what. Why don't you marry me? Take me away and make an honest woman of me. That what you want? Mind you, you'll have to have a big country estate with lots of servants and a carriage. That you, mister?' She laughs derisively.

There is one sure way to get rid of her. 'I've no money, only a few pennies.'

I expected her to swear and go at once but she resumes her softer tone. She patronises me.

'Pity! Never mind, you save up your shillings and come back when you think you can afford a proper woman. I promise to make it an experience you won't forget. Cheers.'

She winks, turns, and heads into the crowd in search of new prey.

Then there are the booksellers. Each shop is a treasure-trove of wisdom. The Strand has half a dozen such, and I move from one to another as if on a pilgrimage. Some are very grand, forbidding and expensive, their windows displaying handsomely tooled leather volumes destined for the libraries of great mansions. Some are small and more affordable, such as Alexander Donaldson on the Strand. I watch the tall Scot move about his shop tidying and arranging volumes to best advantage. He plainly loves his books and is knowledgeable about their contents. I overhear his recommendations to a customer and wait for an opportunity to ask my own questions. Has he a copy of Hume's *A Treatise of Human Nature*? The bookseller reaches

to a shelf and places it on the table before me with a triumphal flourish.

'Our very own reprint!' he proclaims, 'complete and unabridged and for only a shilling.'

When I ask why his editions are cheaper than elsewhere, I receive a messianic address on the need to make printed books available to all. For far too long the world of ideas has been the preserve of wealthy men with private libraries. He and his brother will use new techniques, cheaper paper, and better presses to make knowledge accessible. I buy the Hume volume and Jean-Jacques Rousseau's *Julie, ou la nouvelle Héloïse*. These I devour in my small, cold room warmed by the idea that the education of our emotions and placing trust in our human sympathy for each other are the keys to a better world.

I spend much time in the shabby alleyways of St Giles' Cripplegate, the habitat of impoverished writers, journalists, ballad vendors and the cheapest of booksellers. The frontages of the ancient buildings lean out perilously over the narrow lanes until, in places, it is possible for people at the upper windows to shake hands across the street. The result is a gloomy foul-smelling passage, off which run several courtyards where cafés, bookshops and brothels jostle comfortably together. I move from one to another, at once repulsed by the airless reek but also attracted by this community of poor but literate people. I so want to be a fellow amongst those whose nobility of mind transcend the poverty and the squalor of their environment.

I engage booksellers in conversations, valuing their knowledge. I sit in the coffee houses reading newspapers and listening to heated discussions on the war in America. I have my purse stolen twice but each time it was all but empty. I watch as the literary giants of the day pass through on their business. Twice I identify Dr Samuel Johnson, once holding forth in a coffee house against Rousseau's treatise on the inequality of mankind, and a second time in a bookseller's. I feel awkward in the presence of someone so famous. This is the very man the Reverend John Walters had praised to the heights. I look for an excuse to strike up a conversation, a functional exchange as might occur naturally between fellow bibliophiles. I ask the great man which of three alternative English grammars I should buy. The doctor's large, shapeless form turns slightly towards me but says nothing. I cautiously repeat the question, extending the three books for better inspection. The doctor's eyebrows rise.

'Any one of them will do for you, young man.' And he turns away to read.

Why does he slight me in this fashion? Is it the poverty of my attire or the manner of my speech? No, my question was well phrased and my clothes are no more threadbare than many others in the shop. Is it on account of my accent? Anti-Welsh jibes from the journeymen of Westminster Bridge I can attribute to mindless ignorance, but such prejudice from a scholar of note is unbearable. I feel my hackles rise as I thrash about for a riposte. I lift all three volumes high and, in a louder voice than I intend, proclaim, 'Then, sir, to make sure of having the best I will buy them all.' The great man does not acknowledge the words and I leave the shop having emptied my meagre purse yet again – but having maintained my dignity.

The exchange with Dr Johnson rankles deep. I have had enough of being an observer of the London aviary. I want to unfurl my own feathers. I want to fly.

3

The fog

I EMERGE FROM my lodging this morning to find that I can
hardly see a pace forwards in any direction. What is this? I am
staring into a coarse wool blanket which wraps around me, on
top of me, in front of me, behind me. I can scarcely see anything
but soft dirty grey. I hold up my hand. Eight inches from my
face it is a blurred outline only. I see lanterns floating along,
presumably with bodies supporting them. The bodies call out
'By your leave' to warn those they cannot see of their approach.
I am rooted to the spot, unsure whether to go back into the
lodging or venture further.

I move forward, using the slope of the pavement to keep
me clear of the gutter which runs down the centre of the alley
carrying rubbish, cooking waste and excrement. It takes an age,
maybe twenty minutes, for me to move a hundred yards, groping
along the edges of buildings like a blind man. I reach a corner.
This must be the end of the alley. I continue step by step until
I reach another corner. What corner is this? There shouldn't be
a corner here! This should be the main road but I can only see
grey in every direction and a light bobbing in the distance. Or
is it close by? Sounds are indistinct and uncertain. I feel my way
along the street. The fog is choking, making me struggle for each
breath. Something soft brushes against my legs, some evil thing
that walks under cover of this greyness? Don't panic, it's only a
cat. Or maybe rats? The rats of London are huge and fight with
dogs. I continue to walk but the realisation is growing that I am

lost. Not just uncertain, totally lost. I tell myself to stay calm. I reason that I cannot be a great distance from my starting point, but I have no idea in which direction I should move in order to return. I stand quite still, quite isolated. The mist appears to be thickening. It not only surrounds and swaddles me; I can feel it entering my mouth, my nose, invading my lungs. I am seized with fear.

Breathing is so hard. The air is thick with dirt and I cannot force it down my throat. My asthma has returned, aggravated by the dust, the damp and the coal fumes. Each day I watch as a forest of chimneys belch into the London sky, driving away any last vestige of clean air. But never, till now, have I been seized in the manner I suffered as a child, forcing me to gasp and battle for each lungful. I am coughing mucus. I spit. I lean back heavily against the wall, exhausted. I command my legs but they will not move. I slide down the wall to a sitting position, legs spread before me, dematerialising into the greyness, waiting. Waiting for what? For the wind to change and gather enough strength to clear the sky? I wait, because I can do nothing else. I close my eyes and try to think of the mists which descend on the Vale of Glamorgan in the morning like a fine veil, softening but not hiding the features of the land. Mists that caress rather than suffocate. I cannot doze. It is too cold. I just wait. I despair of ever leaving this place. Might I die here? I have seen dead men in the gutters of London ignored by others as of no more significance than a dead mouse. When this fog clears, will they find my corpse?

'Mr Williams, what are you doing here?'

I assume I am dreaming but when I look up I see the wretched woman, my landlady, looking down at me curiously. For the first time I see her as a human being rather than a frightened bag of old bones. She bends over me, her aspect transformed by her command of my situation. Her voice is gentle, full of sympathy.

'Folk 'ow ain't used to it can get lost in these 'ere fogs, easy as anythink. But when you've lived here as long as I 'av you get to know your way about whatever it's like. We need to get you back 'ome and no mistake. Can you get back on your pegs?'

She helps me up and tells me to put my arm over her shoulders. I fear I will crush her. She may look frail but the old woman has muscles like iron. She half-guides and half-drags me over the rough cobbles back to the hovel she calls home. It takes time, for I have to stop frequently to cough up phlegm and fight for breath. She waits patiently, encouraging me with a cheery, 'Ain't much further now, young sir.' We reach the house. She helps me to my room and deposits me on the dirty straw palliasse.

'You rightly need some physic,' she says, looking down at me with the manner of a mother. 'What d'ya take when it strikes you like this?'

I try and recount to her my recipe for an infusion of thistles and mallow leaves. She smiles a mother's smile to a silly child.

'I think I can do better than that. Got thruppence, and I'll have you cured in a tick? Drop of laudanum should do the trick.'

She does not wait for an answer but rifles in my pockets for my purse. I try to stop her, thinking that I am being robbed, but each time I move my whole body seizes up in spasms. I have no choice but to lie on my back waiting for the crone to return – if she ever will.

In time I drink from a bottle which contains dark, thick, sweet tasting liquor. The effect is instantaneous. Warmth spreads through my body, the coughing subsides. My breathing eases. My heartbeat slows. I fall into a sleep deeper than any I have slept before.

I can feel and smell the rich grass where I am lying. I can feel Peggy's hand stroking my hair. I can hear songbirds in the distance.

I am rising, floating above ground. Floating weightless is easy. I just mustn't think. If I think I might fall. Peggy is holding onto my arm and giggling. She's afraid. I tell her that I will look after us both. When we look down I can see the whole of the Vale laid out before me in soft morning light. A book appears in my hand. I don't know where from. I open it and it sings to me beautiful lyrical cywyddau *by the great masters of the craft. As the book sings, delicate golden butterflies swarm around its pages feasting on its sweetness. I try to show Peggy, but Peggy has gone. I hear a human voice. On the ground Dr Johnson is shouting at me, but I am too high up and too distant to make out what he says. He waves his stick in anger. I wave back in friendship. I wave to the people crossing Westminster Bridge. I fly into St Paul's and sit on a ledge high up in the dome where no one can see me. Christopher Wren is sitting beside me. We are discussing the masonry of the cathedral. Kitty Deere is calling. I want to go to her. She is wearing a bright yellow silk dress trimmed with lace and ruffles. Her hair is piled high and she is wearing too much powder. She is showing her dress off, twirling with delight and wanting my approval. I recite a sonnet in praise of her beauty but she laughs at me. I am lying on my back in the grass whilst my mother, the perfection of womanhood, strokes my brow...*

I wake. The old wretch is sitting by my side tending to me as she might her own child. She is mopping my brow with a rag.

'You'll be better now. Does the job and no mistake.'

I look at her face with gratitude and sadness. I still see the discoloured skin, the wispy hair and the bad teeth. I also see a pair of gentle all-seeing eyes that could be those of an intelligent child. How old is she? Much younger than she looks I'm certain. Why is she reduced to this? I do not need to ask. Poverty, abuse, disease and whoredom would be her lot. She tells me how she was once beautiful. She has a name – Ann. She performed with a troupe and danced the part of a dove in a masque at Court. Such things do not last.

I know I dreamed while I slept but I remember nothing of it. For some reason I know that I must write Peggy a long letter and the perfect love song.

4

Hyde Park Corner

I FIND WORK in the statuary workshop of Mr John Bacon and, much as my previous foreman had predicted, it is infinitely more interesting than dressing identical blocks of sandstone. John Bacon is a craftsman who loves fine stone and prides himself on the quality of the pieces that leave his workshop. He is a broad stocky man of prodigious strength, frequently lifting, single-handed, pieces of stone under which two other masons would have struggled. He is self-taught but has gained so much respect as to have been awarded membership of the Royal Academy. His journeymen and apprentices are plainly in awe. Mr Bacon produces monuments and ornamental masonry of the highest quality, working in fine imported stone: Carrara marble, jasper, agate and jet black polished granite. His workshop is one of several clustered round Hyde Park Corner, each housed in a substantial wooden building with its own fenced-off yard. The different 'shops' compete for business, but their proximity also encourages a fellowship. The masons' relationship with their master is close. John Bacon frequently discusses with his men the best technique for the execution of a difficult design, or how to achieve the perfect gradient on the side of a monumental urn.

I warm immediately to this roughly-spoken man who has risen from the humblest origins through his own dedication and skill. When my first assignment is to assist John Bacon in carving panels for a black marble tomb, I am overjoyed. I appreciate his skill but, far more, I value his willingness to pass on secrets and techniques to masons who will live after his days.

If my master is a source of inspiration, his journeymen and apprentices are not. They are scarcely less hostile to me than were the workmen of Westminster, but the workshop is smaller and the watchful presence of Mr Bacon dictates a controlled sober atmosphere. This is not the case after work when, with one accord, the masons head for the taprooms intent on washing down the dust of the workshop with London ale. I prepare for this event, understanding that to avoid being branded an outsider and again being abused, I need to make myself an indispensable insider who appears to enjoy their high spirits, horseplay and bawdy humour. As in the taprooms of Cowbridge and Cardiff, I perform. My stories earn laughter. My antics gain applause. My flute is in demand, but it is my ballads that win me a place in the beery fellowship. I stand on the table. I march up and down, gesticulating and overacting with panache whilst singing my own 'Stonecutters' Song':

A young stonecutter once did in Westminster dwell
Who for mirth and good humour did many excel.
No lad more expert wielded chisel and mallet
He could sing a good song and make a new ballad.

There is a chorus 'Hi do di Hi do di Hi do di ay yee' which the company sings whilst clashing tankards together and banging the table in time. I extemporise verses, adding references to individual masons present or to masters who, in their absence, can be safely reviled.

The day was quite cold and our toil very hard
But purse-cramming masters pay little regard,
(shouts of 'The skinflint')

Yet night is our own, it gives freedom and rest,
Come, ruby-faced landlord, a pint of your best.
(cheers and calls for more beer)

Best of all, the company enjoys any reference to their trade or to bawdy boastful womanising. I contrive to combine the two. I introduce my stonecutter hero to a beautiful maiden. Celia, I confide with a quiet conspiratorial hush, has:

Skin like Carrara, so white and so sleek,
(whoops of appreciation),
The blush of the Jasper enamelled her cheeks
(cries of lust)
Eyes glossier than agate, more black than Vamure.
(stonemasons collapse in mock sexual satisfaction)

Having set up my young Celia as the stonemasons' perfect untouchable romantic woman, I tell, in couplets, a raunchy tale of her erotic seduction and deflowering. Each stage in the maiden's conquest is accompanied by a thrust of the pelvis, a straight arm gesture or even a wriggle of the bottom. Throughout, as a trained stonemason, my seducer employs 'a well tempered tool' (there are shrieks of appreciation).

So I become, in the eyes of my fellow stonemasons, 'a real geezer' – for a time at least.

5

The Gwyneddigion

DESPITE MY DIFFICULT farewell from the Reverend John
Walters, he had been good enough to have written, on
my behalf, to influential figures amongst the London Welsh
recommending me as someone who might make a valuable
contribution to their literary evenings.

In April 1773 I duly appear at the Bull's Head, a spacious and
well-stocked tavern in the heart of Walbrook, City of London.
Here, in a well-appointed upstairs room with two potmen and
several serving girls to provide their needs, the Society of the
Gwyneddigion meet on the first Monday of each month. I am
early, partly out of anxiety and partly because I am hoping to
introduce myself to Owain Jones, president of the Society, and
one of the names to whom John Walters has written.

Owain Jones greets me enthusiastically. I am impressed by
his firm handshake, broad rounded face and warm smile. He has
dark reassuring eyes that inspire confidence. I think he must be
in his early thirties but his full figure and calm authority makes
him appear older.

'You're very welcome. I'm Owain, Owain Jones usually, but
Owain Myfyr in the Society. We like to give ourselves bardic
names even if we don't write!'

Owain Myfyr leads me up the darkened staircase into the
meeting chamber. It's a handsome room with large windows,
a good fire ablaze in the grate, sideboards with trays of food on
either side, a painting of somewhere impressive with arches on

the wall, and a single enormous oak table which fills the centre of the room. As we cross the threshold Owain announces,

"*Nawr 'te. Rheol gyntaf y Gymdeithas. Yr eiliad yr wyt ti'n croesi stepen y drws, bydd popeth yn y Gymraeg.*"[15]

He explains that one reason he and some of his acquaintances started Y Gwyneddigion three years before was the tendency of the other Welsh societies to allow members to slip into English during meetings. That, in his opinion, was a symptom of the way they had lost focus, forgetting their primary aim: the preservation and promotion of Welsh culture. Instead, some societies had become little more than drinking clubs. I glance at the rows of tankards being lined up by the potmen in preparation for the evening. Owain notices my glance and guesses my thought. He smiles.

'*Ysbryd yr oes yn anffodus. Diod a rhyw ymhobman. Ond o leiaf fi fydd yn cadw rheolaeth yn ystod y cyfarfodydd.*'[16]

And so it proves. When the assembly of bankers, merchants, periwig makers, clerks and lawyers are assembled, Owain calls them to order. My tankard is filled by a young woman who, to my delight, speaks to me in Welsh. Tankards charged, with one accord the company rise to their feet and make the rafters shake with a resounding toast,

'*Hir oes i'r iaith Gymraeg.*'[17]

Owain welcomes the company and introduces their latest member, Iorwerth Morganwg. I stand and am warmly applauded. The business proceeds. There are announcements about publications. The members each pay an annual subscription of 10/6*d.* so as to fund research and the printing of volumes. The

---

15 Now then. The first rule of the Society. The moment you cross the threshold, everything will be in Welsh.
16 Spirit of the age, unfortunately. Drink and sex to be found everywhere. But at least I am the one who keeps charge during the meetings.
17 Long live the Welsh language.

chairman reports that Ieuan Fardd has accepted a commission to collect and edit a collection of ancient Welsh proverbs and triads. I am delighted by this news. That the brilliant, but impoverished, scholar whom I so admire should be supported by this Society, far away in London, must say a great deal for the scholarship and seriousness of Owain. He declares his intent to commission a similar collection of the poetry of Llywarch Hen. I note the power of patronage. This is what Rhys Thomas the printer promised I would find in London. There follows a tedious series of reports from members on their contacts with Wales that appear little more than guides to taverns of distinction.

The main speaker is introduced. Siôn Ceiriog thanks the chairman not only for his inspired leadership but the pleasure he had given those present through his own transcriptions of the work of Dafydd ap Gwilym. These were copied from ancient manuscripts belonging to Richard Morris, a man from Anglesey, now working as a clerk in the Navy Office of the Tower of London. It is from the well-thumbed pages of Owain's handwritten volume that our speaker will read today. There is loud approval. Those who have borrowed the volume tell their neighbours how excellent the contents are. Those who had not yet had the privilege express their hopes of an early opportunity.

He chooses '*Trafferth mewn Tafarn*',[18] a comic account of the poet's failed attempt to seduce a serving girl and his escape from the wrath of three Englishmen and the staff of the inn. How, when tiptoeing down a corridor towards safety, he knocks over a large metal bowl which clangs and wakes the entire house. Siôn reads the piece well, then debates the more obscure phrases. He praises and analyses the complex versification and explains why the bard's first-person style had been so revolutionary

18 Trouble in a Tavern.

four hundred years before. Although scholarly, this is no dry lecture. The speaker entertains his audience, emphasising the knockabout comedy of Dafydd's situation, the general bawdiness of the fourteenth century and comparing it, with some apparent justification, to situations some of the present company might have experienced.

Gradually, the tone of the meeting deteriorates into a more literate version of the bawdy evenings I endure in the company of my fellow stonecutters. Siôn apologises to the chairman for the necessity, but ends with a section from Dafydd ap Gwilym's '*Cywydd y Gal*', a poem warning of the uncontrollable nature of the author's penis. '*Trosol wyd a bair traserch*'[19] complains Dafydd of his own member and its endless capacity for getting him into trouble.

I cannot describe the excitement I feel. I have never felt more certain that this is a company in which I can shine. These are subjects where I am knowledgeable and skills of which I am a master. I wait to impress myself on the company. As soon as Siôn sits down to loud applause, raucous cries and much banging of the table, the newly introduced Iorwerth Morganwg gets to his feet. I improvise a few lines in the same strict and complex metre used by Dafydd ap Gwilym. I thank the speaker for his scholarship and wit, then acknowledge his expertise as a sexual adventurer and stud.

Bwch ydyw i'w ryw a'i rin,
Diawlig am ledu deulin,
Marchaidd ymhlith y merched.[20]

Siôn looks uncertain whether to be flattered or embarrassed

---

19 You are a crowbar of lust.
20 A stud by nature and sort, / A devil for spreading thighs, / A stallion among the girls.

as his fellow members shout raucously or demand him to confirm the extent of his private parts. The applause tops everything that has proceeded. Faces turn wanting more, and I feel the charge that comes from knowing that I have an audience under my control. I am surrounded by admiring company as I command the table with invention and verse. If only I had brought my flute! Iorwerth Morganwg has started to make his mark on London.

6

Good company

M ANY OF THE Gwyneddigion are good company. But not all. I am impressed by the genuine dedication of people like Owain Myfyr and William Owen[21] to academic research. They give me access to important documents, some of which I have been seeking for years, but none so precious as the copied verses of Dafydd ap Gwilym. Owain professes an ambition to publish a definitive edition of the surviving work of Wales' greatest poet. I cannot image a more fulfilling project and I assure him that I will do all I can to carry out his mission. I assure him that I am well equipped to root out surviving manuscripts wherever they may be.

At Owain's request, I compose and perform for the Gwyneddigion several times more, but never with the same success. Each time I feel my welcome fade a little. Some, who consider themselves most learned, are becoming critical of my verse. I fear their observations. They are disparaging, not just of my technique but of what they consider to be my base vocabulary. Glamorgan words they consider more suited to the conversations of peasants than the compositions of poets. As I deliver my latest piece I see them exchanging knowing looks and supercilious glances. I see notes passed, and asides whispered whilst I declaim. One sniggers. Standing in front of the big table

---

21 William Owen is better known as William Owen Pughe, a surname he adopted in 1806 to acknowledge an inheritance. A solicitor's clerk with a passion for all things Welsh.

becomes a trial. I want to crawl underneath. I limp to the end, cutting several good lines in my haste to finish. I know that they are criticising, belittling my work. The fact that I cannot see what they write or hear what they say makes it worse. I imagine their condemnation of my humble beginnings.

William Owen tries to convince me that I'm mistaken, that much of what I fear is the product of my imagination. I do not believe him. The truth is that for many of the Gwyneddigion, Wales beyond Gwynedd scarcely exists. If they are conscious of a Wales beyond their mountains, they regard it as a hinterland, an untidy and unnecessary fringe worthy only of mockery.

Nevertheless, I find several individuals of the Society to be invigorating companions with a refreshing approach to life. Naval surgeon David Samwell tells wildly improbable stories of adventuring on the southern seas and supplies me with good-quality laudanum made to his own formula. Richard Glyn works in a City counting house. He earns good money and spends more on a single meal than I can earn in a week. He is full of brash confidence. What appeals to me is his unexpressed belief that, with enough endeavour, anything is possible. He invites me for dinner at the Bull so that he can talk of Wales. He is patriotic beyond doubt and very sentimental. He boasts that he will happily donate up to ten guineas – no, twenty – if it will assist in the salvation of the ancient poetry of our forefathers. What are ten guineas to a partner in Hoare's counting house? As the port flows he explains his love for Wales: the sounds of the language, the soulful link between the landscape and its people, the way Welsh poetry resonates in his head, the laughter of Welsh children, the gentle dimpled smile of a Welsh maiden.

After half a bottle of port the language changes to English, but the passion doubles. He came originally from the Clwyd Valley, the most beautiful, most fruitful valley in Wales. Why did he ever leave? How often does he return? It's difficult when life and work keeps him so busy, but he will soon, maybe? Like so many others in the society, Richard's dedication to Wales is not based on personal connections or affection for his '*milltir sgwâr*'[22] but is generalised, a love of the concept of Wales that can be discharged without the inconvenience of leaving London. The second bottle appears. I drink little. I do not have a strong head for port and on these occasions I sip whilst others swallow. I do not expect my companion to manage two more glasses before collapsing, but I miscalculate the capacity of Richard Glyn.

With a start he springs to his feet and declares that the time has come to show 'his bardic companion' the joys of London. Whilst he loves Wales, he confides that there is nothing to compare with the refined delights of Covent Garden. I do not understand, but I follow, I know not where. I cannot resist the spirit of those like Richard who are prepared to take risks, to extract every last ounce out of life's rich experience. How could I possibly refuse his invitation into the unknown?

We take a carriage from the City to the piazza of Covent Garden, and alight in front of St Paul's Church where, Richard informs me, we may hear a sermon in Welsh nearly every other Sunday. On the journey Richard has been thumbing thoughtfully through his notebook as if selecting from a menu. Now he seizes my hand, pulls me from the carriage and runs excitedly under the long portico to the side of the piazza until we reach a fine green painted door. Richard knocks. He rings. He cries, 'It's me: Richard. Let me in, my sweet.'

Eventually the door is opened by a turbaned Indian pageboy dressed in fine green and yellow silks. He whispers something to Richard about 'a special guest' being in the

---

22   Home territory, literally 'square mile'.

house and there being a need for discretion. Richard nods conspiratorially. The boy leads us into a small but opulent chamber decorated with a richness that overwhelms my senses; fine, exquisitely carved French furniture upholstered in rich brocade, silk wall hangings, marble surfaces, thick Eastern carpets over a geometrically patterned marble floor. The air is heavy with rich scent. Five doors lead off the room to other chambers. But what really astounds me is the sight of three voluptuous ladies reclining on the various couches, draped lazily in coloured silks. They smile at Richard who is obviously a regular visitor. I curse my stupidity and naivety. I have allowed myself to be taken to a bordello where my companion is clearly set on buying time with one of the ladies before us. I know that Richard and his friends are fond of sexual bravado, but I had assumed that that bravado was where it ended. I am panicking. Do I want to have sex with one of these women? Do I want to have sex with a whore? What about the risk of catching the pox? How could I ever look Peggy or Kitty in the face again? Just being in this place is a betrayal of my mother. Of her memory. Would I be able to perform as expected? I feel fear, not arousal. I remember I have only pennies in my pocket. What will happen when they discover I cannot pay? Richard is now deep in discussion with two of the ladies. One rises and hangs on his arm, whilst the second is walking in my direction. I take a step back until I am wedged against a side table. She places one hand on my shoulder and brings her face uncomfortably close to mine. For a moment I think that she is the same whore who had accosted me in the Haymarket, but it is only the powder and paint that coincide. This woman's paint is better applied and her clothes are finer, if even more revealing. I try the line that had worked before.

'I've no money.' She is unabashed.

'Don't worry, me luv. Richard will look after that side of things. Hoare's Bank has enough money for all of us. You're his guest. So aren't you a lucky boy? By the way I'm Polly, and I'm going to give you the time of your life.'

I glance past Polly in the direction of Richard who waves briefly before disappearing with the whore of his choice through a door into another part of the building. Polly takes my hand and gently but firmly leads me towards another door. I consider running away. The door consumes us. Once inside, I have come too far to retreat. The inside of Polly's boudoir is painted deep red, with gold-painted furnishings and portraits of reclining voluptuous ladies. All such details are insignificant compared to the large feather bed which dominates the room and sets the agenda.

'I take it you're another of Richard's Welsh friends. My, you're a wild bunch and no mistake.'

Polly starts without ceremony to unbutton my jacket.

'We've a Welsh girl here, you know. Proper Welsh. Speaks Welsh and all.'

Now she removes my waistcoat and pulls at my belt.

'Not that she's as good as me, of course. Take your shoes off, there's a luv.'

I am reduced to my shirt when the noises start from the other side of the wall. I am startled by what sounds like the crack of a whip and a groan. Then another, and a louder groan. Polly grimaces in annoyance.

'Sorry about the noise. That's our "special" guest so we have to put up with his little… peculiarities. Normally Madam doesn't offer that sort of thing but you can't say no to the special guest, can you?'

The whip cracks continue and the moans became louder. Then there is a crack louder than all the others followed not by a groan but by a scream. Polly looks exasperated.

'Now, how can a girl concentrate on her work with all that going on in the next room?'

I sympathise.

'No matter, I'll just have to keep your mind off the distractions.'

With that Polly shrugs off her robe which falls to the floor leaving her standing quite naked before me.

'All right luv? Like what you see? Come on then. Let's get on with it.'

At that there's a loud knock on the door.

'What the fuck!' exclaims Polly. 'Go away!'

Instead the door bursts open and a large red-faced woman strides into the room.

'Polly, come with me. You're needed next door with His Highness.'

'But...' Polly gestures towards me.

'Our special guest has suffered an injury. That silly girl Sarah has whipped him too hard and drawn blood. He wants you, and *only* you, to bathe his wounds. Bring a clean rag and that camphor liniment.'

Polly grabs her robe from the floor with a gesture of hopelessness.

'It'll fucking cost him.'

She ferrets in a drawer for the liniment, and then turns to me.

'Sorry about this, luv. You just wait there and I'll be back as soon as I can. If you're in a hurry, Madam will fix you up with one of the other girls.'

There is a loud groan through the partition.

'Coming, your Highness, coming,' Polly yells as she sails off.

The Madam does not leave but stands listening anxiously to the sounds from the next room. I stand in just my shirt feeling very exposed but mildly curious.

'Who's the special guest?' I inquire.

Madam notices my existence and looks at me in disbelief.

'You really don't know? Where have you been living?' A thought passes through her head.

'Best stay quiet about this, I suggest. Don't want any scandals about the Royals, do we now? Good customers but dangerous people to upset, if you get my meaning.'

She leaves the room. I see my chance to escape. I dress hurriedly and try to let myself out unnoticed. I would have succeeded if it had not been for the large beaten bronze bowl in the entrance hall which I knock over. The resounding clang brings heads round doors and the Indian pageboy comes at a run. I do not wait to explain but escape into the night.

I blunder around the colonnade of Covent Garden, still buttoning my waistcoat. It is a cold night and I wrap my jacket tighter about me. I am relieved to have escaped. I wander without thought, down Southampton Street, across the Strand and down to the Thames. I stand for a while trying to collect my thoughts. People like Richard do not think in the same way as me. It is so easy to assume that, because we both speak Welsh, we have more in common than is the case. He is a product of London, first and foremost. For him, being Welsh is a pastime, an amusement. I shiver. It is very cold. I must get back to Holborn. The fog is descending once more, smothering the lanterns of the carriages and filling the lungs of this dirty city with grey poison. I start back towards Drury Lane. From there I know I can walk north to Holborn. Somehow, I go too far east and find himself in Fetter Lane, then Dean Street which I do not know, then Shoe Lane until I have to admit that I am, again, lost. This time Ann, my ministering landlady, will not be able to rescue me from my soft grey cell. The fog is making breathing difficult. My limbs ache with the cold and damp. My head throbs. The smell of sweet perfume from the bordello will not leave my nostrils. It makes me feel bilious. There is escape. I might not have Ann to save me but I do have David Samwell's special laudanum prescription. I now carry a small bottle with me at all times, just in case... I squeeze into a deserted doorway and drink. Within minutes the warmth floods through my veins, London fades, and I am flying in a clear blue sky over my beloved Vale, Glamorgan's happy land.

When I look down I can see Peggy and my brothers, and Father. They are all pointing at me whilst I fly overhead. I am reciting. I am reciting the greatest poetry ever. All the animals, wild and tame, are looking up at me and listening to my words. The Gwyneddigion are here too. Some are applauding, but a few are shouting, telling me that I'm not using the true, the pure north Wales Welsh. I raise my voice and all the animals join in with me, Peggy and my brothers until we drown out those ignorant north Walians. I'm racing now. Racing across the fields and racing towards Peggy. Oh, Peggy! I try and reach her but I'm caught in a roomful of tall frightening ladies with enormous hairpieces. They won't let me go. My mother is telling me to get out of that evil house, but I can't. They are holding my arms and legs and their faces are getting closer all the time. I can smell their perfume and their sweat. I fight through them but, when I try to escape, I'm in a hallway full of ringing bells and clanking metal bowls. I move a bowl but it falls. The noise is deafening. Instead of dying down the clang grows louder. Peggy takes my hand and drags me clear. We run. We are running across green fields. I can see the church in Flemingston and inside Kitty is marrying, marrying someone else! The Gwyneddigion are in the congregation. When I appear they turn and point and laugh nasal north Wales laughter. Now my mother is in the pulpit reading. I am the only one in the church. She is reading Paradise Regained *to me. I am close enough to hear. 'Great acts require great means of enterprise.' Oh yes, Mother. Yes. Give me time. Just give me time. I'm in a lane, a green lane somewhere in the Vale. I'm not alone. There's a strong well-built fellow walking at my side. His clothes are odd. Clothes from another age. He is reciting to me. He smells of beer and garlic. He is reciting* 'Trafferth mewn Tafarn'. *It's Dafydd. It's Dafydd ap Gwilym come to tell me where I can find his lost poems. He's whispering lines to me, such beautiful lines. I want to write them down. I can't find my notebook. Can I remember them? Will I be able to remember them? Owain will be so pleased if I can remember them.*

Darkness.

7

A falling out

L ONDON IS NOT a comfortable place for me despite its excitement and attractions. The fog, dirt and its stinking immorality make me long for an easier clime and honest people. At least I am reasonably at ease with my work. My effort to become the toast of the stonecutters at Hyde Park Corner has not led to friendship but it has occasioned a truce in which they accept me as their honorary court jester. I am well aware they still look on me as an outsider, not just because of my Welshness but because both they and I sense an indefinable gulf in values, assumptions and understanding. I fear tensions will surface.

John Bacon's men occasionally have the task of transporting a monument from the works to a final location outside the city. This is viewed as a 'good number'. It allows those concerned to escape the noisy, dusty workshop and spend time in a horse and cart trotting through the lanes of Bloomsbury or Edmonton. It sometimes provides the extra bonus of being entertained with drink and food at the house where the installation takes place. I have never been selected for such an errand. I put this down to desire on the part of longer-serving masons to safeguard their privileges. I do not complain.

It is a fine spring morning when the master asks me to be responsible for the delivery and installation of a new gatepost finial. I carved the round ball on a square plinth to the exact dimensions he specified. It has to match the opposing twin in every detail. It is to be mounted on the entrance gates to the property of a leading wine merchant.

Two fellows accompany me on the task. The cart is loaded with the finial, sand, cement, ropes and lifting tackle required. It is clear from the first that Harry, the oldest and longest-serving of the stonecutters does not want me on the trip. He is accustomed to making such ventures in the company of a single apprentice and cannot see the need for another mason to join them. John Bacon insists. The task of matching an existing finial is demanding. He would rather have replaced the two, thus ensuring symmetry, but the owner was not persuaded. Our master wants the stonecutter to be present to make whatever final adjustments may be necessary.

It is a glorious journey in spring sunshine. The cart moves slowly as the horse battles with the weight of the load. None of us feel the need to urge the poor beast to move faster as we breathe in the sweeter air of the countryside around Islington. We stop to give the horse a rest and drink in Finsbury Park. Harry approaches me awkwardly.

'Look, cock. I've been doing these installations for many years and, well, there are ways we do things. Get me?'

I do not understand and look blankly at him.

'Just let me do the talking and the arranging. Right? You just take care of the stonework. Agreed?'

I agree. We are at the mansion for three hours whilst the column is prepared, the mortar mixed, the finial is raised and finally deposited in its rightful place. I look with satisfaction at the completed work. Although obviously new, it otherwise matches the original on the other gatepost in every way. Time and weather will make them twins.

I try not to hear as Harry and the steward of the house agree to add amounts to the bill for 'unforeseen alterations' – of which there have been none. I remain silent as the hospitality we are offered expands from bread, cheese and beer to the taking away of several fine bottles and a large cut of meat from the kitchen. I say nothing as the unused sand, cement and two lengths of good rope are quietly offloaded, for a consideration, at 'a place Harry knows' in Islington. Although I am seething with indignation at the way these masons dishonour their trade, I know it is better to say nothing.

At the end of the journey Harry approaches me awkwardly and tries to put a half-guinea into my pocket with a quiet, 'That's your cut, Taff, OK? Not a word now.'

I instinctively refuse, holding my hand over my pocket to prevent him. I hope and expect that he will shrug, dismiss me as a fool and be all too ready to pocket my share of the stolen money. But Harry reacts badly. He curses. His face distorts as if he intends to stuff the money down my throat.

'You stuck-up little prick. Think you're so fucking superior don't you? Too good, too shogging clever for the likes of us.'

As he walks away, his hunched shoulders eloquently express his dislike of me and disdain for my actions. Why does he want me to share his stolen money? Because he wants me implicated in his petty criminality. If we are all involved, theft ceases to be a crime. It is just 'the way we do things'. Theirs is a fraternity to which I will not belong.

There is also calculation. Self-preservation dictates to Harry he cannot leave me in a position of innocence from where I could accuse others. In case I think of talking to John Bacon, Harry strikes first. He confidentially reports to the master that there had been 'irregularities' committed by 'that Taffy' which he feels it his duty, as a loyal employee, to reveal. John Bacon is not fooled. I am not dismissed, but from that moment forward, the air in the workshop becomes as poisonous as any fog. As at Westminster Bridge, no chance is missed to make my life unbearable. Comic ballads are not going to help me this time.

I have had enough. After less than a year in London I fear that the caustic pollution will erode my weak lungs and corrode my morals. The place is a physical and moral cesspit. I write to Peggy to tell her that I am escaping the 'silly city's malignant sneer, the coxcomb's hissing cry'. I can no longer live amongst such a vile debauched race of men. But neither can I return to Glamorgan. John Charles is still actively pursuing me for damages. The hurt of Kitty's betrayal remains too fresh. I will head into the English countryside, although it takes me ever further from Wales.

I tell Ann that I am leaving. She looks genuinely sorry to the point of tears. I ask if she would keep some of my books for me until I return. She agrees greedily as if she were keeping a set of love letters. I ask her if she can read. She cannot, but promises to learn. I promise to teach her one day and head for Kent.

8

Kent

I FEEL NO love for Kent or its coastal towns. I am here because I cannot be in the places I love. As I walk across the flat level landscape, I long for the green vales and mountains of Glamorgan. I long for the literary success that only London can award. Kent offers neither. But it does offer sanctuary, employment and clean air.

I sit on a wall in the docks at Sandwich watching barges pass to and fro. The sight is soothing, hypnotic. I feel that I have escaped, for a time, from the most persistent of my persecutors. I have escaped the cry of my south Wales debtors and the critical carping of the Gwyneddigion. I feel Kent is a place where the world cannot see me. It is a place where I am unknown except as a stonemason, and in that work I can be quietly secure in my skill. For a long time I write nothing, enjoying the feeling of calm and the numbness that results. Sometimes ideas and rhymes force their way into my head. I write, both in Welsh and English, but I show the work to no one. I cannot endure the criticism or ridicule that might follow.

After much hesitation I send three poems called '*Cywydd y Daran*' to Owain Myfyr. These are written in the manner of Dafydd ap Gwilym and I acknowledge this. It took many months for me to convince myself that they were of a high enough quality. I always make endless revisions before reaching a final version. Not that any version ever feels final.

I could revise for ever. My fear of criticism is such that, even after months of careful preparation, I protect myself by pretending to Owain that these are no more than rough amusements. I warn of the imperfections he may find. The poems contain Glamorgan words and I can imagine the sneers that will evoke amongst the Gwyneddigion. Why do I send them at all? Much as I fear criticism, I need someone to affirm that my work is good. I need applause and praise as much as clean air.

From my Kentish retreat I write letters. I have always written letters but in Kent it has become a daily habit. A table in the corner of the taproom of the Ship Inn, Faversham, has become my writing desk. I write to Owain in London, to Peggy in Llanfair, to John Walters in Llandochau, to Rhys Thomas in Cowbridge, to Ieuan Fardd in Towyn, even to my father in Flemingston. My correspondents are all so different. Each letter I write brings out a different aspect of whoever I am. When I write to my father, I write as a tradesman and talk of the new skills I have acquired. In my letters to John Walters, I am a studious disciple determined to learn. To Ieuan Fardd, I'm an antiquarian with a profound knowledge of the ancient ways. To Owain Myfyr, I write as a bard but cover myself by proclaiming my total absence of ambition, writing 'only for my own amusement'. To Rhys Thomas I am a poet down on my luck, oppressed by the philistinism and ignorance of the public. To Peggy, I am a romantic who praises nature and sees the hand of God in every flower. Which of these is the true Iorwerth? Sometimes I recognise none of them. They all appear to be masks I choose to wear, behind which cowers a wretched thing, adrift and rudderless. I would no more face the world without a mask than I would walk naked down the main street. I even wear a mask to hide myself from myself. When I do not, my thoughts become melancholy and self-destructive. I may be able to escape my persecutors in Kent. I cannot escape my own demons.

The flatlands of northern Kent are a good setting for melancholia but they also provide ample work for stonemasons in the ports and towns. I find work in Margate, Deal and Dover before being offered a more permanent position in Sandwich. This small port is booming and there is no shortage of merchants who want to improve their old wood-frame houses by the addition of a classical portico. My skills are admired and I am offered not just a job but a foreman's job directing the work of a team of masons. This is not a good experience. The masons I am sent to lead are an ignorant set of blockheads. Their skills are poor and they dislike it when I correct or try to teach them. I lose my patience with several of them and in return they openly refuse to follow my orders. They complain to the Master that all mistakes are down to my incompetence. Abuse as to my Welshness follows as night follows day. I walk away and attempt to rid myself of anger by writing a furious verse denouncing the English.

Ni feidr y Sais brwysglais brwnt
Na gwawd y tafawd na'r tant.[23]

I am worried as to how I may ever earn a decent living? I have watched Owain Myfyr establish himself as a prosperous trader in fine furs from his unpromising start as an apprentice from Wrexham. I see that it is through trading rather than plying a trade that men like him become wealthy. How will I ever earn more than a labourer's hire? I study the shipping companies, hotels, even the famous gunpowder mills of Faversham trying

---

23 The ignorant English with barbarous tongue / Know nothing of verse or how praises are sung.

to understand the mechanism by which men become, if not wealthy, at least secure against want. It would be good to set up a business, particularly one that did not involve stone dust.

Then again, why should I? I am a highly-skilled craftsmen and a member of a proud trade. I and my fellow men deserve better. When scholars admire the civilisations of Greece or Rome, they hang on their walls images of the work of masons, great creations in marble and granite which express the highest achievements of classical civilisation. Does anyone know the names of the skilled men who wielded the chisels? No, they are forgotten, whilst others, wealthy but unworthy, inscribe their names on the arches and entrance halls. The injustice tortures me.

My asthma is much improved but other health problems beset me. Whilst working in Sandwich, building a chimney, I suffer an attack of the palsy which leaves me unable to use my left arm for three days.

As months, as the years, pass, I become convinced that I am wasting my youth on 'useless rambles'. I am becoming desperately homesick. I write verses praising 'Old Cambria' and eulogising the beauty and fruitfulness of the Vale. In my loneliness I long for female company. I have banished Kitty from my thoughts. It is to Peggy I write. I bombard her with poetry in which I name her as '*Euron – the Golden One*'. I receive few replies but enough to know that my letters have been received and are treasured.

I have too much time for thought. I need direction. I want to know what I am trying to do with my life. Could I make it as a businessman? Could I build my reputation as a poet? Could I perhaps build my reputation as a self-taught scholar and win commissions from Owain Myfyr and others? What do I really want?

To Peggy I write, 'No idea can be more grievous to me than

that of quitting this life without having been, in some degree, the benefactor of mankind.'

Now, is that my true voice or am I donning a mask that I hope Peggy will admire?

Part Three:
Vale of Glamorgan
1777 to 1786

1

Avebury, Bristol and Minehead

I STAND IN the centre of one of the inner rings of stone. Around me the ancient Avebury outer henge stretches two hundred yards or more in all directions. It is late afternoon and the sun's rays cast dramatic shadows on the rings of stone. I place my hand on a block of Sarsen stone that towers twelve feet above me. I do so with quiet respect, just as a small boy might touch the knee of a giant. I look upwards, hoping for acceptance and a caress. I know stone. I see its grain and formation. I admire the craft of those who had hewn, carried and erected so great a piece. It does not require imagination to be awed and humbled by the physical enormity of this ancient construction. But I find it a Herculean task to grasp the uses of the place and the ancient and divine purposes of those who built it. Not just this place, but Silbury Hill and Stonehenge, all of which I have visited on my slow journey home.

What is this place? Certainly a scene of ritual and ceremony. There is plenty written about the ancient druids – most of it rubbish written from an English, rather than an ancient British, viewpoint. Even those who are aware of the ancient origins of druidism come out with some strange ideas. Owain and the Gwyneddigion make much of the oft-stated belief that the druids had their stronghold on Anglesey. But how could that be when these massive stone works exceed in size anything that could be found on that island? Plainly just another instance of north Walians trying to persuade the rest of Wales that anything and everything of significance took place in Gwynedd.

I'm sitting in one of the inner circles of stone, trying to reconstruct the ancient splendour of this place in my mind – how it might have looked at the height of its glory. I hear the spirits of ancient druids chanting as they move with slow and dignified steps through the stages of their rituals. I can feel the stone I touch tremor in union with the chanting, the incantations and invocations of a hundred, two hundred robed priests as they move in patterns around the circle and its centre stone. These sequences, these incantations have been passed on from one priestly generation to the next since the dawn of time. They tell of the secrets of the Earth, the stars, of fire and water, light and dark, life and death. The words are indistinct. I cannot make out the meanings but they are chanting in the ancient ancestor of the language I speak daily, the language of the Britons from the age before the invasions of Saxons, Angles, Normans, or Romans, before Arthur or Vortigern. The rhythm of their words dances in my ears as they danced on the lips of my forefathers.

They carry wreaths. They carry ceremonial banners adorned with mystic symbols of druidism. Animals are being led forward: a white goat, a foal. For sacrifice? There is a cage of doves and a giant sword. There are maidens carrying armfuls of flowers. A bard steps onto the stone in the centre of the circle and recites an ode to the one living God. It is an ode of unimaginable beauty, written in the bardic metre passed down from generation to generation in an unbroken line. The bard praises God. He praises the God who inspires this ceremony of adoration. This is the only God: the God of nature, of peace, of purity, of innocence, of pity, but above all, the God of understanding.

I am bewitched by the sounds. Cadences rise and fall in

complex harmony. These are not made by crude instruments of horn or catgut. These are not sounds made by human voices but are the sounds of the stars and planets revolving around this astonishing place, these circles of wonder and truth.

I have nowhere to sleep this night, so I spend it as the uninvited guest of a farmer in the next village. As I struggle to make myself comfortable in the straw of the cowshed, I muse on the wonders I have seen. The contact with the circle imbues me with strength. Whereas only days ago I felt alone and adrift, uncertain of myself or which direction to take, now I feel certainty coursing through my veins. I am part of... no, I am a direct descendant... no, I am heir to this druidic tradition and to the bards of the Islands of Britain. They show me who I am. I am what I have been. Despite the cold, I drift into a sound comfortable sleep.

I am woken rudely by a shout. It is light. I look up to see an angry farmer threatening violence and brandishing a pitchfork. Thankfully he is old and slow. I grab my bag and run for my life, pursued by the derisive jeers and vulgar insults of unlovely milking maids and the barking of dogs.

I have been promised work in Bristol. John Bacon of Hyde Park Corner gave me a letter of introduction to the renowned statuary workshop of Mr Henry Marsh. I had intended to stay for no more than a week to replenish my purse. However, I am so delighted by the quality of the work I am being offered and the excellent rate of payment that I am extending my stay. For once I am in luck. Henry Marsh has received more commissions than he can easily fulfil. I appeared on his doorstep at his hour of greatest need, vouchsafed for by no one less than his old friend John Bacon. I am warmly welcomed as the answer to the prayers of a hard-pressed man. It's not only the much-needed sovereigns I value, but the chance to add another eminent name to the list of master masons who speak well of my work.

I reach Minehead on a warm summer's day in 1777. From here I will find passage on a sloop trading across the Bristol Channel to Aberthaw – my beloved Glamorgan and home. The boat on which I negotiate my passage is a tired, overloaded vessel, one of many trading between Aberthaw and Somerset. They leave the Welsh coast loaded with Glamorgan limestone for building and agriculture, and return with Somerset broadcloth, canvas, oil, pitch and rope. The sloop wallows, rather than sails, across the calm water, but even so there is something splendid about making a return to the land of my birth by sea. As I watch the coast getting closer, feel the wind in my hair, excitement mounts. I look forward to boasting of my success in some of the best statuary works in the land. I am confident that this will generate new commissions for my father, my brothers and me. I also look forward to sharing what I have learnt with the Reverend John Walters who I'm certain will be greatly impressed. More than all of this, I look forward to seeing Peggy to whom I have written such fulsome love letters and by whom I have been given reason to hope. This morning, the world is a truly beautiful place and the ever nearing coastline promises much.

2

Welcome home

I T WAS NAÏVE of me to anticipate a hero's welcome for the homecoming of the prodigal son. True, my father is greatly pleased to see me but scarcely half an hour passes and things are as fractious as if I had never been away. It is good to be reunited with my brothers but, here too, joy is short-lived. They, like me, have been travelling – along many of the same routes but with less success. They complain at length how far they had to travel and how uninteresting and poorly paid was the work they found.

Miles and John explain that many of the big houses where we used to work are falling into the ownership of absentee English or Scottish families. The Duke of Beaufort, the Lord Vernon, and the Earl of Plymouth have all acquired vast Welsh estates they seldom visit. Many only bought the land so as to claim the parliamentary seat. As a result they have little interest in maintaining, let alone improving, the big houses. John believes that Wales can offer him and his brother precious little. He is all for buying a cheap passage from Liverpool to the new Americas. Miles does not openly agree, but one look at his face reveals that he sees little alternative.

I am dismayed, but determined we shall not be so easily defeated. I tell them that we should be more ambitious. We should not be content with patching up barns when we might build palaces. I remind them that I have worked in some of the most fashionable and distinguished statuaries of London and Bristol. The world should be told of the skills the Williams family can offer. I will produce printed handbills to be distributed in the more respectable taverns and coffee shops of Cowbridge, Llantwit Major and Cardiff.

I renew my acquaintance with Rhys Thomas, the printer, who is very happy to print a sheet to my directions. The handbill advertises the services of 'Edward Williams Jun., Marble Mason at Flemingston, near Cowbridge'. I inform readers that I have worked in London and the large cities with experts in the field, whereas local masons have never had the opportunity to work with such masters and learn such skills.

'I thought by now I would be printing a volume of verse,' remarks Rhys Thomas with unnecessary relish.

My father dislikes the wording of the handbill, objecting to the suggestion that Glamorgan masons have anything to learn from London. 'Just fawning to the English you are, suggesting that anything from London is bound to be better.'

Mr Richards, the landlord of the Horse and Groom, praises my efforts as 'appealing to quality'. He agrees to display one at his doorway for a small payment.

The work is not flooding in. True, I have received a few commissions for memorials and a few porticos to town houses, but never enough to keep three brothers and their father in work and bread. I am impatient for results. I write to Mr Thomas Mansel Talbot, the owner of Margam Park, offering my services as a mason and architect. Word has it that the landowner is planning to landscape the area around Margam Abbey by demolishing the village housing that surrounds it. I propose rebuilding the houses on the Talbot estate in a variety of styles so as to create an 'earthly paradise' with clusters of buildings in Grecian, Gothic, Italian and Chinese styles. I receive thanks but no commission. I try to persuade other landowners to adorn their estates with towers, gothic summer houses, ornamental bridges or romantic follies. I provide, free of charge, designs and impressions of how the works would appear. When this fails, I try to persuade the Cowbridge councillors that the Guildhall would benefit from a fine arcaded extension suitable for holding Courts of the Great Sessions and assemblies of quality. The lack of response leaves me fuming over the lack of imagination and foresight of those in authority.

It hurts me to admit that my brothers are right. The old landowning families are rapidly being displaced by richer, distant estate owners with no Glamorgan associations. When these need work carried out on their houses, they bring in masons from Bath, Bristol or even London. The new owners are a curse, lacking any sense of responsibility for the well-being of the tradesmen and artisans of Glamorgan. I am forced by financial need to make regular journeys from Aberthaw to the West Country. In Bath and Bristol I can still find work as a journeyman mason. I am just a labourer paid for my work by the piece. I want more. I spend time on the sloop travelling across the Severn thinking of Owain Myfyr and other successful businessmen amongst the London Welsh and trying to work out how to imitate their achievements in gaining prosperity.

The best part of coming home is to be reunited with Peggy, although even that has not been as easy as I had hoped. She does not run into my arms but makes me work hard for her smiles. We sit together on a bench in St Mary's Church only yards from the door of her parents' house. We walk in the woods around Beaupre. I do all I can to win her over. My protestations of love are heartfelt. I tell her how I longed for the sound of her voice and the touch of her hand during my long exile. I play my flute to her. I bring her presents: bags of sugar, spices and tea from Bristol. I write her poetry: beautiful melodious rhymes far finer than those that had first turned her head as a girl. But Peggy, like me, is older now and wiser. She accepts my gifts. She responds with gratitude and affection, but with a reserve I did not expect.

She teases me. She tells me that she has waited a long time for me and it will do no harm for us to wait a little longer. She teases with oblique references to Kitty Deere or by rebuking me for the periods when I had not written during my absence.

She tells me she must have time to think. This drives me to distraction. I am even more in love than I had thought possible. I find her as good natured as ever, and even prettier and shapelier. She is a woman of sensibility, innocent simplicity, delicate modesty and unaffected sweetness of temper. I adore her gentle features. Her eyes miss nothing. Her fair hair falls in swirling tresses like a brook running with molten gold. I am a slave for her kisses and the passion of her embrace. Sometimes, when we are alone in a discrete place, she insists that we cool our ardour and talk of things other than love. She wishes to read poetry. She surprises me by quoting Shakespeare, discussing philosophy and even debating the significance of the ancient Celtic monuments of the Vale. Whilst I have been away she has sought to better herself by borrowing books from the young parson. She reminds me that she can both read and write. If we were to become man and wife, she would not be some sweet silent kitchen slave but require to be treated with respect as a woman with a brain of her own. Then she permits me to embrace her.

She asks me what future we could have together. I tell her of my schemes to become an architect, to build great palaces, to write the finest verse, to revive the greatness of Glamorgan and bring new honour to the bardic tradition. I talk. She listens. She nods but there is a small frown on her brow. Why?

My brothers tell me that I should not despair. It is common knowledge that she had other suitors during my absence. One had been a farmer's eldest son from Llantrithyd, heir to a sizable holding; the other a thatcher's apprentice from Llanfaes who makes the prettiest corn dollies and who dances brilliantly. She refused both and both eventually despaired. Either would have made a good match but she had saved herself... for me?

I have, of course, met her parents several times and they are aware of my intentions. I fancy her mother has softened towards me. I recall she considered me wayward in my younger days. I try to convince her how much I love her daughter and describe Peggy's purity, patience and virtue. Peggy's mother laughs and tells me that I should get to know the girl a little better before taking her as a wife. Something tells me this is going to be a very long courtship.

The least pleasant welcome home I encounter is in Cowbridge, where I discover that, although the threats of legal action have gone, there are many who still remember that I left owing money and are not prepared to forgive.

I am building a portico on the front of a house in the main street. I have constructed the columns and the front lintel is ready to be mounted. At the end of the day's work I ask the client, a local doctor of renown, if he would be prepared to make half of the payment now that more than half of the work is done. He throws out his chest and in a pompous tone announces, 'not a penny before the work is completed'.

I ask him why? After all, I have the expenses of materials I have had to meet and I have a household to maintain. Without looking me in the face, the doctor announces to an imaginary audience that I am an excellent mason but an unreliable businessman. Over several quarts in the Horse and Groom he had been advised that, despite my clear accomplishments as a mason, 'any man who extends credit to Edward Williams before the work is finished will live to regret his foolishness'. So much for Christian charity.

John Walters' family

I HAVE BEEN looking forward to calling on my old mentor again for several reasons. The most personal is to establish that we are now equals, partners in a great endeavour rather than master and pupil. I have written long and learned letters to the rector outlining my research and theories as to the derivation of words. I have, on one occasion, filled several pages discussing only the various uses of the prefix 'al' in Latin (Alps/Albia = very high); Welsh and Cornish (Alwyn = very white); Irish (Alan = very noble) and Gaelic (Alban = high lands). I sent many such, all designed to impress on the rector the high standards of scholarship I have reached.

I knock on the familiar door, clutching a large sheaf of notes, the product of my research into how words travelled across Europe and through time, adapting their usage and precise meaning to new climates and peoples. I have also brought some of my latest poetry.

The door itself suggests change. It has been repainted from the previous dull brown to a severe black. It is opened by the same Mrs Walters whose manner has increased in severity to match her front door. She looks blankly at me for several seconds before recognition dawns.

'Edward Williams, do come in. We haven't seen you for some time.'

It has been four years since I last visited the house. It is intriguing to see how things have stayed the same, yet how things have also changed. I notice small things: a new umbrella stand and a black statuette of rearing horses that might have been moved from elsewhere in the house. No changes of significance, until a tall figure emerges from the direction of the kitchen to reintroduce himself as John Walters Junior. He shakes my hand warmly. I look up at this well-built handsome young man with strong features and gentle smiling eyes. For a second I remember the boys I met in the kitchen years before. Some things *have* changed. The young man speaks with easy confidence.

'Father told us you were coming today. You've been doing good work with the Welsh societies in London I hear. I would dearly like to hear more. Perhaps we could meet up before the start of term?'

I do not understand. Mrs Walters gladly and proudly explains.

'John is doing his degree at Jesus College, Oxford, where, he assures me, life is far more exciting than in Cowbridge. So we only see him when he comes down.'

I wonder to myself why Oxford colleges 'come down' whereas schools have an 'end of term'? It appears to be the obscure language of a privileged world denied to ordinary people, however clever or hardworking. I banish resentment from my mind for the moment, chiefly because John Walters' welcome is so open and obviously sincere. Maybe, through him, I may glimpse that world of privileged academia? I hear myself reply, rather more stiffly than I intended, 'I'll be delighted to meet up when it's convenient to you.'

'Excellent, and I'll tell Daniel as well. You'd better not keep Father waiting. I know he's been preparing for your visit.'

If 'preparation' suggests that the rector now sees me as more than a pupil, the illusion is dispelled the moment I enter the familiar room. Here nothing has changed. The furniture and ornaments are as they have always been. Only the piles of books on the desk are higher. The rector gestures me to the pupil's customary chair at the side of the table rather than to the upholstered armchairs which the rector would use for visitors of rank. He professes himself pleased to see me fit and well but there the informality ceases. The rector discusses and analyses my letters at length in the manner of a tutor marking the work of a promising but careless pupil. He praises my efforts and thanks me for the small number of commentaries which might be of use to him in the next volume of his dictionary. My work is being diminished, belittled, and dismissed. I feel confused and despondent. This turns to anger as the rector explains that, 'Your research shows great enthusiasm but lacks academic rigour. I'm afraid the fact that you have not had the benefit of grammar school and university education means that you conduct these inquiries in a somewhat haphazard manner.'

My chest swells with indignation. I am wounded. I feel bruised and misused by the ingratitude of the rector. I struggle to control my voice as I try to challenge these dismissive comments.

'Could you explain what is amiss with my commentaries?' I ask in a quiet strangulated tone.

The rector is quite oblivious to the hurt he is inflicting. His emotional detachment makes him atypically cruel. Where potential contributions to the dictionary are concerned, the feelings of others are of no consequence. His own high academic standards cannot be threatened. He replies in a matter-of-fact manner, 'There are, for example, no references, no citations to establish the veracity of your statements. You assert, rather than prove, by reasoned steps. Let me illustrate.'

The rector takes my analysis of the prefix 'ar-' and for a full ten minutes dissects the work, line by line. I have stopped listening long before he ends. When the steady stream of unwanted criticism eventually subsides, I try to win ground in other ways. I report on my various meetings with the London

Welsh, especially Owain Myfyr, and the backing I have won for the publication of future volumes of the Walters' dictionary. I pause, anticipating some gratitude. The rector blinks.

'Yes, thank you for that,' he mutters before adding ungenerously, 'I'm pleased I gave you that introduction.' Rather than give me thanks he makes himself the architect of whatever progress has been made!

Without hope I try to interest the rector in my latest compositions. I explain that I have been very productive since returning to Glamorgan. Would the rector care to read a selection? One look at his stiffness of form tells me the invitation is not wanted but will be accepted out of politeness. The sheaf of poems is placed on a side table, where, I fear, it will stay till my next visit. I marvel how this studious man, with his huge passion for the history and technicalities of the language, has so little time, or desire, to enjoy its poetry. As I walk away from the house I decide that the Reverend John Walters' view of the world has become so narrow as to blind him to the true purpose of his own work. His vision has become microscopic rather than telescopic.

I am determined to scan wider horizons.

4

Glamorgan

T HERE IS ONE aspect of returning home that gives me pure pleasure, presents no unpleasant surprises and provides unlimited inspiration. The unchanging countryside of the Vale of Glamorgan embraces her prodigal son with unconditional affection and showers him with favours.

I am walking the lanes around Flemingston, St Mary Church, Beaupre, and St Hilary intoxicated by the beauty and bounty of nature. I watch as the farmers of the Vale harvest the richest crops and raise the healthiest cattle. I revel in the wildlife, be it a buzzard, fox, badger or deer. I compose endlessly. I have to do so or else the pent-up joy would burst my breast. I compare the gentle fruitfulness of my native land to the unfavourable filth and corruption of London. I see the honesty and virtue of its inhabitants to be in stark contrast to the lewdness and immorality of the capital – and even the rest of Wales.

> *Rhodiais Loegr oll o'i bron*
> *A Chymru lon ddierthwg,*
> *Ond na welais unrhyw dir*
> *Mor deg â Sir Forgannwg.*[24]

I confess to God, to the sky and to the cow parsley my trials of the flesh amidst the evil temptations of London:

---

24 I've travelled all of England's dales / Crossed Wales in all directions, / But never saw another a vale, / So fair as this Glamorgan.

Mi weddïais i ar Dduw
Am nerth i fyw yn ddiddrwg
A fy nhroi yn ôl mewn pryd
I gyrrau clyd Morgannwg.[25]

and how I prayed for deliverance from that sink of vice and depravity.

Now I stand on the top of Bryn Owain imagining Peggy and I living a life of pastoral simplicity immured from the temptations and false idols of riches and luxury. Not just London but Cowbridge now has a smack of the fox about it. Its population have become sly, cunning and thievish.

I revisit all the ancient stoneworks of Glamorgan: the massive dolmen at Tinkinswood, the shattered remnants of Sweyne's Howes, the extraordinary carved faces of Tarren Deusant and the ruined grandeur of Maen Ceti. What could these be but evidence that ancient druidism had seen Glamorgan as its capital?

I write of the common labouring people of the Vale, of simple village events which have survived the centuries. Peggy enjoys the poems but asks why the characters from the Vale are so virtuous.

'Ned, don't make us all out to be saints. There are plenty of unpleasant people in the Vale and I'm sure we have our fair share of thieves, swindlers and murderers.'

I tell her that the function of a poet is to make the world a better, more inspiring place. I show the world as it could be, not always as it is.

'So is that the truth?' she asks.

'Truth of the highest kind,' I reply. She looks at me strangely.

---

25 I prayed to God to keep me strong / Away from all temptations / And bring me home where I belong / To safe and pure Glamorgan.

It is good to once more be able to spend time with the bards of Glamorgan, my literary friends and acquaintances. We are a network of poets and antiquarians. I meet with John Bradford of Betws and Edward Evans of Aberdare to exchange compositions and debate the intricacies of strict-metre poetry. We exchange views on the evidence that survives of ancient druidic practices and the poetic traditions of Glamorgan. I believe that I have failed to understand the true significance of our network of scholars and poets. We have been too prepared to accept the low opinion of others. In truth we are heirs to, and custodians of, a tradition that reaches back to the time when Avebury was in its pomp. When I was instructed in the techniques of *cynghanedd* by Lewis Hopkin, he was passing on to me the heritage of a line of bards stretching back beyond record. Since Lewis died, and others of the tradition – Rhys Morgan of Pencraig Nedd and David Nicholas of Aberpergwm – we are the only real heirs, the only true keepers of the flame that makes Wales uniquely honoured and civilised amongst the nations of Europe.

I have decided not to write to Owain Myfyr or any other of the London Welsh who have offered their support. I resent their assumed importance in the task of asserting Welsh identity and proving the quality of Welsh culture in the face of the damnable prejudice of Samuel Johnson and his kind. In truth, they are only money grabbing spectators. Their only role is to supply finance by which the great chronicled traditions of the ancients might be recorded, published and applauded. Here, in Glamorgan, we *are* that tradition, a living tradition that runs from the age of druids through the ancient guilds of master poets who plied their trade in the halls of the princes, to Lewis Hopkin and his fellows, and then to me, Iorwerth Morganwg.

What significance has the London Welsh apart from that which their money buys them? Why should the great bards of

Glamorgan have to bow the knee to the fat wallets of those who make their fortunes in the open cesspit that is London?

I'm standing before the great dolmen at Tinkinswood and I swear that I will find a way of publishing the works of the medieval masters without tainting the venture with money earned in the corruption of London. What is needed is a man with a fortune. What is needed is a man who can establish a successful business that will itself support the publication of the scattered works from the great age of Bardism. I will be that man.

5

Beaupre

I'M WALKING IN the Beaupre Woods between John Walters, the son, on my right and his brother Daniel on my left. I was a little surprised when they called on me, but it was only as John had promised. I suspected, at the time, he was only being polite and, once caught up in the excitement of Oxford, he would forget. I was wrong. He calls to see me quite often. Daniel usually comes with him. I am reciting for them as we walk. They like the new pieces I have written about the honest country folk of Glamorgan. I think they see me as a country bard, unsullied by the sophisticated mannerisms of more academic poets. I play up to the image. Sometimes they recite too. Often we debate. Always we compose together, competing to find the cleverest rhyme or most ingenious couplet.

They treat me with deference. I think that's just because they are younger than me by ten years – more in Daniel's case. He likes to remind me of the time I entertained them with doggerel verses in the rectory kitchen. Amazingly, they both remember the lines and embarrass me by chanting the verses together by heart. I'm flattered to hear that these became part of their childhood, taking a place alongside the usual children's songs and rhymes. I tell them that I always hoped that I would get another chance to rhyme for them all the other times I visited the rectory. It never happened. Did their mother ensure that?

'Plenty of time now,' remarks John, avoiding the question, 'whenever I'm down from Jesus College, that is.' We walk in silence for a while, picking our way along a muddy track. They are waiting for me to perform.

'Go on, Ned,' urges Daniel at last.

I have a new satirical verse for them but I'm going to make them wait. Instead I talk. They are happy to indulge me whilst I lecture them on nearly everything: antiquity, nature, husbandry, architecture. I talk to them of the poetry of Dafydd ap Gwilym. They listen as I recite in Welsh. When I finish, Daniel apologises that their Welsh is not as fluent or as natural as they would like. John explains that their father always taught them to respect and honour their language but the language of the home was English and the stress in their lessons had been on ensuring their Latin and Greek were of the highest quality.

'Without the Classics we will never fulfil the ambitions he has for us, and I would not now be at Oxford.'

He hesitates. There is plainly something he wants to tell me – or ask me, so I wait, leaving a longer silence than is quite comfortable.

'Ned, I've been looking through some of the Welsh manuscripts in the Bodleian Library. They hold several collections of Welsh medieval manuscripts including the poems of Llywarch Hen. I've been trying to translate some of these into English. If I brought home some copies would you be prepared to help me?'

I agree readily. Why doesn't he ask his father? I know why.

We have reached one of the clearings in the wood and Daniel suggests we rest for ten minutes. I sit on a fallen log with the brothers beside me. From here we can see the valley below through a break in the trees.

'Do we get to hear the new verse yet?' asks Daniel in the tones of the impatient schoolboy he still is.

I stop teasing and give them what they want. Not the verses of rural tranquillity but one of my more biting, scurrilous compositions. These I write at the expense of anyone who has incurred my displeasure. I include customers who had not paid their bills, tradesmen who withhold credit, pompous landowners and their conceited wives, but particularly overweight, egg-brained churchmen of the kind their father is forced to entertain at the rectory.

Verses satirising clergy contain the spice of forbidden pleasure. None of us would have relished the rector overhearing my satirical lampooning of the doddering doom-intoning 'Parson Gravelocks' or his waddling overweight colleague 'Parson Pot'.

They laugh heartily throughout. Perhaps this is because we all feel the rector himself to be an unacknowledged presence, even here. I respect my stern unsmiling mentor, even if I now find his lack of imagination unbelievably frustrating. They plainly love their old greying father, but get great pleasure out of being able to share with me how difficult it has been to live under his discipline.

We walk to the ruins of Old Beaupre castle, a fortified manor house of splendour and mystery. Here we unpack the ingredients for a picnic. I proudly demonstrate my country craft by building a fire, boiling water to make some of the exotic Indian tea I bought in Bristol.

Whilst we sip I cannot resist reminding them of the skills and techniques that went into the making of the fine Italianate carving on the front of the main gatehouse. Daniel points out the initials of the Bassett family who, he claims, had built it. I contradict him sharply.

'The Bassetts didn't build it.'

'I'm certain they did.'

'No,' I insist. 'They ordered it to be built. They paid for the work. They put their names on it and dedicated it to their family's memory, but it was a forgotten craftsman of great skill and his apprentices whose work so impresses you today, not Bassett money.'

'It might have been you.'

'It might indeed, if I'd been here two hundred years ago, but I'll tell you who carved it.' I stand up to help me make my point. It's the point I've already made to them, but to make a message memorable you have to people it with characters. They watch whilst I improvise the story of the Twrch brothers.

'There were two brothers, like you, who worked the Seaton Quarry in Bridgend, William and Richard. They were good, competent craftsmen but not skilled enough to create a gatehouse of this splendour.'

I walk about the courtyard gesticulating.

'They both fell in love with the same girl who rejected Richard and favoured William. They fought and they rowed bitterly and in the end Richard decided he had no option but to leave the Vale and go far, far away. He took his broken heart to London where it might mend and where he might seek his fortune.'

'This could have been you as well,' interrupts Daniel. I ignore him.

'There he worked for an Italian master. He was so good that his master insisted that the young Richard accompany him to Florence where he became a famous master of masonry, sculpture and architecture and even worked on the building of the Ponte Santa Trinita, a bridge renowned for its rich classical decoration. When news reached him of the death of his brother, Richard returned home where, as you can imagine, his skills were much in demand by the gentry. It was then that Sir Richard Bassett asked him to design and build this great gatehouse.'

The brothers look at each other and back at me. A moment's silence.

'Did you make that up?' they challenge.

'Why should I? It's well known amongst the masons of Glamorgan, of which I am one.'

They look dubious. I think hard. I will give them the sort of evidence they cannot refute.

'If you want proof ask Richard Roberts of Bridgend whose family are descended from the Twrchs. Or go to Florence and check the records of the statuary workshop of Bernardo Buontalenti.'

They say nothing as I list other sources they could consult if they continue to doubt my word and are prepared to travel a thousand miles to Italy or root out the descendants of the Twrchs in west Wales. I think I'm safe.

6

Dafydd ap Gwilym

*F*LYING HIGH AND *free. Sublime verses of Dafydd ap Gwilym are in my head, in the wind, in the fine spring rain. I hear them whispered. I hear them roared. The words circle, soar, climb and swirl in ordered formations around me, exotic birds reaching out for the sun. I rise and fall with their rhythms. I hang in air on each caesura. I swoop low with each rill and rise on each rhyme. I touch the words with my hands and they are part of me. I am of them.*

Dafydd is beside me. He is spreading his arms in welcome. He is urging me to do likewise. We are bidding, imploring summer to fly with us, from the north, from the sea, from the sweet places where the sun stores her warmth. She must fly to wake the trees, the hedges, valleys and fields. All will be fruitful.

He is telling me to sing. He is telling me I must sing of summer if the land of Glamorgan is to flower again. I must sing as Dafydd sings. As only Dafydd can sing. I'm trying. It is difficult but he has taught me well. I open my mouth. I hesitate, but then the words start to flow, to fly. Are they mine or are they Dafydd's? Does it matter? My words join his, tumbling, laughing, dancing and playing in a ferment of joy. My song is called 'Sending the Summer to Greet Glamorgan'.

Clyw fi Haf! O chaf i'm chwant
Yn gennad di'n d'ogoniant,
Hed drosof i dir Esyllt,

O berfedd gwlad Wynedd wyllt.
Gyr onis boch i'm goror,
Anwyla 'man, yn ael môr.

F'anerchion yn dirion dwg,
Ugeinwaith i Forgannwg
Fy mendith, a llith y lles,
Dau ganwaith i'r wlad gynnes.[26]

---

26 Hear me O Summer and my high demand, / That you, an envoy clad in Summer's
    gold / Fly south for me to Esyllt's blessed land, / So far from Gwynedd's mountainous
    stronghold / Fly on until you reach the country's edge / A place beloved where sea
    and pasture meet / Bestow my benediction and my pledge / Glamorgan's warm and
    fruitful pastures greet, / Two hundred blessings to the growing wheat.

7

The promised land

I LOOK AT my father. His shoulders are drooped and his head bowed as a man defeated. He sits in dejection by the unlit fireplace trying to take in the enormity of what he has just been told. He says nothing. Behind him, I am arguing with my brothers and our excited voices fill the small cottage. I am doing all in my power to persuade Miles, Thomas and John to change their minds, but they are having none of it.

They repeat once more.

'We've booked passages from Bristol, two weeks from today.'

They had originally intended to go from Liverpool to America but their plans have changed and they are off to Jamaica. There they have a promise of work, not as masons but as plantation managers and slave drivers. They will be earning a regular income. Miles boasts that, if they are lucky, they might, in time, come to own their own plantations.

'Sugar! That's what it is. Everybody wants sugar now. You've seen that. Since sugar started to be imported you can't move in Cowbridge for cake shops and tearooms. Where do you get the best sugar? From the West Indies!'

Thomas explains how they had met a sugar merchant in Bristol docks who owned a plantation with six hundred slaves. He has more than enough work on his hands shipping the cargoes back to Bristol and distributing it to merchants here. He needs some respectable white single men to go out there and run the plantation to his orders.

'It was as if it was meant to be. Don't you see? It's the kind of chance that comes up once in a lifetime,' says Miles.

I do not answer. Thomas continues, 'And the good thing is it's still British. Not part of the new America. So it's a lot safer. We'd be fools not to go. There's nothing here for us. There's precious little work about and when any of these new estate owners want a big job done they call in some big name from Bristol or Bath.' He repeats with finality, 'Nothing for us here.'

'There's your father!' I remind him, my temper frayed. 'The man who brought you up, looked after you and fed you since you were born. Doesn't he deserve to have his sons around him, caring for him in his old age?'

There is an awkward silence. Thomas tries to answer, 'Well... we knew *you* wouldn't want to go – even if you'd been offered, which you haven't. Can't see you leaving Peggy and Glamorgan and that.'

Miles cuts in helpfully, 'It'll be easier to find enough work as a mason here without us about. We weren't able to bring much home as it was. Maybe now we'll be able to send money from Jamaica.'

He looks at Thomas who nods earnestly, 'Soon as we can, we will honestly.'

If our father is appeased by their charity, his shoulders do not betray the fact. I appeal to their consciences.

'So... you intend to desert your father and disgrace your family by earning your living through the suffering of slaves; men forcibly kidnapped from their homes, transported across the oceans and made to work like cattle for no money. And you call yourselves Christians?'

'That's not fair!' counters Thomas. 'Black savages they are, not normal people. In any case, they get better food and better quarters on the plantations – and they learn to speak English.'

'And,' adds John in triumph, 'they get converted to

Christianity whether they like it or not, so it's for the good of their souls. If you are so full of your Christian principles you'd be pleased about that.'

Further conversation is pointless.

8

Peggy

I AWAKE SHIVERING with a fever. It is still night and I lie trembling in my cot. Today of all days is not a day to be unwell. By mid-morning I am to be married to Peggy. Peggy's family and her girlfriends have been preparing for weeks. Her mother has cooked enough to feed a regiment. Her father has engaged a fiddler. The Reverend John Walters is to marry us. The old Norman church of St Mary's has been decked with flowers. There are friends, fellow masons, and bards from all the Blaenau descending on the small village for the event. I even have new clothes; a smart blue high-collared jacket with gilt embossed buttons, a buff-striped waistcoat, grey breeches and shiny buckled shoes. They hang over my chair mocking my inadequacy. I have no option but to face the day. But how? I search for the laudanum that has been little used since I returned from London.

***

The walls of the church have never looked so white nor the roof so high. The rector is not in his pulpit but has floated high above the congregation. His voice booms. The church is a sea of flowers and lace. Peggy sails on that sea accompanied by mermaids from the village who throw flowers and rice and rings. I look behind me. I see my mother smiling at me. I see all the Walters brothers. I see the bards of all the ages. They are all talking at once! There

144

is discord – an argument about the rules of poetry. Llywarch Hen is here dressed in bardic robes. He carries a mystic staff with which to bless us. He calls for silence. Silence! This is a deep silence as profound as that hour before the making of the world. Then a sound as of rushing water, and Peggy arises out of the sea of lace and rose petals and flying cherry blossom in all her naked glory. Her skin shines, her hair falls in tresses, her breasts swell with the ocean.

The rector is talking now but I do not hear. The bards are asking me to sing in honour of my bride. I am the bard of the ages. I have in my head the voices of those who went before. They implore me to compose, to recite, to declaim, to make my marriage holy. They are watching from the pews, urging a consummation in great verse. Where's Dafydd? I need his help. Why is he not here? I see all of the ancient bards but not him. Now I hear him! Of course, he is not in the pews. He is inside my head. I am him. He is I. One flesh. Now I hear the rector, 'And they twain shall be one flesh: so then they are no more twain, but one flesh.' I will sing to Peggy in the voice of Dafydd,

Y ferch dan yr aur llathrloyw
A welais, hoen geirwfais hoyw.[27]

---

27 Before me came a girl with golden hair / As lithe and joyful as the dancing waves. [*Dafydd ap Gwilym*]

9

Business

M Y FATHER IS obviously in love with Peggy. He watches
her every move and will hear no criticism of her. He
tells me again and again how good it is to have a woman in the
cottage once more. Since my mother died he has been deprived
of female company and cooking. Peggy's pastry is rich and her
wit is even richer. He also never tires of telling me that Peggy
has twice the common sense of all his sons combined and that I
should be happy to be ruled by her. I agree.

Now I have a wife to support, I am all the more determined
to emulate the successful businessmen of the London Welsh
and provide generously for my family. One lesson I have learnt
from observing the master masons of Bristol and London is
that they employ skilled men to do the work whilst they spend
time with potential clients, designing and drawing plans to their
requirements. I feel insulted when some owners of Glamorgan
estates go to masons in Bristol when they need major work to
be done. I believe that part of the problem comes from our
being based in Flemingston. Landowners of quality like to visit
cities when they commission work, not hamlets. In cities they
can dine and entertain their friends after spending time in the
statuary workshop of a fashionable stonecutter.

I decide to set up a workshop in Llandaff, as close to the
cathedral as possible. Being in the shadow of its towers will
associate the name of Edward Williams with stonework of
prestige. I have found a suitable building but am finding it

difficult to persuade the owner to accept the rent I can afford. The man has several properties around Llandaff and insists that he has many other potential tenants just waiting for me to drop out of the agreement.

'I'm already letting you have it at well below its proper price,' he explains. 'It's only because my wife comes from the Vale that I've been so soft as to let you have it this cheaply.'

It is a well-known business maxim that to make money you have to invest, so I agree. I take on two apprentices: James and Owen. Both come with letters of recommendation and promises to pay five guineas for their indentures. The money is not forthcoming. After only two days James complains that the workshop dust is causing him to cough. What did he expect? Owen turns out to be the slowest workman I have ever met. He is frequently late and a positive liability, particularly if he spends his lunchtime in the tavern. Some work is coming in but, frustratingly, I find myself back in the position of being sole working mason.

Peggy is keeping a sensible eye on my books and complains, 'Ned, we're losing money we can't afford.'

But I do not believe I am mistaken in my strategy. 'The idea's right,' I insist, 'but I should have set up the workshop in Somerset or somewhere outside Wales. The problem is that these big landowners are all English and they don't think that anything can be of quality if it comes from a Welsh workshop.'

Peggy sighs. I plan to open a second workshop in Wells which, I explain to Peggy, 'is quite close to Minehead and even closer to Weston, so good for travelling. It's a cathedral city but it's cheaper than Bristol to rent property. It's surrounded by some very prosperous estates with owners anxious to outdo their neighbours in the construction of romantic towers and gothic follies. I'm certain we've got it right this time.'

Peggy says nothing for a full minute, then she lectures me

on the need to avoid distractions whilst I am in the process of building up a business. I should put writing and antiquarian research to one side for now. She tells me that I have more responsibilities than I am aware. She is pregnant. Soon there will be another mouth to feed.

1 0

Ieuan Fardd

T HE TALL OLD man is moving across the piles of fallen masonry. I watch him carefully, concerned that he may fall. He is so very tall and unsteady. The site where he searches is a mass of broken stone and jagged remains, sections of arches, pieces from the great fireplace all rapidly sinking beneath a rising sea of brambles. We had great trouble finding the place. Villagers in Basaleg didn't know it by name but, when I questioned a young farm worker, he told me of a ruined hall which local farmers plundered when they needed stone for building. That turns out to be what little is left the great court of Ifor Hael.

His excitement is making old Ieuan reckless and he stumbles but, thankfully, does not fall. Now he calls to me, 'Over here. Over here. Look, you can clearly see where the main fireplace of the hall would have been. The Lord Ifor would have had his tables facing the fire, about…'

Ieuan Fardd scrambles over one pile of masonry before announcing, '… Here! So now you can construct the scene. Ifor Hael at his supper there, and Dafydd ap Gwilym would have sat in front of the Lord's table… here! … singing for his supper. He wrote four *cywydd* to Ifor – that we know of – and more after the Lord's death.'

Ieuan talks about the medieval bards as if they are old friends.

I admire his knowledge and scholarship more than any man in Wales. He knows so many of the secrets of how the bards worked. I tremble with anger at the sight of his threadbare jacket and worn shoes. A man of his standing should be valued by the Church as a prince; instead he gets passed from one poor parsonage to the next.

Now the old scholar looks to the heavens and cries:

Llys Ifor Hael, gwael yw'r gwedd, – yn garnau
  Mewn gwerni mae'n gorwedd;
  Drain ac ysgall mall a'i medd,
  Mieri lle bu mawredd.[28]

He is overcome with emotion.

'Ned, I am so overjoyed we found this place. Thank you for helping me find it. So sad to see its condition, true, but I'm certain there are spirits about, an energy held within the stones that saw so wonderful a flowering of never-to-be-forgotten verse.'

I take him back to the latest small damp parsonage in which the Church has housed him. If anything, it is smaller and more miserable than the one I visited in Towyn. I have brought him some food and some brandy. He ignores the bread and cheese but the brandy gives his body warmth. He is not well. He has aged and is painfully lean. His skin is thin and yellowing and stretched tight over his bones and skull. But he talks so very well. His greatest worry is that he will die before he is able to publish his collection of ancient manuscripts. It is early morning before the bottle is drained and Ieuan falls asleep. I leave him to rest and let myself out.

When I reach Flemingston the next afternoon Peggy is angry with me. She is now large with our child, tired and anxious. She wants to know why am I not in Wells doing all I can to make the

---

28 The Court of Ifor the Munificent / Now hurts my sight / Weeds and thistles in abundance, / Where once was light.

new workshop a success. I tell her that I could not ignore the needs of that ill-treated old man. She is not convinced. I try to explain,

'Peggy, he is perhaps the greatest Welsh scholar of our time and does the Church value him? No. He's been bundled from one miserable curacy to another all his life – eighteen in all, he tells me he's held – and none of them giving him more than a pauper's income. And why? Because the old Church which we all once loved is now in the hands of scavenging ravens, Anglo-bishops who give the best parishes and richest livings to their own sort regardless of the needs of their parishioners. Look! The Bishop of Bangor had a vacancy in Trefdraeth on Anglesey where no one speaks English. It's a living that would have been perfect for Ieuan Fardd and he would have been perfect for the parishioners but, instead, it has been given to an English cleric eighty years old without a word of Welsh! What's he going to do but stay in the rectory by the fire getting fat on the tithes of the same poor parishioners he can't possible serve?'

Peggy understands but she is worried. There is a trembling in her voice as she talks. She's developed a steely way of saying my name. 'Ned, you have to be careful. You can't go on saying things like that about the clergy. If you do they'll make sure that you never get any work. You know the parsons and the landowners are all one.'

'Peggy, I can't ignore the truth.'

'No, but you don't have to be the one that tells the truth so loudly that it makes us poor. You are the one who has to earn our bread and you've already got a name as a troublemaker. In a few months you'll be a father. Please think of that. Think of me.'

Peggy's eyes are watering. She is so full of child and tears that she fills my world. I hold her close to me. I love her so and tell her so. I promise to care for her and our child, but I do not, and cannot, promise to lie.

11

A business opportunity

O N THE DECK of a sloop coming back from Minehead, I'm angry. The workshop in Wells is not going well. I had a row this morning with the journeyman I left in charge. He has plainly been doing work on his own behalf in the workshop and probably in my time. The workshop is a mess and I'm certain that two pieces of fine marble have disappeared. He swears they were used for a monument last month, although there is no entry in the ledger. Why is the world full of cheats and liars?

I am watching the captain of the sloop. He works well with his men. It's only a sloop, so there's a small crew of three. They all appear to know their tasks and work together like dancers. Why can't my journeymen work like that? Maybe it's something to do with being on a boat? Everyone has to do whatever they do or you all end up on the rocks. I like being on this boat. I'm a familiar sight to the captain, as he is to me. I've talked to him before, mostly about lime. His cargo from Aberthaw is always lime. There are limitless tons of limestone to be had on the shoreline along our south coast. To builders, farmers and ferry captains, it's the secret ingredient. To builders it makes cement and mortar. To farmers, ground fine, it's the best fertiliser for the fields and, for captains, it's the perfect cargo.

What a beautiful evening. The captain comes over to talk.

There's something peaceful about talking on a boat. On a crossing there's nothing to do apart from wait for the distant shore to approach. One can muse, compose or converse. He asks me if my life is good. I tell him I am awaiting my first child and he tells me of his family. We talk like contented men. I ask him about his trade. He tells me that the trade is good, particularly for men who understand limestone.

'I'm doing alright, but a fellow captain of mine carried a cargo of stone which, when crushed, turned out to be pure sand. There was the devil to pay. Poor man had to give the farmers their money back and still they blacken his name.'

He stares out towards the coast as one does on a boat. I want to know more.

'Was that enough to ruin him?'

My captain shrugs his shoulders.

'Had enough, he has. Says he's going back to his old trade as a smith – if he can only find someone to take over his ship; fifteen-ton sloop in good order. There's a good opening here for a man who knows good lime when he sees it.'

I want him to say more, but he does not. I know about lime. Surely he remembers? The seconds are ticking by. He is turning to go. I reach for his shoulder to stop him.

'I know about stone. All kinds of stone.' Suddenly I feel stupid. I add, 'But I know nothing of ships.'

He is looking at me kindly.

'No problem finding crew in these parts – plenty of sailors about. Old hands who don't want to sail the Atlantic again are the best. See Jim over there? Seen the world he has, rounded the Horn five times but now wants to be able to go home to his own bed of an evening.'

We both watch Jim as he does complicated things with ropes.

'Might you be interested?'

'In buying a boat?'

'Just asking, you being a businessman and obviously knowing about limestone.'

I've never been called a businessman before. I like it. I don't answer him at first because I'm very tempted. I could combine running the workshop in Wells with carrying cargoes between Aberthaw and Minehead. I spend days doing the journey as it is and every time I pay for the pleasure. Why not do the journey on my own boat and get others to pay me?

'How much would your friend want?'

12

Margaret

I'M A FATHER. I'm cradling the infant Margaret in my arms. She looks up at me with wide blue eyes, the same blue eyes as her grandmother. When I hold her like this, I feel I have the future of the world in my arms. What more could any man wish from life than this? What greater responsibility than ensuring the future? She is smiling. At least I think she's smiling. Peggy spoils my pleasure by telling me that it's just wind. I don't believe her. Margaret burps and the illusion is broken. Peggy and I both laugh. Peggy is looking tired but joyful. Her mother has been here all morning helping to organise the cottage to cope with a baby, but she has left us now, thank goodness. I take the fragile bundle over to the corner where my father now spends most of his days. He is very proud, although he annoyed Peggy at first by complaining that she had not produced a boy. Now he's more besotted than we are, except when she cries. My father is a light sleeper and little Margaret has good lungs.

I hand the baby back to Peggy who wraps her in a shawl. Now she's rocking and singing an old lullaby. I join in, playing the same tune softly on my flute. Margaret is soon asleep. Was there ever such peace? My father sleeps, the baby sleeps in Peggy's shawl, and Peggy rests. I should be at ease too and, for Peggy's sake, I rest my head on the high-backed chair as if dozing. In truth, I cannot stop worrying. I have a family to support. I need to start making money out of my business ventures but at present there appear few good prospects. The workshop in Cardiff I have had to close. The workshop in Wells needs my continuous presence which cannot be. I sought to build on the fashion for Indian teas nowadays. I bought a considerable quantity in Bristol with thoughts of selling small quantities at a profit in Cowbridge. So far I have met with little success and the sack of tea is taking up space behind the door, space which Peggy tells me she must have back.

We have little left of our savings or of Peggy's dowry, yet I believe I must invest in the captain's offer. After weeks of thought it still sounds to me like the best opportunity to date. I look across at my wife and child. I resolve, for their sakes, to pay yet another visit to the bank and to those lenders where my credit remains good. I despise the bankers with their aloof manners and language designed to mystify an honest man. But, for the sake of Peggy and our new daughter, I will suffer their condescension. I will have that sloop.

The Lion

THANKS TO THE good offices of Captain Meriwether, I am now the owner of *The Lion*. It was not the sloop he spoke of originally which sold for more money than I could raise. True, *The Lion* is in need of a coat of paint, but she's a fine fifteen tonner. With his help, I have engaged a crew of three and spent some days prospecting along the coast for the best lime pebbles I could find. I had not reckoned on the dues charged by the harbourmaster merely for tying the craft up against the harbour wall. Neither had I expected that the crew would demand half-payment before sailing. I am unused to the ways of the sea but I anticipate that I will swiftly learn.

I stand on the deck enjoying the feeling of being on my own boat. There are fellows on the quayside pointing at the craft, presumably praising its lines. The loading is going well. Two cartloads have already been sent clattering joyfully into the hold. I have three more lined up, which will give us our full complement. The crew have been doing things with the sails. I have learnt that the front sail is called the 'jib', a word I will drop into conversation whenever I wish to appear practised in the nautical crafts.

One of my crew, Will, the bosun, is going onto the quay to talk to the observers. I think to stop him but decide against it. I can see him chatting to a friend in time I am paying for and I feel cross, but say nothing. I reason that our maiden voyage is not the time to kindle ill will. Will is coming back on board and is approaching me.

'Beg pardon, sir. Permission to speak?'

I find it hard not to play-act the sea captain when they talk like that, but think better of replying with an 'Aye aye, Bosun.' I respond politely.

'Of course.'

'Lloyd's Rule, sir. You can see from the quayside that the old *Lion* is sitting low in the water as it is. Beg pardon, sir, but if those three carts I see waiting are intending to deposit their stone into this old tub, I would respectfully advise against it, sir.'

I do not know how to respond. Old tub! I look around hoping that a Captain Meriwether will appear to engage this sailor with talk of 'freeboards', 'holds' and 'Lloyd's Rules'. No one is coming to my aid.

'But this sloop is a fifteen tonner. That means she can carry fifteen tons, does it not?'

'When trim and new, yes sir, but this 'ere *Lion* is not a young cub any more. Most round here thought she had sailed her last a year ago, until Captain Meriwether told us he had found a buyer, sir.'

I must look panicky for he continues swiftly. 'She'll be alright in the water, sir. But it's just that her keel is heavy with wood that is a little swollen and barnacles and the like. One more cart is the most she will take, sir, if you follow my meaning?'

This statement is delivered with polite certainty. It sounds less like the passing of information than an instruction. I am not going to stand for this! I have calculated the income from the trip on the basis of fifteen ton of limestone. To deliver only six or nine tons would mean I was losing money, even if I manage to sell it all at the full price. I start to tremble with rage at this man who is clearly trying to trick me into giving him and his crewmates an easier time with less cargo to shift. I try and talk with a calm authority I do not feel.

'Please continue loading.'

'Just the one cart more, sir?'

'No, all three carts.' I'm nearly shouting. I had not meant to shout but these people who try and cheat me at every turn make me lose control. Will backs away and shrugs his shoulders. He goes off and gives the orders.

I can feel the eyes of the crew on me as the loading continues. Why are they so slow? I think about Will's comments. I know this is not a new ship but Captain Meriwether would not have recommended her if she had not been seaworthy. Would he? I start to doubt. I watch as the deck slowly but certainly sinks lower below the level of the quay. When we started loading I could step off the deck onto the shore. Now I would have to climb a six-foot iron ladder to reach the top. I look over the side. The water was some ten feet below deck level. Now it's scarcely half that and lessening with every shovelful that goes into the hold. I look at the shore. Still one cart to go. The hold is full and the men are now piling the stone around the deck. I take another look over the side and call,

'Will, tell the men to stop loading. I think this will do.'

'Aye aye, sir.' They are all looking at each other with knowing smiles. They go about their business with conspiratorial understanding. Will tells me that at least the tide is with us. We can be on our way in minutes. They cast off and *The Lion* slowly drifts away from the harbour wall. For a moment I breathe a sigh of relief. With the cargo as it is I will still make a profit when we reach Minehead. *The Lion* is moving very slowly now into the open channel. When do we raise the jib? We are moving so slowly that it will take a week to reach Minehead unless we get some sail up. I ask Will who looks at me as if I am mad.

'Permission to speak plainly, sir?'

How infuriating are their forms of assumed deference!

'Granted.'

'If you were to look over the side, sir, I think you'll see that we're settling in the water.' He leans over and points. I follow his gesturing arm and I am horrified. Whereas the water had been five feet below the deck level when we cast off, it is now no more than three.

'What's happening?' I demand.

'To be plain with you sir, we're sinking.'

I cannot believe I am hearing correctly. Will appears quite calm and his voice as level as if he is describing fair weather. I know myself to be frozen, unable to believe my situation. For a moment we look at each other in silence. It is only a second or two but it is long enough for a thousand images to flash through my mind. 'Death by water.' 'These are pearls that were his eyes.'

'Suggest we try and tack to starboard so as to keep away from the deep water, sir. Soon as we will hit the main current, we're done for.'

I try to say something but Will does not wait for a response. He gives an order and someone does something at the tiller end. They start shovelling stones into the water. Will throws me a shovel and I join them. We shovel for five minutes or so until our lungs are bursting. I look round. Water is starting to creep across the deck. Will has seen it too. I look back towards Aberthaw. We have drifted down channel but are still less than a hundred yards from the shore. A large group has gathered and is watching our progress. I cannot hear their comments or see their faces, for which I am grateful.

'Beg pardon, sir. Can you swim?'

'Not very well.'

'Best wait here then, sir.'

'And wait to drown?'

Will laughs at me. He actually laughs! Is he hysterical? Is this what happens to people a moment before death?

'Bless you, sir. I doubt we'll do more than get our socks wet. I suggest we all move onto the deck and wait.'

'To go down? To die?'

'To settle, sir. We're already aground on the sandbar if I'm not mistaken. If you notice, sir, we're not moving.'

I look. There still is water flowing past and over the deck. But he's right, there's no movement, no rocking. We are grounded on the sandbank. I cry with relief and throw my arms around the small wiry seaman who looks, for the first time today, slightly panicky. He pulls away.

'We'll just have to wait here until someone from the port is kind enough to come and get us in a dinghy. Now if we only had some cards…'

14

A letter to Owain

I AM BEING pursued by my creditors. I am certain that some of them exaggerate the amounts I owe. John Walton, the Cowbridge surgeon, has sent me an account totalling seven guineas for nothing but medicines, tinctures and oils he claims to have supplied over time. This cannot be true but I have no means of disproving it. I have debts for workshop rent, debts for lawyers' fees, and debts for materials. I have debts for loans and debts on interest on loans to repay other debts. My debts breed like vermin. Is there no end? I have not been truthful with Peggy about our finances. She is pregnant once more and I wish to save her the anxiety. However, she appears to know without being told.

I am considering writing to Owain Myfyr in London. It pains me to do so. I had hoped to build my fortunes so as to myself sponsor a great volume of the work of our medieval poets. Instead, I can scarcely put bread on my table. I learn from the Reverend John Walters that Owain has been very generous in providing support for the printing of further volumes of his great dictionary. The London furrier thrives and he is apparently now master of the company where once he was an apprentice. He has in the past paid scholars to research and transcribe ancient poems for his collection. How can I persuade him to support my work?

I am at my table writing him a learned letter. I want to impress him. It includes my latest discoveries on the ancient druids and some poetic pieces. I am excusing the fact I have not written for years by telling him that I have tried on several occasions, but that the results were unworthy of being sent. There! It's done. Can I send him some Dafydd ap Gwilym? I have none from the libraries I have visited of late but I do have the pieces I composed to his dictation. Should I rather say 'the pieces I wrote under his spell'? They are so much in his manner and style that I truly cannot say where Dafydd ends and I begin. Should I describe how these pieces were coined? I will not be understood should I try to explain. Better to let the works speak for themselves. I shall send him four of the finest *cywyddau*. I will not ask for payment. I shall trust in his generosity.

Chatterton

A S IF TO confront me with my actions, Daniel has brought a copy of the Rowley poems with him to one of our meetings in the Beaupre Woods. These purport to be the work of a fifteenth-century monk at St Mary Redcliffe, Bristol, but the theory now abounds that they are in truth the work of a young poet, Thomas Chatterton, in our own time. Chatterton took his own life whilst still only seventeen. There is much debate as to who is truly the author of the work. Daniel wants my opinion and I ask him,

'Why would a poet go to all the trouble of forging a masterpiece only to credit it to someone else? I don't believe it. We bards are vain and jealous of our reputations. Eisteddfodau are full of poets complaining that someone copied their best lines. I can't imagine any poet asking that another poet be given the credit for work over which he has laboured.'

Daniel nods but comes back at me. 'But what if he did? For whatever reason, what if he did?'

'Matters not at all,' I insist. 'Do you like the Rowley verses?'

'They're beautiful.'

'Do they speak of wisdom? Do they show you truth?'

'Yes.'

'Then it matters not who composed them. And if, for some unfathomable reason, Thomas Chatterton gave credit for his glimpse of perfection to another, that is a matter for gossips and tittle-tattle. What matters is the truth of the verse.'

Daniel looks at me and nods.
'You're right as always, Ned.'
Bless the boy!

16

Truth

I HAVE COME to an important conclusion.
Truth must triumph.

Truth must emerge unsullied from the attacks of the myriad forces that seek to besmirch her name. To pursue truth is to hold fast to God's purpose whilst all those around assault and deride His messengers. It is to rise above the petty dealings of clerks and tellers. It is to gainsay the tedious disciplines of academics and the self-serving strictures of clergymen.

When the truth is clear before me I will proclaim it. Those lines of Dafydd ap Gwilym I have sent to Owain are one such truth. There are other grand truths that are becoming clearer to me. Truths which will be ridiculed and disregarded by the clerks, clergy and academics who seek to frustrate me at every turn, who cannot see past the pettifogging detail of the tedious present. For the sake of my country, my Vale, my family, I have to find the means of building a greater truth which reflects the glory of the past and projects it into the future. The truth must inspire my countrymen to greater acts.

Truth against the world.

17

The Reverend James Evans

I AM IN Marshfield, Monmouth. I have been repairing the gateway of a big house and am returning home. It is dusk.

'Stop, sir. I wish to know your business.'

The voice is nasal and challenging. I peer into the gloom at the figures before me. I see the gaitered legs and dog-collared neck of a stout clergyman. Beside him is a country man in a rough wool jacket. He holds a lantern out in my direction to assist his master's vision. I know the cleric to be the Reverend James Evans, a man famed for his limited wit and boundless intolerance. He preaches weekly against Catholics, Methodists, Baptists and Congregationalists. Any whose conscience leads them away from the Church of England are, in the sight of the Reverend James Evans and therefore God, damned for eternity. I am not prepared to indulge the man. I move to pass them.

'I asked you to stop, sir, I believe. I know you to be a man of poor reputation given to penning scandalous verses against the Church and her servants. I will not have you spreading your damnable poison amongst my flock.'

I should be aware. He is carrying a riding whip and his servant a cudgel. But I feel my blood heating. What right does he have to question me as to my business? Before me stands a servant of the Lord threatening violence in the name of divine love. I am tired and I have a long walk ahead. I do not seek trouble. I am about to assure him that I am in his parish on lawful business as a stonemason, not an agitator, when his voice threatens again, high and excited.

'I will have none of your dumb insolence, man. Tell me your business or it will be the worse for you.'

I meet his aggression with calm and with the Gospel. I spread my arms in a gesture of concord: 'Blessed are the peacemakers, for they shall be called the children of God – Matthew chapter 5, verse 9. Now if you don't mind I have a way to go this evening.'

The Reverend James Evans is puffing up like a toad. Without warning he takes a step forward, raises his whip and aims for my head. It's a poor blow which does not catch me but throws me off balance. The strong hands of the country man push me to the ground. I fall on the rough road. The servant has taken my satchel and pins me down. The Reverend raises his whip once more. Now he is above me and can scarcely miss. I try to protect my head with my arms as his whip descends once, twice, three times, catching me on my arms and chest. I hear the heavy breathing of an overweight man unused to exertion. Now he tries again, one, two, three lashes. The last catches my cheek. Does it bleed? The Reverend James Evans takes a step back. I think he is done. I pray he does not hand the whip to his servant to finish the task. He speaks to me as if to a rabid dog.

'And be warned, sir, that I am not a man to be trifled with.' He pauses gulping air. 'I would further advise you…' another pause for breath, 'never to set foot in this parish again on pain of a proper thrashing.'

His servant loosens his hold on me and enquires of his master, 'Do I let him up, Reverend?'

'You may, but watch him for he's an artful felon.'

The man stands, steps back, and I feel a sudden violent pain in my stomach and again in my crutch. He kicks me three times in all. I am in great distress. They start to move away. I remember they have my satchel – my chisel, my mallet and, more importantly, my notebook containing three weeks of composition. I appeal.

'My satchel, sir. Would you deprive a poor mason of the tools of his trade?'

The servant holds the satchel out towards me, 'There you are, villain.'

Instead of dropping it on the road he throws the bag over the hedge into a mess of brambles, thorns and nettles. They both laugh. The Reverend James Evans returns my biblical reference, 'Lord, now lettest thou thy servant depart in peace, according to thy word. Luke chapter 2, verse 29.'

'And don't come back,' adds the man with the big boots.

I vomit involuntarily.

***

Peggy is bending over me trying to clean and dress the whip cut on my cheek. For a second she might be my own mother, and I a child once more. She is heavy with our second child and smells of womanliness. She tells me the cut is surprisingly deep, as if made by a jagged knife. She is angry; thankfully, for once, not with me. She tells me I should sue. I should have a lawyer acting on my behalf by the morning. I tell her that it would be pointless. The clergy and the landowners are all one – as she well knows. The landowners appoint the magistrates, so any action against a cleric of the Established Church is doomed to fail, and, in consequence, would cost the litigant (us) money we can ill afford.

'But don't fret, *'nghariad i.*[29] Vengeance will be ours. Even

---

29 My sweetheart.

as you bind my wounds I am composing an artful ballad of retribution to be called "The Marshfield Parson". If I can make this as playful and defamatory as I believe I can, I will have the young bucks of most of Monmouth singing it with glee whenever they are in the alehouse. The Reverend will be a laughing stock in his own parish within a month.'

'I'm still angry.'

'Of course! Your husband has been hurt.'

'Not that you don't deserve it! How often have I told you that you're getting a bad name? But he had no right. If anyone is going to try and knock sense into my wild handsome uncontrollable man – that will be me.'

At that she puts down her cloth and I feel a slap on my undamaged cheek. I cry out more in surprise than pain. Peggy laughs. We kiss. She pushes me away and looks me full in the face as if surveying my features in disbelief.

'What a mess! At least the outside of your head is now as disorganised as the inside.'

I'm wondering whether to broach the subject of religious affiliations but decide against it. I have not attended the church at St Mary's for six months or more, but Peggy remains loyal. Despite all our unhappiness with the Church, it is where her parents worship, where her old friends gather to gossip on a Sunday, and where several generations of her family are buried. It would be unfair to put more pressure on her. The 'Old Church' has been our home since the days of the Celtic saints Illtud and Cadoc. But the rectors of our grandparents' days were local people who knew their parishioners and cared for them as their own family. The new estate owners, Mount Stuart, Beaufort and the Earl of Plymouth, have brought with them a new breed of clerics with no regard for Welsh culture, who appear to believe that the only function of parishioners is to pay the tithes that support their port-swilling extravagance.

Resentment is common. Some local people have joined the Methodists in Llangan. Their services are lively enough, if you like your worship to be full of wild arm-flying emotion and spiritual pretension. A strange lot they seem to me. They think that they can stay faithful to the King whilst rejecting his Church. Nonsense!

I tell Peggy of a preacher, Josiah Rees, with whom I am corresponding. He is a Unitarian, a believer that there is but one Godhead, not the three represented in the Trinity. I have heard him, and others of his church, preach. Theirs is a simple message of love, tolerance, social justice and fellowship. They believe in rational thought and free will. I talk with enthusiasm of how this accords so much more with the modern thinking of Locke, Hume and Rousseau. But I am talking too much. Peggy stops my mouth with a kiss once more. We embrace. There is a moment of bliss but I cry with pain when her hand touches my bruised parts.

The happiness
of Glamorgan

P EGGY IS DELIVERED of our second child, a daughter we have
named Ann after my mother. She is as sweet and pretty
a child as any man might wish. As if by providence, the next
morning I receive a reply from Owain Myfyr. I walk away from
the cottage to open it. I have set great store by its contents. I not
only sent my Dafydd ap Gwilym poems to him but proposed a
project which would be close to his heart; a quarterly magazine,
entitled *Dywenydd Morganwg*,[30] containing selections of the
great medieval works in need of preservation and deserving of
fame.

My initial disappointment is that no paper money flutters
from the envelope. I had not asked directly for such support,
but our need is great. The letter is long. He apologises for his
tardiness in replying but explains the stresses of business life. He
is now installed in new premises, at 148 Upper Thames Street,
a fine address not far distant from the Mansion House. He
assures me that this is significant. He is enthusiastic about the
idea of a magazine but believes that this should be published in
London where there are collections of manuscripts, printers and
booksellers he can command. He offers me a bed, good working
facilities, candles and a wage if I will join him.

---

30   The Happiness of Glamorgan.

How frustrating is this? It is as if he torments me by dangling unimaginable delicacies before my nose only to cruelly dash them from my sight untasted. I have to compose myself before I reply that I cannot accept his offer, however delightful the prospect appears.

I explain that, 'I have tied myself firmly to a post in Glamorgan – in short I have married a wife.'

I reread the sentence. Its tone suggests that Peggy is a burden. Perish the thought. I add much more of the joys of life in the bounteous Vale with a fair wife, two thriving daughters, and the glory of God all about. I will not have the man pity me.

I turn to the other pieces of mail I have received today. I know too well their contents, some by recognition of the handwriting, some by the stationery, but mostly by the knowledge that 'all things do conspire against me'. There is a letter from John Wood, Attorney of Cardiff, threatening me with seizure of my goods if his account is not settled forthwith. There is an abusive letter from William Rees of Court Colman promising to have me before the magistrates, and half a dozen similar.

I open my book and so escape this malevolence into a world of rhyme and sweet reason.

19

Beaupre Woods

I HAVE JOHN and Daniel Walters with me and we are brewing tea. The darker my circumstances, the more I desire their company. John is done with Oxford and is now installed as the headmaster of Cowbridge Grammar School. I am grateful that, despite his success, he still treats me with a respect I receive from few others.

Together we escape into an altogether more amenable world of lyric poetry. I read to them my 'Shepherd's Song'.

Mewn tawelwch y mae'n byw
Gan ofni Duw'n wastadol,
Dyn serchogaidd yn ei blwyf
Ac ynddo nwyf rinweddol;
Einioes hir a gaiff o'i swydd
Ac iechyd rhwydd naturiol
A phan dderfydd yma'i fyw
Caiff nef gan Dduw'n dragwyddol.[31]

As always they are receptive and appreciative. As always John makes the best analytical comments, but Daniel is the one who rhapsodises over the sentiments. Suddenly there is an awkward silence of the kind that is unknown between us. Something is

---

31 A man of quiet country ways, / A loyal child of God / The parish where he spends his days / The pathways he has trod / A long life is his just reward / With natural good health / When called at last, he'll join the Lord / In heaven's eternal wealth.

wrong. Their company should grant me a brief escape from my money concerns, but this is not to be. The brothers' trade glances. They have agreed a course of action. John sits up and puts his hands on his knees in studied concentration.

'Ned, may we give voice to our concern?' He speaks with hesitation. 'We've heard and believe me we don't go looking for gossip, but I think it's pretty common knowledge…'

Daniel comes to his rescue, '… that you are in financial difficulties… that William Rees is filing a complaint with the magistrates against you.'

'What of it?' I snap back. I am angry. What right have they to interfere? They are undermining our friendship when they take liberties like this. I tell them so. I stand up and deny that there are any money problems.

'I would have thought you'd be the very last to listen to and spread malicious gossip against me.'

'Ned!'

The two of them are on their feet and talking at the same time. They are trying hard to placate me, apologising for any offence, assuring me of their friendship, insisting they only have my best interests at heart, asking me to hear them out, imploring me to listen to what they have to say.

It would be churlish to refuse. I say nothing but sit again on the forest floor.

'I'm listening.'

John repeats that they are both great admirers of my writing. They believe that I write equally as well in English as in Welsh. In his experience of preparing his own small volume of the work of Llywarch Hen, he learnt how difficult it was to be published in Welsh. On the other hand, he also became aware that there is an explosion in English-language bookselling. London and Oxford are alive with booksellers looking for publishable material – and there is a good income to be made by a popular, accomplished poet. I am impatient at being told of the sophisticated ways of John's world and my attitude demonstrates as much. I have had enough. I prepare to leave.

Daniel takes over. These two brothers, close in age and fellowship, often come at matters from remarkably different directions. Daniel talks, not about his world but about my verses, about Glamorgan and the Vale. He talks about the link between poetry and countryside and how rare it is to have a writer of greatness who is close to the lives of real country people, a writer who is a country craftsman, self-educated and able to avoid fogging his verse with pretentious fashionable ornamentation. He tells me that I am unique in his experience and that, were I to write in English, there would be a wide readership.

John re-enters the conversation. Whilst at Oxford he developed alliances with several poets. He would like to show any English-language poems I produce to booksellers of his acquaintance who, he is certain, would be prepared to advise and support.

I reply emphatically that, 'I do not need or want advice on how to write my verse.'

Our goodbyes are stiff. I tell them that they have changed the carefree nature of our friendship and I am not pleased. I do not need them to tell me the problems of publishing. I certainly do not need them to direct my writing. But I temper my words. I am aware that they are friends – good friends – and that I appear to have few of those left in the world.

2 0

A knock at the door

A LONG PASSAGE leading to a door. A knock on the door. It opens. A huge roaring fire in a vast, stone, fire grate. Long tables. Burning torches. Fine wall hangings. Rich foods and fine wines. My mother is at the table looking at me with expectation. I take my seat by the fire. Ifor Hael bids me sing. I have no words prepared. I am afraid, but in my head Dafydd prompts me with lines of unsurpassable ingenuity and beauty. I close my eyes as I recite. The words are filling the air, mingling with the smoke of candles. They are leaping in the fire flame. I watch as the words caress the red flushed faces. When I look again, Ifor has gone and in his place Owain Myfyr is standing applauding. He is telling the world of my brilliance. He throws a bag of gold which opens in the air. The coins change into small golden birds that fly in evermore beautiful formations, singing and crying in ecstasy. I go to gather the golden birds but they are flying out of reach. Owain tells me that they are things of great beauty, beyond value, beyond the shoddiness of coinage. He has gone. Around me there are creditors. They are advancing out of the gloom demanding, demanding, demanding…

There is a knock on the cottage door. Peggy is feeding our infant Ann. Margaret is playing by the fireplace. I answer the summons. Standing on the step is a magistrate's clerk and a special constable. They tell me that they have a writ for my arrest on account of non-payment of sums rightly due to John Walton of Cardiff and Evan Griffith of Penllyn. I offer myself to them as a songbird to be caged.

Part Four:
Cardiff Gaol
1786 to 1787

1

A small world

FIVE YARDS BY five yards of grey, rough-hewn granite. That is the size and texture of the world to which I am now confined. How cruel is this to a man who lives his life according to the rhythms of the open countryside? Or to a mason, forced to stare at these ill-hewn blocks of stone which are an insult to the craft? As I stare at them I try to understand my emotions. I am uncertain whether my anger and indignation for being locked away are greater than my sense of shame and ignominy.

In my cell I have a bed, two chairs, a table, a pair of shelves, a bellow, a poker, a teapot and some rudimentary cutlery. I also have a gaoler, Thomas Morgan, who goes out of his way to be disagreeable. When I was delivered to the prison he had the audacity to seek payment for admission. I replied that I was quite content to be refused entry, which did not amuse him. Apparently, debtors are required to pay for their room and any food the warder sees fit to provide. The man demands half a crown for providing a thin gruel which might be purchased in any tavern for a few farthings. Even if I choose to comply, I cannot. I have only thruppence in my pocket.

Peggy and my father are permitted to call and they bring me food, books and the money to appease the gaoler. I will not allow them to pass it over. I explain that I am composing a letter in my head to the Chief Justices complaining of the behaviour of the gaoler and his efforts to extract money by extortion. My old father shakes his head.

Peggy pleads, 'Ned, please don't. If you upset him he can make your life most unpleasant.'

When I look at her I feel even more wretched. Has she not enough work to cope with our young daughters and my ageing father without the problems of a husband imprisoned? I want to agree to her request but I cannot. I ask her if she will step out of the prison and return with paper and pens. She does so. My father shares his knowledge of debtors' prisons. He tells me that he has escaped them narrowly several times in his life, but many of his contemporaries have not been so fortunate. He advises me to do all I can to avoid antagonising Mr Thomas Morgan.

When Peggy returns with stationery, I write a simple but elegant letter arguing for the legal rights of debtors to be respected. We are not felons and, as useful citizens, have rights and privileges. I make no complaint for paying for food, were it at the same prices as elsewhere, but it would be an injustice to pay half a crown for so little. Light is poor in the cell, and I struggle to maintain a clear hand as I finish, sign and seal the letter. I pass it to Peggy and make her promise to deliver it, in person, to the Court of the Great Sessions in Cardiff. She agrees reluctantly.

I ask my father to obtain a copy of *The Gentleman, Merchant, Tradesman, Lawyer, and Debtor's Pocket Guide, in case of Arrest* as I clearly need to make myself knowledgeable on the law of debt and insolvency if I am to assert my rights and obtain a speedy release. I forbid them to canvass my friends for help. Those in Glamorgan do not have the money and those in London would be certain to regard incarceration for debt as so shameful as to cause them to lose whatever regard they may have for me. Peggy suggests the Walters brothers might be an exception. I point out that John is now working in Wrexham, but Daniel is master at the grammar school and might be approached. What of my brothers? Could they not afford to help, given their good fortune in Jamaica? I forbid any suggestion that we might benefit from the evil trade of slavers.

As they prepare to leave, Peggy is in tears. Her weakness prompts me to appear stronger than I feel as I try to comfort her. I give her a list of additional books which I wish her to bring as soon as possible. Giving her something to do appears to help. She tells me what I already know, that the cell is damp and that my chest is weak. Do I want her to bring more physic? I always need to have my laudanum about me. What of the children? I insist they are not to visit. The foul confines of Cardiff gaol would only corrupt the innocent spirits of my sweet Margaret and our infant Ann. They leave. I sit still on the side of the small bed. The cell is cold and I do not have the means to light a fire. I must have some coals to drive away the damp. The cell feels very empty. I usually do not mind being alone. It gives me time to think, but tonight I do not want to think. I reach into my bag for my flute and play. Playing replaces words with sounds that are both simpler and more profound. My repertoire is narrow, mostly tunes my mother taught me and a few I have devised. I can't even name the air I'm playing now, but it is old and gentle and soothing. I play for a long time, repeating phrases and extemporising. It fills the cell with sad comfort until someone bangs on the door and shouts,

'Quiet, you in there. Some of us need our sleep.'

2

Fellowship

WE ARE ALLOWED out of cells during the day to work, socialise and to exercise. There is a yard which at least enables me to walk about and look up to the sky. I travel around this at speed, trying to imagine that I am walking along the pathways of the Vale. I am far from alone. There is a significant company of other debtors. They come out to enjoy what unpolluted air there is, but few of them exercise as strenuously as I do. I recognise William Freme, a fellow stonecutter, who sits slumped against a wall mindlessly scratching with a stick in the dirt. He is most surprised when I greet him. He reacts with a mixture of pleasure at reunion and dismay that I should witness his reduced state. I know him to be a stonecutter of average, but honest, skill. What brings him here?

He tells me how he had overreached himself in the building of a stable block for a country squire. His skills as a stonemason were not equalled by his experience as an architect. He failed to ensure that the walls were built on firm foundations. Before the building was complete, cracks appeared and sections started to give way. Unable to afford to do the work again, his client had him thrown into debtors' gaol. He avoids looking at me as he tells his tale. His voice is quiet and his mood morose. He has lost both spirit and self-belief.

He introduces me to others; William Evans, once a man of substance who borrowed too much money at too high a rate of interest and was unable to repay when the bank called in the loan. I can picture him as one of the prosperous figures sitting in the Horse and Groom. His clothes betray his former wealth, even if they are now ragged. I note the worn waistcoat buttonhole where once his gold watch chain would have hung. He frets for the well-being of his destitute family.

John Griffiths is a tradesman who fell on hard times. At least he had the spirit to punch the bailiff sent to appropriate his family possessions. I want to laugh but there is no humour in the conversation. He is a large man whose fists appear permanently clenched as if willing the next attack. He is unsettling company.

Across the yard there is a man standing alone in a corner talking to himself. I ask who it is.

'Henry, Henry Meyrick. He does that all the day long,' explains John. 'He's been petitioning for release for years and it's slowly driven him out of his mind.'

'What's he saying?'

'Mostly he asks God why he is being punished in this way. Sometimes he reels off pages of legal words he learnt writing petitions for release. Most of the time he talks gibberish.'

Conversation lapses. These are not men who enjoy idle chatter. They see little point in their own existence. They appear embarrassed that, whilst their lives have ended, their bodies still live. I feel removed from them. I refuse to be party to their defeatism. I do not want to join a fellowship of debtors. I intended to ask them to share their knowledge on the processes of petitioning for release, but I do not. Any knowledge they can offer will be tainted by failure. I shall do my own research. I move away, anxious to escape.

I return to my cell along a narrow corridor which leads to a stone staircase. As I mount the stairs I become aware of a figure standing in my way. The light is poor. I move to one side to allow the figure to pass, but instead I am thrust hard against the iron railing. A hand twists my arm behind my back and pushes me hard until the air is squeezed from my lungs and my ribs are at cracking point. A hand grabs my hair and pulls my head back. The voice of Thomas Morgan, the gaoler, sounds threateningly in my ear.

'So my new debtor's been making complaints about the standard of my hospitality has he? Thought you'd go over my head to the justices, did you? Well, Mr Williams, I think you'd be better off remembering that there's not much that happens that Thomas Morgan doesn't get to hear of. Whilst I have the pleasure of your company I suggest it might pay to be a little more appreciative of the service.'

With that he thrusts me hard against the railings one more time before letting go. I slip to the ground, struggling for breath and nursing my bruised ribs.

Sitting in the darkness the truth dawns that I am enrolled in the fellowship of debtors, like it or not. They and I are victims of a tyrannical law which oppresses us as much through the manner of its enforcement as through its strictures. I am determined not to surrender to the violence and crude intimidation of Thomas Morgan.

3

Come read my new ballad

I MOVE THE piles of books and papers around my desk. I am becoming an expert in the laws governing debt and debtors. It appears that Parliament is forever tinkering with the law without ever doing much to improve it. Our gaols are full of people like me who have committed no crime and are prevented from earning the money that would repay their creditors. Appalling though Thomas Morgan may be, he is, I discover, a saint compared to some of his counterparts in the debtors' prisons of London where charges are made against prisoners for all kinds of 'services', so that a man may enter gaol owing five pounds and find himself owing a hundred before a month has passed. I will not be alone in campaigning. Many writers of note, including Dr Johnson, have written condemning the current state of the law.

In theory, getting out of debtors' prison is simple. All I have to do is construct a schedule of my assets demonstrating my solvency. This is placed before the justices who, if they agree, can order my release. I don't even need to have repaid the debt for which I was detained, but must promise to do so out of the proceeds of my industry. In practice, it's a lot harder and, even if one obtains a hearing, the original complainant can object all over again. It would plainly be best to pay off John Walton for his pills before petitioning the justices. For that, I have to earn some money and that is going to be difficult from inside the prison.

I have a visit from Peggy who brings me news of my father and our infant girls. She brings supplies of paper, pens, ink and books. She brings my beloved copy of *Julie, ou la nouvelle Héloïse* by Jean-Jacques Rousseau and Carl von Linné's volume on the classification of plants which I had requested. She brings me a pound in silver coins. She brings bread, cheese and apples and a supply of laudanum. She informs me that several orders have come to the cottage for monuments. My father, God bless the man, is trying his best to fulfil some of them but he is old and frail. I tell her not to turn orders away. She stays with me for the night. For this I have to pay a supplement to Thomas Morgan. My accommodation is not commodious but it is worth it to have my darling wife in my arms once more. We talk of the girls. Margaret has sent me some dried flowers. She misses me and particularly the sound of my flute. Ann is teething but she can be charmed asleep by song. We make love with great tenderness, a consummation which will give me fulfilment and strength in the face of my trials.

In the morning Peggy departs and I seek out Thomas Morgan. That in itself requires courage and a certain swallowing of my pride. I mention money as quickly as possible to keep his interest. I offer two shillings and sixpence for the use of a room in which I can prepare and cut a limestone monument for a gentleman from Ely. He is surly and suspicious, demanding to 'see the colour of my money first'. To his surprise I produce a bright half-crown which he pockets greedily before promising to reserve me a place in the old brewhouse.

I am determined to free myself from this confinement. I am equally determined to carry out a campaign to change the iniquitous and tyrannical law which licenses Thomas Morgan and his kind to practise intimidation and extortion under the pretence of being agents of the Crown.

My next act will be to instil some heart in the broken bodies of my fellow debtors. I do this by composing a spirited ballad which I will perform for their enjoyment. I have entitled it 'A Callendar of all the Debtors now Confined in Cardiff Gaol, who in the Creditor's opinion deserve to be hanged'.

I start thus:

Come read my new Ballad and here you shall find,
A list of poor debtors in Cardiff Confined,
Convicted of poverty, what a vile thing,
And doomed by their creditors shortly to swing.

I start with myself, lest my companions might fear that I seek to censure them in any way.

Ned Williams, a mason whose case is not rare,
Stands indicted for building huge castles in air,
And also for trespass, a scandalous crime,
On the grounds of Parnassus by scribbling a Rhime.

Now the tricky bits. I need to list them by name to bring their predicament to the attention of those who know them. I also want them to recognise the truth in what I write and, if possible, to laugh at the wild folly of the situation. I face William, ruined by a failure to build secure foundations:

The next William Freme, one well known thro' the land
As a Mason of note, but he built on the sand,
Hard blew the fierce tempest, high swell'd the rude stream,
And down came the building of poor William Freme.

I watch as he listens, looks dubious, then smiles, then laughs, then thanks me, then asks me to read it again, then asks if he may have a copy. I go to the cell of John Griffiths. When he opens the door his body looks like a massive slab of granite on which I might inscribe. On top of that is a head, and by the sides dangle those enormous fists. I hope he approves or I may be pulp in short time.

> The next is John Griffiths, who fiercely can fight,
> He drub'd a Bum bailiff, a thing very right,
> And sure out of prison he never shall come,
> Whilst Lawyers deserve a good kick in the Bum.

When I finish reading his face distorts into a grimace which I mistake for pain but turns out to be the closest thing to a smile he can manage. Next William Evans, who listens with the air of a man listening to fine music.

> And now William Evans, attend to the Rhime,
> Over-reaching himself is his capital crime,
> Dear Judge shew thy mercy, Release him from jail
> But confine him for life in a butt of good Ale.

He turns and shakes my hand, 'Well done, my boy. You plainly have a talent for these things.'

He reaches to his waistcoat pocket, presumably for a florin to hand me, before remembering that he has no money to give.

I visit eleven debtors in all, gaining their approval for the verses. I return to my cell pleased with their response and hoping that it may make the ordeal a little more bearable and their suffering a little more acknowledged. I make fourteen copies, one for each of the debtors named, one spare for me, and two which I will ask Peggy to dispatch for reading in the taprooms of the Bear in Cowbridge and the Old Globe in Cardiff. From there I have confidence that more copies will be made and wider recitations given.

Within four days, the piece of limestone which I have ordered arrives, to be transformed into a monument for the gentleman from Ely. I direct the carrier to take it down to the brewhouse as I have agreed with Thomas Morgan, but when we open the door the whole space is full of vats and stills and all the paraphernalia of a distillery. The gaoler is nowhere to be found. I am forced to request the carrier to move the piece, which is of some considerable weight, to my own cell. He is unhappy about this. I am unhappy about this. Stone cutting causes dust which affects my asthma. I have always tried to avoid working on stone in the same space where I have to eat or sleep.

It is a full day before I have a chance to remonstrate with my gaoler. At first he pretends not to hear me. Then he listens whilst I complain that he has reneged on an agreement, and taken money under false pretences.

He replies, 'I was going to be kind to you, Mr Williams. I was indeed. But then you go and upset me all over again with your verses. And not just me, but their justices too. There's a whole bench of angry lawyers who have seen your ballad and who would wish me to do all in my power to make your life as miserable as possible. So I tell you what. Why don't you make another complaint and see how far that gets you? You could even do it in verse.'

He turns to go but pauses to add, 'Your sort never bloody learns, do you?'

4

Succession

I AM BESET by enemies on all sides. Wherever I look men wish me ill and denigrate what I have done, and even who I am. John Walton is looking in through a jagged hole in the wall of my cell. He smiles with pleasure when he sees my suffering. He turns to whisper some vile suggestion to Thomas Morgan who nods in agreement and departs to prepare some further misery for me. Behind them stand a row of grim-faced justices in wigs and robes, mouthing doom in unison. When I look away I am confronted by clergymen waving sticks in anger and money lenders demanding payments. I try to speak to them, to offer words which will pacify them, but I am drowned out by a chorus of London Welsh splitting their sides with laughter and mocking my Glamorgan accent and peasant words. Behind them stand a row of London stonecutters waving tankards and chanting 'Taffy' and 'Toasted cheese'. Samuel Johnson is in their midst mouthing pompous insults to all things Celtic. Will no one help me? I call to Owain Myfyr but he does not hear. I run towards him. He has his back to me and is in his counting house totalling columns of figures. I shout but he does not turn. What of Daniel and John? Where are they now, despite their protestations that I was a bard who deserved fame throughout Britain? I look for them in Beaupre Woods, running through the bracken, tearing my flesh on the brambles, but I can find no trace.

I sit on the ground and weep. I feel my mother's arm around me and her voice in my ear. As always she is right. Of course! My

persecutors fall silent when Dafydd ap Gwilym walks into the cell
complaining about the food and drink – or rather the absence of
either. He asks why I brought him hither when neither the place
nor the provision is worthy. I plead my excuses but insist that I
need his fellowship now more than ever.

He sits with his feet on my table, picking his nose whilst I pour
out my heart. I explain that whilst I am a bard, the equal of any in
Wales or England, I cannot practise my craft for want of a patron.
I am forced to spend my days not in the making of great verse but
in the carving of epitaphs, and even then I cannot make a living as
my desperate predicament illustrates.

He looks dubious. 'I cannot believe the world is rid of the rich,
powerful and vain?'

I confess that they inhabit Glamorgan and London in
abundance.

'And if sufficiently rich and sufficiently vain, easy prey for a set
of verses written in their honour and praise?'

I try to explain that the wealthy landowners of today prefer
to aggrandise their positions, not through such simple devices as
verse, but by increasing still further their wealth, as if their bank
account was a more certain paean of praise than the exquisite verse
of a bard of note. I add the additional problem that many cannot
read Welsh. Dafydd waves his hand dismissively.

'No matter! You just have to persuade them that there's no
replacement for the quality item, the very best verse. Providing
they believe it's the finest available, they'll pay. They pay
gold for all sorts of things they don't understand or can't use,
even horses they can't ride, just to impress everyone else. The
important thing is to keep the competition under control, keep
out balladmongers and street artists, amateur rhymesters and
the like. If you don't have strict rules about who is a proper bard,
you'll soon be submerged in doggerel verses delivered by farting
jesters.'

'How?'

'How what?'

'How do you prove to someone with no taste that you're the best? And keep out the rubbish.'

'I can't believe my ears. The guild of course, the assembly of bards, the Gorsedd, whatever name it gives itself this month. Don't tell me it doesn't exist any more? Look! Who taught you the rules of cynghangedd?'

'Lewis Hopkin, till he died; then John Bradford of Betws.'

'So you are an accredited bard, instructed in the craft and approved by those who went before you?'

'Yes. I suppose so.'

'I suppose so! Presumably there was some ceremony? Never keen on ceremonies myself. Too many elder bards treat it as a chance to have fun at the expense of their juniors – initiation ceremonies involving horns, broomsticks, nettles and the like, but important all the same to be in or out.'

'In or out of...?'

'The bardic succession. Like the Papal succession but more important! The lineage of those of us who form a link in the unbroken chain of tradition from the first druid to... me, or even you.'

'How do you know this?'

'No idea. But that's how it is. Now, if you really have no food worth eating, or drink worth drinking, excuse me if I try to ease my hunger elsewhere. Good luck.'

And with that Dafydd saunters off towards a tavern I had not previously noticed, not a hundred yards from my barred window.

Now I sit in darkness. All my tormentors and my one self-assured friend have departed. But the darkness is not oppressive. Dafydd has left me a single candle, a strong steady thought, an idea which, if I tend it, will flare into a splendid flame. The succession of *which he talks is a truth that must be acknowledged, a benefaction not to be denied.*

It shall be my task to bring this truth out of the shadows and into the light where it can be admired by all.

5

Ancient secrets

I AM ONE *of very few who have been taught the secrets of cynghanedd in the ancient way. Techniques and rules passed down by word of mouth during those long sessions I spent in Lewis Hopkin's small kitchen learning how to make the chime, where the stress should fall, and how a line must be constructed. I shall lay out the rules and trace their origins back to the great meetings of bards.*

I write at speed because I know these secrets as do few others. I write on the first page 'The Secrets of the Bards of Wales'. No, I cross out 'Wales' and rewrite 'The Secrets of the Bards of the Island of Britain'. This is a tradition that reaches back long before the Saxons and the Angles or the Romans – to a time when the Brythons ruled all of this island, when the monument at Avebury would have echoed to ceremonies conducted in our ancient language.

I use all that I have read or been told of the work of the old masters and seek to codify their work into a classification of twenty-four poetic measures which I will call 'Glamorgan Measures'. I am astounded by the resonance with Carl von Linné's volume on the classification of plants from which I borrow ideas.

I explain the rules of the Guild of Bards and the process by which it governs itself. Not 'Guild' – that makes us sound too much like cobblers. We need a more dignified name. Dafydd mentioned Gorsedd – a court, an assembly, a gathering – good!

The first and overriding purpose of the Gorsedd is to ensure the continued practice of writing strict-metre poetry according to the rules agreed democratically by the members:

Membership is restricted to those properly trained and licensed in the craft of poetry;

Training shall be in the oral tradition, ensuring purity of language;

Language and thoughts should always be such as to inspire the readers to live pure moral lives inspired by the example of Jesus Christ;

Bards must be men of peace and reason, knowledge, morality and truth.

I write many pages explaining how the Gorsedd was and should be again, at the heart of the nation. I explain how the function of a bard was always to teach the nation to aspire to the highest moral standards. There is a link between maintaining the purity of the language and purity of thought. Above all else, bards should teach that disputes should be solved through debate and wise judgments, never through violence.

I write of the nature of meetings and how they would be conducted. I write as one possessed until at last I stop, not because I have finished but because the vision I have witnessed now surrounds me. The cell is full of curious figures talking quietly to each other about my writing. A bard of great distinction steps over to my desk and looks over my shoulder to read. He nods in pleasure and signals to the circle of watchers. His lips start to move but out of them come no sounds. I can read the soundless words on his lips. I must take his lead and turn his mouthing into lines. I write:

Tra fod dy feirdd yn cadw'th iaith
Na foed eu gwaith yn ofer,
Boed ar eu cerddi o bob rhyw

Llais deddfau Duw'r uchelder,
Barddoniaeth yw'th gelfyddyd fawr,
Bu gynt yn fawr ei lleufer,
O bydded fyth yr hynn a'i gwedd
Yn addysg hedd bob amser.

A thra bo cynnwrf mawr y byd
Yn arwain bryd annwyfol,
At waed a rhyfel ymhob mann,
A sarnau'r gwann cystuddiol,
Bid iaith dy gerddi 'mhlaid y gwir,
Drwy gyrrau'th dir yn hollol,
Na ddeled byth ond iawnder hardd
O Benn un Bardd awenol.[32]

The circle of druids and bards applaud.

---

32   Whilst your bards protect the word, / Their striving has a purpose, / Proclaim the laws of God on high / In verses free and fearless, / Our verses are our greatest art / Whose light was once resplendent, / Her beauty to your lives brings peace / And to our hearts, atonement.

Whilst tumult and confusion reign / Men's actions are unworthy. / Blood is shed and brothers slain / A cruel war, ungodly. / In every part of this fair land, / Your poets' words are truthful, / Let nothing but the voice of peace / Be heard within their circle.

6

A petition

I AM DISTURBED in my writing by William Evans, the ruined businessman, who brings information about the Insolvency Act of 1781. I had forgotten that I had requested this. It is so much more pleasant to ignore the stern reality of the gaol by finding comfort in the civilised world of bards and druids. However, the *Gorsedd* itself would instruct and impel me to act to secure the liberty of good men such as these.

William Evans produces pages of notes he has made during his imprisonment. He now talks freely about his predicament and the circumstances of his falling into debt. He does so in the manner of a wealthy merchant recounting a humorous episode after a good dinner. But there is no humour in his account. He has followed the proper procedures to obtain release several times, but each time his application has been blocked by an attorney acting on behalf of 'men who prefer to see me humbled and out of their way'.

Given the problems of petitioning the justices and the fear that Thomas Morgan may, as he claims, be in league with them, I believe our best course of action is to petition Parliament directly in the hope that some, at least, of our MPs are men of conscience. I have written an address outlining the iniquity of the system by which honest tradesmen can be thrown into the loathsome apartments of a prison and detained indefinitely. They are tortured by having to watch their debt grow daily, so making any prospect of release retreat to a far horizon.

He confirms what I know – that insolvency acts give the justices a responsibility to hear submissions for release but, as no act has been passed for seven years, their legal lordships see no need to stir themselves or leave their expansive suppers and fine port for the confines of an undistinguished local court.

My petition to Parliament requests a new insolvency act that will require county magistrates to arrange hearings every month and, if they are satisfied, to administer the oaths that the law requires before a debtor is released. I need several pieces of information to make the petition sound. William Evans' notes help, although I rely far more on the books and pamphlets Peggy brings me. My father also writes regularly, and with a passion which surprises me. Many friends of his have suffered detention of this kind and his indignation at the injustice brings him closer to me.

I still need more information as to the provisions of the 1755 Insolvency Act. William Evans shakes his head, admitting the gap in his scribbled archive. Then his head lifts and his eyes widen. He issues one word, 'Meyrick!'

He races ahead of me towards the corner of the yard where Henry Meyrick always waits, staring at a vision apparent only to his eyes. He stands like a puppet waiting for a puppeteer to jiggle the strings.

Williams Evans leans over to him and whispers the words, 'Insolvent Debtors Relief Act 1755.'

Henry Meyrick looks confused for a second before his lips part and out pour the word-for-word contents of that Parliamentary bill. It is recited in a steady stream without pause or punctuation or expression. I have a pencil and paper. I would like to stop and ask him for the particular clauses, 24 and 30, which I need, but plainly there is no control over the flow and the only order is a recitation of the whole. Consequently, I am in a state of high nervous tension when Clause 23 approaches its conclusion. Whilst weak, his voice is clear and I have no difficulty in gathering its meaning. I have more problems with Clause 30, perhaps because of the strain of sustained concentration. Despite that, I have most of that which I require. William Evans offers to prompt Meyrick to make the recitation all over again, which I decline. I do so out of consideration for the old man who is plainly exhausted, but also out of consideration for my own sanity. I believe I have more than enough law for my purposes.

Henry Meyrick reaches the end of his recitation and freezes like a statue. A tear drops from the corner of his eye. What hell is going on inside that fine head? The giant John Griffiths places his arm around the shrunken form and soothes him, just as a mother might hold a frightened child.

I spend hours incorporating the details I have gleaned into my submission. I revise it the following day, and that afternoon read the whole to William Evans for his comments and approval. He sits in my other chair, his legs asunder, as if a pendulous belly still hung before him. In truth, the deprivations of the prison regime have left him a thinner, sadder man. His posture describes only his memory of his former prosperous self.

'Well done, my boy,' he intones and reaches to his empty pocket for the half-guinea that is not there.

Tomorrow Peggy will be here to see me and I have to have the submission ready, together with instructions as to who she must contact to ensure that the papers reach the correct parliamentary authorities. When she arrives she is quiet and mysterious. I ask her why she smiles so. She teases me before confessing that she is certain that she is with child once more. A child she reminds me, as if there were need, who would have been conceived within these prison walls. I am awed and overjoyed. I am each time fulfilled beyond expression when I learn that I am to be a father. There is additional symbolism to this child-to-be. A child conceived in the walls of a prison has to be a champion of freedom. I embrace my Peggy's beauty, her glorious ripeness and bounteousness and I love her more than even I, a poet, can declare.

She asks me to play my flute for her, for our daughters and for our unborn child. I do not regard myself as a musician of note but tonight, in the luxury of my cell, my playing expresses beyond words my love of my wife, my child and sweet life itself.

7

Rhys Goch

B EFORE SHE LEAVES, Peggy breaks bad news. I have been asking why the Walters brothers have not come to my aid when their praise of my verse was so generous. She tells me that Daniel is ill, afflicted by the most brutal attacks of consumption; that the young and vigorous young scholar and poet is thought to be but a short time for this world.

I cannot help but contrast my joy at news of my new child with the shadow of death that now hangs over the Walters family. I owe the father so much. I love the brothers as if they were my own. In truth, more than my own. This juxtaposition of the promise of new life with the prospect of the grave is too stark and violent to comprehend or endure.

Peggy departs purposefully with my papers and instructions, and I am left to consider. The pain is great and the sense of desolation, of pointlessness, returns. I need support.

The bardic world I am recording is a complete and perfect truth. It is also a symbol of a greater certainty. Whilst I browse its features and refine my descriptions of its secrets, I understand that I need company. As in all I have ever done, in all I have ever created, I understand that I will have enemies, gainsayers, those who will dismiss my truth as apostasy. To resist this attack I need witnesses. I need testimony from the bards of medieval Wales that the Wales of which I give evidence is based on truth unimpeachable.

I call on Dafydd ap Gwilym who wanders back from the tavern up the road still chewing on a chicken leg and looking as if the ale had been more than satisfactory. He resumes his position with his feet on my desk and looks at me wearily. I explain that I need voices to sing in support of the great vision I have designed.

'Why would you want others when you have me?'

He is offended. These bards can be very touchy. I tell him that I need voices from different ages and different backgrounds to be witnesses to my account.

'I am the best.'

I agree with him, partly because I have to, but mostly because he is.

'Why not choose some names from history and see if you can make them sing?'

'Have you suggestions?'

'Well!' The great bard belches, shifts himself and farts loudly. 'Ah, that's better. As I was saying, I am the best, so you will have to calibrate your history around me. There are those who came before me, as prophets foreseeing the greatness to come, and those who came after who had to live in my shadow. For the prophets, why not look for a voice from the Norman period. Plenty about, I'm sure.'

'Llŷr ap Gerallt?'

'No way. Upstart rhymester and far too late. Now there was a Rhys Brydydd who was a fair rhymester. If you go back through his family history: Fat Gwilym, son of Rhisiart ap Rhys, son of Lewys Morgannwg, and so on, you get to Rhys Goch ap Rhicert. Twelfth century with a good pedigree. A son of Glamorgan, which will please you. Try him.'

The great bard falls off his chair. I think for a moment he is going to fall asleep and snore on my cell floor but he raises himself and stumbles off uncertainly into the gloom.

On the other side of my cell Rhys Goch ap Rhicert appears, standing on a piece of high ground surveying the landscape. He *is everything I might have hoped; a nobleman, proud and full of swagger, but with great sensitivity. His long red robe displays the coat of arms of his family, and his posture betrays the manner of a man born to rule. He is, I soon learn, a confused man, full of resentment at the displacement of his father from his seat of power by the Normans and caustic in his low opinion of the new masters. He grants that they can fight and they can construct fortifications, but after that? Nothing to enchant the soul.*

It is cold up here. I don't know exactly where we are, but somewhere in the Blaenau. Rhys points out the places I should know. Where I expect to see towns there are only hamlets. Pontyclun is a dirt track with a few shepherds' huts.

I tempt him to compose. I plead with him to sing. He is willing but he tells me that he will only do so with my assistance. It takes but a short while before his words soar in praise of the Glamorgan the conquering Normans have traduced. His lines concur with the 'Glamorgan Measures' I laid down in my 'Secrets of the Bards'. I hear in his words the progenitor of Dafydd, the true voice of romantic poetry. If Dafydd is the high noon of pastoral love, then Rhys is its dawning. He is as lascivious as Dafydd, his praise of a girl requires him to list each part of her anatomy and praise each part in great detail: lips, brow, shoulders, breasts, nipples, belly, thighs and then the most secret parts. He is more explicit even than Dafydd. He whispers his sensuous lines into my ear and I scribble.

We stay out on the hillside until night falls. Rhys fades. I reach for my flute and play until sleep overtakes me.

8

My own petition

WHEN I AWAKE my flute is missing, my precious German-made flute which my mother gave me so many years ago. At first I do not panic. I have mislaid it many times and, like a good friend, it always forgives my carelessness. I search all parts of my cell, which does not take long. I do this again until it becomes clear to me that it is indeed missing. It has been stolen whilst I slept. I know it is not of great intrinsic value but, to me, it is a most precious possession. Not only is it one of my last links to my mother, it is also a source of comfort and solace when the world is unkind. It is like a limb or an ear or eye; a part of me that is always there and always ready to function – except that now it has been severed.

I charge out of the cell raising the alarm, shouting news of my loss down the cold corridors. I stop when I realise how selfish, how irrelevant this must sound to the ears of debtors whose despair is based on far greater, less redeemable burdens.

Who should I suspect? The gaol is full of thieves but I suspect none of them. Thomas Morgan has to be the culprit. Why? Because in this sad environment, the debtors' value any source of comfort or hope. My poor music spelled hope to me and to others who listened. Who in this gaol would wish to see us so deprived of comfort? There is but one answer.

It is late morning before I find the gaoler inspecting the trays of food lest there be too large a portion of thin gruel in any. I inform him of my loss. He smiles with open villainy.

'Too, too bad. Lots of nasty sorts in 'ere – sad to say.'

'And I am looking at the most villainous of them all.'

I should not have said it. I regret it at once. Not because I doubt its truth. I need no more proof of the way this selfish, self-serving, callous, mean-spirited, heartless man will behave towards those who do not bow to his regime. His eyes widen in wonder and he cries,

'I don't believe I have ever met anyone more foolish than you, you, you… scribbler!' (This is his worst insult? I am proud of the title.) 'You just wait. I know all about your little petition to Parliament.' (I do not doubt it.) 'You'll suffer for it. I'll make sure of that. Don't you think because you can read you can get the better of Thomas Morgan.'

He stalks away, slamming doors along the corridor. I am stunned by his admission that he cannot read. To run a gaol with all the letters and messages from justices and the like without being literate. How does he manage? Does his wife read? Does he guess? That would explain much in his erratic behaviour. Does he feel inadequate as a result? Plainly. For a fraction of a fraction of a second I feel sympathy. I imagine myself teaching him the alphabet and correcting the way he shapes his letters on the slate. This is not the first time I have had revealed to me the pathetic truth that behind the fists of the bully lies the heart of a fearful frightened child.

I return to my cell. After all the work on the petition to Parliament I now must complete my own petition to the justices for release. My father, God bless the man, has been out in the yard in Flemingston inscribing monuments, finishing and polishing stone for other masons as if he was thirty years younger. Peggy tells me that she is amazed by the vitality he displays. He has decided that he cannot afford to be an old man hugging the kitchen corner whilst his son is behind the walls of a debtors' gaol. God provide that he will not suffer for this generosity after my release. For my own part, I have completed half a dozen significant commissions in the cramped confines of my cell which have brought in a significant purse of golden guineas and much suffering with asthma. I have no difficulty in submitting an account that demonstrates that Edward Williams, master mason, is financially sound and should be released from this abominable place forthwith.

I wait for Peggy who will come to spend this night in the gaol. She is now heavy with child. When she arrives I remark on how she has grown since her last visit. She grins ruefully and tells me that the village women all convince her that such increase is a sure sign that our new child will be a boy. I tell her that I adore our girls and will be beside myself with joy whatever we produce. I give her my petition for release which I assure her makes a strong case. She takes it and embraces me sensuously as only Peggy can. I tell her that we should not make love because I fear that it might be injurious to the child-to-be. She pouts but tells me that nevertheless she wishes to *cwtsh*, to lie with me, to embrace and to fondle.

She is half undressed when there is a banging on the door and the man-monster Thomas Morgan appears. He is plainly drunk. He slurs his words as he shouts,

'I'm not having your woman spend another night in this gaol whilst I am its master. The King cannot be held responsible for midwifery services. Given that Mrs Williams could be about to hatch at any time, I wish to serve notice that I'm not prepared, given the authority invested in me by officers of the Crown, to permit her to lie within these walls another night.'

He sways. I am inclined to laugh at his idiocy which I cannot regard as serious. He explodes, 'I mean it you – you – you poet!' (Another insult I find hard to recognise as such.)

He returns to the door and calls the assistant turnkey. I protest and cry in outrage whilst the two men manhandle my half-naked Peggy around the room. Without allowing her time to refasten her stays or don her cloak, they bundle her down the passageway. The cell door is slammed in my face and the key turned to prevent my following.

It is twelve miles from Cardiff gaol to Flemingston; a hard walk in the dark for a young man, but a torture for a heavily pregnant woman. I sit in silence for maybe an hour considering. Am I responsible for the suffering that Thomas Morgan has inflicted on my Peggy? Or is she suffering for the failure of the world to teach people that their first duty is to the care of their fellow men – or women. Human sympathy, the virtue my mother embodied. Fellowship, the value the *Gorsedd* holds sacred. My bardic circles are not the stuff of idle dreams; they are the basis of a new and better world.

I reach for my absent flute. In the darkness my fingers curl round its remembered shape. I blow real breaths and finger imaginary stops to create music that expresses my pain more than anything I could really play. I am comforted, but the sadness is that no other being can hear my song, my pain, my triumph.

9

Will Tabwr

I HAVE TALKED *to many poets during my time here. I approach each of them in turn and ask for their conspiratorial involvement in my project. All are willing, although some take more persuading than others. I now have all I need. Indeed the cell is often crowded with bards from Rhys Goch to the group from the seventeenth century, all of them skilled practitioners in one or many of the poetic forms I have classified as the 'Glamorgan Measures'. Their pedigrees and the periods they represent all contribute to prove the truth of my 'Secrets of the Bards' and demonstrate beyond doubt that Glamorgan was a far more important centre of bardic creativity than any other part of Wales – including Gwynedd.*

They can be a very boisterous bunch, much given to flights of ecstatic joy, sloughs of depression, quarrels, revelries and, when questions of primacy are concerned, challenges to personal combat. This last, I insist, is not part of the bardic code which abhors violence of any sort. I have had to be resolute on this point, sometimes in the face of open rebellion. Although I have become used to their ways and am more than able to cope with the lively spirited word play that persists whenever they are present, I experience one moment of delightful surprise.

I receive a letter I wrote to myself from a remarkable but little-known Glamorgan poet from the time of the Civil War. It reads:

Mr Iorwerth,

I have heard that you are in the business of raising some of our wise old heads from their graves. I would most appreciate an opportunity to have another go at satirising the foolery to be found amongst the nobility of Glamorgan. When I lived, there was no shortage of thick-skulled ignorant fools amongst the nobility, and my main task in life was to make fun of them and to ridicule their stupidity to my audience of common decent folk.

I have no doubt that your current generation of lawyers, landowners and clerics will be equally deserving of ridicule, and I would be most pleased to leap from my grave at a moment's notice if I might be of service to your cause.

Your entertaining and satirical servant,
Will Tabwr.

He arrives in my cell dressed in simple country attire but with the demeanour of a king. He greets me in the simple honest language of a son of Glamorgan, but his swagger is the swagger of one who knows the truth. He will have no part of my incarceration. A gaol cell is no place for this free spirit. He takes me out to county fairs and village greens, to maypole dances and sheep shearings. He is the king of the pastoral romance, willing to make a fool of himself for the love of any pretty shepherdess.

He is not content just to be another of my versifiers. He wants to dance. He wants to roam with me across the county. In Llangynwyd on a summer evening we attend the Mabsant where we compete to be the quickest stepping dancers, then delight the audience with short poems. We meet two of the prettiest young women. Mine is Peggy. His is a wild untameable wench, half-bird, half-girl, who runs and teases and fights and shies and argues and cries and laughs and loves. Will is the spirit of freedom. He tells me with pride that he is proud to be of my company but that he cannot spend a moment longer in that granite cell.

Peggy remains. She smiles and extends her arms. She is holding a baby, a boy, our new son! He will be called Taliesin. I am father to the King of Bards.

1 0

Julie

I KNOW NOT if I have gaol fever or cholera, but I fear that I shall not survive this attack. My throat is so dry. I vomit and sweat. I feel the moisture running from my pores. I lose consciousness and dream the most vivid visceral dreams. I am hot. I am cold. I tremble. I shake. I shiver. I believe I am to die.

But I do not. Peggy is with me. She is by my bedside. She braves whatever disease I have and any scorn the Morgan creature throws her way. I am so blessed and undeserving of her. She gives me laudanum. I sleep and phantoms rise.

I am with my mother declaiming Milton. I am a rebellious Satan. It feels good but is it proper to glory in the acts of darkness? How do I know what is right? All the time the world calls on me to compromise, to take an easier option. Am I right to refuse or am I merely proud? To be proud and rebellious makes the blood run faster and the heart to beat. Have I any right to make choices that inflict suffering on others, particularly my family?

Jean-Jacques Rousseau is visiting my cell. He sits on the hard chair with poised elegance, his right hand resting on the top of his silver-topped cane. He is dressed plainly but elegantly in the French manner. He sips the tea I have made for him. He holds the tin mug with the elegance of one attending a Parisian salon. After re-reading his great novel Julie, *I have asked him here to help me better understand myself. I know that we have much in common. We are both great lovers of sensibility, expressed in our close identification with nature and our fellow human beings. We are also driven to create art, bring people to life and to seek truth underneath the superficiality which passes for reality. But do I do so for reasons that are good or bad? Does my desire for fame make my efforts unworthy? Jean-Jacques has little English and no Welsh. We speak in French. I am confident of my vocabulary but fear my accent will offend his ears. I ask my questions.*

He has a gentle, beautiful smile. He listens intently then asks my permission before rising and walking over to the tall elaborate French windows that have appeared in the wall of my cell. Beyond the casement I see green pastures, clear blue sky and snow-topped mountains. He opens the windows and steps out. He looks about and then calls gently, 'Julie'.

Of course! He is summoning Julie, the heroine of his great novel. The magnificent landscape I see must be her Switzerland. She suddenly appears, elegant and fine featured and a little startled by his summons, the very image of sensibility. He takes her hand and leads her into the room, announcing,

'Madame d'Etrange – Julie. May I introduce Monsieur Williams.'

She inclines her head graciously. I stand and bow in return. He leads her to the chair he has vacated and she sits, gathering her skirts with the grace of a white gull settling. He stands to her side and explains,

'Monsieur Williams wishes to know more of the secrets and subtleties of the heart. I explained that I have created you expressly so that men and women of feeling may learn such secrets.'

The great philosopher turns to me, 'You may ask her what you will, but remember she is a character from a book I have created. She can only repeat for you the truth I have placed on her lips. You, who create the words of great bards, will understand. You and I will learn and change from our encounters with each other. Julie d'Etrange will never change because she does not exist.'

I tell Madame d'Etrange how moved I was to read her story, her troubles with her husband, her letters to her lover and how she had found a path through a complex maze of passions. How was it that she maintained her virtue, her purity of soul, when her actions had so often offended against conventional morality?

'What is your name?'

'Williams.'

'No, your familiar name. The name your wife or mother would use?'

'Ned.'

'May I call you Ned?'

'I would be honoured.'

'And you may call me Julie. But to answer you as milord would wish – each of us has a secret in our own heart which makes us who we are. I had to ask myself continuously whether to follow the teachings of Church and society or to listen to the moral commandments of my own heart.'

She produces several sheets of notepaper which she holds before her. A flagstone in the centre of the floor melts, and a roaring fire leaps hungrily through the gap as if from hell. She walks over to the inferno. She holds the papers over the flames.

'If I had listened to the Church I would have cast away St Preux, my lover. I would have taken his letters and destroyed them. Had I done so I would as surely destroyed myself.'

She turns to the fire.

'Yet, that is what the Church demanded of me in the name of duty, to destroy my soul in the name of salvation.'

Jean-Jacques speaks quietly from the window, 'Remember Ned, Julie has only to be accountable to her maker – a mere author. You and I have to be answerable to a far more powerful creator.'

I spring up in alarm as Julie appears to walk into the flames but, as she steps, so the leaping fires turn from fire red to corn yellow and from corn yellow to grass green. She sits on a small rock at the side of a mountain stream that runs through the cell. She looks at me inquisitively, 'Come and sit at my side, Ned. Tell me more about your work.'

I do as she asks. Jean-Jacques chides, 'He is a writer. And you are supposed to answer questions not ask them.'

'Ned, you see what a tyranny it is to have a creator who forces his rules upon those he has created? At least your own creator gives you the freedom to make mistakes.' Julie looks reprovingly at her creator who laughs. Julie continues to question.

'Of what do you write?'

'Of the countryside, of the bounty of nature, of love.'

'Do you write the truth?'

'I believe so.'

'Who tells you so?'

I hesitate. I am uncertain and she can see that.

'Do you trust those who read your work to tell you so, or do you listen to your own heart?'

She stands up and walks across to Jean-Jacques. She stands behind his chair and places a hand confidently on his shoulder.

'This man, the great Rousseau, warns the world of the dangers of seeking esteem through the applause and adulation of others. The true writer acts in accord with simpler individual instincts of what is right and true. The false writer loses any vision of truth in their desire to please and entertain. Correct milord?'

'Correct,' he affirms.

'That, at least, is what he tells the world. But then he creates me and I am a sensation. I am on the shelves of every bookseller in every language in Europe. He receives adoring mail by every post. Do you smell hypocrisy? I am firmly of the opinion that he created me because his books of philosophy sold so badly.'

Jean-Jacques shrugs his shoulders as if to admit that purity is not always possible in those less than angels.

Julie continues, 'So do you write to entertain or to seek the truth?'

I want to portray myself as pure, but an image of myself standing on a table entertaining the Marble Arch masons with bawdy songs springs into my conscience. I admit to Julie that I have a love of pleasing the crowd, but I protest that in other work I write according to the truth in my heart.

Julie sighs. 'I pray that it is so, but writers are an inconstant breed. The only ones I trust are those who write as if their words will never be seen or printed, who publish anonymously or under another's name. If that was a condition of publishing I suspect there would be few books. But at least then I could be certain that what I read is written from the purity of their soul and not to satisfy their vanity.'

From the corner of the room Jean-Jacques announces quietly, 'Ned, it has been a great pleasure but – it is time.'

Julie gathers her letters from the grassy floor. 'See?' she affirms, 'he is a tyrant. Au revoir, Ned.' And with that she walks across the grassy floor towards the window. As she steps, the grass returns to cold stone behind her. As she passes through the windows she and the landscape fade. I turn to Jean-Jacques, but in the place where he sat there is only an empty chair.

The fever is past.

11

Release

I HAVE BEEN granted a release. At the second attempt I have been judged sufficiently solvent to resume my trade as a mason and my life as a free man. I have spent a full year in Cardiff gaol and do not want to prolong the experience one hour more than is necessary. I am free to go from midday.

Peggy is here, slim once more and smiling broadly. There is no sign of Thomas Morgan who has sent the assistant turnkey to release me. A dozen debtors stand together in the yard to see me go and wish me well. William Freme shakes my hand and I see in his eyes a small glimmer of hope that if I can escape, then so might he. Big John Griffiths stands with his arm around Henry Meyrick who stares at the floor. At their head is William Evans who makes a short speech. He thanks me for my company, for my verses, for my work petitioning on behalf of all debtors and for the hope that I have engendered. It is a pretty speech, delivered in the tones he would have used addressing men of substance in the upper room of the Horse and Groom in his other, more prosperous life.

He concludes, 'And finally, we have a little something, a very little something which, we trust, will serve to remind you of your friends and might help fill a gap in your life.'

He calls on John Griffiths who hands me something wrapped in a blue cloth. When I open the parcel I find a tin whistle.

'We had not the means to buy you a new flute,' apologises

William Evans, 'but we hope this will help a little to ease the pain of the loss.'

I am deeply touched. I tell them that they will never be forgotten. I tell them that I am inspired to work for the cause of freedom and justice. I tell them that they suffer beneath a barbarous law and under a vile system. I pledge to devote myself to the cause of all the downtrodden peoples of the world, but first and most importantly, to the inmates of the debtors' prison in Cardiff.

They applaud. I collect my packages and turn to leave. No one moves until I have stepped through the prison gate. The door clangs behind me.

Part Five:
Glamorgan and Bath
1787 to 1791

1

Family

I DEPOSIT SOME of my books at the Tinker's Arms to be
collected by carrier before Peggy and I begin the twelve-mile
walk to Flemingston.

The joy of release. As we walk along the road I demand of
Peggy news of the son I have yet to see. Peggy reports that he
is two months of age and a strong child with good lungs and
a healthy appetite. Margaret, our eldest, dotes on him. I tell
her that Taliesin was the greatest of the ancient British bards. I
cannot help but imagine a great future for him, fulfilling all the
failed dreams and unfulfilled ambitions of his father. Ann, our
second, also thrives.

Peggy talks incessantly, but after her news of the children I
find it hard to listen. My senses are overwhelmed. I have loved
the lanes and byways of the Vale all my life but today I see things
afresh, as would a child. My eyes hurt at the colours of wild
flowers, at the abundance of greenery, at the proud dignity of
trees. I had almost forgotten the smell of grass. I am enchanted
by the patterns of the sky, the ever moving drama of clouds.
Rain is so sweet.

Peggy is describing our finances. I assure her that after months
of writing statements of our accounts I know how poor they are.
She tells me that they are much worse than the accounts show.
She tells me we must be grateful for financial support no matter
from what quarter it comes. I do not understand. I protest
that today of all days I will not be made to feel downhearted. I

explain to her how wonderful and bounteous is nature. Peggy lapses into silence and so we walk until we reach the cottage.

I have longed for this moment. I stand in the door and look at my family. I try to hide my disappointment at my welcome – or lack of it. Margaret looks at me and runs to hide in Peggy's skirts. Ann looks up briefly and then cries. Taliesin sleeps. In the centre of the floor stands Jane, Millicent's daughter, who has been minding the children. Jane is only twelve but possessed of the same dignity as her mother. She is cradling Taliesin. Peggy bids her hand me the babe which she does in too casual a manner for my liking. I want this to be one of the great moments of our lives. I am being introduced to my son for the first time – a son whom I will nurture and educate with all the dedication my mother showed to me. Taliesin wakes, looks up at me, refuses to recognise the significance of the moment, wriggles a little and cries.

'He's hungry,' explains Jane. Peggy takes the babe from me and retreats into a corner to feed the infant.

'Welcome home,' greets my father from his corner seat. I had scarcely noticed him amongst the hustle and bustle of children. 'I advise you to stay well out of the way, my boy. Babies rule this house now.' His words are slightly resentful, but his tone is generous. I remember when I married Peggy how much he enjoyed having a woman in the cottage once more. I remind him.

'Well now there are three of them, four if you count Jane who might as well live here.'

We sit together and I thank him for all he did whilst I was in gaol. He dismisses my thanks as 'merely doing what I had to'. But I can see how proud he is of his efforts. He tells me in detail of each of the pieces he cut and the difficulties he encountered. He shakes his head in sorrow at the state of the world. He grumbles at the behaviour of the new landowners, the Duke of Beaufort and the earls of Bute and Plymouth. Their local officers are the worst abusers, for the owners themselves are seldom in Wales and never seen. He has received letters from my brothers in the West Indies. After some bad experiences early on with hurricanes and fever, they have saved enough money to buy their own plantations. They boast that they are both established growers and their further expansion is limited only by a shortage of new African slaves, a deficiency which they hope will ease as new boatloads arrive.

Father knows how much I disapprove but reveals to me that my family has been eating only because of the benevolence of Miles who had sent five guineas to ease matters. My father tells me that, whatever I think of their trade, I cannot be other than grateful for the brotherly support. I am stunned into silence, knowing it would be cruel and pointless for me to argue with the old man, but I decide to make it clear to Peggy that I will not have my family supported by the proceeds of a trade in human misery.

Peggy serves us a stew that Jane had placed on the fire some hours earlier. It is full of good roots and herbs but there is no meat. There is some fresh bread. We eat heartily and a feeling of well-being is restored. Peggy and I leave the children with my father. We stand some distance from the cottage and, out of earshot, I remonstrate with her for not having told me of the gift from Miles.

'It was not sent to you, but to your father.' Peggy's response is defiant and her eyes glint.

'It matters not,' I protest. 'It is money that has been won through the merciless exploitation of helpless Africans. I will not have my children's upbringing tainted by such blood money.'

Peggy looks at me with a steady, determined gaze. She speaks with intensity.

'Ned. You are a good man, a clever man, a true husband and,

though I know not why, I love you dearly. But you are a child with money.'

I start to protest but my few words are drowned by a torrent of pent-up fury.

'Now listen to me Ned Williams, and don't you dare say a word. You are the most exasperating, vexatious, infuriating husband any woman has ever had to endure.'

Peggy's calm tone has given way to high passion and shrill protest. I have no option but to bow before the storm.

'Now understand, husband. We have survived, no more than that, whilst you were in prison; survived, filled our bellies with roots, dressed ourselves in rags. Those five guineas not only helped feed our children, the same five guineas appeared on the accounts that got you released. Understand now?'

She is shaking and shouting, moving closer as if to defeat my arguments with the might of her onslaught.

'I *had* to take it *or* leave my husband to rot in gaol and let my children starve on a diet of nettle soup. My children come first, not your precious principles. Real people have to do what has to be done to survive in this unfair, unjust world. Understand?'

2

On Affric's beach

P EGGY HAS PLACED me on the rack. How can a man choose
between allowing his children to go hungry and abusing his
fellow man in so unchristian a manner? Such choices should
never be commanded. My instinct is to blame myself for failing
to support my family adequately. Had I done so, my brother's
five guineas could have been returned and consciences kept
clear. A clear conscience should not be an extravagance reserved
for those with money.

I cannot blame Peggy. What simpler more noble instinct
exists than the instinct of a mother to feed her children? Even
if I had provided well for my family, would that excuse my
own shame at the actions of my brothers? Would it lessen the
responsibility of each and every one of us towards our African
brothers? If any man were to be so grossly abused, as are those
slaves, on the streets of Cowbridge or Cardiff, even the most
heartless drunkard would be sure to intervene. Because it
happens across the seas we can avoid knowing of the practices.
We can turn our backs. We can choose not to see. We can pass
by on the other side.

We must not allow our brethren to ignore the cries of those
suffering. I am in the taproom of the Old Globe in Cardiff, a place
where I was wont to recite scurrilous satires against whoever
had offended my dignity. My purpose today is more serious.
I am to support a speaker from the newly-formed Society for
the Abolition of the Slave Trade in his campaign against this

abominable practice. I am determined to make amends for any part my family have played in perpetrating this offence against humanity.

The room is far from full and it appears sadly that some of those present are only here by chance, unaware of the address to be given. We are awaiting a Thomas Clarkson, who is one of their committee of twelve. I have written to him beforehand volunteering my services, and received a pleasing reply. As a result I am now worrying a sheet of paper with adjustments to a short ode in support of their cause.

When Thomas appears he does so in style. Two men are required to carry before him a trunk, several large drawings, a set of iron manacles and a whip. He is a good speaker. The drawings display the layout of a slave ship, drawn to exact dimensions by a naval architect, showing how hundreds of men, women and children are chained in layers with less than two-foot headroom to the row above them. In such quarters they endure the journey across the Atlantic. We wince in horror. From the chest he produces all manner of exotic goods and artefacts: intricate metalwork, exquisite woodwork, fine cloth, sandals. Why he asks, instead of trading *in* Africans do we not trade *with* Africans for the glorious things they can produce?

His final objects are the whip and manacles and an iron collar with spikes protruding round the rim. He tells us of the horrors of life on a plantation; how slaves are worked relentlessly from morn to dusk, beaten if they slacken, are fed on little but a bowl of porridge and are locked in chains at night lest they attempt to flee.

He reminds us that these are not acts perpetrated by unknown merchants of far distant lands. Whilst Bristol is the port with the greatest record of shame, Cardiff is not without infamy. I begin to fear that he will reveal the record of my family but, instead, he tells us of Richard Priest, a Cardiff slave trader, who since the 1760s has captained a Cardiff-built ship on slaving runs from Sierra Leone to Antigua, capturing four hundred at a time and transporting them in conditions unfit for animals.

When he finishes he beckons me to his side and I read.

I ask my listeners not to think of themselves as observers considering the plight of slaves but to place themselves in the position of one who suffers. I ask them to close their eyes, to stand on the shore looking out to sea, to scan the now empty horizon and to weep bitterly for their lost families. To weep for their lost wives, their strong brave sons captured, bound and manacled and cast into the hold of a craft such as we have heard described. When I perform my verses I usually do so with fabled vigour. Today my voice trembles with emotion. I can scarcely see the audience through my tears.

> Behold on Affric's beach, alone,
> Yon sire that weeps with bitter moan;
> She, that his life once truly bless'd,
> Is torn for ever from his breast,
> And scourged, where British Monarchs reign,
> Calls for his aid, but calls in vain:

I ask them to imagine themselves manacled or collared with the evil instruments we have been shown, punished for life for having committed no crime, no felony, no debt. And why? Because the British Parliament approves, even applauds, the practice! And we have the gall, the hypocrisy, to call ourselves Christians.

> His sons on slav'ry's shameless land,
> Now bleed beneath a villain's hand;
> Their writhing frames now sorely gall'd!

Still Britons must be Christians call'd
Their groans the wide horizons fill!
Vile Britons 'tis your Senate's Will –

I stop, unable to continue.

I cease – these cruelties affright
A Muse that shudders at the sight.

There are only some twenty of us present but each and every one swears to do whatever we can to press for the abolition of this detestable practice. Thomas Clarkson shakes my hand vigorously and tells me that, whenever I am in London, I am to make his acquaintance. He tells me I could be of great assistance in making the public truly understand the horror of the acts being performed in their name.

I explain that, given my family circumstances, visiting London is most unlikely but I thank him for the invitation and pocket his address.

3

William Owen

I VISIT THE Reverend John Walters at the rectory. It is the first time I have done so since my release or since hearing of Daniel's death. I had expected the visit to be difficult, but am somewhat awed by the refusal of the rector and his wife to do other than briefly acknowledge my expressions of sorrow and loss before continuing with whatever business or routine they have in hand. Mrs Walters' face is drawn and expressionless.

Daniel, I try to explain, was as a brother to me. I start to recount the pleasure we had walking in the Beaupre Woods and composing verse of variable quality. I mean to say more but the rector stops me.

'It is God's will, Edward. It is not for us to question his reasons. We shall all treasure Daniel's memory and thank the Lord for the precious gift of the time we had him with us.'

I have thought often of our last meeting in the woods when John and Daniel – but Daniel most insistently – had tried to persuade me that I might earn more as a professional poet in the English language than I ever might as a stonecutter. Although Daniel has left me, that thought has not.

The rector lapses into silence. I look at his face closely, wanting to find signs of pain and the suffering of a bereaved father. I have no doubt that the loss has caused much anguish but, by choice, he shows no emotion. He moves swiftly on to discuss the contributions I have brought to the dictionary and to give me the latest news of the London Welsh. I watch him talk rather than listen. I see how the continuity of work provides the means by which this man, these parents, will survive so cruel a blow. I am unsure whether this is a mark of his strength or his weakness, but all I can do is to assist his endeavours in any way I can.

I ask the rector for his opinion of William Owen of London, from whom I have recently received a letter. The rector tells me that he is a solicitor's clerk, originally from Meirioneth, who has taken the role that I was unable to accept as a literary assistant to Owain Myfyr, chairman of the Gwyneddigion. He believes Mr Owen to be a diligent and hardworking researcher. Mr Owen has contacted the rector several times to clarify elements of the dictionary or to seek advice as to where he might obtain copies of early manuscripts of the work of Dafydd ap Gwilym. The rector tells me that he suggested that I might be of assistance.

This explains why I have received letters from William Owen soliciting my help. I have not yet replied. I remain resentful of my past treatment by Owain Myfyr. I sent him some of my Dafydd poems three years ago, for which I received scant thanks and no payment. When I was most in need of a sponsor, he was silent. When I was a prisoner, he did not stir to help despite his wealth. I suspect he learnt of my imprisonment and deemed me unfit as a colleague to a successful merchant. Why should I now answer his request? Why? Well, there are reasons. Because this might be a means of getting some of my Dafydd poems into print? Because there may be a way of being paid for my work? Because my London Welsh acquaintances may still be of great value to me – even if I am uncertain how, at present?

The letter tells me that Owain Myfyr is well advanced in his plan to publish an edition of all the known works of Dafydd ap Gwilym. He is unaware, of course, of the extensive series of works that Dafydd has imparted to me – works which are amongst the very finest of his creations. I will reply and I will send some more of my Dafydd ap Gwilym poems. But this time I must ensure that they are aware of my value to them. They must be made to work for my favours.

I write a letter excusing the delay in replying. I blame this, quite justly, on the pressure of earning a living as an itinerant stonecutter and the demands of family life. I make it clear that I am hurt by their neglect of me over the past two years; how I received only the briefest acknowledgement of my earlier Dafydd ap Gwilym discoveries, how I received no word or support of any kind during my time of greatest need in Cardiff gaol. Indeed, their unkindness had led me to lose interest in pursuing the collection of ancient Welsh poetry.

'I know not why I even answer your letter, but perhaps it is because you approach me as a stranger and a man with a pure and honest love of Dafydd's work. I can never refuse a stranger's honest request. But if you wish me to continue to assist in your great endeavour, I would expect a request to do so from Owain Myfyr himself.'

There is, of course, a risk that they may decide they can do without my contribution, so I include twelve of my Dafydd *cywyddau*. These are pieces in which I have complete confidence. They are in style and sentiment as good as any William Owen will already have, and ring with the authentic voice of the medieval master. It is not possible that they could disregard such treasures. I end my letter by hinting at other greater riches, twenty or so *cywyddau* written for Ifor Hael which are to be found 'in an old book' owned by 'someone in the Blaenau'. I do not ask for payment. Instead I offer, should the volume be published by subscription, to myself pay for a subscription in the name of my newborn son, Taliesin.

I doubt their scholarship and fear some of the footnotes they may write, so I make them the offer of an essay explaining the place of Dafydd ap Gwilym in the development of Welsh poetry and offer some notes to assist in the meanings of some of the less familiar medieval words, particularly those of Glamorgan origin which appear in my new discoveries.

I seal the letter with some satisfaction, imagining the reaction it may cause.

4

July 1789 – Wyndham for ever

I N THE BEAR I find myself part of a lively debate with several of the gentry. The 'gentry' I refer to are the old Glamorgan squires, landowners whose families have lived in the Vale since Norman times: the Jones family of Fonmon Castle whose crenulations my brothers and I have shaped, the Bassetts of Bonvilston, the Treharne family of Beaupre, the Matthew family of Llandaff. It is not unusual to find these gentlemen here, drinking and talking at length. I observe that the subjects of their discourse are seldom different from that of common men: horses, money and women.

Today they are at their most animated. There are raised voices, fists and tankards being smashed hard on the tables to emphasise their points despite the fact that they are plainly all in agreement. Robert Jones of Fonmon asks me across to their table. I am curious to learn what has caused this outbreak of unanimous indignation.

They are annoyed at the actions of the new large absentee landowners. Robert describes the lords Vernon and Mount Stuart as 'the new parasites', whilst the Duke of Beaufort and the Earl of Plymouth are 'foreign titans'. The particular cause of their outrage is the joint decision of the 'new parasites' to nominate a minor relative of the Earl of Plymouth as a candidate for the county seat in Parliament. Thomas Windsor is, in their opinion, a failed businessman and a failed sea captain. He has no local connection, no understanding or sympathy with Glamorgan. He is being foisted upon us. He will do nothing for us. He will live in London and protect the interests of their earlships in Parliament. They fear the final demise of the local squirearchy were this to happen. They call on me to assist them in preventing their own imminent eradication.

I despise aristocracy in any form. To me it is a fundamental tenet of the Bible, and of modern philosophers such as Rousseau, that men are born free and equal. But I have more time for the old gentry. Firstly, they are my main source of employment. Secondly, in the darkness of the Bear it is easy to miss the signs that men use to mark themselves out as superior in rank or wealth. Finally, I share their most frequent complaint; the growth in power and influence of the new absentee landowners who, estate by estate, are buying up the land only to have them managed by unscrupulous agents and stewards who rule brutishly without care for the tenants. The Glamorgan squires belong to a class whose demise I would not mourn, but at present they appear the lesser evil and some of them even have a conscience. They support local tradesmen. They consider the needs of the poor and, even if they do not speak Welsh, for the most part they respect and honour the language.

They ask me to assist them in ensuring the election of their candidate, Thomas Wyndham of Llanmihangel, son of an established Glamorgan family. They fear that many of the tenants of the 'foreign titans' may be intimidated into voting for Captain Windsor. They will pay for whatever printing I need, for free beer at any meetings, and any other reasonable expenses. I agree to adopt the cause as my own.

***

I speak in the Horse and Groom to a gathering of tenant farmers, freeholders and small businessmen, most of whom have the property qualifications to enable them to vote. To these people I describe the actions of the stewards of the Duke of Beaufort in Swansea where rents have been increased and where they have blocked any developments by tenants which do not please the Duke. I warn them of the folly of putting Captain Windsor, a Beaufort steward in all but name, into Parliament to act against local interests.

I write a lampoon of Captain Windsor to be printed and distributed wherever voters may be found. I congratulate him on becoming 'the tool of a few tyrannical noblemen'. I applaud his courage, given that he has never set foot on Glamorgan land, knows nothing of Glamorgan customs, and won't be able to understand Glamorgan people.

In an open letter to the Nonconformist chapels of Glamorgan, I warn how the ancestors of the Duke of Beaufort had been amongst the very worst oppressors of Nonconformity and remain zealous opponents of religious tolerance.

I praise Thomas Wyndham as coming from a family of landowners who have been merciful, generous and protective of their tenants and the poor, particularly in times of severe need.

I whip the meetings into a frenzy in support of Thomas Wyndham by writing songs to be sung to simple, rousing, well-known tunes including 'Britons Never will be Slaves'.

I am most content with the reaction to my endeavours. Elections are seldom held in Glamorgan, and when they are the numbers able to vote are small, so it is hard to create a meeting with any intensity or fervour. But this campaign is a great exception.

***

I receive a swift reply from William Owen. It is gratifying for several reasons. He and Owain Myfyr are plainly delighted and excited by the Dafydd poems I sent. They recognise their quality and there is no questioning their authenticity. William regrets that they arrived too late to be properly placed in the forthcoming edition of Dafydd's poetry. He reproaches himself for not have waited until he had heard from me. He has ordered the poems in his volume according to subject and the date, as far as ascertainable, they were composed. Those pages have been printed so he regrets that the pieces I sent will have to be included as an appendix.

He is hungry for more, asking if the poems to Ifor Hael I mentioned could be found and dispatched. I will make him wait for those. I am more concerned to persuade him to include in his book my commentary or introduction to explain the meanings and correctness of the Glamorgan words used in the appendix poems.

He grovels an apology on behalf of Owain Myfyr and the London Welsh for any perceived slight or neglect towards me. As he was not party to the events, I don't know why he is doing the apologising but he assures me that Owain Myfyr was quite unaware of my imprisonment. He is reported as expressing great sorrow and lamenting his ignorance of my troubles. William quotes him as saying, 'Had I known it was thus with Iorwerth I would have set him free'. Fine words but why, if his regret is so heartfelt, does he not write in person?

As I expected, my offer to subscribe towards the costs of the publication is declined. Owain Myfyr will meet all costs from his own pocket. It makes me uneasy that this publication is dependent on the wealth of a powerful but ignorant merchant.

***

In Cowbridge Town Hall the waiting crowd, including many women, and others who have no vote, are singing:

Rise Glamorgan, sing with me
Wyndham, peace and liberty...

until the roof trembles. When the young candidate appears he is cheered and applauded before he says a word. He delivers a reasonable speech, promising to do his very best for the people of Glamorgan should he be elected. I would dearly have liked a more inspiring address, better representing the causes of liberty and equality, but it is not to be. We end with another song written for the occasion,

And Wyndham we find
Was the man to their mind,
When he nobly for liberty stood
My brave boys,
When he nobly for liberty stood.

***

I receive a letter and a volume from John Walters, Daniel's brother, who is now headmaster of the grammar school in Ruthin. It is a reply to my letter of sympathy on Daniel's death in which I recalled our wanderings in Beaupre Woods and the joy of our improvised compositions.

John's reply is similar in tone, sorrowing for the loss of a brother who was, in his view, the most talented rhymester of the family. The book he sends me is entitled *Poems, Chiefly in the Scottish dialect* by Robert Burns. They comprise a lively collection of rural ballads and lyric poetry. The volume, John reports, has become an immediate and profitable success, with copies disappearing off booksellers' shelves as fast as they can be printed. The reason, he argues, is that Burns is an authentic voice of the countryside. Sophisticated Oxford and London readers have acclaimed this self-taught ploughman from a remote part of Scotland as the voice of simplicity and directness because of his humble origins.

John reminds me of Daniel's urging the last time we met in the woods, that I should endeavour to make my fortune through writing instead of stonecutting; that I should do so in English and proclaim myself as the authentic voice of the Welsh countryside. John suggests that the Burns phenomenon has proved his late brother correct.

He adds, modestly, that he has had some small success in publishing his own translations into English and could put me in touch with some influential literary figures in Oxford who might be of help.

5

Great means of enterprise

A LETTER FROM Owain Myfyr! It is short, written in haste. He proclaims his friendship, protests his innocence of my complaints against him, encloses a ten-pound note and bids me drown any animosity in a quart of ale. He tells me that Dafydd ap Gwilym needs me; that I should do all in my power to ensure he appears at his best when his glory is unveiled to the world.

He little understands that Dafydd and I are as one. I will do all within my power to ensure his work is presented to the very best advantage.

***

The writ for the by-election was issued in August. Nominations closed some weeks later for the election in September but, to our amazement and delight, Captain Windsor's papers do not appear. The 'new parasites' have decided to retreat in the face of a determined and united opposition. A victory has been won!

There is much celebration and I am not short of offers of free ale from the delighted squirearchy. But my mood is sober. I read of the events in France, of the storming of the Bastille, and the release of the wronged inmates. What have we succeeded in doing on behalf of the debtors of Cardiff gaol? I read of the banner unfurled in Paris proclaiming 'Liberty, Equality and Fraternity'. Fraternity! I am inspired and I am shamed. In Glamorgan we have campaigned and won a victory just to keep things as they are. Fraternity? Universal brotherhood? I must find better ways of spreading the values of the Revolution.

Robert Jones of Fonmon takes me to one side to repeat his thanks for my efforts. Should I be in mind to publish any of my poetry, I can rely on him and his companions for generous subscriptions. I am effusive in my thanks. He offers to use his good name on my behalf amongst others of his acquaintance.

***

I have an article published in *The Gentleman's Magazine*, a London literary journal, for which I am paid two guineas.

I look for the right moment to have a serious word with Peggy. This is not easy. The cottage has become a factory for the upbringing of children. There is always washing, crying, feeding, nursing, cuddling, scolding, mending, patching and a myriad other maternal necessities to be attended to.

Peggy knows that since coming out of prison I have done all in my power to bring in the money that we need to raise our family. She knows, without my having to tell her, that it is a struggle. Well-paid work is hard to find and, when I do, it usually involves long journeys. It is hard because I am forced too often to accept low-skilled work building walls and the like. It is hard because of the effect on my health. Apart from asthma, aggravated by the dust from carving, I am now experiencing severe attacks of sciatica and suffer pain from rheumatism in both knees. Peggy suggests that my knees would gain some relief if I were to walk less and, when long journeys are unavoidable, ride our old horse to my places of work. This last suggestion I will not accept. Our old horse is a friend whose company I treasure. He is not a slave to be whipped and made to bear my weight.

Taliesin has been fed and she can put him down to sleep. She waits for me to speak. I hand her the two guineas and she smiles with pleasure.

'That's twelve pounds that I have won through my pen in the last month,' I inform her with satisfaction. She is pleased but she looks at the money dubiously, as if it were obtained dishonestly.

'Well done, Ned. Well done, my husband.' She leans over and kisses my cheek. 'But you could also say that it's the only twelve pounds you've earned though writing in the past forty years.' She pauses. She knows me well enough to know that I have more to say.

'Peggy, I am afraid that I will find it hard to earn the money we need through stonecutting. Work is scarce and I am not as fit or as active as I once was. That's why I tried to find other ways of earning a wage after we were married.'

She is tensing up. She believes that I am going to suggest buying a boat or selling tea or opening a workshop, any of the other schemes which ruined us and ended up with my time in gaol. I carry on quickly.

'I know that none of these worked out Peggy, and I know why. I was trying to change my work to an activity about which I knew little or nothing. No wonder I failed. Earning this literary money, rather easily, persuades me that perhaps I should instead look to earn money out of the one activity, apart from stonecutting, that everyone openly agrees I'm good at – writing.'

I tell her of the success of Robert Burns, of the similarity to my writing, of the support of John Walters, of the support of Jones of Fonmon, of my correspondence with the London Welsh and of my success with *The Gentleman's Magazine*. She sighs deeply and shakes her head.

'Ned, I don't know. I just don't know. But I suppose at least this is something you can do as well as stonecutting. It doesn't have to be a choice, does it? Maybe you can spend days writing in Flemingston when you haven't got mason's work to do.'

She has not convinced herself. A thought strikes.

'But, Ned. Would you ever be happy to write to order?'

I don't understand.

'You always write what you want to write. It so happens that this time two other people have decided it's also what they want to read. If you write for money, don't you have to write what readers want? Would you be able?'

Two days later a handsomely bound copy of *Barddoniaeth Dafydd ab Gwilym* arrives, together with an ecstatically happy letter from William Owen. It is a delight to see Dafydd's poems in print at last, but I turn first to the appendix. I sit down to enjoy a sight that has eluded me for the first forty years of my life – my own work in print.

6

Sampson's Pillar

I AM IN the graveyard of Llantwit Major. It is a gentle, warm September day – the harvest time. I am adding the name of a Mrs Wilkins to the large stone I placed here some eight years ago to mark her husband's grave. I record the fact that they are united once more in the earth and in heaven. My work is done but I need to wait until men return from the harvesting to help me replace the headstone. I look about. The church at Llantwit has always provided me with distractions and today is no exception.

'A fanciful tale and nothing more,' exclaims the sexton as I remind him of the story of Will the Giant. I have testimony from more than one old inhabitant of the town that buried in the churchyard is a man who reached a prodigious height in his youth and died through the strain this put on his heart. When they dug his grave they had to excavate so far, to accommodate his length, that they undermined the footings of a close-at-hand ancient monumental stone which, according to the tellers of legends, tumbled into Will's grave and was left to lie where it fell. My interest in the story is revived by finding a record in the parish register of a 'William Williams, called the Giant, who was buried here in 1724'. Maybe there is truth in the tale?

'Stuff and nonsense!' asserts the sexton. 'If I let you do as you please, half these graves would be permanently open whilst you search for ancient remains. Let the dead rest where they are, I say.'

I try to persuade him that it would do no harm to turn a clod, just to test the possibility. If there is a stone it will not be far below the surface. The sexton sighs.

'All of these stories get built up over time,' he insists. 'Will the Giant grows in height every time the story is told, and the stone, if there is one, becomes bigger at the same time. I suspect he was no taller than I, and this old stone is no larger than the one you carved just now for old Grace Wilkins. You mark my words, these old stories always exaggerate whatever truth may lie behind them.'

I deny it. I insist that sometimes when we resurrect the past the reality is more glorious than the pale version that survives in folk memory. We debate for some time. The day is warm and, after a weak verbal struggle, the sexton gives way. I fetch a mattock and spade and excavate a small hole in the centre of the suspected grave. The sexton watches with folded arms, anticipating vindication. I only have to go down a foot before I strike stone. I clear enough soil for us to see the surface of a monument covered with small, ancient inscriptions. In half an hour I have cleared the soil away along the entire length which is an amazing eight foot or more. When the men return from the harvest they are overcome with curiosity and I have no difficulty persuading them to help. With the aid of a block and tackle, and an hour of hard labour, the stone is soon lifted back to a precarious perpendicular.

The setting sun casts shadows across the inscription which I attempt to decipher. It is a monument to two ancient kings of Glamorgan, Ithael and Arthmael. The inscription suggests that it was erected in their memory by Abbot Sampson more than a thousand years ago. As the sun sets behind the stone, we all sit on the ground in a circle, awed by its physical presence and enchanted by the sudden and unarguable manifestation of the heritage of Glamorgan.

Despite having done a day's work in the fields, and an hour more for no pay in the churchyard, the men are slow to leave. They stare in the fading light like men enchanted. When they do depart it is to tell their wives, girlfriends or fellow drinkers that they have tonight become part of history. The sexton and I are the last to go. I resist the temptation to insist to him that sometimes the old stories of the past become even more glorious when the truth is revealed in the light of day.

There could be no better metaphor for my work.

7

First impressions

I AM WITH the rector discussing the origins of a new crop of words. He is even more remote than usual. He works his way through my notes with care but without his accustomed pedantic scholarship. I start to wonder if he is unwell. It is only when I raise the subject of my correspondence with his eldest son John that I realise that something is seriously amiss. I remark that John has plainly been very busy in his new role as rector of Efenechtyd which is why I have received no replies to my latest letters. The rector looks at me with disbelieving eyes. His pupils glow like slow-burning coals in his white, white face.

'You have not heard? Oh God forgive me Edward that I have so neglected you.'

He falls silent. I say nothing as it is clear that he has more to report. I anticipate all the possibilities I can imagine for John: illness, rows with his bishop, overwork, being sent on a mission overseas but never the cold cruelty of the truth.

'John died two weeks ago of consumption, following a pattern of decline similar to Daniel's. Given fears as to the contagious nature of the disease, his body was not brought home and the burial took place in his own churchyard officiated by the bishop of St Asaph. I had assumed that word would…'

He stops. The rector looks like a man on the point of breaking. I am of little help. I should probably ask him a technical question about something grammatical and obscure to offer his brain a straw of normality to grasp at but I feel myself unable to do that or anything else of use. We sit in silence for a very long time before the rector struggles out of the dark pit of his misery into some dimly-lit corridor of conversation.

'There will be a memorial service in the Church of the Holy Cross at the end of the month. Notices will be read out in the churches of the diocese for any who wish to remember him.'

***

My tin is boiling well on the little fire in Beaupre Woods. There is laughter around me as I brew the tea that everyone is expecting. Dafydd ap Gwilym looks dubious. He tells the company that he only drinks infusions of leaves when his stomach is unwell. Daniel tells him that as a bard he should never refuse any new experience, that he will soon be able to enjoy the product of the mystic orient. Will Tabwr takes Dafydd's side, proclaiming that he will drink only the product of a clean spring or well-brewed barrel. There is much laughter as I pour the tea. Dafydd sips and makes a face.

Spirits are very high and the conversation sparkles. John and Daniel are delighted to be back in Beaupre where, John proclaims, they have unfinished business. How, they demand, are we to make Ned the greatest, most successful poet of the age? Dafydd insists that they rephrase the question as he, Dafydd, is obviously the finest poet of every age. Will asks why there is need. Does Ned not command the respect of a line of ancient bards stretching back to the earliest records? Was he not acclaimed a bard by those who have inherited the right to do so?

'Of course,' replies Daniel, 'but we are not talking about Ned's prestige amongst the Welsh. We wish him to become a prosperous and well-respected figure in English poetry.'

'Because it pays better?' asks Will Tabwr, slightly disapprovingly.

'Of course because it pays better,' snorts Dafydd. 'I never wrote

if it were not for reward. Fine to write odes to a woman you wish to bed but otherwise I write for silver or gold. A poet has to eat.'

'And so does his family,' adds John.

John talks of the London fashion for poetry of the countryside, of primitive originality and the success of Robert Burns. 'If a Scots ploughman poet can have such a success,' he asks, 'why not a Welsh stonecutter poet?'

Dafydd protests, 'Ned is more than a stonecutter who scribbles. He is a bard by virtue of his being trained, examined and initiated into the guild of poets. That is all the commendation any bard should need.'

'Not in London, I'm afraid. I don't believe any of the literary magazines have heard of Lewis Hopkin of Llandyfodwg, nor of the Guild of Bards. To win a readership Ned is going to have to win the hearts and minds of the fashionable elite and, at the moment, they are obsessed with the idea of the pure voice of the simple self-taught man in touch with nature. You can blame Rousseau for this. If we can all get closer to nature we will be closer to our true selves.'

Daniel tries to reconcile Dafydd and John. 'If the London critics want an authentic voice, what could be more authentic than the last surviving bard of the ancient British tradition?'

'He's not the last,' snaps Dafydd. 'What about Edward Evans?'

'Well, nearly the last! Look, I grant you that they will not have heard of Lewis Hopkin outside the circles of the London Welsh, but why not tell them of the Guild of Bards, the Gorsedd?'

'How?' asks Will.

'Tell them!' replies John. 'The Gentleman's Magazine *has already printed some poems and articles by Ned, have they not?'*

I agree they have.

'Well someone – not Ned, should write an article about Ned explaining what we know. Apart from anything else it will give Ned a chance to gauge the reaction to ancient British Bardism. It would be good to add some suggestions of the connection with the

ancient druids as well. They appear popular at present. Daniel, will you write it?'

'We'll do it together.'

'Agreed.' The two brothers wander away composing between them. Their voices fade. Dafydd and Will go off in search of a tavern and I am left alone.

Two weeks on and *The Gentleman's Magazine* prints the following:

> Edward Williams – about the age of twenty, he was admitted a Bard in the ancient manner; a custom still retained in Glamorgan, but, I believe, in no other part of Wales. This is by being discipled to a regular Bard and afterwards admitted into the order in a Congress of Bards assembled for that purpose, after undergoing proper examination; and being also initiated into their Mysteries, as they are pleased to call them. Besides Edward Williams, there is, I believe, now remaining only one regular Bard in Glamorgan, or in the world: this is the Reverend Mr Edward Evans, of Aberdare, a Dissenting Minister. These two persons are the only legitimate descendants of the so-long-celebrated Ancient British Bards.

Alongside it appears my 'Ode Imitated from the Gododdin of Aneirin' and the article is signed 'J.D.'

8

'The Fair Pilgrim'

S O ONE THING leads to another. Robert Jones of Fonmon has prevailed on his neighbour, the Reverend Carne of Nash Manor, and a Mr John Curre of Chepstow to support my cause. Whilst Robert Jones would not know a good poem from a grocery list, Mr Carne and Mr Curre are, he assures me, well connected in the literary circles of Bristol and Bath. They have read of my work in *The Gentleman's Magazine* and would be pleased to introduce me to others who may be able to assist me in obtaining more subscriptions.

***

I am looking out of the window of Mr Curre's carriage as we trot through the old city of Bath towards the Royal Crescent. I am uncomfortable spending so much time in a carriage. I prefer to walk. Mr Curre is amiable but appears on edge. I suspect he is a little anxious as to how I will appear to those he has prevailed upon to entertain us. If I am judged lacking, he must fear censure for making the introduction. For the third time, he emphasises to me the status of our host.

'Make no mistake, Mr Anstey is a very distinguished author and scholar. Very distinguished. Very scholarly. Famous for the quality of his Latin translations but also known for his... unconventional attitudes.'

'Has he read any of my work?'

'Indeed, yes. He praised the samples I sent him and I suspect that is because he is himself a master of satirical verse. His *New Bath Guide, or Memoirs of the Blunderhead Family* has offended countless and sold hundreds. He is also immensely wealthy. It is most promising that he should take an interest in you.'

I am bemused and dizzy at the speed with which events have moved. The fast-moving carriage appears appropriate. We reach the splendid Royal Crescent. I have seen this great curved façade before, but never looking as grand and as stately as it does today. This may be because, on my previous visit, I was a humble stonecutter dressing masonry, whereas today I am a guest. Indeed, I am the guest of honour at one of the great houses.

The carriage stops outside number four. I make to open the carriage door but am restrained gently by Mr Curre.

'Let the footman open the door, Edward.'

If the footman is supposed to be at my service, then the contrast between his rich costume and my worn jacket is in itself a satire on our relative status. We descend from the carriage and I climb the steps up to the open door as if on a royal progress. The owner, Mr Christopher Anstey, stands at the top to greet me. He is of medium height, broad of build with a full fleshy face, bright red cheeks and two pleasant twinkling eyes that appear at the same time welcoming and mischievous. Although not a man of the cloth, he is dressed in a sober black topcoat with white cravat which conveys a ministerial air. He welcomes me and leads me through the elegant hallway with its large oriental vases and gilded mirrors to a set of doors which, miraculously, open as we approach, revealing another footman.

Inside, I survey a pleasant, elegantly-furnished drawing room. To my relief it is not imperial in scale but is of perfect proportions and furnished in the latest fashion. I have only seconds to take in the fine hangings, the panelling, the paintings – Italian perspectives, I think, and the rich Indian rugs. I am trying to focus on the people. It is important that I see and register the other guests whom Mr Anstey is introducing. I am given no time at all to focus my senses. There are two ladies sitting or reclining on sofas, placed to perfection like objects in a painting. An elderly man holding a small dog under his arm stands by the window. Are they real?

'May I introduce Miss Fanny Bowdler?'

The lady before me is in her forties, pleasantly plump and displaying an excess of satin, lace and cleavage. She reclines on a striped sofa. An action is obviously expected. I feel panic within. I nod and mumble something which I know betrays my lack of breeding and social skills. Should I have kissed her hand?

My host explains that Miss Bowdler is the most unconventional of the Bowdler family, the one more prone to flights of creative misbehaviour than her sisters. He floats around the room as he speaks, his hands and arms a flurry of gestures. Miss Bowdler knows all there is to know about writers and, as a result, has refrained from writing anything herself. He adds that she is single, despite her evident talents and his best attempts to marry her off. Miss Bowdler scolds him for his crude presumption. There is a light-hearted understanding between these two which licenses the saying of the unsayable. Miss Bowdler laughs flirtatiously.

'Take no notice of Christopher, Mr Williams. He is an outrageous man. It's why we get on so well. As a member of the family whose literary name is founded on the removal of all of the shocking lines from Shakespeare, I feel the need to redress the balance through a modest display of the socially outrageous.'

'Which you do *so* well.'

Miss Bowdler sticks her tongue out at her host, and then returns to me.

'They tell me you are a druid, Mr Williams. Is that so?'

'Not quite, my lady. I am a bard initiated into the Ancient

Order of Bards descended from the earliest bards of the Island of Britain. Our forefathers were bound by the mystic orders of druidism to use the power of their verse only to inspire faith in the Lord or the enlargement of human understanding.'

'So what's the difference between a bard and a poet?'

'A poet writes for whosoever he pleases in whatever style he wishes. A bard writes according to the ancient rules of British versification. He attends regularly at meetings with his fellows to review and revise such rules. A bard in our tradition is the guardian of all that is true and valuable.'

Did her eyes glaze at my answer? Her warm smile suggests otherwise.

'How very original.'

My host turns to the next lady.

'May I introduce Miss Hannah More?'

Miss More is a severe tight-lipped woman in an uncompromising grey dress devoid of lace. She sighs in anticipation of her host's inevitably flamboyant introduction.

'Poetess, novelist, philanthropist and playwright of great note. Authoress of *Thoughts on the Importance of the Manners of the Great to General Society*. She has been wooed by the brightest luminaries of our age, including Walpole and the immortal Garrick, but has refused them all, preferring to spend her best years in rural retreat providing education to the poor. Hannah writes fine moral tracts designed to reform unreformable sinners such as Fanny and I.'

During this Hannah More's eyes have rolled heavenwards as if in despair at the outrageous behaviour of her host. She does not bother to correct or reprove him but immediately demands of me,

'And what is your attitude to the slave trade, Mr Williams?'

I am pleased to recount that I am most passionately opposed to slavery, that I have written against the trade and read, at public meetings, verses designed to condemn what I believe to be an inhuman practice contrary to the law of God. She nods with obvious approval.

'You are an unschooled poet I understand; one who has learnt through the inspiration of nature rather than the disciplines of scholarship?'

I do not need to consider my answer.

'In my culture we depend on the triads, a simple poetic form of three wise statements to enshrine our inherited wisdom. One of our most important runs:

Three things a bard must own,
An eye that sees Nature,
A heart that feels Nature,
The courage to let Nature rule his actions.

Would she prefer me to recite it in the original British?

'The English will suffice, thank you. What is your attitude towards the French?'

This is a test. Should she be against all sympathy with liberty I am lost. Despite her uncompromising manner I feel her to be of my persuasion.

'I am a lover of liberty as I have already proved through my verse and actions. I have been prepared to sacrifice for my beliefs and will do so again. I would only add that I am an opponent of violence and murder wherever it appears. Liberty bought at the expense of a child's death is not liberty.'

To my surprise she rises and applauds. She claps joyously.

'Well done, sir. Well done, Mr Williams. You are a creature I would deem it an honour to count as my associate.'

I am introduced to the elderly man with the small dog. Mr Melmoth is a retired bookseller from Bath who, Mr Anstey assures us, writes 'works of such literary distinction and deep scholarship that there can be no more than a dozen people in the kingdom who can understand their contents or appreciate their quality.'

Mr Melmoth enquires as to dinner.

***

Several other guests join us at table. This I must endure. The food is too rich and indulgent for my taste. We are served course after course laced with sweetmeats, sauces, spices and brandies, against which my stomach and eyes rebel. I survive by moving the carcasses of small birds and the bodily remains of great mammals around my plate but not on to my tongue.

I do not believe that my lack of appetite is remarked upon, as Miss Bowdler alone devours enough for the entire company. Besides which, I am allowed little time to eat as I remain the focus of attention. I am expected to entertain. I tell them my story. I expound further on the nature of Bardism and my hope to publish *The Secrets of the Bards of the Island of Britain* in the near future. They appear entranced.

After dinner I am to read to them. We return to the drawing room where chairs are arranged in a half-circle with a footman on each side for no reason I can discern. I am invited to stand in the centre and recite. I do so, mostly from memory. The pieces I choose are my pastoral poems, a selection of pieces I have written over many years. I vary the diet with a story of love betrayed, 'The Maid of Cefn Ydfa', which is a great success. I end with a new translation of a poem by Dafydd, 'The Fair Pilgrim'. When I finish Miss Bowdler applauds with passion. Miss More applauds with studied deliberation. Mr Anstey nods judiciously. Mr Melmoth smiles weakly. Mr Curre looks relieved.

9

The prospect
fair before me

M R ANSTEY SITS opposite me in a genteel tearoom in Bath. We study the list of fine Indian teas before choosing. This is a matter of importance to both of us. Taking tea has become one of my greatest pleasures.

Mr Anstey gives me his assessment of my appearance at 4 Royal Crescent, having had an opportunity to solicit the private reactions and opinions of those present. He rates highly the good opinions of Miss Bowdler and Mr Melmoth, but most highly the detailed analysis provided by Miss More. Hannah More, he tells me, is not only a highly accomplished author and celebrated bluestocking; she has previously nurtured primitive poetic talent. He recounts her rescue from poverty of Ann Yearsley, a milkmaid of Bristol, in whom she has detected a pure unspoilt poetic genius. It is a name I know but I stay silent. With Miss More's guidance Ann Yearsley published *Poems, on Various Subjects* only three years ago to loud critical acclaim. She continues to enjoy success, although not as much as had once appeared possible. Mr Anstey had hoped that Miss More would have seen fit to propose a similar mentoring relationship with me, but she did not.

I enquire why? There is some duplicity in the query as I suspect I know the answer. It is common knowledge amongst those who read *The Gentleman's Magazine* that Miss More and Miss Yearsley are engaged in a bitter dispute in which the milkmaid accuses her mentor of seeking to control and own her talents, her mind, and most particularly, her money.

Mr Anstey merely replies that the partnership has not ended well, hence the reluctance of Miss More to engage in a second such venture. However, she is convinced of my talent and has urged Mr Anstey to take on the same mentoring role in my case. He announces with a generous flourish that he is willing to do so.

It is clear that I am supposed to express my gratitude and I do so genuinely but with some fears. He begins immediately. He instructs me at length in what he calls 'the mysteries of authorship'. Despite my suspicion I am astounded by the practical common sense of the advice he gives. He tells me how to make the greatest use of my new acquaintances to persuade others to join the subscription list. I should aim for persons of stature as subscribers, as their status will immediately cause another twenty to contribute. He tells me to polish my drawing room performance. The folk story was a particularly good touch. I should develop a repertoire of similar pieces and be prepared to respond to other invitations whenever they arrive. He assures me that arrive they will as I am now 'the latest sensation'. He particularly enjoyed 'The Fair Pilgrim' and makes an urgent proposal. I should visit a printer of his recommendation and have it printed as a single sheet. This, together with a prospectus, should be offered through reputable booksellers. It would serve as an example of that which subscribers find in abundance were they only to subscribe to my new edition of poems.

This all makes sense. I am even more impressed when he advises me on the price to be set for subscriptions. He tells me that I should calculate not only what it will cost to print, bind, cover and distribute, but also what it will cost me as an author to live and maintain my family during the month or so that I am seeking backers and correcting proofs.

I am most pleased to have landed in the care of such a knowledgeable man. I am certain that Peggy would be reassured were she able to hear our conversation.

***

I write to Peggy to tell her of my good fortune. I am touring the fashionable salons of Bath reading, recounting Bardism and entertaining. Bardism enraptures each salon. I have developed my repertoire of Welsh stories. These I have taken from folk tales or ancient lore and shaped for English ears. To 'The Maid of Cefn Ydfa' I have added an old tale of the boy who stumbles upon Arthur and his warriors asleep under the holy mountain; the tale of the fairy harp and, from the ancient chronicles, the story of a cruel maiden created from flowers.

I had not anticipated the flattering reactions of women. There are some who appear anxious to provide for my every need. The Reverend John Nicholl of Henley and his wife Mary are in Bath for the waters. They appear at several different readings. He professes himself an admirer and adds his name to the subscription list for three copies. Mary Nicholl smiles at me in a manner I find disconcerting and even predatory. She misses no opportunity to bring me tea or elderflower should my cup or glass stand empty. She looks at me with eyes that suggest a deep admiration and a bond of private understanding. If I did not know her to be a woman of the utmost respectability, I should have mistaken her behaviour for that of a flirtatious tavern maid. It is as if the small fame I now enjoy makes me once again young and dashing in her eyes, whatever the truth I see reflected in Mr Anstey's large gilt mirrors.

As a result of my readings, I can record thirty or more

subscribers of rank and status whose presence on my list is certain to inspire others. I have several lords, a gaggle of ladies, many reverends, one countess and the Duke of York. Each appears ready to swell the list further by making recommendations.

Mary Nicholl and Mr Anstey have discussed how the list may be lengthened with subscribers of nobility and substance. They have determined that I must now move on to London where Mrs Nicholl promises to arrange opportunities for me to present my work in the drawing rooms of the wealthy and fashionable.

Without my stir, I have a printer. Mr John Newbury, publisher of *The Gentleman's Magazine*, who is now familiar with my work, has proposed that he should print my volume of poetry and is even now taking subscriptions on my behalf at his shops in London, Oxford and Cambridge.

I write to Peggy that 'the prospect, for once in my life, seems to be open fair before me'. I promise her that I will take care not to disturb my good fortune with some rash impetuous act.

***

Mr Anstey has been the most energetic of patrons and I have benefited greatly from his advice. But now he sits with a copy of 'The Fair Pilgrim' on which he and Mr Curre have written notes and 'improvements'. He has not sought permission to alter my work but clearly sees doing so as part of his role.

He explains, 'Mr Curre and I are greatly concerned about the last couplet but two. Although I was at a loss to explain why, Mr Curre is more perceptive. He pointed out that it is in conditional mode. Therefore, would it not be better to omit the "s" in "heaves and bedews"?'

He does not pause for my answer. I watch as he makes another mark on my sheet. He continues in this manner, making minor and unwanted changes throughout the text. I am at a loss how to prevent him disfiguring my work without causing offence. I know what I must do.

'I think you know how truly grateful I am to you and Mr Curre for all you have done, and continue to do on my behalf, but you must forgive me if I cannot accept your guidance in this. I have from the first been determined not to impose on the public by giving them anything that was not absolutely my own.'

Mr Astley looks at me in some surprise. The surprise turns to annoyance. I feel a moment's terror lest he declare his support at an end. How could I report such a disaster to Peggy? He puts down his pencil and takes a studied draught of tea before speaking. He tells me that I am unwise to insist, and may well regret refusing assistance when the critical lions of London point out the technical faults he is endeavouring to correct.

'Perhaps I should have been forewarned. This is an exact repeat of the problems that arose between Ann Yearsley and Miss Hannah More when that distinguished patron attempted to assist her inexperienced pupil. In that case, matters became most unpleasant. I pray God no such conclusion will be seen between us.'

I do not retract. Rather, I add to his discomfort. There have been letters of subscription from booksellers in Bristol who are known to have rejoiced at the defeat of Mr Wilberforce's recent abolition of slavery bill. I tell him that I have a clear and fixed resolution that my subscription list shall not be disgraced by the inclusion of such villainous abettors of the slave trade. I am certain that Miss More will support me in this.

Mr Anstey is further displeased. He leans across the table.

'Enjoy the fame that your work is now bestowing upon you, but do not let it go to your head. Were I in your position, I would value this brief fame far less than income it brings. I suggest you do all you can to increase your financial emoluments whilst fashion smiles upon you. I warn you not to be careless of the opportunities I present or else you may quickly relapse into a life of labour and penury.'

With that, Mr Astley gathers his cane and hat and leaves the tearoom.

Part Six:
London
1791 to 1795

1

Mrs William Owen

I AM TRULY grateful for this deep soft armchair, the ample stew and the warm fire. Although I wish to deny it, I do not have the strength I once owned. I was determined to walk the whole distance to London but, after several nights in cold damp cowsheds, by the time I reached Slough I resigned myself to taking a seat in a coach.

'I would have been so much better walking!' I tell my hostess, Mrs Sarah Owen.

'After only seven or eight of the most uneven tempestuous miles, the inebriated coachman mistook the road, drove over the edge and we tumbled, coach, luggage and all, into a ditch. Good lady, you cannot imagine the distress not only to the occupants but also to those poor horses. I credit myself with having cut them loose and set them free. This act, I must report, would not have pleased the coachman had he been conscious and several on board sought to question the action. Nevertheless, I believed that I was correct. I trusted once more to my legs and a hazel staff for support and, in good time, I made it to your door.'

My audience for this account looks at me strangely as if at a creature from another world. I had expected to be greeted by William Owen who has offered me temporary lodging in Pentonville whilst I seek my own accommodation. He is away, but is promised to return soon. I find myself entertained by his wife, a slight, sickly woman of poor posture and her maid of burly manner, generous proportions and suspicious eyes. They are both, however, most attentive to my well-being, as this accords with the instructions of her husband.

Mrs Owen is troubled by a persistent troublesome cough for which she apologises constantly and suffers persistently. I desist from my narrative to inquire if she has tried an infusion of hyssop and red fennel?

The maid shows an interest, protesting that her grandma believed in fennel for a bad chest and that some might be found on the marshland towards the river. She and I discuss the rival virtues of nettles or marchalan and before long she heads off into the gathering dusk, intent on her mission.

Mrs Owen and I struggle to sustain conversation. She appears nervous and totally self-effacing. I try to question her about herself but she wants only to talk of her husband and his work. She tells me how much he admires my scholarship and how greatly he appreciates the help I have given him. After this our conversation lapses and we sit in silence. She is as relieved as I when the knocker announces that her husband has arrived home and she is discharged from the duty of entertaining.

William Owen is scarcely more robust in appearance than his wife. He is slight of frame and has a fine delicate face which might grace a maid. His hands and movements are similarly deft and dainty. I imagine he might have made an excellent clockmaker. He is, thankfully, more voluble than his wife. Although his voice is quiet, he talks readily on all the subjects we have in common. We have previously corresponded at length over the search for ancient manuscripts. He has all my letters to hand, with his own annotations. I have to respect his diligence and organisation. I can see why Owain Myfyr has appointed him as administrator of his publishing projects. As we talk, it is clear that beneath the tidy, calm exterior beats a heart passionate for all things Welsh. He questions me at length about the secrets of the bards of the

Island of Britain. He was excited by the description of me by 'J.D.' in *The Gentleman's Magazine* as the last of the true bards. He wants to know more of the secrets of Bardism. I am ready for this. I have been rehearsing my answers on the long road from Glamorgan.

I explain to him that the ancient bards were the keepers of the rules of poetry handed down in the oral tradition and regulated in their eisteddfodau. But that only starts to describe their importance to Wales. They were the keepers of the wisdom and values of the Ancient Britons: peace, love of God and respect for learning. The learning was crystallised within odes which had to be learnt by each new initiate into the order. Most important were the triads, brief memorable statements of wisdom. He asks if I can recite any. Of course! I am a fully initiated member of the order. I offer him, '*O dri pheth y cafwyd barddoniaeth; awen o Dduw, synnwyr dyn, a syrth anian.*'[33]

I watch his face as I declaim. He appears transported with delight and rapidly reaches for a pencil.

'Please no! Better for you to emulate the bards and learn from me as I learnt from Lewis Hopkin of Llandyfodwg. Memorise!'

He nods and repeats the words after me as an incantation. We repeat this triad and several more until he protests that his memory is overloaded, but still I will not permit him to write.

I describe to him the meetings of the Order of Bards, the *Gorsedd*, a practice which has sadly lapsed due to the death of so many of the order but which I, one day, hope to revive.

His excitement is palpable. He is a prominent member of the Gwyneddigion and insists I attend one of their meetings to talk at greater length on the subject of Bardism. I will, of course, be

---

33 Poetry came from three sources: the muse of God, the senses of man and the presence of nature.

delighted, although I am uncertain if they will make as uncritical an audience as William Owen.

The maid has returned and I retire to their kitchen to assist in preparing an infusion that will relieve Mrs Owen's cough. The maid inquires whether I am some sort of Welsh wizard. I deny it strongly, but such perceptions may do my reputation no harm in London.

2

London

Y ES, I AM in London again! I know I must focus on the purpose of my stay for the sake of Peggy and the children. I am here to get my verses into print. My next calls should be at my printer and those who are being kind enough to pursue more subscriptions on my behalf. I know I will have to perform in drawing rooms and entertain literary gentlefolk over teas. Before I do so, I am anxious to renew my acquaintanceship with London, a city I despise and by which I am also enthralled.

From the house in Pentonville it is but a short walk to the Thames and the Strand. London is truly a place of wonders. In just a few days I have seen a live rhinoceros at the Lyceum. I have marvelled at a mechanical menagerie in the Strand. I have sat in the pit of the Parthenon Theatre listening to the most sublime Italian opera. I have visited the British Museum in Montagu House and stared in amazement at all kinds of exotic artefacts, natural curiosities and rare antiquities.

All that is but nothing to the uplift of my spirits as I visit the coffee houses and taverns. There are more than I remember, but what is more extraordinary is the ferment of ideas and philosophies. Almost without seeking, I attend lectures on astronomy, Eastern religions, and science. I am welcome, as are all freethinkers, democrats, republicans and Jacobins. The feeling of liberation comes from a common understanding that logical disciplined discussion should be the means by which intelligent men determine the truth, rather than relying on the random decisions of 'authorities', be they Church, king or landowner. I find it hard to sleep when I consider the implications of this.

The booksellers are my greatest joy. There are so many great texts on so many subjects; so many more than when I was last in London. I spend far too much on volumes of history, philosophy, politics, religion, India and the mysteries of the East.

**

I receive a note from David Samwell, the dissolute poetry and laudanum-loving naval surgeon I know from my earlier time with the Gwyneddigion. I am pleased that he is the first of my former friends to contact me. He invites me to a supper in the company of liberty-loving free men to celebrate the anniversary of the French Revolution. The event is to be held in a tavern in Leadenhall Street. There must be over a hundred or more crammed into the rooms of the Crown and Anchor. One excited speaker after another proclaims the new values of the revolution: liberty, equality, fraternity. A Frenchman wearing a red cap and tricolour cockade gives a dramatic account of his part in the storming of the Bastille; how he had been part of the crowd who had stormed the inner courtyard despite the hails of gunfire and cannon shot. The fall of the Bastille, he tells us, proclaims a new age; an age when every man and woman will accept their responsibility for the sufferings of their neighbour, when every landowner who refuses such obligations shall be driven from their property and replaced by a committee of citizens. We cheer loudly.

We end with the singing of '*Ça Ira*' and '*La Marseillaise*', the new anthem of French liberty. As most of us do not know the words, we are instructed by a French-speaking musician of good humour. Thanks to my knowledge of the language I have less difficulty than my colleagues, but it matters not. The music and the all-conquering emotion of the occasion fire our passion. We are energised for revolution tomorrow, if too exhausted to consider further action tonight.

***

The next morning at breakfast I address William Owen on the subject of Bardism. He and his wife sit at opposite ends of the kitchen table and I in the centre. I suspect there is usually little talk over breakfast and I am aware that Sarah must see my presence as intrusive, but my experiences last night leave me with a strong desire to talk. I am at pains to stress the importance of equality and fraternity to the discipline of bardic practice. Equality and word of a Christian God, I stress, are incompatible with the actions of kings and the corrupt princes of the Church. Equality is enshrined in the values and recorded practices of the Ancient British order.

I offer him another triad of the old wisdom, '*Tri dyn a fynnant fyw ar eiddo arall: brenin, offeiriad a lleidr.*'[34]

There is a silence as Sarah studies her egg fastidiously. I suspect she resents me greatly. William clears his throat before responding. He believes the enshrined values of the bardic order to be pertinent to the modern age. It is of the utmost importance to perceptions of Welsh culture amongst the English that knowledge of our ancient traditions be better known. He has already asked Owain Myfyr for a date when I may address the Gwyneddigion. He finishes his egg, makes his apologies, and

---

34 Three men live on the property of others: a king, a priest and a thief.

leaves for the solicitor's clerk's stool where he spends his days. I am alone with his wife once more.

I enquire of Sarah Owen if the infusions her maid had prepared had any beneficial effect on her cough. She looks embarrassed. I tell her that she should not worry about my feelings if they failed. I should be delighted to explore alternatives.

'Mr Williams. Oh dear, I never know what to call you. William sometimes calls you Edward and sometimes Iorwerth. What should I call you?'

'Edward will suffice, or Iolo.'

'Then Edward, let me confess I did not take the infusion as I believe I may be with child and I have heard that doses of fennel can occasionally cause a miscarriage. Is that so?'

I am taken aback by her directness and trust.

'I have not heard this said, but you are plainly right not to take the risk. Does William know?'

A pause. 'Not yet. You see we have been trying for a child for some time with little success, so I did not want to raise his hopes before I am certain.'

There is such innocence in her eyes. They are both admirable people.

'Your secret is safe with me. I am honoured to have been admitted to such a confidence.'

To my relief Sarah smiles, 'I had little choice, I think.'

This is the first smile I have seen cross her face and it is a warm sunny sight. She relaxes somewhat and starts to talk.

'May I ask another kindness, Mr Williams… Edward?'

'Name it, dear lady.'

'You are aware how important Wales and the language are to my husband. Please be aware that, although I am endeavouring to learn, I understand almost nothing of your language. When you talk in Welsh could you please translate the important pieces, such as the proverb you quoted earlier? I do so much want to understand and support William in things that are so close to his heart.'

I reprove myself for my dismissive assessment of this woman. Beneath the gentle, meek exterior is a determination as strong as her husband's.

3

This business of publication

I VISIT THE printing shop of Mr John Newbury. I am greeted warmly and treated as a visitor of importance. From that start I cannot help comparing Mr Newbury with Rhys Thomas in Cowbridge whose business collapsed, or rather drowned in a bath of brandy. Whereas Rhys would distance himself from the realities of commerce by donning a mask of sardonic humour, John Newbury is exhaustingly concentrated, watchful and analytical. As he shows me around his shop with its three large printing presses, he is constantly adjusting screws, observing ink levels, removing waste and advising apprentices and journeymen, all of whom listen attentively to his words.

He waves his arm in the direction of several massive pillars of printed sheets, partly printed books awaiting stitching and binding. He explains that authors' works have to be put aside on Wednesdays to allow for the printing of the great love of his life, *The Gentleman's Magazine*. I cannot demur. It is a great thrill to watch copy after copy of that famous publication roll off the presses in a constant stream.

At the front of the shop he displays my specimen sheet, 'The Fair Pilgrim'. This is arranged alongside the prospectus for potential subscribers. He tells me that he has arranged for the specimen sheets to be available at shops in Bath, Oxford and Cambridge, and even at the famed bookshop, G.G.J. and J. Robinson, Paternoster Row. I ask about other shops in London, Joseph Johnson for example, the radical bookseller in St Paul's Churchyard? He shakes his head and tells me that London is full of booksellers and some offer better profit margins than others. I want to protest and insist that my purpose is greater than mere 'profit margins', but I choke back the words. I assume this is one of those compromises I will have to make. It does not sit easily.

Then, without my asking, he consults his list, excuses himself whilst he requests the help of a clerk and, as a result, hands me five guineas as my share of recently collected subscriptions. I am delighted, not only by the success of the venture but by my ability to send money home to Peggy and the children as promised.

'Sorry it's so little,' apologises the industrious printer, gesturing at the coins. I had thought the payment bounteous. 'We'll have to do a lot better than this to satisfy those hungry brutes.'

I am unsure whether he is pointing at the presses or the journeymen who work them. He then tells me that he has been visited by a Mrs Nicholl who tells him that there are scores of fine gentlemen and ladies who will gladly subscribe if they were only to be requested by the bard himself. He trusts I have this in hand?

***

I have only met Mrs Mary Nicholl in the chambers of polite society in Bath. I remember her as a gracious and endlessly accommodating lady with time at her disposal. Here in the rectory at Remenham, Henley, she is scarcely recognisable. She greets me politely but with studied formality before ushering me through to the drawing room where we are to take tea.

The rectory is larger than its equivalent in Llandough and the furnishings lighter in the modern style. There are more servants, who scuttle around Mrs Nicholl like a well-disciplined army. No cutlery is dropped, no drop of milk spilt. The scones are laid out with precision. The teapot is primed and the maid pours hot water over the leaves with meticulous care.

'Thank you, Lucy. You may return to the kitchen. I will ring if I need you further.'

The maid bobs and, with a 'Yes Ma'am' and a rustle of starched linen, vanishes, closing the heavy, oak-panelled door with a resonant click.

The moment we are alone Mrs Nicholl's manner softens. Her voice loses its shrill commanding edge and assumes a warmer, more intimate tone. She hopes that the journey out to Henley was not too wearisome. She is astounded that I have walked the whole way and is full of admiration for my 'country fortitude'. She pours my tea with tenderness, caressing the delicate china cup as she places it in my hand.

She leans across and almost whispers, 'I am so delighted to have a few private moments with you, Mr Williams, just to be able to tell you how much I admire your work. There is perfection to the rural simplicity you describe that can teach us all more about ourselves and the true nature of human riches. If only those rebellious peasants of France had a bard of your calibre, then I am certain that they would learn to value that natural order in society they now appear intent on destroying.'

I thank her for the excellent tea and ask from where it was obtained. She asks me to address her as Mary when the servants are out of earshot.

Mary puts down her cup, reaches for a set of papers and moves to sit next to me on the sofa. She has before her a list of some twenty names, together with their titles, addresses and a short note as to why they are of importance, or to whom of significance they are related. She has personally solicited each of them and extracted promises that, subject to a visit from the bard himself, they will subscribe. My heart sinks when I realise that I am to call on each of these in turn to read, make idle conversation, and perform. But... I express my gratitude for all her work on my behalf and express disbelief at the extent of her social circle.

She smiles, 'Comes of being the eldest daughter of Viscount Ashbrook, certainly not from being a rector's wife! Here I am expected to visit the poor and sick. It is a great pleasure to be able to use my place in society to be of service to one so obviously gifted.'

She places her hand on my arm and moves closer as if to impart a great confidence. 'Some of my acquaintances would be quite outraged that a woman of my station would be so dedicated to the success of an unschooled countryman such as yourself, but I have always had a wild streak in me that cannot resist challenging convention.'

She sits closer than is quite proper. I fear this woman. She would control me, own me as her toy, and display me as her trophy, but this is an accommodation I must make if I am to achieve my high designs.

4

Welsh Indians

I HAVE LONG since learnt not to mistake the quietness of William or his wife Sarah for lack of commitment or courage. They can so easily be mistaken for belonging in the ranks of the timid and the docile that will be downtrodden. In truth they are the meek who shall inherit the Earth.

Even before I arrived in London, William had written me long and detailed letters about the Welsh Indians. He is not the first to become enchanted with the story of Madog ab Owain and how this Welsh prince sailed to the Americas many hundreds of years before any other 'discoverer'. He never returned, but legend has it that somewhere in the vast American interior there survives a tribe of white-skinned, Welsh-speaking Indians. It is a popular legend, much repeated but not too closely questioned lest the truth disappoint.

William is obsessed with the story, particularly since the arrival in London of a red-skinned Indian chief by the name of William Augustus Bowles. He is here as a novelty, appearing nightly at Astley's Amphitheatre, and billed as the chief of the savage Creek nation. He rides bareback, together with six other Native American Cherokees. Mr Bowles is said to have great authority based on experience, knowledge and having married daughters of four great chieftains.

William has met with him twice and questioned him in detail about the Welsh Indians or, in his account, the Padoucas. Chief Bowles claims to be familiar with the tribe, having travelled west of the Mississippi for eight hundred miles along a mountainous range in the company of a Welshman escaping the horrors of the Spanish gold mines of Mexico. On entering Padoucas territory, his companion was astounded to hear the Welsh language being spoken with great purity. The Padoucas had in their possession several manuscripts which they considered as mysteries, containing the lost account of their origins. They are longing for a visitation from one who might explain their existence and their history.

I am annoyed by Chief Bowles whom I suspect of invention in furtherance of his own fame. I am also concerned that he will undermine rather than strengthen belief in the Madog story, giving it the appearance of a fairground boast. I write to *The Gentleman's Magazine* to lay before its readership scholarly evidence based on conversations and research I have undertaken. I quote a Mr Binon from Coity in Glamorgan, who spent many years as a trader in Philadelphia and journeyed up the Mississippi and came across the Padoucas. To this I add excerpts from the accounts of French explorers of the American hinterland, who attest to the existence of a tribe speaking a language they did not know, who lived in a manner and style more associated with Europe than America. This is all written in a restrained academic style.

I have orders from Mrs Mary Nicholl to call on the Honourable Miss Nevill, 6 Curzon Street, Mayfair, at eleven in the morning. I have now made eight or more such calls and have come away with a subscription in all cases. The process plainly works but the experience palls quickly. In the beginning I quite enjoyed being entertained in the houses of the privileged and wealthy. But as the novelty wears thin I have become increasingly repulsed by the extravagance, the lavish furnishings, decoration and clothing which is wasteful beyond all reason. Some hostesses are harder to entertain than others. I spent a pointless two hours shouting into the ear trumpet of a stone-deaf Miss Winford of Berkeley Square, and several hours sitting in servants' kitchens whilst another potential subscriber completed her round of whist or woke from her afternoon nap. The tea, on the other hand, is consistently excellent.

The Honourable Miss Nevill, I am promised, can hear and see, and is a fine judge of literature. She will provide me not just with her own subscription but payments from two or three of her acquaintances. As always I am briefed to refer to the Mary who guides my footsteps as 'daughter of the Viscount Ashbrook' *not* 'Mrs John Nicholl'.

My hostess turns out to be a lady of great charm, wealth and eccentricity. She is attended on by two Indian footmen whose natural height is exaggerated by turbans. She reclines on a day bed surrounded, and occasionally submerged, by a constantly moving infestation of miniature dogs with long flowing coats. Her hand shoots out from the hairy mass requiring me to take it and bow. I introduce myself. She has an engaging smile and a way of addressing me as if all her words conveyed intimate secrets. She hands several of the dogs to the footmen so as to aid her concentration. Several more appear from beneath her cushions to take their place. I am reminded of a bed of maggots.

I have developed a shortened version of the readings I gave in Bath. I introduce myself as the last genuine bard of the Ancient British tradition. Miss Nevill confesses herself honoured. I read two or three of my warmest pastoral poems. Miss Nevill swoons with pleasure. I usually end with a story from Welsh legend, but this morning with the details of the Padoucas fresh in my mind I substitute a retelling of the journey of Madog ab Owain for the story of 'The Fairy Harp'. This produces an even more ecstatic reaction. Miss Neville asks me if any expedition is planned to visit the lost tribe and reunite them with their Christian heritage. If so, I may put her down as a subscriber to the costs of the expedition.

I leave with a total of four subscriptions. This money I have to take immediately to the printer to pay for paper and labour. He is able to show me a dozen printed sheets. They look very fine and I am content to hand over every last penny.

***

I receive a letter from Peggy reproving me for my failure to write and, more especially, for not having sent money for two weeks. She accuses me of 'building castles in the air which will fall and crush you under their ruins'. I am beset with guilt.

5

Radical thoughts

S O MANY BOOKS. So many printers and booksellers. After a lifetime of semi-starvation when printed matter was scarce or poor in quality, I find myself in a maelstrom of ideas, words, booksellers, books and readers.

I visit as many booksellers as I can. They are concentrated along the Strand, in Covent Garden, Soho, and the streets around St Paul's Cathedral. Each bookseller attracts authors and readers of a distinctive sort. I avoid Tom's in Russell Street, which is a hotbed of King-loving loyalists. William Stratham in Shoe Lane is always stimulating, and Thomas Rickman, the Quaker bookseller, is a haunt of true radicals. My favourite place of all is the bookshop of Joseph Johnson at 8 Paternoster Row, St Paul's Churchyard. This is a home to Dissenters, Unitarians and revolutionaries alike. The list of authors he has published is impressive, most notably Joseph Priestly, the theologian. Mr Johnson himself is to be seen working in his shop but is not given to casual conversation. He appears to me to have the manner of a fastidious small bird carefully building a magnificent nest many times his own size. Like the wren, he is totally concentrated on the task in hand.

As with other booksellers, writers and their supporters bring trade to the taverns and coffee houses nearby. I sit in the Chapter coffee house, next door to Joseph Johnson's bookshop, listening to a fine discussion on the reform of Parliament. I am a stranger here but there is a fellowship within the coffee house which makes introductions easy and nurtures friendship. I tell those at my table that I am a poet collecting subscriptions to finance the publication of my book. They want to know more about me. Who I have as a printer? What he is charging for his work? Where I have my prospectus on display?... and more. Why is it not on display in Joseph Johnson's? I explain that Mr Newbury was handling the matter and had given reasons I did not understand concerning profit margins. They laugh, and warn me that I should be suspicious of Mr Newbury who, in their view, is manipulating matters to his own advantage. They suggest I talk to Mr Johnson who has a reputation for assisting new authors of a radical inclination.

Across the room an eloquent speaker is complaining of the absence of fair parliamentary representation and is loudly cheered. He continues with a tirade against the follies of the aristocracy and the idiocy of kingship.

'What is government more than the management of the affairs of the nation? It is not, and from its nature cannot be, the property of any particular man or family.'

The speaker is a large man with a memorable head. His hair is thick, his chin pointed, his forehead wide. He has a large Roman nose and two of the most penetrating blue eyes I have ever seen. He plainly knows how to hold an audience.

I ask who the speaker is. Should I know who he is? When I can, I make my way through the group anxious not to lose the chance to talk with Thomas Paine, the radical thinker who has so impressed me. I praise his earlier book, *Common Sense*, which I regard as a work of the greatest importance. He thanks me and urges me to read his next work, a defence of the French Revolution entitled *Rights of Man*. When I enquire where I may obtain a copy he shakes his head and tells me that there has been a delay. Joseph Johnson was his preferred publisher but that is not now possible due to the unwarranted pressure of the authorities. I do not understand.

Thomas explains, 'William Pitt's secret police have been issuing threats against the gentle Joseph Johnson which he has not been able to withstand.'

I must look incredulous, for Thomas laughs.

'Do not blame him. I do not. The authorities are becoming frightened and thus liable to behave unpredictably and with great malice. In any case the *Rights of Man* will be published but a little late and by a publisher who is, as yet, unknown and beyond the reach of Pitt's spies. In the meanwhile I am taking myself to France, lest the reaction to my book land me in the dock and in gaol.'

By the time we part Thomas Paine has asked if he might join my list of subscribers. He tells me that he will await publication with anticipation.

'And one last thing. Be careful who you talk to in here and how much you tell them. You can be certain that even in this happy company of comrades there will be several informers anxious to be paid in pieces of silver for whatever betrayal they are able to make.'

6

Bard by
rite and privilege

O WAIN MYFYR IS even more corpulent, more authoritative and more welcoming than he was twenty years ago. The Bull's Head has altered not a jot; the same paintings on the wall, the same enormous oak table, and a very similar team of potmen and serving girls. The membership is also familiar in aspect and dress, although names have changed, faces have fattened, and waistlines have thickened. Instead of the spontaneous lively exchanges I remember, there is a settled predictable rhythm to the meeting. Owain still rules. The all-Welsh rule is maintained, although I find much of the Welsh language spoken to be over-ornate and self-conscious. The society has aged.

But the biggest alteration I perceive is in myself. Last time I was here I felt a desire to be accepted on any terms. This time I am determined that I will dictate their perceptions. Owain rises and bangs the table for silence. He welcomes me back, regrets my long absence and praises my work in uncovering lost works of Dafydd ap Gwilym. There is polite applause. He introduces me, as I have requested, not as Iorwerth but as Iolo Morganwg. As I rise to speak I sense expectation. Many have read the articles in *The Gentleman's Magazine* and have an appetite for more. I see David Samwell to my left and, of course, William Owen on Owain's right taking notes. Good to have friends. I look for

Richard Glyn, frequenter of Covent Garden bordellos, but in vain. All other faces appear distant and anonymous.

Since I had the pleasure of addressing them last I have been initiated into the Bardic Order, hence my new name, Iolo. I explain that I am now one of only two surviving bards who have been fully initiated in the ancient traditions. I explain something of the fundamental values of the order – how we exist primarily to ensure that the standards and forms of composition are maintained from one generation to the next; how the succession is maintained from one bard to their pupil. I briefly outline the 'Glamorgan Measures', adherence to which is basic to the standards we seek to uphold. There is some uncomfortable shifting in the seats of those who resent the suggestion that anything of value might emerge from outside Gwynedd, but this I ignore.

I describe the ancient rituals of bardic initiation and the conduct of the *Gorsedd*. I stress how the fundamentals of the *Gorsedd* reflect and, over centuries, have inspired the values that make Wales a distinct civilisation, superior to its Saxon neighbour. The *Gorsedd* demands that all its members accept a commitment to equality, to Christian behaviour, to the truth. Members of the order set their faces forever against the rule of tyrants or kings and abjure the use of violence or the call to war. To the *Gorsedd*, the voice of the Lord comes from the scriptures, not from the mouths of prelates or archbishops. It speaks to the free spirit of every man.

I declare that I intend to revive the ancient ceremonies of the Bards of the Island of Britain and will do so by proclaiming, to all who will hear, that a year and one day hence, on 21 June, the summer solstice of 1792, there will be held a *Gorsedd*. I announce that it will take place on Primrose Hill to the north of Regent's Park, the finest spot in London from which to observe the movement of the heavens. All who wish to be admitted to the ancient order should attend. The *Gorsedd* is commanded on my authority as the last of the true bards of the Island of Britain. I am '*Bardd wrth fraint a defawd Beirdd Ynys Prydain.*'[35] The society of Glamorgan bards, whom I term as the 'Chair of Morgannwg' authorise my actions. Whilst there were once similar chairs throughout Wales to regulate the initiation of bards to the order, the tradition survives only in Glamorgan. I also deposit some copies of 'The Fair Pilgrim' with prospectuses, and invite subscribers.

After the address I am as popular as a prince, at least with a few. There is a circle of the curious and the deferential around me at all times asking questions. Owain Myfyr shepherds me around the room to prevent a small number monopolising my conversation. I am aware that the reaction is complex. For most, my revelations are a welcome proof of the ancient lineage of the Welsh. There are others who stand back in small groups shaking heads and conversing in whispers. No matter. I was prepared for that.

One man in particular, for whom Owain wishes me to allow time, is the rounded Edward Jones. He is a short, soft-spoken man with grey, thinning hair and a very ruddy complexion. There is a robust stockiness to the way he stands as if he might survive the blowing of a great tempest. He tells me how moved he was by my address, and how hopeful he is that the *Gorsedd* revelations may increase the esteem in which the Welsh are held in London.

Owain interrupts to inform me that Edward Jones is no less a person than the 'King's Bard' who plays the harp in the royal nursery. The musician lowers his head and raises one hand as if to ward away the resultant expressions of admiration which he expects and which I am in no way anxious to bestow.

---

35 Bard by rite and privilege of the Bards of the Island of Britain.

William Owen insists we share a carriage for the journey home to Pentonville. For once I do not object. My legs feel heavy and my breathing is laborious. The effects of returning to the damp, fetid air of London are starting to show. As we trot north through Charing Cross towards Islington, William tells me how successful he believed the evening to have been. I am always delighted to receive praise but even for William the words appear excessive. He is nervous. Why? He has a conversation in mind that makes him so. I try to help. I tell him that I am a little concerned as to Sarah's digestion. I have heard her retching of a morning. May I prepare an infusion of herbs for her?

It was the opening he wanted.

'Dear Iolo. The sickness is not caused by a poor digestion but is part of much better news. We would like you to know that, if all proceeds well, my wife should be born of our first child some months hence.'

'That is splendid news, William. Congratulations. I had no idea.'

'Thank you.'

'And you would prefer it if I were to find alternative lodgings. You will have more than enough to cope with without a troublesome Welsh bard to entertain.'

William is plainly embarrassed and explains that Sarah is delicate but that she also worries too much.

'She is concerned lest we – you – are being drawn into support for organisations which may be disapproved of by the authorities. You know how protective she is of…'

'Quite so, William. Please do not apologise. I have already presumed too much on your generous hospitality.'

I watch the streets give way to countryside as we journey through Clerkenwell.

7

Mrs Nicholl
and the Bowdlers

T HE STREAM OF messages from Mrs Nicholl is unrelenting. Each day I receive another set of commands to attend 'The Honourable Mrs This' or 'The Gracious Lady That'. When I first saw a rhinoceros on display at the Lyceum, I pitied the poor animal being paraded for the amusement of all. Now I envy the creature! At least his audience come to him, whereas I have to travel all over London. He does not have to perform or smile or pretend to be honoured by the attentions of deaf, insensitive patrons. He is, as I recall, fed well, whilst I survive on cups of tea.

No matter – I have striven to do all that Mrs Nicholl required. I have smiled, told the story of my life, recited, recounted ancient tales and provided a view into the secrets of Bardism. I have done this scores of times in grotesquely furnished, violently perfumed drawings rooms to audiences of the decrepit, the ignorant, the incontinent and their pampered pets. Often I judge the coiffured miniature dogs to have more literary discernment than their owners.

Now I am judged to have given short measure! In her elegant manner Mrs Nicholl scolds. She complains that the abominable Miss Flower thought I displayed a 'coolness' towards her and failed to demonstrate appropriate gratitude. My behaviour is deemed 'unfitting' when attending a 'lady of rank and status'. I puzzle as to what I did to offend and conclude that it is what I did *not* do that has caused displeasure. I did not kneel, lick her shoes or prostrate myself before her.

By the same post I receive a delightful letter which restores my spirits. Fanny Bowdler, whom I met in Bath, has written to her mother and sister in London informing them that I am a writer whose acquaintance is worth cultivating. She enclosed a copy of 'The Fair Pilgrim'. The letter is from Fanny's sister Henrietta, herself an author of improving moral texts. She invites me to take tea with her mother and herself in Bloomsbury any Tuesday or Wednesday morning at ten. What sets this letter apart from the usual round of visits is the language. Dry formality is replaced with simple enthusiasm. She explains that Fanny, whilst not a writer, is a better judge of literature than any of her sisters. Henrietta boasts a distant Welsh relation, which makes my work all the more welcome to them. She has already collected five subscriptions on my behalf and the money is available to me at my pleasure.

***

The house is modest but very well maintained; one of the smaller terraced houses behind Russell Square. I knock, expecting a footman or maid to answer. The door is opened by a tall woman in her forties, dressed all in grey apart from a white linen collar and cuffs. Her hair is pinned back. I could have been mistaken for assuming this to be the maid but...

'Mr Williams. How delightful. I'm Henrietta.'

She shakes my hand vigorously, and then springs to one side to invite me over the doorstep. She has the manner and movement of a young girl. She raises her head and shouts, 'Mama! Fanny's Welsh bard is here. Do follow me, Mr Williams.'

She leads me into their drawing room. The floor is polished wood with no carpet. The furnishings are simple and functional:

plain hard chairs, a small round table, a writing desk and a coal scuttle. There is a carriage clock and small set of miniatures on the mantel, possibly portraits of the family. A small but vigorous fire burns in the grate. Bookcases cover every available inch of the walls apart from the window overlooking the street. Thankfully, there are no dogs or other animals of any sort.

By the side of the fireplace sits an older version of Henrietta, dressed with similarly severe grey simplicity plus the minor frivolity of an amber brooch at her neck.

'Mr Edwards, may I introduce my mother, Mrs Elizabeth Stuart Bowdler.'

We shake hands and I am gestured to a chair. Unnervingly the mother and daughter start and end each others' sentences seamlessly. It is hard to determine whom to answer or in which direction to look. My head spins from one to the other as they speak.

'We've been doing our very best for you, Mr Williams, and we have…'

'… five names. I do believe it's five…'

'… not including ourselves of course…'

'The Reverend Davis of Trinity…'

'… a fine judge of verse. Then there's the Reverend J. Jones of Bletchley…'

'… and Mrs Lockwood of Mayfair…'

'… who will do whatever Mama tells them to do.'

Their duologue continues in this vein for some time, requiring no response on my part apart from an occasional nod or expression of thanks. They have not only the names but the money waiting for me in a neat envelope. I thank them again. They advise me on the process of publication. I must not allow the book to come out in the summer when too many people are away. The winter is far better, when the evenings are dark and readers crave entertainment. I repeat my thanks.

'We do so approve of your expression of simple virtues, Mr Williams. Your verse might serve to remind…'

'… those who…'

'… in the modern age…'

'… have become obsessed…'

'… not too strong a word…'

'… with the accumulation of useless possessions…'

'… and pointless luxuries…'

'… which merely distract them from prayer…'

'… and the true reasons for our existence.'

I agree heartily. I express my fear that the building of factories will continue to take people away from a pastoral life and draw them into the corruption and filth of towns and cities.

'And for what?' adds Henrietta.

'To ensure the production of more and more unneeded…'

'… frivolous items…'

'… which through ownership…'

'… men can ostentatiously parade their wealth.'

We agree heartily. There is a slight pause before Henrietta completes a whole sentence without interruption. She boasts that the family have noble Welsh blood on her mother's side which leads her to be fired with curiosity by my 'Padoucas' article in *The Gentleman's Magazine*. She has since read widely on the subject: the works of Gutun Owen, Cynwrick ap Grono and Sir Meredith ap Rees. The matter has been discussed at length amongst the literati of her acquaintance, including Mrs Elizabeth Montagu, queen of the Blue Stockings Society.[36]

'You must forgive my Welsh blood being up when I hear the story denied. I do so hope you will enable me to ascertain the right of my Uncle Madog to the discovery of America.'

---

36 A London-based women's literary discussion group founded by Elizabeth Montagu in the 1750s. It advocated the importance of women's education.

To this end she would like to introduce me to two poets of her circle. Had I heard of Robert Southey or Samuel Coleridge? I confess not.

8

Southey and Coleridge

THE Madog story is everywhere. I begin to regret associating myself so closely as I am daily pursued for more information. Weekly there appears new testimony affirming the survival of the Padoucas up the furthest reaches of the Missouri. I care deeply about this important piece of Welsh history but I have many other pressures on me. I wish to concentrate on preparing my poetry for print but the distractions are impossible to resist.

William Owen is in a state of high excitement following a new account by a Captain Chaplaine of Kentucky. During the war the Captain's troop was garrisoned at Kaskaski Fort, Lake Kinkade. He hired scouts of the Padoucas tribe who conversed in Welsh with Welsh soldiers under his command. He recalls that there was amazement amongst his men over the quality of the Welsh spoken. In addition, there is a letter circulating from a Mr Howells of Philadelphia affirming that the 'Welsh Indians' have been found and visited. He can confirm the Welshness of their language and the whiteness of their skins. William is anxious that an expedition be formed.

'*So* important! This would mean so much to us. It would prove that Madog ab Owain discovered America well before Columbus. Think what that would do for Welsh self-esteem.'

I look at his face, as illuminated as a child being promised sugar.

'You are correct Owen, but to me there is even greater

symbolism in the idea of a community of Welsh people living free and equal in the Americas; a land outside the reach of kings, tyrants or priests.'

His eyes gleam with pleasure. He is not alone in his enthusiasm; witness the Bowdlers. I am becoming concerned lest this publicity and 'Madog fever' spreading over literary London causes the tribe to be visited not by friends who would wish to support them, but by unscrupulous merchants or imperialist adventurers who will exploit their innocence. It would indeed be an act of benevolence to mount an expedition.

***

I am sitting in the Chapter coffee house in Paternoster Row, this time in the company of Henrietta Bowdler's two young poet friends, Robert Southey and Samuel Coleridge. They are very young, not yet twenty I would say. They are committed to all things progressive in a vague impetuous way, which is why they use this fashionable meeting place. Samuel is the elder but also the quietest and the most nervous. Robert is the most vocal and intense of the two. He is explaining at some length why the Madog story means so much to him personally. It is a story he has been obsessed with since boyhood. He is currently composing an epic poem on the subject which he intends should rival *Paradise Lost* in the grandeur of its themes. I admire his ambition. He believes the Padoucas to be our potential saviours and role models, men of our race who have preserved their innocence and refinement of emotion through their isolation in a wilderness. They are untainted by the corruption of modern life. Robert quotes Rousseau and tells me of the need for mankind to recover its natural nobility by returning to a simpler form of existence. Southey and Coleridge intend to travel to America to establish a colony based on simple living;

a community dedicated to the principles of peace, harmony, equality and fraternity.

My concern for the Padoucas grows. I do not want these two venturing up the Mississippi. The Padoucas are a Welsh tribe and their very existence reflects great credit on a hero of our nation, Madog ab Owain. Any expedition must be led by Welsh-speaking Welshmen.

***

I inform William Owen that we, he and I, must mount an expedition. He says nothing at first, and then he pours out excuses.

'I would love nothing more Edward, you know that. It would be the greatest achievement of my life and I do not fear the hardship and privation... but... there's Sarah and our unborn child and my work in the solicitor's office which is our sole source of income – apart from the payment I get from Owain Myfyr, of course.'

He apologises at length and repeatedly. He cannot be part of the venture, though he will do all in his power to support it. I am angry and tell him so. Do I not have family, too? Three living children deprived of their father whilst I endure the cesspit that is London to pursue the betterment of all things concerning Wales? Do I not have the pressures of writing and of preparing my work for the printer? Do I not have to spend my days entertaining the imbecilic, but fashionable, in order to feed my printer's avarice? Am I not twice William's age? Yet even so, when I see the need for Welshmen of principle to act – I will do my duty. I intend to place an advertisement in *The Gentleman's Magazine* inviting adventurous patriotic Welshmen to join me. I will, from this very night, begin my preparation for the expedition by accustoming my body to sleeping on the bare earth. The green of St James' Park will toughen me for the wilderness of Kentucky.

***

Only laudanum sees me through a night disturbed by revellers, mad dogs, degenerates and the hardness of the earth. I thank David Samwell who keeps me supplied with the source of all release from trials of the flesh. When will I ever learn to let my brain stop my impetuosity ruling my actions?

9

Joseph Johnson,
Paternoster Row

I AM IN the bookshop of Joseph Johnson in Paternoster Row, anxious for a conversation. As an antidote to the endless grovelling for subscriptions, I need to profess my true self to the world. I have written a pamphlet entitled *War is incompatible with the Spirit of Christianity*. It is one of several such essays I have composed attacking kingcraft, priestcraft and the glorification of war. Joseph Johnson has previously published anti-war and anti-slavery pamphlets. I wish to contribute to his crusade. I must profess my truth, lest I turn into Mrs Nicholl's pet rhinoceros.

Joseph Johnson orders affairs with care. He counts copies, tidies shelves, and instructs his assistants with quiet unhurried authority. He is today engaged in conversation with a man with untidy ginger hair in a green coat and an ingratiating smile. Unusually the bookseller appears edgy. Having waited several minutes for the conversation to end, I feel justified in edging closer so as to make my presence obvious.

They both notice me and the man in green declares, 'Don't let me take all your time, good sir, gabbing away as I do. This gentleman plainly wishes a word.'

I protest that I will wait but the man in green insists that he is in no hurry. I should take as long as I wish and not mind him in the slightest. Any matter concerning books and radical thought is 'food and drink' to him. He will bide his time whilst I discuss my business.

I start by reminding Joseph Johnson of the pamphlet I left for his attention. Had he been able to read its contents? Did he think that it was suitable for publication? If not, I had several others in similar vein attacking kingship and the licensed butchery monarchs and priests call war.

I have had conversations with Mr Johnson before. He has been very helpful in advising me over the progress of *Poems, Lyric and Pastoral* but today he appears anxious to avoid conversation. He is expecting a package which has not arrived, and needs to send a message lest he disappoint some important customers. He offers one of his assistants to answer any further questions either of us may have, and disappears into the rear of the shop like a small finch flying to safety.

The man in green looks momentarily annoyed, then composes his face into its previous fixed smile. He wishes me good day and swaggers out and down Paternoster Row.

***

'Forgive my cautiousness, Mr Williams, but I suspect that man. I had fear of what you might reveal were you to talk further. I do not want to provide him with matter that he might report against you or I.'

It is an hour later and we have moved to the discrete surroundings of Mr Johnson's office, a small room with ledgers, files and bundles of paper lining every wall to a height I suspect the small man would not be able to reach unassisted.

'You know him to be a spy?'

'I do not *know* such a fact, but I have come to suspect it. He is around constantly and uses tactics of assumed politeness in order to encourage others to speak of their business in his presence. It may be that I am over-cautious but you will be aware, as I am, that the authorities have become far more active since the Royal Proclamation.'

Mr Johnson refers to a proclamation by the King declaring 'seditious' writing to be 'treasonous'. I am affronted by his remark.

'Is it not our duty to refuse to be cowed by such threats?'

The bookseller looks at me as if shocked by the talk of a foolish child.

'Mr Williams, you talk honestly but rashly. That is why I did not want you to speak where spies might report your words. Tell me, have you a family?'

'Yes, a wife and children.'

'Then may I suggest that your first duty is to them. For their sakes they do not want their father in gaol. Have you any concept of the nature of prisons in this realm?'

'I have. I was gaoled for debt for a full year.'

'You did well to have freed yourself. But let me assure you that a debtors' prison is fine hospitality in comparison to the treatment His Majesty affords those he deems traitors. Treason is punishable by death – violent, slow, painful death. I have no desire to be a political martyr, Mr Williams. What I wish to do is to help my writers influence their readers so that person-by-person we grow to an understanding that we are all equal before God.'

'Amen.'

'Amen indeed, but I suggest you be ruled by me as to how to make the greatest impact at the least cost to yourself and those you love. There is no virtue to a pointless show of defiance. That would be glorious self-indulgence.'

'Thomas Paine was not cowed.'

'No, but he is now in exile in France and knows he would be

arrested the moment he set foot on Tilbury docks. We can't all hide in France. We can work stealthily. I did not myself publish the *Rights of Man*, yet copies are everywhere.'

I look at this slight, wiry elderly man with admiration. He continues,

'The London I knew is changing. The authorities fear that the Revolution that took place in France may happen here and, heaven will witness, there is poverty enough to precipitate such an upheaval. They incite their followers to mob rule based on hatred of the French, crude patriotism and an inexplicable adoration of George III.'

'So you suggest that we should now fall silent?'

'No, but I suggest that we need to confront crude force with craft. Open criticism of the King will not be tolerated. So our criticism will be covert, devious, executed with guile.'

'For example…?'

'Once a month we print our periodical, *The Analytical Review*. When all the presses are running I myself take the opportunity to print forty copies of some articles I would not dare sell in the bookshop. These are not displayed but are distributed through trusted associates in a manner that prevents the government acting against my bookshop.'

'And my pamphlet?'

'Is too long for that, but reduce it by a half and I will distribute it in the manner I describe.'

'Thank you.'

Mr Johnson looks at me quizzically and asks as to the progress of *Poems, Lyric and Pastoral*. I complain about Mr Newbury and his ever-increasing charges. He tells me that I must take some of the blame for the way the work keeps growing in length.

'I am most impressed with the accounts I have heard of your discovery of the ancient British bards. I would suggest that you look to include more details of this in your volume, particularly those aspects where their values appear strikingly congruent with those of Thomas Paine and the cause of liberty.'

For the first time I see a twinkle in his small blue eyes as he adds, 'I do not think I am alone in deploying craft and guile in the service of liberty.'

10

This wilderness business of publication

M R NEWBURY TAKES the corrected proofs I offer. He does not look at them and deposits them in a basket already piled high. I give him some new sheets of work that I have completed only days before. I hand them over as I would a precious gift. He looks at them as if at a turd.

'More? How much more do you expect to pack into that volume? You have already added more than thirty additional pages.'

All three of his presses are in operation and the noise levels are high. I have to shout as I explain that these are my latest pieces, written under the inspiration of the French Revolution and the dawn of rational thought. The anti-kingship poems are crucial to my vision.

'Poets have visions. I just have costs. More pages mean more paper. More ink, more typesetting, more proofing, more hours at the press.'

'Which I suppose you will pass onto me.'

'Well, of course. And another thing. You've now gone far beyond what we can squeeze into one volume. I thought we might still manage, but these additional pages…'

He waves the new sheets in the air with no respect and adds with a note of supposed despair, 'And I don't even suppose that this lot will be the end?'

'There's an essay yet to come for the front of the book.'

'So there will have to be two volumes. That doubles the binding costs, of course.'

I am annoyed at the way he loads more and more costs onto the project every time we meet. More than that, I am incensed by his manner and lack of understanding of the process of writing.

'This means no more to you than printing a livestock catalogue, does it?'

He turns at the challenge, correctly detecting the anger in my voice. It does not cause him to soften his attitude. He shouts over the noise of the presses.

'Not a jot more. Indeed, livestock catalogues are always twelve pages. No more, no less. Much less trouble.'

I threaten to take the printing elsewhere. Mr Newbury laughs.

'By all means. But you'll find that no other printer is going to take on a half-printed book. And you'll end up with a mess of different typefaces and styles. No, I'm afraid you and I are stuck with each other until this blessed volume appears.'

He is right and my impotence makes me even more furious. But if I cannot take the printing away from Mr Newbury, I can take the publishing. I will speak to Joseph Johnson. Everyone of a radical opinion praises him as an honest man with real concern for his writers. I will say nothing until I have his agreement. Mr Newbury mistakes my silence for surrender.

'Well, it's been pleasant talking to you but there's printing to be done. And can you let me have another twenty shillings as soon as possible so we can make a start on setting these latest pages?'

Twenty shillings! A sum that would have lasted a family for a month in Cowbridge is here a trivial amount that disappears in the wink of a printer's reckoning.

***

I look across the table at John Evans, a serious-minded young man originally from Waunfawr who has answered the advert for brave explorers who will travel up the Mississippi river in search of the Padoucas. He is quietly spoken, God fearing and very patriotic. I tell him of the need to practice the skills of survival in the wild. He assures me that he is well prepared by virtue of his upbringing helping his father tend sheep in the mountains of Gwynedd. He appears quite focused and determined. His single-mindedness forces me to confront my own confusion.

***

An angry letter from Peggy protesting, again, that she cannot live on the money I am able to send them. They have had to survive for seven weeks on only six shillings. Life has been a continual and painful struggle since I left. They have now eaten the last crust of bread. She tells me that I am a heartless cruel husband and father. She signs it 'Yours affectionately'. I send them every last penny I can command.

***

I am summoned by the industrious Mrs Nicholl in language of the greatest urgency. She has news of such importance that she has to convey it in person. To that end I am to meet with her at 14 Curzon Street, the home of Lady Caversham of the Sunbury Cavershams. I will be expected at ten sharp, Wednesday next.

The urgency of her tone incites my curiosity and ensures my punctuality, although I fear her news. I imagine she has arraigned a battalion of aged nobility of title and wealth but without a pennyworth of wit between them all. They will bay and cackle their self-importance whilst requiring me to throw the pearls of my labours before their illustrious swineships. This is the worst I can image. The reality is infinitely more horrendous.

Mrs Nicholl sits before me in a printed silk robe. Her head is covered by a ridiculous turban which has to be a dictate of fashion to persuade an otherwise reasonably intelligent woman to so decorate her person. How I would love to snigger. How Peggy would roar with laughter at the pretension. I sit respectfully. She is speaking in the same low intimate voice she employed at the Henley rectory. Lady Caversham mouths the Nicholl words as if auditioning for the role of a mirror. She makes no sounds of her own. Mrs Nicholl speaks,

'Mr Williams. As a man of humble origins I pray you will not be too overwhelmed by the magnitude of the honour you are to receive. I take it as a tribute to my late father, the Viscount Ashbrook, that my loyal application has secured favour in the highest circles of the realm.'

She stops as if she has explained all that needs to be explained. She is awaiting thanks but I do not understand. With some slight annoyance she clarifies,

'I have it from the Court of St James itself that His Most Gracious Highness, George, Prince of Wales, is disposed to become a subscriber to your volume of poetry. His Majesty, as you will be aware, is a fine judge of literature and has condescended to bless your 'Fair Pilgrim' with his seal of approval. All you need do is to submit a suitable dedication to His Highness for the approval of his courtiers and you will have the inestimable advantage of a royal endorsement.'

Her voice gradually rises in register during this speech, in step with her levels of excitement. She is now speaking at so high a pitch that I doubt any of the sopranos of the opera could match her endeavours. Lady Caversham claps her hands together and emits a strangulated 'Bravo'.

A royal endorsement. What am I to do or say? The volume

itself will contain no shortage of verses condemning kings and kingship as those who trample on the rights of the common people. I should refuse the endorsement of our fat indulgent prince. On the other hand, to do so would be tantamount to an act of treason. I would be suspected and condemned as an enemy of the true order. If I accept this 'honour', my book will be guaranteed sales throughout London society and will make a profit that will secure my family's well-being for years to come. I look at Mrs Nicholl and Lady Caversham who have reached a summit of exhilaration, and are now awaiting my effusive thanks for their obtaining so great a largesse. I do what I can but the words are torn painfully from my being.

Fortunately, they excuse my lack of eloquence on the grounds of shock. It is hard for one of such humble origins to comprehend the enormity of the honour.

It is a fine day. I lie on my back in Hyde Park watching the clouds form and reform. They do not drift, they race across the sky and cherubs play hide-and-seek between them, screeching with laughter when one is caught. The obese Prince of Wales appears from behind a cloud and spoils their play. He belches loudly and scratches his crutch. The cherubs laugh. I roll over to avoid the sight. A cherub tickles my face with a feather. I brush him aside. Another sits on my legs.

'Why don't you come and play?' they chime in high silly voices.

'I cannot.'

'Why not?'

'Because I have to guard my truth.'

'Truth!' squeaks the first cherub. 'What's that?'

The cherubs are joined by two more who carry bowls of sweet-tasting honey. They feed me off golden spoons. The honey tastes of fame and riches.

'There you see! Easy, isn't it?'

'Now you're ours.'

'Just because you fed me?'

'Because you ate Kingy's royal porridge,' they chant in triumph. I spit it out.

'I will not. I must not!' I shout.

The cherubs look at me in amazement. 'But everyone wants Kingy's royal porridge! Are you sure?'

I feel a hand on my shoulder. I turn and see above me the perfect image of womanhood. My mother drifts in a cloud of white silk. Her face is painfully beautiful but so stern. She holds a book, Paradise Regained, open before me.

'Great Acts require great means of enterprise,' she quotes. Behind her stand rows of the Matthew family urging me to do what I must.

'Sometimes it is necessary to pretend, to feign, in order to reach the goals you seek in this world.'

'But Mother,' I whisper hoarsely, 'this is beyond dissembling. If I publish to the world a professed loyalty that transgresses against all my heart holds dear, I put my very truth in peril. Look what you ask of me!'

There is the sound of splintering and a grinding of mighty forces; cracks and coruscation as if the world were being torn in two. An enormous ravine is opening to split Hyde Park; violent nature asserting itself over cultivated garden. There is a widening chasm where there was green grass. I peer into its depths. A thousand feet below a waterfall crashes on the rocks. Steam rises. In the depths serpents writhe. Strange evil creatures fight over the bodies of the newly dead. I am confused and unsure of my footing. I step closer onto a jutting rock which provides a clearer view and greater peril. There are inches only between me and a downward plunge into oblivion and death. I have to walk this ledge and not fall.

'Take my hand,' she commands.

Her fingers are cold and white as alabaster, but steady as she leads me like an infant along the ledge.

'Do not look downwards, Ned, just follow my voice. Remember... "All thy heart is set on high designs. High action. But whence to be achieved?"'

Brook's Market, Holborn

I MOVE MY lodgings again. This is chiefly to secure somewhere even cheaper. All of my money goes to the printer and what little is left I send to Peggy who, even so, tells me they are destitute. I return to the back streets of Holborn where I stayed twenty years before. Beauchamp Street is filthier and more vermin infected than I remember. Ann, the dancer, is no longer to be found, and the room I used is now part of a warehouse. In my poverty and my misery I am drawn to these poor streets. I am drawn to converse with my former self. I am drawn to a place where I can write undisturbed by Mrs Nicholl and all the other chattering monsters of society. I am drawn to this place by the ghost of Chatterton. I recall the Walters brothers discussing him and the world he created: the gentle world of a fifteenth-century monk described in filigree. It was at Brook Street, only a door or two from my own, that he took his life, leaving his creation, Rowley, to walk into the souls and hearts of readers.

I talk to some who remember him, some who claim they cared for him, but in vain. They describe him as slight and boyish in form, but do not understand his pain. They express surprise that he was revealed as a 'forger'.

'Did him no good though, did it? I ask you – forging poems! Where's the sense in that? Forging letters of introduction or money, I can see the profit in that, but poems? He'd have been better off writing honest letters for folk. There's few round here who can write for themselves and a scribe can always scrape a living. Anyway, what's it to you? You a relative or som'at?'

'Of a sort,' I reply.

***

We sit together in the gloom of the small attic. His silhouette is striking but I can scarcely see his features. His voice is quiet and rolls with a soft Bristol accent.

'Have you a sponsor?' *he asks.* 'Writers have to have good sponsors. I was promised. Horace Walpole promised but the promises were seldom kept.'

'No I don't, but I have many subscribers.'

We talk of the parsimony of today's sponsors. Of how they take so much and give so little. Of how they are not content until the work they profess to promote is defiled by association with the foul baseness of their power or fortune.

He turns to face me. I see my own face of twenty years ago as if in a mirror. We talk about the problems of getting anything published, of the resistance in London to anything that comes from the country.

'Bristol could be a place on the moon as far as London people were concerned. And if you speak with an accent like mine they know you're from humble origins and that places you outside their comprehension.'

I want to ask him how and why he died. Had he lost his way in the world of his own creation? Did he die so that Rowley could live? Did he go against the teachings of his own heart? Did he betray himself before God?

'I could not live in the world I had created and I could not live in this one either. My soul lived with Rowley in old Bristol whilst my body starved in London.'

He rises and we walk together down the nave of St Mary Redcliffe, Bristol. Chatterton points out the graceful vaulting of the roof. He takes me to the room above the south porch where he studied the church records. It was here, he explains, that he first met the medieval monk Rowley who took over his life. Rowley sits at his stool writing with great care and concentration. He does not see us.

Chatterton asks about the Gorsedd, *my creation. I tell him of the poets with which I have peopled the bardic tradition, of their collective strength, of the inspiration they afford others. I boast that they are now a force in the world quite free of their creator.*

'Do not let your creation live outside you,' he warns, 'or you will die. Be the centre of your new world if you wish to live. Mark me!'

His voice weakens and slowly his form fades before me. I see only the elderly monk hunched over his work.

***

My health is poor again. I am plagued by headaches and bouts of asthma. My joints creak and my lungs ache. I have sought help. Quack doctors draw my blood with leeches. I live for days on water to purge my system. I attend a clinic in Soho where they send electrical charges through my body. All to no avail. The excellent bottles of sweet laudanum that my friend David Samwell supplies bring sleep but also nightmares, horrid visions of home. In one dream Peggy has died and in another Margaret has breathed her last. One night Ann had fallen into a fire and burnt; another night Taliesin had lost a hand and a foot. I send word urgently to Peggy, begging her to write to me to tell me that my little darlings live. If they are troubled by whooping cough, which is here a great threat, I have recommended a remedy of garlic beaten into a soft pulp in a mortar to which should afterwards be added a little rum and so used to anoint the child's back, soles of the feet and the neck under the chin. I beg her, when she replies, to name the children each in turn for my better assurance. Her answer arrives swiftly.

Dear Ned,

We are alive, though we live but poorly. The children are tolerable in health. Tally is mostly over the fever, Margaret's foot gives her trouble and Ann has pains. Your father grows frail and forgetful and sometimes cries. I am sorely tried with a cough and a tightness of my chest. Otherwise, we are well. Our living is humble and I am reduced to joining the poorest women gathering the fallen grain from the margins following the harvest. This is what you have brought us to. You say that your children are most dear to you, yet this is hard to believe when you prefer to abide in London rather than take your place by our hearth.

My great fear is that you are involved in such concerns that can only heap ill repute on your name and bad fortune on your children. Last Sunday the Reverend John Walters took as his text a verse from Corinthians 15:33: 'Be not deceived: evil companions corrupt good morals.' He did not mention you by name but others in the church did look my way with meaning in their eyes. I so fear the company you keep. I beg you to reflect what will come of making friends with those who would drench their country with blood. I fear you are being led into bad ways. I am in poverty and distress but clear in my conscience.

Your father sends his greetings,

Peggy

***

I am besieged by angry subscribers. Leading their charge is Mrs Nicholl, dressed as one of the whores of Covent Garden with a dirty silk gown, too much powder and her breasts exposed. On her head she wears a statue of her father on horseback. She shouts obscenities demanding the copies she has paid for. I try to explain that the printers... No one listens. Beside her comes an infestation of overdressed gentry with small dogs crawling over, under and through their arms, legs and hair. Preening strumpets and haughty courtiers follow, loaded down with their endless possessions, pointless, gaudy and ostentatious. They wear enormous hats and carry pomanders to drown the stench of the poor.

The Prince of Wales and his cherubs descend on a cloud. The debauchees all applaud. He steps onto firm ground and strikes a ridiculous noble posture awaiting the words of my dedication. There is a silence of expectation. I try again and fail, and try again. I kneel on the filthy ground. He frowns.

I prostrate myself, face down, the filth filling my mouth as I try to speak, 'not deficient in humble respect... it is with the greatest humility... solicit the great favour... permitted to dedicate... fervent supplication to heaven... hand of great benevolence... supplicate myself before you.'

What more can I give?

I have prostituted myself until my body rebels. My stomach heaves and I vomit real words in torrents over his cherubs who squawk and cry and shriek in horror. They pick the words from off their sticky pink flesh and out of their stubby wings. Each word is held up in turn and read with great distaste. I have betrayed myself to them! 'Liberty' reads the first and cries as if whipped. 'Equality' reads the second and screams as if prodded with a hot poker. 'Justice' reads the third and falls into spasms of torment.

A priest steps forward to rid the court of my odious spirit. He calls me to confess that I am a sinner, that I am the Antichrist, that I am at his mercy. If I do not worship the thumbnail of St Nebuchal the Nice, brought from the Holy Land and available to worshippers for silver or gold, he will see me damned. He demands his just tithes. 'You are my lamb,' he cries. 'Let me roast you on a spit.'

The Prince now opens my book but he holds it upside down. He commands me to kneel. 'Remember you are my obedient subject,' he shouts and points at the floor. I do not kneel.

Mrs Nicholl and her debauchees step forward and demand that if I will not kneel I must perform. They command me to recite, to declaim, to walk a tightrope, to jump through hoops, to ride a camel, to imitate a rhinoceros.

'You are our darling rhinoceros,' they chorus, 'our toy, our amusing little poet.'

Generals appear, demanding that if I will not kneel or perform I must be struck through with sabres, peppered with musketfire, shot by a cannon and declared a military hero.

'You are our loyal cannon fodder,' they bellow.

I must declare myself against this torrent or I will become who they say I am. I try but all I hear is the chanting of priests, the cackle of courtiers, the bawling of commands. If I die now, then all I ever worked for will die with me. My children will die. Oh pity me, God. Not my children. Please.

I hear Chatterton in my ear.

'Be the centre of your new world if you wish to live.'

I struggle to stand but the noise is deafening and a great wind blows. I walk to the top of a grassy mound. There is a rock awaiting me. I stumble but do not fall as I mount the rock and face the rising sun. I search in my head for the fragments of verse I have composed which I can use to profess myself part of a new tomorrow, free of kings, priests and fawning courtiers. My voice sounds distant and unreal. I shout into the wind:

Mine is the day so long foretold
By Heaven's illumin'd Bards of Old,

To feel the rage of discord cease
To join the Angels in the songs of peace.

The wind drops. The crowds are still. I spread my arms and shout, 'I am Iolo. I am what I am for all the world to see!'

I fall, but I fall onto a bed of down. Ann, the dancer, is beside me. She wears a costume of silk and silver feathers. She tells me it is time for the masque. It is time to step.

It is time for me to follow my truth once more. I have been driven by the will of others. They have compromised my verse but they cannot compromise the Gorsedd.

Gorsedd, 21 June 1792

I HAVE LAID out the *Gorsedd* on the summit of Primrose Hill. A ring of small stones marks the outer circle or *Cylch Cynghrair*[37] whilst in the centre I have placed the *Maen yr Orsedd*[38] from where I will preside. I have previously rehearsed those who will be initiated into the bardic order. These are David Samwell who will take the bardic name Dafydd Ddu Feddyg; William Owen; and Edward Jones, the self-styled 'King's Bard'. I have also enlisted several members of the Gwyneddigion to assist in the ceremony.

I would have preferred to robe those present according to the traditions of the order, but cost dictates that instead of robes we will make do with coloured armbands. I explain that there are three sections of the order: the Bards of Privilege, who wear light blue symbolising peace; the Druidic Bards, who wear white symbolising truth; and the Ovate Bards, who wear the green of learning. There is no hierarchy. All members of the *Gorsedd* are equal.

The day is bright and clear as we process up the hill. This is as it should be. Ceremonies of the *Gorsedd* are never secret or clandestine. They take place in the open air in the eye of the public when the sun is above the horizon. Some twenty members of the Gwyneddigion are here, plus friends and relations, including

37 Circle of Federation.
38 Throne Stone.

Sarah Owen, anxious as always to support her husband. There are small clusters of the curious, a few children and, to my delight, a reporter from the *Morning Chronicle*.

The *Gorsedd* begins with the rite of the sword. I place a naked blade on the *Maen yr Orsedd*. We stand in a ring to protect the world from the threat it symbolises. It is fundamental to the order that no ceremony may take place whilst a naked weapon is exposed. I raise the sword and hold it horizontal, whilst David Samwell and William Owen sheath it and put it safely to one side.

I proclaim the Bards of the Island of Britain to be the heralds and ministers of peace. It is unlawful for any present to bear arms during the progress of the *Gorsedd*. I ask three times:

'Is there peace?'

To which all present reply: 'Peace.'

I start the recitations with my new composition, 'Ode on the Mythology of the Ancient British Bards'. The verse and all proceedings today are in English, and I have copies available for the correspondent of the *Morning Chronicle*.

The ode describes the sense of fulfilment and transformation I felt on being initiated into the bardic order years before. How I had turned my back on the evil of this world. How the bardic principles of peace, equality and love of God are potent answers to the tribulations of life.

I call on all present to share the love of liberty celebrated through verse.

Come LIBERTY! With all thy sons attend!
We'll raise to thee the manly verse,
The deeds inspir'd by thee rehearse;

I praise Wilberforce and look forward to the end of slavery.

Great WILBERFORCE! for thee they bring
Yon chariot of th' ETERNAL KING!

I praise the new enlightenment in the United States.

New time appears! Thou glorious WEST!
How hails the world thy rising Sun!

But, following the advice of Joseph Johnson, I am oblique in
my prediction of the fall of kings.

Now glancing o'er the rolls of HEAV'N,
I see, with transport see, the day,
When from this world, OPPRESSION driv'n
With gnashing fangs flies far away.

I watch Edward Jones, the self-styled 'King's Bard', whilst I
recite these verses. His brows are furrowed as if uncertain as to
their propriety.

David Samwell and William Owen recite their compositions
in turn and I initiate them by the award of the appropriate
ribbon. When it is time for Edward Jones to step forward to
recite, he does not. I invite him once more but he remains rooted
to the spot. What is the problem? Can the man be affected by
nerves? Has he lost the poem he is to declaim? We wait for a full
minute in silence. Nothing happens. I lose patience and begin
the closing *Gorsedd* prayer.

I declare the ceremony at an end and prepare to lead the
procession back down the hill towards Hampstead. I would
prefer to be outside the circle before I demand an explanation
from the 'King's Bard'. To my amazement Edward Jones suddenly
recovers his voice and starts to sing 'God Save the King'. I am
furious. This is the very last tune that would be appropriate to

this place and this ceremony. I will not have that Prince of Blood praised through the singing of that vile murdering bloodthirsty song which demands the slaughter of innocents to extend his dominions. I command the snivelling harpist to cease. He ignores me. Several in the crowd have taken up the tune. Is this a rebellion?

'It does not mean anything,' hisses David Samwell in my ear. 'It's so often the way in which anything ends; any concert or performance. I don't think anyone realises the significance.'

William Owen is restraining me on the other side.

'Even if he is doing it out of mischief, it would be dangerous to be seen refusing to sing 'God Save the King' at a time like this.'

They are both right. By this point the imperial dirge has thankfully ended and no one appears to have the appetite for a second verse.

This will not be forgiven.

I seek out the reporter from the *Chronicle* who has a number of questions. He asks if there will be another *Gorsedd* at the next equinox. I assure him that there will. A competition has been proposed for an English-language ode telling the story of Rhita Gawr the giant. This chief of the Ancient Britons was a famous slayer of despots and kings.

1 3

Southey, Coleridge, Evans and Louis XVI

R OBERT SOUTHEY IS reading to me from drafts of his epic
poem *Madoc*. The language is magnificent and his style
is suited to epic events. He has previously asked for my help
in researching the history of Madog ab Owain. Following
the death of his father, Madog's older brothers fought for the
throne. Madog sought to escape the internecine strife by sailing
westwards until he reached the New World and began to explore
the Mississippi. So far so good, but then in his poem Robert has
described Madog and his party coming across Aztecs and being
revolted by their practice of human sacrifice.

'There is no historical basis for any of that,' I protest. 'Do
we even know that Aztecs existed on that continent? Don't they
belong in the South Americas?'

Robert does not answer. Instead he explains that his poem
is about rescuing the noble savage from superstition and
religious exploitation: 'A gentle tribe of savages delivered from
priesthood.'

'By violence? By going to war against Aztecs?'

'Yes, but to establish a society free of priests and superstition…
in the longer term.'

I snort. 'Wars are always justified by those who propose
them on the grounds that they will bring peace – in the longer

term. Instead, they bring slaughter and pestilence. Wars breed resentment in the hearts of the defeated and arrogance in the hearts of the victorious. Their evil heritage survives for centuries. War can never be a healer.'

He looks at his papers with embarrassment. We sit in silence. He is abashed by my outburst. I must learn to control my tongue. I do not ask about his and Coleridge's plans for a new colony in America. I have been warned by the Bowdlers that Coleridge now wants to move the project to Wales. Hardly a country free of priests and tyrants. I doubt their motives. I need to be free of these distractions.

***

In a different coffee house I break the news to John Evans that I will not be leading the expedition to the Mississippi. I express earnest apologies and give my reasons. These are numerous and sincere: my health, the importance of bringing my book to publication, my bardic duties, my researches on behalf of the Gwyneddigion, my work for the Unitarians, my political involvement. The list is long but must sound pathetic to his ears. It does not even include the protection of my poor neglected family.

He nods and admits he was expecting such an announcement. He tells me I am too old and too immersed '*yng ngwallgofrwydd Llundain*'[39] to be able or prepared to make such a trip into the unknown. He appears neither surprised nor particularly dismayed. He tells me that, if needs be, he is determined to make the trip alone. All he asks is my blessing and the details of any arrangements I have already made. He is calmer than I, quite relaxed in his decision.

---

39   In the madness of London.

I promise him all the support I can provide, organisational, journalistic, financial, moral. I ask him why he is so determined to venture on such a perilous mission.

'Mr Williams, you have done many great and wonderful things in your life: poetry, history, politics, Bardism and much more. I have achieved little, apart from helping my father and learning to read and write. I am a humble servant of God. I wish, whilst I am young and strong, to accomplish something which will be worthy of the people of Waunfawr – and of Wales. I will not give up this opportunity to serve my Lord and honour my country.'

I am greatly moved and reach for his hand. I suspect he is embarrassed but he will have to suffer. We stare across the table at each other in splendid silence. I tell him that I am honoured to count him as my friend and will visit Waunfawr at the first opportunity to thank his parents for bearing him and to thank the community that raised him for giving Wales such a champion.[40] I should add that I bless him for releasing me from an impossible promise.

***

The King is dead!

I sit quietly and digest this news. The French have decapitated their vile Louis. He was the great slimy serpent, the slithering viper, the fat glutinous toad that squatted on the lives of his people. He was the gorged ogre who seized food from the mouths of children and played courtly games with the bones of the newly starved. He was the perfumed, coiffured, coutured

---

40 John Evans did explore the Mississippi, travelling two thousand miles to the upper reaches of the Missouri, but found no Welsh-speaking Indians. He died of a fever in New Orleans in 1799.

monster whom the French people did well to identify as their prime enemy. This fiend, this abomination, deserved to spend his remaining days in penance contemplating his crimes. He should have been sentenced to a lifetime of scrubbing floors in the cottages of the poor, digging cesspits, carrying coals and cleaning slaughterhouses, but he should never have been killed!

I weep. Not for the vile Louis but for the people of France. Once they believe that bloodshed is a cure, a means of reconciliation and a road to peace, they are doomed. Great evil will come of this act. The worst is that they have sacrificed their claim to fraternity. If any life is cheap, even that of despised Louis, then we are all cattle.

14

Poems, Lyric and Pastoral

T HE PRINTING PROCEEDS, but at the slowest pace imaginable. Whenever I visit Mr Newbury's print shop it appears that some other pressing priority has caused my work to be put aside for another day. Every Wednesday, the presses are fully given over to printing *The Gentleman's Magazine*. Other work, which he deems urgent, such as playbills or notices of sales, have the next priority. I suspect I should not have announced my intention of transferring the distribution of the book to Joseph Johnson. Mr Newbury just shrugged his shoulders at this news as if to wish good riddance to the whole venture, but he shows no urgency in achieving this end.

The delay in publication is causing unease amongst some subscribers. There is even a rumour that I am suspected of planning to defect with the subscription money to a hiding place on the Mississippi river. Would that there was any subscription money left!

When I remonstrate over the delays, Mr Newbury tells me that he will ask some of his staff to work into the late evening. He tells me that it is customary to ease proceedings along on such late shifts by providing free ale, porter and gin at the client's expense. This costs me four shillings. Some progress is made.

When I think we are at last in sight of the end, Mr Newbury informs me that we have exhausted the stocks of paper purchased for the purpose. I protest that this is his oversight, but he insists that the quantity originally ordered was correct. The additional pages mean there is a significant shortfall. He can obtain paper of the same colour, weight and texture as soon as I furnish the thirty-eight shillings this will cost.

I tell him that I do not have thirty-eight pennies let alone shillings. He is unmoved. With unnecessary directness he orders work to stop on my account and other clients' printing to occupy the presses. I am at my wits' end. I write in desperation to some of my backers explaining the situation. All the replies I receive tell me that I have mismanaged my affairs. Mr Curre's reply is curt. If he has to face a loss, this is regrettable, but I cannot possibly expect him to throw more money after bad. One letter alone provides salvation. Miss Henrietta Bowdler writes on behalf of her mother. The elderly Mrs Bowdler is too unwell to put pen to paper but encloses eight guineas. They are truly sorry to hear of my distress and sincerely wish that I may find means to extricate myself without delay. They also pray that events be brought to a swift conclusion so that I may return to my family whose well-being is of great concern to them.

So there are good, trusting, generous people in this vile city after all.

***

January 1794, and *Poems, Lyric and Pastoral* is complete. I say complete rather than published, for the bookbinders sew a score at a time. I distribute these twenty when they are ready, collecting additional payments which, in turn, enable me to pay to bind another score and so on. It is a great relief to be able to deliver copies to subscribers whose patience deserves my gratitude. The Bowdlers are the first.

Second recipients are the reviewers of the London journals:

The Analytical Review, The Critical Review, The Gentleman's Magazine and *The Monthly Review*. The success or failure of my book will depend crucially on their reports. If positive, I may expect the book to reach a second edition which would be highly profitable. To my great relief the reviews are good, sometimes excellent. *The Analytical Review* writes:

> From the simple stock of his own observation and feelings, he writes pleasing pastorals, songs and descriptions of nature; moralises agreeably; and sometimes pours forth animated strains in the cause of freedom.

The Critical Review is equally appreciative, if patronising in tone. It praises the pastoral poems as being 'equal to any in the English language' and judges this particularly remarkable from a writer suffering the disadvantages of my background. None of the reviewers appear able to analyse my innovations in introducing internal rhyme schemes in the Welsh manner into English verse, but then I had not expected perception of a high standard.

The only really negative comments are directed towards my footnotes in which I draw attention to the deficiencies of contemporary poetry. *The Critical Review* judges me guilty of 'strokes of petulant sarcasm which greatly blemish the general tenor of his productions'. Fools! Nevertheless, I am pleased.

It is a while longer before I begin to receive the reactions of my subscribers. William Owen is the very first, but then he has been the willing audience for so many drafts that the final volume must have felt familiar. David Samwell is ecstatic in his praise. He claims not to have slept the night he received his copy, being awake till the dawn reading and rereading the sections concerning Bardism.

I had feared that some readers, less sympathetic to the cause of liberty, might be surprised by the sentiments of the second volume, particularly the 'Ode on converting a sword into a pruning hook'. Even so, I am stung by the acidity of the letter from Mrs Nicholl, my (former) benefactor, the daughter of Viscount Ashbrook. She writes in the third person as she cannot bear to imagine us having any personal contact ever again.

'Had Mrs Nicholl known Mr Williams' principles, she would not have subscribed to any of his writings, for she would not purchase poetry written by a republican.'

I am derided as a Jacobin, which has become a popular form of abuse amongst anti-libertarians. I write her a long and considered reply which she does not deserve and will probably not understand.

There are others in the same vein. An anonymous contributor to *The Critical Review* tells me 'to stay in my proper sphere… retire into a remote corner of Wales where [I] never may be seen or heard of more'.

I am not displeased by the fierceness of some of these reactions. I am proud to be perceived as a banner bearer for freedom. I am proud not to have been sucked into that vortex of conformity where weak poets turn grey and die. Mrs Nicholl's anger gives me new strength.

Peggy is delighted by news of the publication and demands my return home. I disappoint her as I still have much work distributing copies and collecting subscriptions. I also report that I have high hopes of a second printing or of selling the copyright for a considerable sum. That I cannot do from Flemingston.

I receive a speedy reply which scorches the paper on which it is written.

Husband,
You do me no credit to take me for such a fool. You have written the poems and we have waited for many long months

and years for them to be printed. We have endured with patience. Your children need their father. I see no reason why others cannot handle the business matters you refer to. I fear the truth is that you remain out of pride and vanity. You wish to strut about like a cockerel on the dung heap glorying in the fame your book has brought. Remember Matthew chapter 23, verse 12: 'And whosoever shall exalt himself shall be abased; and he that shall humble himself shall be exalted.'

Is this how you honour your marriage vows?

Your loving,

Peggy

***

I write back enclosing two guineas, a petticoat worth eighteen shillings and printed cotton material for a dress. I urge her to be more temperate in her words to her husband. I explain that I see the establishment of the *Gorsedd* as the way in which I may achieve my ambition of not quitting this life without having been, in some degree, the benefactor of mankind. I tell her she has a sacred duty to support her husband in his great work.

15

The second Gorsedd

T HE WINTER EQUINOX approaches and with it the next
Gorsedd ceremony. I have been discussing the arrangements
with Samuel and Owen in a tavern in the Strand before
scurrying back to my cold garret in Holborn. Even that feels
a haven compared to the badly-lit streets. Britain is now at
war with France and the mood of London is threatening and
febrile. Groups of thugs and bully boys take advantage of the
times, roaming the streets, supposedly patrolling for Jacobins or
republican sympathisers. They hunt blasphemously in the name
of the Lord, choosing those they waylay at random. The penalty
for being caught varies according to the amount of alcohol
they have consumed. One may escape or receive a beating or be
murdered without the perpetrators fearing punishment.

I am accosted by such a group the wrong side of Shoe Lane.
They are led by a butcher who waves a meat cleaver to reinforce
his arguments. I am pushed to a wall and held whilst a dozen
ruffians chant,

'Blast your eyes, cry Church and King, damn your soul!'

I say nothing. This angers their leader who raises the cleaver
which, on close inspection, appears to have recently been used.
With this above my head he shouts,

'Down on your marrow bones, blast ye!'

I kneel without hesitation. This is not an occasion to be over
principled.

'In the name of God, cry Church and King!'

He waits. I will do so if the alternative is that cleaver in the top of my skull but I try other tactics first. I recite several Welsh children's lullabies at great speed in a terrified, beseeching tone that requires no pretence:

Hai gel i'r dre, hai gel adre,
Ceffyl John bach cyn cynted â nhwnte,
Hei'r ceffyl bach i ffair y Bont-faen,
Cam, Cam, Cam.[41]

I add for good measure, 'Church *sans* King, Church *sans* King.' I trust I appear quite without deceit?

He looks around his followers.

'Dutch?' he inquires, 'and an obvious idiot?'

They all agree. I am released and they move on in search of more obvious English treachery. When they have passed out of sight a man crosses the road and helps me to my feet.

'*Da iawn 'ngwas i,*' he reassures me, '*Twyllest ti nhw'n llwyr.*'[42]

This is no light-hearted encounter but we embrace and laugh with a mixture of relief and hysteria. I know not if I should exalt in my escape or allow myself to be cast down into the deepest depression by the foolery of such men.

***

As to the *Gorsedd* plans, the 'King's Bard' continues to give us cause for concern. Edward Jones failed to complete his initiation on Primrose Hill for reasons known only to him. He continues to use the term Bard as a title despite being unqualified to do

---

41 Hey ho for the town, hey ho for home, / John's little steed as early as any, / Trot little steed to the Cowbridge fair, / Step, Step, Step.

42 Well done, my boy. You have fooled them completely.

so according to the rules of the *Gorsedd*. Tonight we agreed that he would be presented with a requirement to complete his initiation at the next *Gorsedd* or cease to use the title. He will be presented with a set of alternative tasks: a bardic composition, a prayer or a learned discourse.

I raise, in William Owen's presence, the question of admitting women to the *Gorsedd*. I explain that I have had applications from two ladies who would wish to be admitted. One of these is none other than Sarah, William's wife. There is a brief discussion of precedent according to the laws of Hywel Dda. No objection can be found. I suggest that, in the circumstances, I should convey the conclusion to Sarah to avoid any suggestion, or possible accusation, of nepotism on William Owen's part.

***

Sarah is holding her son, the young Aneirin, on her knee whilst we talk. Their Pentonville home is not large and this ever-growing boy makes it feel smaller. At the same time the house feels immeasurably livelier. During my earlier stay here I always felt as if William and Sarah were playing at being a family, like a pair of under-rehearsed actors, unsure of their lines or moves. Aneirin has banished such awkwardness, causing his mother to react spontaneously and speedily as he toddles about the room threatening to demolish all and everything of value.

She hands the infant over to the same large maid whose humour has also benefited from tending to an inquisitive child. Maid and infant disappear in the direction of the kitchen where Aneirin will be bribed with sugar. I tell Sarah that motherhood appears to suit her.

'Possibly. He is a darling child and yes, I do feel happier as a mother than I had ever expected. But it is very exhausting and I have never been strong. I would not survive without the help of a maid as efficient as Phoebe.'

I tell her that her application to be admitted to the *Gorsedd* has been approved. She looks slightly startled, expresses her thanks and surprise.

'I feared that I would have to speak Welsh and write a poem in Welsh, neither of which things I am capable.'

I explain that she will not be confirmed as a Druidic Bard or a Bard of Privilege but as an Ovate or learning member. This still leaves it open for her to apply for these divisions in the future if her skills have so improved. I explain that I intend to initiate my young son Taliesin in the coming *Gorsedd*. He too will be an Ovate and I anticipate his applying for Privilege status years hence when, as a young man, he has completed his bardic apprenticeship.

'So may we also introduce Aneirin? William would be so delighted. Our child already has a very bardic name I am told. This is all so very, very important to my husband as you know.'

Was her application only to please her husband?

'By no means. How could you think such a thing? Women are permitted to have minds of their own Edward, even if some men wish otherwise. Unless you change your mind about admitting me I shall be a proud and faithful member who shares and celebrates the values you stand for. I am conscious I do so at a time when such values are under threat and much needed.'

I apologise for doubting her conviction. I stay longer than I had intended. Sarah asks many questions about the original sixth-century Aneirin after whom her son is named. When I rise to leave she bids me stay. Her tone is urgent. Her manner reverts to the shy and deferential Sarah I remember from our first encounters, apparently fearing my reaction.

'Please do not be angry with me Edward, but I wish to speak privately over matters that concern me greatly.'

She twists a lace handkerchief nervously.

'Let me be frank. I am increasingly worried for the safety of you all – my husband and the rest of the London bards. You must see – William is in some ways an innocent. He thinks the best of everyone and finds it hard to believe that anyone could be so foolish as to regard the *Gorsedd* as a threat. He is right, of course; any reasonable examination reveals an institution devoted to peace and a threat to no one. But I am worldlier than William and understand that headstrong men seldom listen to reasonable argument. I heard with pleasure of the way you dealt with the Church and King ruffians. But not all enemies will be so stupid or so vulnerable to manipulation. I am more concerned by the activities of the government whose spies are everywhere.'

I try to reassure her but she will not be stilled. Had this conversation come from any other direction I would have left by now, but I have built a high regard for the intelligence and directness of Sarah Owen. She is well read. Her frail form houses a powerful intellect and determined will which reminds me of my mother.

'Edward, the government intends to suspend Habeas Corpus! You realise what that means? They will not need a warrant before they lock anyone up. They will be able to hold people indefinitely without trial. The King's declaration makes it possible for people to be transported just for saying the wrong things.'

'Why should you think that we are targets?'

'Edward, if you think that you are not, then I am truly worried. Anyone can be a target, just by saying something which your enemies interpret as treasonous. It's important not to give the government any excuse.'

'You clearly have something in mind?'

She hesitates and reaches for the book on her side table. Out of it she produces a paper covered in my handwriting. It is one of a series of satirical letters addressed to the King. These have not been printed, but handwritten copies circulate. She also flourishes an essay of mine, *Demophobia*. This single sheet warns of an outbreak of a medical complaint known as 'King's Evil', a canine disorder resulting from contact with a royal 'German Whelp'. No cure is known apart from the dispatching of all such dangerous animals to Botany Bay. This essay has been secretly printed by Joseph Johnson for distribution amongst trusted friends only.

'Please do not mistake me, Edward. These are highly satirical and I enjoyed every word. You are a very clever writer – but you must confess that to be caught with these would be disastrous. Can I persuade you to move whatever copies you have from your lodging, which Pitt's spies would be certain to search were you to be accused?'

I do not like being told what to do, even by Sarah. She senses as much.

'Please do not be angry with me. I speak only out of a genuine concern for the men I love, and whom I fear to be in more danger than they will admit.'

'If you fear this contact so much, how is it that you are prepared, apparently anxious, to become a member of this "dangerous" *Gorsedd* and put your young son in danger's way?'

'Because I reason that an organisation that numbers amongst its members frail young women and young children cannot appear threatening even to a government as fearful as Mr Pitt's. I hope to help keep William and his dearest friend safer than might otherwise be the case.'

'So it is a tactic only.'

'You have apologised already for suggesting that. But it is true that I don't want Aneirin to see his father bound for Botany Bay.'

***

Against my will I am persuaded that the winter equinox will be celebrated not on Primrose Hill, which is judged too exposed and distant, but on the Long Field behind the British Museum. Although held at midday, the light is poor and the rain steady. It does not extinguish my fire. I have been waiting for my opportunity to declaim the ode which so upset Mrs Nicholl, her fellow royalists and those who support this bloody, wasteful war.

Ode on converting a sword into a pruning hook

Aloud the trump of Reason calls;
The nations hear! The worlds attend!
Detesting now the craft of Kings,
Man from his hand the weapon flings;
Hides it in whelming deeps afar,
And learns no more the skills of war.

I care not who hears me. I will not bow to that infernal goddess prudence. There is very warm blood in my heart and every drop of it is solemnly dedicated to the cause of 'truth'.

16

A time of turbulence

O WAIN MYFYR HAS, to his credit, set a clear direction for the Gwyneddigion in troubled times. I hear him declare to a full meeting that the Society's goal must be, '*Rhyddid mewn gwlad ac Eglwys*'.[43] I believe him sincere but fear that he is compromised by his involvement in the worlds of commerce and finance. It would take a man of superhuman strength to stay untainted in the position he occupies.

At Gwyneddigion meetings I detect factions. For years the fault lines have been visible. Whilst Owain has sponsored eisteddfod medals for poems in praise of liberty, the winners have too often been faithful royalists who condemn democracy. There are far too many who are content to embrace Welshness for one evening a month but spend the rest of their lives bowing obediently to any earl, marquis, baron or blue-blooded baboon with title and land. In short, they are more compromised than Owain Myfyr but in their cases willingly.

The advent of my *Gorseddau* has been the occasion for the fault lines to become visible cracks and unbridgeable fissures. When I recited 'Ode on converting a sword into a pruning hook' it was clear who was with me and who preferred to sulk in corners whispering, 'God Save the King'. David Samwell has warned me to be suspicious of several. I receive a letter from him with an afterthought scrawled along the edge of the page:

---

43   Freedom in state and Church.

Iorwerth, despise that foolish harper
He's a little better than a sharper.

He refers to Edward Jones who still titles himself the 'King's Bard' on the basis of providing entertainment in the royal nursery and publishing some unoriginal collections of Welsh songs. He is a prime example of one who derives whatever prestige they enjoy from their role as obedient, fawning, drooling lapdogs of our vile ruling class.

Enough of the Gwyneddigion. They were ever whimsical, then became ridiculous and are now detestable. I have other places I can visit for intelligent discourse. The Unitarians provide religious discussion to my taste. The Caradogion Society addresses the problems of our age fearlessly on Saturdays in the Bull's Head at Walbrook. Then there is the London Corresponding Society. This society of craftsmen, shopkeepers and small traders suffer an excess of shoemakers who hammer their points home relentlessly. I would prefer more watchmakers, who talk with precision. We discuss the reform of Parliament and the better representation of working-class people. My voice is raised in praise of the skilled worker and against the practices of the monopolising merchant, the slave-possessing planter, the land-engrossing farmer, the all-grasping manufacturer, the blood-sucking usurer or the common purse-proud master.

Lest I should be allowed to take Sarah's warning too lightly, I am shaken by the arrest and conviction of the Reverend William Winterbotham, an assistant minister at a Baptist church in Plymouth. His crime was to deliver two sermons of great moderation which I seek and read. He told his flock, 'Take no doctrine on trust; you have the Scriptures in your hands, use them as the touchstone of truth.' For this intelligent and helpful advice he is fined £200 and sentenced to four years in Newgate gaol in London; the most foul of all the prisons of England. I will not be cowed. I present myself as his visitor and fellow. I sign the official Newgate visitors' book as 'Edward Williams: Bard of Liberty.'

The gaoler is a mass of white superfluous flesh with a small mouth in a piggish face out of which emanates a thin callous voice. 'Bard of Liberty?'

'Yes.'

'Then, Mr Bard of Liberty, understand that the only liberty allowed you here will be to walk out the way you came in.'

It could be worse.

'I wish no Bard of Liberty may ever meet with worse treatment than being told to walk out of a prison.'

I enjoyed that.

***

Thomas Spence runs a radical bookshop in High Holborn called the Hive of Liberty. I have become a frequent customer, enjoying the pamphlets he produces and the manner in which he refuses to be cowed into moderation. He greets me with the greeting of the French Revolution, 'Citizen!', delivered in a broad Newcastle upon Tyne accent. He tells me how he was dragged from his bookshop on no fewer than four occasions by Bow Street Runners and arrested for seditious libel. Each time he was released but expects that one day soon they will charge him. I am not alone in displaying bravado and courage in the face of intimidation and threats.

His publications aim not to inform the modulated debate of the educated but to incite the multitude. I am well-practised in the art of composing scurrilous anti-royalist satires. For Thomas Spence I write a series of anti-King pamphlets. As all his publications are anonymous, I sign myself, 'Wicked Welsh

Bard at the sign of the Golden Leek, Liberty Square'. How many of those can there be in London?

I will not have dealings with the coward compromise. I involve myself openly in anti-war and anti-slavery campaigns. We visit the counting-houses and warehouses where slave traders do business, and interrogate them as to the morality of their practices. Abuse or physical threats are common. Often we are threatened darkly with retribution from 'higher authority'.

These activities have further enhanced my name in radical circles as a leveller and Jacobin. I have become a regular guest at Joseph Johnson's dinners. The quiet bookseller holds these fine affairs monthly. They are fine in the sense of the quality of the guests and the high level of discourse. The food makes no pretence to be other than simple fare and I am all the more comfortable for that. This appeals to the puritan tastes of Henrietta Bowdler who attends together with authors, Nonconformist ministers, anti-slavery campaigners, booksellers and academics. Whilst the food is plain the discourse is frequently so rich as to keep us at table until cockcrow.

Tonight, I suggest the constitution of the ancient *Gorsedd* as a potential model for an egalitarian, democratic government freed from the antique idolatry of kings, nobles, pomposity and imagined greatness. I am applauded.

***

A letter from Peggy in high anguish. Not her usual worries about money, the children or even my safety, but dismay over accounts circulating amongst the gossips and slandermongers of Penllyn. She writes:

Dear Ned,
It was Elizabeth Davis who asked me if the reports that she

had heard of you be true or not. If they were true then I was greatly to be pitied and no good would come of it. When I asked what reports she spoke of she looked away as if afraid to voice such an enormity. I had to hold her arm and pinch her before she would say that the word amongst the men was that my husband is guilty of treasonous correspondence and makes common cause with the most bloodthirsty of the French who are sworn to kill King George with their own hands. They report that even now you are in Paris with Thomas Paine assisting the Jacobins in planning revolution that will see the blood and terror of the guillotine on the streets of London. I told her that this was all a lie, and that those who spread it should be made to repent before the altar three Sundays in a row. She protested that she repeated only what the men were saying. And, did I know for certain where my husband might be? Send me word that I may silence these evil tongues.

Affectionately yours,

Peggy

I reply at once that she should believe none of these tales. I laugh at such lies and so should she. How can a man maintain a bright character when so many endeavour to besmirch it with fanciful slander? To make my point I send a printed sheet of my 'Ode on converting a sword into a pruning hook'. This contains the severest things that I ever wrote against government and not a single exhortation to violence.

***

Two Scottish Unitarian ministers, Thomas Muir and Thomas Fyshe, have been tried and sentenced to seven years transportation for writing a leaflet calling for universal suffrage and protesting against the war taxes. To express my solidarity I send them a copy of *Poems, Lyric and Pastoral*. I am astonished to receive a reply from Australia thanking me for the gift and welcoming my support.

With such people being arrested how do I stay at liberty? I have published many strong pieces attacking the government. I wonder if the presence of the Prince of Wales as a sponsor of my poems makes the authorities cautious.

There are other voices, apart from Sarah, warning me of the dangers I am running. The loudest is Peggy's, who writes weekly pleading with me to avoid putting myself in the way of danger. She begs me to return home for my own sake and for the sake of my family. Henrietta, her sisters and her mother implore me to leave London for the same reasons. There is no doubting the danger. In my letters I protest that I am working towards a second edition of *Poems*. This is no longer true. Joseph Johnson tells me that my reputation as a republican and Jacobin has greatly reduced the potential to attract new readers. My pamphleteering earns me infamy and friends but no money. The mild-mannered publisher suggests I write more on the history of Bardism as a means of promoting libertarian values from behind a camouflage of antiquarianism.

***

I sit with David Samwell before a good fire in the Bull's Head.

'Why do you not go home?' asks the naval surgeon. 'You are too well known here for safety.'

'I still have work to do.'

He leans forward to poke the coals before responding.

'I suspect you cannot help yourself! It is good to be in London at such a time. I know I feel more alive at this moment than I have ever felt before. We are at the centre of history.'

'That is true of both of us.'

'Yes, but you are in greater danger and I fear the sensation fires your blood. Danger heightens the senses more than laudanum and is just as hard to do without.'

We lean back in our chairs whilst I weigh his words. I think of Peggy and the children I have not seen for so long.

'Is it that you want to be tested before you leave London?' he queries.

'I do not understand.'

'Maybe you wish for martyrdom. Do you feel it fitting that you should be gaoled or even transported for your beliefs?'

'I do not.'

'Even so, I think that you are thrilled by flying closer and closer to the flame. You still crave to snatch a supreme moment of triumph without burning your wings. Be warned, Ned. The dangers are real. For every good friend, you have two determined enemies and the fire burns hot.'

17

The Crown
and Anchor

I AM AT the Crown and Anchor where nearly a thousand people
have paid seven shillings and sixpence for a grand dinner and
celebration to mark the release from custody of three members
of the London Corresponding Society: Thomas Hardy, Horne
Tooke and John Thelwall. The government accused them of
treason for campaigning to reform Parliament and introduce
universal suffrage. The defence pointed out that even the Prime
Minister had, at times in his life, campaigned for the reform of
Parliament. Pitt is forced to appear and cuts a sad, fumbling
figure as he protests himself 'unable to recall' or 'devoid of any
recollection' of meetings that are a matter of public record. The
case is dismissed.

I have been asked to compose and sing a celebration piece at
the dinner. The result is 'Trial by Jury, The Grand Palladium of
British Liberty'. I rise to sing:

Come hither ye Spies and Informers Of State
With Consciences offer'd for sale.
Come hither and all your achievements relate
Whilst Ridicule joins in the tale,
Or will ye, disgrac'd, to your PERJURER throng,
Nor Memory wish to possess?

Then haste gnash your fangs whilst we call for the song
Of Triumph's exulting success!

I look at the packed benches who roar with pleasure and demand refrains and choruses again and again. I believe I can see the spy in the green coat roaring out the chorus.

William Owen sits on my right. He congratulates me heartily. As we eat he conveys Sarah's apologies. Aneirin has been unwell. William is nevertheless charged with a message. Nothing written, he explains with a grin.

'Sarah said she did not want to add to the stock of potentially incriminating evidence.'

He chews his celebratory beef before adding,

'She worries too much but she is convinced that this failure by the government will only make them more dangerous. In the case of Hardy, Tooke and Thelwall they believed the law would do as they wished and so they failed to prepare a good case. She reasons that now they will be more careful to gather evidence before accusing those they wish to silence. She has made me dispose of anything that might be used to prove treasonous conspiracy. She tells me she has urged you to do the same. Have you?'

At this great celebration of liberty we are forced to talk in whispers like guilty men.

'I have stuffed a large tin box with papers of the sort and intend to dispose of it shortly, although I am uncertain where to send it for the best.'

'There. I told her you would have things under control.'

William Pitt and the Privy Council

I AM ARRESTED on my way home. A pair of oversized Bow Street Runners step from either side of an alleyway, grab an arm each and growl something threatening but incomprehensible.

I ask the reason for my detention but the officers are not conversational. I am marched the mile or so through Covent Garden to the office of the High Constable. Here I am left for the night in a cell with five others. After a cold, noisy twelve hours disturbed by the nightmares of one of my cellmates, the door opens and I am reunited with my companions in blue who march me along the Thames to Whitehall. I feel my time of trial has truly arrived when we reach Downing Street and a sergeant steps forth to take me into his custody.

I am ushered through an impressive double door into a dark-panelled room. I face a long table behind which sit three men in periwigs. Behind them stand two clerks and, in the corner, an armed soldier.

'Good afternoon, Mr Williams. Would you like to take a seat?'

The polite voice comes from the middle periwig.

'You are Edward Williams, occasionally referred to as the Bard of Liberty?'

'I am.'

I wait for the introductions to continue but the middle periwig starts shuffling papers instead. I feel entitled to ask,

'May I have the pleasure of knowing to whom am I speaking?'

I suspect I know but for the sake of politeness.

The middle periwig looks up, slightly annoyed.

'Certainly, sir. I am William Pitt, the Prime Minister.'

I will not be cowed.

He gestures in turn to the periwigs left and right. 'This is Lord Grenville, the Secretary of State for Foreign Affairs, and this is Henry Dundas, the Secretary of State for War. Together we form a committee of the Privy Council, a body trusted to advise the sovereign, in this instance, on potential sedition and threats to His Majesty and his dominions.'

'I thank you for your reply. I am Edward Williams, by rite and privilege, Bard of the Island of Britain. My bardic name is Iolo Morganwg.'

The Prime Minister sighs deeply. I suspect I am one of a long series of interrogations that they have conducted today and the strain is showing.

'I see. Thank you, Mr Bard. William, carry on will you? I have not the strength.'

The Secretary of State for Foreign Affairs looks unprepared. He reaches for a copy of *Poems, Lyric and Pastoral* and flicks through the pages.

'Philip! Where's the passage you showed me?'

The secretary at his shoulder leaps forward and hastily identifies the page.

'Oh yes,' breathes his master and reads badly,

Detesting now the craft of Kings,
Man from his hand the weapon flings,
Hides it in whelming deeps afar,
And learns no more the skill of war.

His voice has a triumphant note.

'There, sir, in four lines you profess detestation of our King George and a cowardly refusal to act in the face of the barbarism of the French. And Philip here found other similar pieces. I suggest you are plotting to undermine the will of the nation to resist the French invader. What say you?'

I point out that I am writing in the global mode, referring to the eventual evolution of the whole of mankind once we have learnt from the follies and foolishness of us all as sinners. The reference to the craft of kings is similarly universal and is in no way a comment or reflection on the skills of His Highness George III. I point out that there is a gracious dedication to the Prince in the frontispiece of the book which has the approval of His Majesty's officials. Would I have sought royal approval if the intention of the book was to traduce His Majesty? I'm certain that Lord Grenville is not suggesting that His Majesty would be so lacking in judgment as to endorse a book whose intention was to damage the monarchy? Is he?

Lord Grenville looks confused. 'Philip! Am I?'

'No, sir, you are not.'

'Good. No more questions. Henry, your turn.'

I look anxiously at the small pile of papers before the Secretary of State for War. They have obviously raided my garret. The box of the most incriminating papers has not been sent away and I shudder in the expectation that they will produce my mock letters to the King or copies of the essay comparing him to a mad dog. If they produce any of these...

To my surprise and relief the minister lifts only an anonymous pamphlet and squints at the print.

'Are you by any chance the same Welsh bard as the...'

He is having problems. His eyesight is poor.

'... as the Wicked Welsh Bard at the sign of the Golden Leek, Liberty Square? Well, are you?'

'No.'

'Prove it.'

How do I prove a negative?

'I am a professional writer. I keep a wife and three children on the proceeds of my labours. Whilst the income from being a Welsh bard is poor, it is an income. The writers of scurrilous pamphlets, such as those you hold in your hand, would be paid nothing for their efforts. I could never afford such luxury.'

'Henry!'

The other secretary leaps forward. 'Yes, sir.'

'What else do we have?'

'We have the reports, sir? The first-hand accounts of conversations and indiscretions.'

'Produced by...?'

'We should not say, sir, at least in the presence of the suspect.'

'What do they tell us?'

'That in the opinion of our loyal informant...'

I have no doubt as to the identity of their 'loyal informant'. I will miss no opportunity to condemn that sad, disloyal, talentless, simpering, spineless, sycophantic harpist. He wears his Welsh identity only as a guarantee of his subservience, of his desire to fawn on any English aristocrat. Now, like a whelp attempting to please his master, he will betray his friends for a hambone. This blunderhead may have some wit at his fingers' ends but where his head is placed he has not a single atom.

'... that Edward Williams has tendencies which might be termed disloyal.'

The Prime Minister is roused from his slumber. He expostulates.

'For God's sake, gentlemen! If we spend our time interviewing every subject who "might have disloyal tendencies" we will still be sitting here when hell freezes over. We are looking for proof of treasonous collaboration. Thank you, Mr Williams... Bard of whatever you are. You are free to go.'

He adds as an afterthought, 'And you may take your documents with you.'

The Prime Minister bundles up the various papers and pushes them across the table. I wish to prolong this moment of victory.

'As these papers have been seized without my consent, I request that they be returned to my lodgings by the men who removed them.'

I enjoy the look of discomfiture, amazement and frustration on the face of the Prime Minister. He plainly itches to kick me into the street and shove the papers down my throat.

I look into the face of a very sick weary man who, for the sake of peace, declares, 'Philip, arrange it, will you please? Good day, Mr Williams.'

That is as close to the heat of the flame as I wish to fly.

I ponder on how the box of incriminating papers could have disappeared from my garret before Pitt's agents arrived? I question my neighbours. A small boy reports seeing a carriage containing two women and a child visit on the evening of the dinner at the Crown and Anchor. I promise him thruppence if he can describe them. The mistress was slight and the maid generous of build. The child she carried was no more than two.

***

Another letter from Peggy which is hard to ignore.

Ned,

I am distracted beyond tolerance. Your poor father is confined to his bed and draws every breath hard as if it would be his last. He knows me not, but calls your name in vain. The children have no shoes and cry with hunger. Part of the cottage wall is falling and I fear that the roof may crush us as we sleep. I am driven to madness by your refusal to play the part of a true husband. Remember 1 Timothy 5:8; 'But if any provide not for his own, and especially for those of his own house, he hath denied the faith, and is worse than an infidel.'

Your loving,

Peggy

It has to be said that she is sometimes given to dramatic exaggeration. I write back telling her to obtain a supporting joist for the roof from William Alexander the carpenter, and enclose a remedy that will ease my father's breathing. I assure her that I will be home as soon as I have been able to collect the last of my outstanding subscriptions.

Word comes from Peggy that my father has died. She did not exaggerate. The box of dangerous papers has been delivered to the cottage. I prepare to journey home.

Part Seven:
Glamorgan
1795 to 1798

1

Books and slavery

I REST IN Bristol. It is not the place I would have chosen, for I despise prosperity built on the blood of Negro slaves. I stop because I have walked the whole distance from London and there is scarcely a half-inch of unbroken skin on my feet.

I derive great relief from a foot bath of red nettles, hemlock and sage which Owen Rees has prepared for me. He laughs as I sigh with pleasure, feeling the caress of the healing herbs. It is good to talk Welsh again. Owen Rees is the eldest son of my old friend Josiah, the minister at Gellionnen in the Swansea Valley. He and his English wife make me their honoured guest, although she understands not a word we say.

The bright vibrant young woman just throws her hands in the air and proclaims, 'Carry on please. I know just how much pleasure Owen gets from being able to speak his language and I would not wish to disrupt in any way. I'll just pretend I understand. Will an occasional smile be enough?'

After a good meal and two large glasses of Bristol port we relate the iniquity of the slave trade. He invites me to attend an anti-slavery lecture the following day. I agree. We discuss his father's Nonconformist ministry and his battles with the mendacious agents of the Established Church. We talk about London. Owen is a bookseller and wants my opinion of London bookshops. I am able to give him a complete review of every shop from the Strand to High Holborn and north beyond Canon Street. He has a shop in Wine Street, Bristol, and a share in Longman

Printers. I am excited to hear of his success. He tells me that there is a huge surge in the number of books available for sale. It is, he tells me, a wonderful time to be a bookseller; the supply of books is unstoppable and the demand is unquenchable.

I have in my purse some thirty-five pounds from the proceeds of my book, and tomorrow I will collect another five as I visit subscribers. Would that be enough, I ask tentatively, to enable me to set up as a bookseller in Cowbridge?

'Is there a competitor, an existing bookseller?'

'Not when I was there last.'

'Would you relish being a bookseller?'

I explain that ideas are my life and to be a bookseller would be a privilege; that my body is weakening; that I had hoped to live from my writing but that appears unlikely. I am a skilled stonemason but my body suffers from asthma, migraine, gout, sciatica, quinsy, rheumatism, kidney stones and occasional melancholy. I would regard the work of running a shop dedicated to the sale of ideas to be a deliverance.

Owen laughs but tells me that I would be the perfect bookseller. Were I to proceed he would be willing to help by recommending suppliers and suggesting stock lines.

***

Attending the anti-slavery lecture means that we must visit the Bristol quay, a place where so many slaves have been held before being shipped to the plantations. I am moved by the experience. The docks are full of ships of many kinds and sizes. The jungle of rigging extends in all directions. On the quays merchants and sailors intermingle on errands of pressing importance. It requires little imagination to reconstruct the scenes of suffering and cruelty that so often occur in these trading houses and in the holds of these vessels.

The Assembly Coffee Shop is civilised and stocked with the finest teas and coffees. The speaker is Samuel Coleridge whom I have already met on several occasions in London. As he speaks I am impressed. From my previous meetings I had judged him to possess a large but meandering intellect, devoid of purpose. Here he speaks with great passion and directness. He castigates the trade and urges all abolitionists to continue to campaign even in the face of such an uncaring government. He points out one way in which those sympathetic to the abolitionist cause could inflict immediate damage on the slave trade despite our failing to win a vote in Parliament. We should refrain from buying slave produced imports: sugars, rum, cotton, dye, cocoa, coffee, pimento, ginger, indigo and mahogany.

He describes cotton and mahogany as the only useful products on the list. All the others fuel the ceaseless quest, by the ostentatious, to create artificial imagined worlds stuffed with expensive, exotic pointless artefacts. Their aim appears to divorce themselves from the beauty and richness of the natural world so freely available to all. I am reminded of the artificiality of the drawing rooms of Mayfair where I strutted like a country cockerel attempting to impress aged peacocks.

He demolishes the usual arguments against abolition and adds another moral dimension. He worries about the degrading moral effect on the crews that man the ships, on the merchants and slavers. It is not just the slaves who are defiled; we are all mentally degraded by this failure of imagination. Our precious imagination is perverted by our isolation from nature. He ends with a piece of his own verse:

... my countrymen! Have we gone forth
And borne to distant tribes slavery and pangs,
And deadlier far, our vices, whose deep taint

With slow perdition murders the whole man,
His body and his soul.

I congratulate him on his address and promise to send him a copy of *Poems, Lyric and Pastoral.* He appears well pleased.

2

A theatrical gesture

'YOU ARE WITHOUT a doubt the worst, most uncaring husband any wife had the misfortune to marry. You take no care of yourself and no care of us. Walking all the way from London – at your age. You could have killed yourself or been killed by any vagabond. You stay away for five years and then just walk through this door as if you'd never been away. You're lucky we're still here. Three or four times we were on the edge of starvation waiting for your promised sovereigns. When they did arrive they were always late and never even enough to pay off what I owed. You just left me begging for more credit just to stay alive.'

Peggy scarcely draws breath. She delivers this tirade whilst moving about the house from the fire to the table, to one child then to the next child, to the window and back to the range.

Then she cries and shouts, 'Ned Williams, you have not dealt fairly with us. You have not!'

At that she collapses into a chair and cries. The children look on silently, waiting to see the outcome of this explosion.

I start to say something but Peggy wails again, 'Children. I should like to introduce you to your father. Yes, you do have a father after all. He's the one that *tad-cu*[44] and I have been worrying about and cursing since any of us can remember.'

Peggy stands up, driven by a fresh impulse.

---

44 Grandfather.

'And now, do you come home with anything in your purse? You wrote again and again how you would be able to sell the copyright on your poetry for a hundred guineas. Did you?'

I did not but I can't resist a theatrical gesture. I take my purse, open it, and pour thirty-five golden sovereigns onto the bare table. The children gasp in amazement. Peggy is determined not to be impressed. She says nothing; then starts counting the coins.

'Nowhere near a hundred is it Ned?'

She stares at the money and then at me in an agony of confusion.

'All my neighbours tell me I should just slam the door in your face; that I would be better off without you.'

'Do you think that?'

A pause.

'Sometimes. Often. Yes! No, I don't. Of course I don't. But I should. Oh, I don't know.'

She looks hard at me.

'But I do know this, Ned Williams. You are *never* going to leave us again as you did this last time, or else we will just not be here when you get back. Understand?'

I plead that I only did what I had to do. That I had to get the poems to publication and it all took longer than anyone could have predicted.

'Ned, your poems were published two years ago.'

'And then there was the collection of subscriptions and...'

'Ned, I don't want to hear another word. You have not dealt fairly with us and that's the end of it.'

But Peggy doesn't end there.

'And your poor old father hoping to see his eldest son for one last time before he wheezed his last. And after everything he did for you, particularly when you were in gaol. Took years off him, the work he did then.'

My father is buried next to my mother in the churchyard

at Coychurch. She has a small simple stone. He has nothing but a poor wooden cross to mark the spot. It's not even good hardwood and will rot away in a year or so. I will inscribe a good new headstone for both of them.

I do what sons do over their fathers' graves. I tell him how I tried and how I'm sorry I never quite achieved those things he hoped I might achieve. I thank him for his love. I remember, but don't mention, the blows, the unpredictable, wild outbursts of temper. I wonder how alike we are... we were? I envy him his place at my mother's side once more.

It is raining. I'm pleased it rains. I can feel the water trickle down my face, making the tears I cannot shed.

***

What to do with the tin box of 'incriminating papers'? I cannot bring myself to burn them but I have to hide them somewhere where spies and magistrates will not think of looking. I send them to Thomas Evans, a newly-ordained Unitarian minister in Brechfa, rural Carmarthenshire. He is a trusted friend and passionate radical. I tell him to keep the box sealed for fear of his being contaminated with liberal ideas.

I make my proposal to Peggy. I do not believe I can return to the life of a journeyman mason and, in any case, she does not want me to roam too far again. There will be some money to come from the book, but not enough to live on. I propose using the bulk of the money to establish a small bookshop in Cowbridge, preferably in the High Street. I repeat to Peggy all the things that I was told in Bristol about the flourishing nature of the trade. Every town will soon have a bookshop which will be regarded as indispensable as the butcher or the baker. No one has yet thought of starting one in Cowbridge, so this is the perfect opportunity to establish a small business that will sustain us in our later years. It is an excellent prospect but I assure her that the final decision is hers.

Peggy nods her head thoughtfully.

'Do you think people will be prepared to buy from you?'

'Why ever not?'

'Because, Ned, people round here are slow to forgive and there are plenty who enjoy giving you a bad name.'

I start to protest.

'Ned, it's true! I know it, even if you do not. And it's not just people with old grudges. Since the war started people have become very watchful for anyone they believe to be against the King or for the Frenchies. Lots of local boys have been persuaded to join the Volunteers and they march up and down in red uniforms singing 'God Save the King' and threatening anyone they think may be a Jacobin. Do you know they even burnt a stuffed figure of Thomas Paine in Cardiff to show how everyone hated him and his ideas? And, there are plenty of rumours about that you were a friend of his and whilst in London you became a dangerous Jacobin firebrand.'

'Not true. At least I'm no Jacobin.'

'I'm glad to hear it, although you know well enough that the truth is no defence when people have made up their minds. Ned, you have to promise me faithfully that you will stay out of gaol – and that means behaving yourself and curbing your tongue even when every instinct in you tells you to proclaim your politics from the rooftops. I give you my blessing to open your bookshop but not to turn it into a hotbed of revolution.'

'Anything else?'

'Plenty. Start with fixing the roof. This cottage has been neglected for too long – like the family inside it.'

3

14 High Street, Cowbridge

As I look about Cowbridge for suitable premises, everything that Peggy warned me about becomes obvious. There are Union flags on several of the buildings and patriotic slogans in windows. It is some time before I catch a glimpse of the red uniforms she mentioned. In truth they are very smart: white breeches and redcoats with proper boots and leggings, handsome soldiers' caps and a flag to lead them. They carry muskets and pikes and have all the outward appearance of an army. They march behind their Captain Beavan who, I am told, was the man who paid for the uniforms.

I recognise several of the boys, the sons of farmers, cowmen, millers and shopkeepers – rural boys from country families who would not wish to attack anyone. I am horrified at the way the uniforms turn these lads into warriors. The boots and leggings make them march with stiff pride and the jackets make their chests push out in a posture of arrogance. They love it. So do their adoring mothers and coy girlfriends. Has anyone told them that we dress troops in red so that their blood will not show whilst they bleed to death?

I find several suitable premises. I am attracted to a vacant shop next to the post office. I could sell stationery items that would compliment their activities. I am refused for no good reason. The agent I contact makes it very clear that my custom is not sought and is not acceptable. No reason is given.

In the end I agree to rent a rather dilapidated premises at 14 High Street near the Town Hall. It is not ideal but will suffice. I have tenure of the shop, a garden, a stable and an outbuilding. The interior will require adaptation but that is easily within my capabilities. The owner, Mr Isaac Skynner, wishes to retain outhouses adjoining Bird Lane to continue his trade as a hatmaker and wishes me to offer his products for sale through the shop. We bargain. He is a deep-voiced, portly Methodist with a permanently red face and an aura of self-importance which does not bode well. We eventually agree a rent of eight pounds a year which is considerably lower than I had projected. I agree to devote a small section of the shop to his hats and take responsibility for the external maintenance. We shake hands and part contented.

To set up a new shop is very public work. Passers-by peer in at the windows as I build a new counter, fit shelves, paint, saw and hammer. Most are content to read the temporary notice announcing that 'the finest books, quality stationery and the choicest teas will soon be available here'. Mostly they move on but a few insist on attempting conversation through the glass.

I cannot but be pleased when I am disrupted in my building of a new counter by the earthy tones of my old friend William Dafydd shouting through the closed shop door. He is a weaver from Aber-cwm-y-fuwch in Ogmore Vale and a poet of quality. He has much news to share and insists we move to the Horse and Groom to continue with the benefit of refreshments.

I am no longer a drinker but I become inebriated by his humour, his conversation and the beauty of the Welsh language as it flows from his tongue. He is here for a purpose. He has read of the *Gorseddau* I have staged in London and demands, in the most engaging fashion, that a similar event be arranged in Glamorgan. He reminds me that he is a bard of distinction who has won prizes at eisteddfodau throughout Wales but who has never had the privilege of being admitted to the Order of the *Gorsedd*.

I do not need William to urge me to such action but I am overjoyed that the events on Primrose Hill have reverberated down to Aber-cwm-y-fuwch. I tell him that in fairness to my family I must make the new shop my priority but…

'That's why I am here, to help. Iolo, we need you to lead us. If getting your shop open will allow you to attend to matters of the *Gorsedd* sooner than you might otherwise, then I am willing to spend a week here for the purpose.'

In the days that follow I have great reason to be grateful for the nimble fingers and engineering skills of a master weaver as he straightens, fixes, repairs, constructs, modifies, finishes and polishes. Now all I need is the stock to grace the shelves.

Thanks to Owen Rees of Bristol I am able to order an array of books which will delight any of a scholarly or radical persuasion. I have dictionaries, works of philosophy and grammars. I have almanacs, Bibles, prayer books and improving tracts. I long to stock *Rights of Man* but my promise to Peggy forbids it. I do stock books of philosophy; Voltaire, Priestley, Milton, Hume and my favourite, Rousseau's *Julie, ou la nouvelle Héloïse.* I stock magazines not previously seen in Cowbridge including *The Gentleman's Magazine* and *The Critical Review.*

I have a splendid stock of stationery: papers in numerous weights and sizes, envelopes of all dimensions, inks in several hues, crayons in all the colours of the rainbow and sealing wax in black only.

After consideration of the words of young Coleridge, I have

ordered from Mr Read of Tucketts and Fletcher, Bristol, a stock of delightful beverages and fine preserves: sugars, teas, chocolate, cocoa, cinnamon, nutmeg and ginger. Whilst these are not usual in a bookshop, I consider that the produce will have great appeal to those of a sensitive nature; that is, those who share my opposition to slavery. Outside the shop I post a notice that my East Indian sugar is 'uncontaminated with human gore'. All who buy will be invited to add their name to a petition calling on Westminster legislators to, once and for all, renounce this barbarous practice.

I write and distribute a handbill to advertise the shop's opening:

> At Cowbridge the name of Ned Williams appears,
> A shop-keeping bard, having choicest of wares,
> To those that have money, be this understood,
> Ring the bell at his door, he sells ev'ry thing good.

My first week as a shopkeeper is both pleasing and worrying. My small shop is consistently full of the curious and the nosey but I sell less than I hoped. There are the usual annoying ladies who finger everything but buy nothing. I suppose this must be tolerated until I am established. What I will not endure are those who tell me that they will not buy my sugar as they see nothing amiss with cheaper slave-produced sugar which is available twenty yards from my premises. Such people receive a shortened version of Coleridge's brilliant anti-slavery address in Bristol climaxing with my own verses:

> Behold on Affric's beach, alone,
> Yon sire that weeps with bitter moan;
> She, that his life once truly bless'd,
> Is torn for ever from his breast,

And scourged, where British Monarchs reign,
Calls for his aid, but calls in vain.

Paper, ink and sealing wax are my most successful lines.

***

The keeper of the neighbouring shop, a Mr Rich, is taking an extraordinary interest in my activities. As he is a staunch loyalist I suspect malign intent. A Mr Curtis has visited several times showing great interest in books written in support of liberty, but buys nothing. If he is a spy, as I suspect, he is remarkably inept. After each visit he retreats into the shop next door where the pair exchange notes and share information.

Not wishing to disappoint them I place in the shop window the cover of a volume entitled *Rights of Man,* well knowing that Thomas Paine's book is now banned and its possession a treason. Like a fish rising to the fly, Mr Curtis is in my shop the same day, paying five shillings for the volume. Once I have the money and he has the book he reveals himself for what he is. Waving the volume in the air he cries,

'This shall go to Billy Pitt himself.'

He is less than amused when I point out to him that he has just bought a copy of the Bible and that William Pitt probably has one already. He is by turns crestfallen, angry and offensive. He demands his money back and calls me a cheat.

'I am no cheat, sir. In the Bible you will find the best and the dearest rights of man.'

4

Bryn Owain

I AM STANDING on top of Bryn Owain, near a grove of trees, a place which must be the physical centre of Glamorgan. To the south I can see the tower of St Hilary Church and beyond that the Severn Sea and Somerset. To the north the Blaenau, the valleys filling with new industry and governed by satanic ironmasters. This is a very public place, but also a place of remoteness where the soul can speak to the body. The circle and the centre stone at Bryn Owain are simple affairs, little more than pebbles I carried here in my pockets. But it is an assembly of the *Gorsedd*, the first in Wales in modern times.

Around me I have seven bards eager for admission to the order. They are an impressive group. William Dafydd I have known for many years. He is a weaver from Ogmore and an established bard. Thomas Evans is a newly-ordained Unitarian minister from Gwernogau, Carmarthen, who previously sold cloth around the fairs. He is a poet of great intelligence, a man of good character, a fiery preacher and a determined champion of the rights of man. When we discussed which compositions each would recite today, Thomas Evans proposed his translation of '*La Marseillaise*' into Welsh which is, unsurprisingly, full of rousing seditious matter of the kind that could land us both in gaol. It took time and persistence to persuade him to substitute his 'Ode to Liberty'. This remains a rousing piece but refrains from personal attacks on George III.

There are five more, all worthy of note. The youngest at

nineteen is my namesake Edward Williams. He came into the shop two months ago and stood diffidently like a child waiting his turn to recite at a Sunday school concert. He is a tall, good-looking boy with a thick thatch of unruly black hair and strong features. With great formality he asked me to confirm that a young bard needed to be taught by an established master if he is to gain admission to the *Gorsedd*. When I confirmed the fact, he asked there and then to become my bardic pupil. He opened his purse to prove that he had the means to pay.

'When I have been taught all I know by wise men who asked of me no more than hard work and loyalty, how could I possibly charge you for tuition? I will be delighted. It will be a part-repayment to those who taught me. Only, remember this. If I consider you have not the diligence or the ability to reach the standards required, I will not spare your feelings or waste my time further.'

He agreed readily. Since then he has been industrious and displays great promise. There is something very satisfying and symbolic in having a pupil with my own name seeking to inherit my knowledge, but it is also prone to cause confusion. At our first lesson I give him a bardic name, Ifor Bardd Glas, as he is wearing a blue coat. He will today be admitted to the Ovates or learners' group.

I debated whether to repeat my London experiment of inviting the newspapers and decided against it. This group is small and drawn mostly from my own and William Dafydd's circle. I think we should feel more certain of ourselves before opening the group to wider inspection. I did not even put a notice in my shop window. Despite that, we have an audience of some forty, spread in groups along the hillside. They start as silent observers, standing well off from the ceremony but, as Thomas Evans begins his recitation, they separate into those who wish to hear – who inch closer – and those who come to mock, who stay at a good distance and occasionally shout obscenities. There are also some who do not move, standing in twos or threes. Spies? I have told the *Gorsedd* we should always assume the presence of malevolent listeners.

Thomas Evans completes his ode and is admitted to the order under the bardic name of Tomos Glyn Cothi. William Dafydd has chosen Gwilym Glynogwr, William Moses of Merthyr becomes Gwilym Tew Glan Taf and Edward Evan of Aberdare becomes Iorwerth Gwynfardd Morganwg.

I am impressed. This small group has more cohesion than the London *Gorsedd*. We are all men who have a trade, who are self-taught, who feel the Welsh language move inside ourselves like lifeblood. I had prepared an address to them on the reasons for the *Gorsedd* but I quickly realise there is no need. They know that this is a powerful means to preserve the language and our traditional poetic forms. They know that it proves that our traditions are ancient and deserve honour. They know it gives dignity to a nation the English are so prepared to ridicule. They know that through its commitment to equality, peace and fellowship the *Gorsedd* stands for values which are the opposite of the imperial thuggery of George III.

5

Defending the cottage

MARGARET, MY ELDEST daughter, bursts into the shop in the middle of the afternoon in a state of high excitement. She has run the whole four miles from Flemingston without stopping and collapses into a chair unable to speak for lack of breath. I wait anxiously whilst she gathers herself fearing some disaster.

'Men… magistrates at the cottage. Tada, you must come. Mother was doing her best but they won't listen. She bid me run as fast as I could to fetch you.'

'Magistrates? What do they want? If they want me, why don't they come to the shop?'

Margaret has no answers but she takes my hand and pulls me towards the door. I lock the shop and run with her down to the Bear. Whilst I would normally never ride a horse, speed is vital and I fear for my daughter's heart if she were to try and run the whole way back. For a half-guinea the Bear supplies a pony, trap and driver. We gallop back to the cottage at a speed that makes the hedgerows blur.

The cottage is full of neighbours all talking at once. Peggy sits in the middle looking flushed and triumphant. Her old friend Millicent is here with her daughters. As we enter the room they all rise at once to tell the story. I have to shout for calm and ask for one sensible person to speak. Peggy starts to explain but Millicent interrupts.

'You've said quite enough for one day Peggy, best if you rest. Ned, it was like this. About one o'clock…'

'On the dot,' affirms Jane.

'Walter Lloyd the magistrate marches up to the door with another man who said he was a magistrate too…'

'Herbert Evans,' claims another voice.

'… and two special constables. "We're here to search your cottage," they announce. That right, Peggy?'

'You don't know, none of you were here then,' insists Peggy, anxious to regain the narrative. 'Only me and the children doing our chores. They came out with lots of important sounding words "in the name of His Majesty… by the authority vested in me" and words like that and told me to stand aside and let them search the cottage.'

'That's when Mam sent me to get *Modryb*[45] Milly,' chips in Margaret.

'I told them that I didn't care if they came from the King himself, they were not looking through my private things and my husband's things and they could just turn about where they were and think again.'

There is a burst of applause from the rest of the room.

'When I came to see,' added Milly, 'Peggy was standing at the door holding an old broom as if it was a musket and threatening to brain the lot of them.'

Delighted laughter from everyone and Peggy takes the cue, 'I told them that if they wanted to enter my cottage then they were going to have to arrest me first! And that I would not be going peacefully.'

By now Peggy is enjoying the reliving of the story and the applause of her neighbours. Milly takes over again.

'They stood there for five minutes trying to work out what

---

45 Auntie.

was best, whilst your Peggy told them straight. Didn't pause for breath. Just kept on waving her broom and telling them what for.'

'But it was when you all arrived that they took fright. I don't know how to thank you all.'

'If those four men couldn't cope with one woman, then what chance did they have against all of us together?' asks Mary. There is much laughter.

I tell them that I am so proud of my Peggy and so proud of the women of Flemingston that I shall compose an ode in their praise.

'That's the least you should do!' retorts Milly.

***

The neighbours are gone but Peggy remains buoyant with victory.

'Mind you,' she remarks, 'if they could find anything in all these piles of papers and books I'd have been amazed. I sometimes doubt if you know the half of what's here.'

We laugh and embrace. Her tone turns more serious, 'I did the right thing, didn't I, Ned?'

'Oh yes, *fy nghariad*.[46] You certainly did. But if they were to come again you should not put yourself in any danger. There is nothing here that would allow them to accuse me of treason.'

'Are you certain?'

'As certain as a man can be. They cannot gaol a man for believing that kingship is a bad system. They would have to find evidence that I am a direct threat to George III. Anything I have written which might be interpreted so, I have removed and hidden in a large tin box.'

---

46 My love.

'Where, in the shop?'

'Certainly not. They already know every book or periodical in the shop. No, those have been sent well out of harm's way. I promised you I would stay out of gaol and that's a promise I intend to keep.'

A pause is interrupted by a hungry Taliesin demanding food. I tell Peggy how proud I was that the women of the village all rallied to help.

'There's a loyalty amongst us that goes deep, even if some of them think you're a madman.'

'Is that what they call me?'

'Oh a lot worse sometimes, and so do I. But it's not all bad. Milly likes to call you our Bard of Liberty. Something she picked up in the town. When I hear that I still feel very proud of my Ned, despite everything.'

6

Defending the shop

I HAVE ADDED umbrellas, fishing tackle and perfume to my stock, as well as a new shelf of Psalters, Hymnbooks and music manuscript paper. I have also started a library of volumes that may be borrowed for sixpence. I advertise that the shelves will contain only volumes of quality, superior to the usual trash found in subscription libraries. I receive several requests from impecunious parsons to acquire expensive theological works such as the six weighty volumes of ecclesiastical tracts published by the Bishop of Llandaff. This is an expense I had not anticipated.

My reassurance to Peggy was not an empty boast. I have no hesitation in openly proclaiming my views, but stop short of any treasonous sedition that would land me in gaol. I have become expert at knowing where the line lies and rejoice in treading right up to the point of danger, but never over. My shop remains full. I meet the most interesting people, attracted by my reputation. Some travel from considerable distances to talk reform, politics, theology and to take tea. They mostly buy small pamphlets.

Unfortunately, the shop's growing reputation has earned the ill will of many King and Country loyalists, particularly the wealthier burghers of Cowbridge. At first some of these enter the shop to challenge me face to face. I am always happy to engage in debate, and after receiving several intellectual drubbings they do not return. Some descend to simple abuse. These receive in reply a premature obituary designed to stun them into silence. Two days ago I penned this response to a troublesome customer:

> Here lies deceas'd a guzzling beast
> Who burst his paunch by drinking,
> A wenching blade – a Rake by Trade,
> His name was Davy Jenkin.
> He, down his guts whole pipes and butts
> So speedily would pour
> That Cowbridge ale grew never stale
> Had never time to sour.

Those who wish me ill have evidently turned to more covert means to undermine my business. They intimidate those with whom they have influence. Landlords tell their tenants they would be wise to buy their ink and paper elsewhere. Unexpected competition arises. The apothecary has taken to stocking papers, nibs and ink. I suspect this unlikely diversification from selling pills to be a suggestion of his landlord.

My own landlord, Isaac Skynner, has transformed from a tolerable business partner to an aggressive adversary. In our original agreement he maintained the use of several buildings to the rear of the shop for the purpose of continuing his hat-making business. For some time this went well but, at short notice, he gave up the business and removed all his furniture and fittings, including the stove, from the section he used. A week later he sent in a pair of men to remove the locks, take the glass from the windows and totally demolish an outbuilding adjoined to my shop, leaving me with the necessity of spending considerable sums to make the premises once more secure against thieves and the elements. He has now issued letters threatening to take me to court because of my failure to properly maintain the premises in accord with our agreement.

Such actions are not to his financial benefit. He is inspired by the malevolence of others.

I refuse to be cowed but it is becoming clear that I am not earning the income I anticipated. I look to supplement my income by applying for a commission to write a report on the agriculture of south Wales for the Board of Agriculture. I know more about the topography, geography, and farming practices of Glamorgan than any man living. It would be a splendid opportunity to reveal the poor husbandry of so many farmers. I spend much time making my application and including a sample report. I take time out of the shop to write a piece that is of a quality far higher than anything they have seen before. My application is rejected out of hand. With reason, I suspect that my submission was blocked by my enemies in high places. I am aware that Richard Crawshay, the tyrannical ironmaster of Merthyr, has done me the compliment of branding me a Jacobin and a dangerous seller of seditious books. He is a vindictive man of great influence.

I receive a letter from William Owen who tells me that many of our fellow radicals have 'gone to ground' fearing persecution. He berates me, for the sake of my family. I could have told 'a few small lies' to have helped my case to the Board of Agriculture. Others warn me of putting myself in the way of those who would do me harm, particularly the devil Crawshay who is known in the Blaenau as 'Moloch, the Iron King'.

7

Tomos Glyn Cothi

Tomos Glyn Cothi has been arrested on a charge of sedition. I receive a letter from him imploring my assistance. He will appear before the Court of Great Sessions in Carmarthen. How could I possibly decline? I lock the shop, post an apology and head west.

Tomos has been a close friend since I took up the Unitarian cause. We share a sense of humour and a love of scurrilous satirical rhymes. It was to him that I entrusted the tin box of incendiary writing that was best kept out of official sight. On my last visit to his home in Brechfa he entertained me with his Welsh translation of 'La Marseillaise'. In the spirit of bardic competition I replied with an English version. These we sang lustily in the private confines of his kitchen. Both versions contained enough ingenious suggestions of how to inflict discomfort on the person of the King to consign us both to Botany Bay. He should be as aware as I of the dangers of repeating such performances within earshot of enemies. This time he appears to have trusted one person too many.

I find him in a cold damp gaol cell, looking unshaven and dejected. He is an untidy character at the best of times and his short round frame squats on the cold stone bench like a bag of dirty laundry. I have a real sense of dread as they close and lock the cell door behind me. This is one place I do not wish to spend another night. Tomos assures me repeatedly that he has remained careful.

'I'm totally innocent, Iolo. You must believe me. I never sang the verses they accuse me of singing – at least not then. Only when I'm with you.' He looks at me as if seeking absolution, then adds in a ministerial voice, 'Innocence is my shield.'

'Who accuses you?'

He shakes his head sadly and grimaces before replying, 'Well that's the most unholy thing about the business, one of my own parishioners, George Thomas shoemaker. He's been criticised by some of the elders before and I've had to have words with him about non-attendance and not helping to maintain the chapel as we expect all the faithful to do. He's obviously nurtured a grudge. You know how grudges can grow in chapel communities.'

'Maybe, or maybe he's a spy, a man paid to hear what he now swears he heard. Who else was there?'

'Oh plenty, about fifteen in all attending a *cwrw bach*[47] to help old John Roberts who's without a shilling to his name. A good evening it was too. The beer was good. I told a ghost story. There were recitations. We had a goose to raffle and a fiddler to help the singing along.'

'Were you drunk?'

'Of course! But not so that I didn't know what I was doing – or singing.'

'What are they accusing you of singing?'

'"*La Carmagnole*," the French song you wrote new words to.'

My hair prickles and a cold tremor runs down my spine.

'My song!'

'Yes. I'm afraid so… but they don't seem to know it's yours. By now I think lots of people have heard it, learnt it and no one

---

47 A tradition of the eighteenth and nineteenth centuries in south Wales by which 'small beer' would be brewed for sale and consumption at an evening of song and recitation in the house of a family in need. The family would receive the proceeds.

knows where it started. Apart from me. It's the fourth verse they are accusing me of singing. You know…'

He does not sing but whispers the words for fear:

… And when upon the British shore
The thundering guns of France shall roar,
Vile George shall trembling stand,
Or flee his native land
With terror and appal,
Dance Carmagnole, dance Carmagnole.

'So this man, George Thomas, says you did sing it, but there are witnesses who can say you did not?'

'Absolutely.'

'Can you give me their names?'

Tomos has no problem listing all present and giving me directions to their houses. Before I leave I ask, 'Tomos, the box of papers I bid you keep safe. Where is it?'

He tells me that it is safe enough hidden in his barn.

Have the constables searched his house?

Not yet.

I feel a sweat breaking. I came here to save Tomos. I must also save myself. I set off at once to gather statements and collect my box.

***

Abraham Jones is a miller with a big heart. He is outraged at the arrest of Tomos who he describes as 'a man of God and servant of his people'. He was present at the *cwrw bach* in the cottage of old John Roberts. He claims to have drunk more than any other man there, to have sung louder than any and still been able to walk in a straight line all the way home. He is incandescent with rage that any man should seek to 'make trouble' for the minister by lying in this fashion. He speaks very little English, so I take a statement which I translate into English and which he signs.

This procedure is repeated with four farm labourers, the smith, a gardener and a cowhand. Their stories are all similar and no one remembers Tomos singing the verse concerned. They are of one in considering that George Thomas is lying. Some hint that there might be 'other persons' guiding his actions. Brechfa is a totally Welsh-speaking village. I think the court will be bound to accept that even if Tomos had wanted to entertain his audience with a treasonous song, there is no reason why he should choose to sing in English.

Tomos perks up considerably when I report my findings and show him the sets of signed statements I have collected. I leave him several books to help him fill the days between now and the trial. The Courts of the Great Sessions will not convene in Carmarthen for some months. I visit his home to support his wife. The tin box is sent back to Cowbridge by carrier. It is proving harder to conceal than I had ever imagined.

***

Peggy is furious. She is convinced that I will be imprisoned alongside Tomos. She berates me for associating myself with his case. If he is condemned, then certainly I will be too?

'You promised me you would stay out of prison.'

'And so I shall.'

'So you say! What, pray, is this?'

The tin box has been delivered ahead of me. She stands with an outstretched arm pointing at it as evidence of a great crime. Does she know its contents? I had previously told her of its existence. Has it been opened? At a glance I cannot tell, but decide not to risk deception. I admit its substance, confess its danger and explain how I had to remove it from Brechfa for fear of detection. Peggy shrieks with outrage.

'So you send it here, where it will not condemn your friend but rather yourself, your wife and your children!'

She paces the kitchen whilst I stand mute and still as a guilty schoolboy. She harangues and scolds.

'Have you no thought for us Ned? Have you no thought for me? Oh, I have been sorely tried. I have been cruelly misused. I warned you that you could go too far and you take no notice. Well this time you will do as I say or I will be done with you for ever.'

I fear she means it. She bids me leave the tin box in her care. I beg her not to burn the contents. That would be to destroy my posterity. She tells me the papers will be stored where only posterity will ever glimpse them. I do not understand and she does not explain.

She demands more of me. She wants me to promise that I will not defend Tomos in court. I meekly agree. That decision is already made. Tomos himself tactfully suggested that to be represented by me might, in the eyes of the judge and jury, be proof of his revolutionary intentions.

Her third demand is more difficult.

'You need to do something which will show people you're not as wild and dangerous as people think.'

She has a scheme.

'People are very proud of the Volunteers. It's not political really. It's just that all of them are local boys, so nearly everyone has a son or nephew or boyfriend involved and they do look so good in those red uniforms. I want you to write a song for them – something spirited and bold.'

I start pointing out that it is hard to remain a bard of peace whilst praising an army. They may be local boys but their muskets are real. Peggy is unyielding.

I protest, 'I am not willing to do anything which goes against my beliefs. I will not pretend to be what I am not. I will certainly not pretend to be a royalist.'

***

For a week my head has been filled with thoughts as to how I may do as my Peggy wishes. Now we sit outside the cottage and I read my song to her with all its spirited cadences and trumpeting choruses. When I finish she looks at me with a bemused air. Does it do as she demands? I explain that the song praises the Volunteers as opposing all enemies who 'would Britons enthral'. I praise them not as the violent servants of a rapacious bloodthirsty king but as the proud descendants of the ancient Silurians, of the great Caractacus, of Ifor Bach and Morgan ap Hywel defending a free Welsh people against any oppression, be it by Romans, Normans, Saxons or Danes. That way I am praising the 'Sons of Glamorgan', of Britain's old race – that is the Welsh – not defending an imperial Britishness that seeks to subsume all the Celtic nations into an English Britishness.

Peggy looks confused. She breathes deeply and laughs. 'Ned, I do not understand all your Britishnesses, but the song is beautiful. Perfect.'

'Even though it contains not one word of praise for the King nor damns the French?'

'I didn't notice. Neither will anyone else. Thank you Ned. I know how much that cost you.'

I even earn a kiss.

***

'Song for the Glamorgan Volunteers' is a great success. Peggy distributes copies to all of Cowbridge. As she suspected no one looks too closely at the words since they sound stirring enough. No one appears to notice the promise that in victory the Volunteers would 'spare the conquered'. The Volunteers sing lustily. Business improves.

I ask tentatively about the tin box of seditious papers. Peggy tells me that they are safe. A 'friend', who I assume to be Milly, although she denies complicity, has sent the sealed box by carrier to the farm of a distant cousin somewhere in a distant part of England. I am not to know where. It is to be stored in an attic with the command that it shall not to be opened for a hundred years. Posterity may claim it but I shall never see it again.

***

At last the date of Tomos' trial is fixed. To my delight I find that the judge is to be George Hardinge, Senior Justice of the Brecknock circuit. My pleasure is based on the knowledge that he acquired six sets of my *Poems, Lyric and Pastoral*. He has a reputation as a man of letters, has written several articles for *The Gentleman's Magazine* and a study of Chatterton and the Rowley poems. I anticipate that his refinement and sensitivity will make him sympathetic to a man of Christian learning such as Tomos. The defendant sits in the dock. He is not a tall man and the two large officials who flank him make him appear shorter.

I will play no part in proceedings as promised, but I sit alongside John Prior Estlin, a Unitarian minister from Bristol who collected all the testimonies and briefed the London barristers who will act for the defence. They sit robed and bewigged in the front, shuffling papers uncertainly. The Carmarthen Guildhall is not large but it has elegant oak panelling and good headroom. A tall bench constructed for the occasion gives the judge the authority of one who speaks from on high. A fine chandelier adds to the sense that he sits in celestial realms. As Judge George Hardinge enters the court we all rise. I suppress a ludicrous desire to call to him. I did consider writing to him before the trial to establish a bond based on our love of literature and his support for my poems. I did not do so, lest this be judged an attempt to interfere with due process, but I still nurse the hope that he will have a copy of my work in his luggage and might be casting an inquisitive eye around for Iolo Morganwg.

When he addresses the court I am sorely disappointed. My assumption of sympathy is instantly dispelled. From his elevated position he looks down on us as an eagle surveying a nest of impudent sparrows. He makes clear in his opening remarks that the courts have a loyal duty to protect the realm from anarchy and rebellion and he looks to the jury to play their part in ridding the land of disobedient species. He continues in this prejudicial fashion providing the star witness for the prosecution all the time in the world to repeat his lies. He encourages George Thomas to repeat his testimony like a pet parrot for no apparent reason other than to better impress his perjury on the minds of the jury. Tomos makes the mistake of shouting 'liar' from the dock, for which he is seriously pecked by the Great Eagle on high.

When it comes to the defence, things start to go further awry. As the lead barrister rises to present the sworn testimony of my witnesses, the prosecution objects to each one in turn on the grounds that whilst all had been present at the *cwrw bach*, they had not been present at the time when the words are alleged to have been uttered! The defence barristers are chickens in a panic, and I am a depressed owl. The people I interviewed were all most anxious to testify to defend Tomos but, out of a total of fifteen, it slowly emerges that only three were entitled to be more than character witnesses. The Great Eagle rustles his plumage in annoyance and sharpens his talons. For an agonising half-hour the hawks of the prosecution disqualify twelve of the witnesses, striking out their evidence with deadly aim.

The miller was most certainly at the *cwrw bach* all evening and boasted the hangover to prove it. He is sworn. He is asked to give an account of the meeting and starts to do so – but in Welsh. The Great Eagle lets out a fearsome squawk and insists that in a British court of law testimony has to be given in King's English. The miller glances up at the fearsome hooked beak that threatens him. He tries, but he has little English. We watch as his confidence crumbles away and his words shrivel to a squawk.

In desperation he looks around the court, summons up the best of his vocabulary and shouts,

'Tomos. A good man he is!'

The prosecuting hawks and the Great Eagle find this greatly amusing and, as he cannot be eaten, the miller is dismissed.

Both the remaining witnesses fare slightly better, having just enough English to make statements asserting that Tomos did not sing any song in English and certainly not the one of which he is accused. The bench appears unimpressed and even disinterested.

In his summing up the Great Eagle casts serious doubt on the truth of the two allowable defence witnesses, given the obvious attempts by the defence to deceive and frustrate the court. He reminds the jury of their duty to defend George III, the most innocent and the best man in the kingdom. He suggests as a dissident, a Unitarian and an enemy of the Church of England, Tomos is trebly guilty. Just in case any jurist remained uncertain of how he should cast his vote, they are told that the accused is a man of dangerous character.

Having treated the court with total disdain, the Great Eagle now proceeds to rip each heart into shreds. He strikes and tears at the cowering body and mind of Tomos, sentencing him to two years imprisonment. The great bird of prey glories in his cruelty, adding that each year Tomos should be placed in the public pillory where the crows and jackals may pile filth upon his head and hurl abuse at his beliefs.

Judge George Hardinge takes wing, content with having struck fear in the hearts of another dangerous nest of rebellious sparrows.

This small bird stays sitting in the court long after the crowd has flown. I am terrified. Let me admit it to myself. I am terrified for Tomos, for his wife and six children, for my family, for myself, for all of us who would stand in the way of this tyranny but are helpless to confront the forces of a ruthless, vengeful state with no weapons other than our beliefs. Where do beliefs get us? Like Tomos, a place in the pillory to be abused by any lout who can drink the King's shilling?

What is the alternative? To lie to your soul? To be damned?

So many others have been imprisoned, exiled or deported. So many who once espoused brave words have retreated into the safe tent of conformity. So many who tried, like me, to be cleverer than the storm, have fallen.

I grip the seat before me and stare to the oak as if it bore the words of the prophet. There is no other way! We will use what liberty we have to build foundations for tomorrow. The Unitarians in Wales must group together to support each other. The *Gorsedd* must continue to meet whatever the persecution. That is where I will preserve my truth. They cannot condemn us for reciting poetry in strict metre.

Gorsedd Glynogwr
1798

THIS CEREMONY IS long. We have four new initiates and a number of substantial odes to be delivered. I wondered if the cordon of magistrates, constables and Glamorgan Volunteers would retire once we start but the magistrates give no such order. They plainly hope to witness or hear something which they can use against us. The clouds have moved away and the sun is asserting its power. For two hours on a hot sunny day the magistrates and their men stand sweating in their smart clothes and woollen uniforms. The *Gorsedd* often attracts an audience of the friendly, the curious and the haphazardly hostile, but this is different. At first it feels as if every word we use is being weighed and judged by a uniformed jury of half-a-hundred.

The ceremony of sheathing the sword provides some anxiety, lest they mistake our symbolic actions as threatening. No mistakes are made and I detect no reaction, although several of the magistrates are in discussion. We read from the psalms and sing a hymn. The hymn is well known and some of the watchers might have been expected to join in had goodwill been evident. None do so.

I start the process of inviting candidates for initiation to step forward. Ifor Bardd Glas is today being admitted as a Bard of Privilege. He declaims his ode '*Cartref*'.[48] It is a fine

---

48 Home.

piece with much moving sentiment telling of the love of a young man for his home, his hearth and the woods and fields he played in as a child. He delivers it well, but not just to me and his fellow bards. He is projecting the verse in his strong youthful voice out to the circle of watchers. Some shoulders appear to relax. Some of the Volunteers exchange comments which I cannot hear, but their manner does not suggest displeasure. Whilst Walter Lloyd, the magistrate in charge, makes a snobbish virtue of his ignorance of Welsh, many of his fellow magistrates and most of the men under his command will speak the language. Ifor Bardd Glas is using the verse to plead with the circle of watchers. He knows many of them as young men of his own age. To Ifor, this is a proclamation of all things good and important and Welsh. He offers his verse unconditionally to all who love Wales and who value the things that make Wales different.

I recall so many occasions when I have looked down from a platform and read the signals of how spectators react. This circle of watchers has softened into an audience. Young Ifor has turned the tables so that now we are commanding their emotions. Not all, of course. Walter Lloyd is unaffected but he cannot see what I see; that around him, his men are warming to an appeal to their childhood memories and their mother tongue. They are loosening their jackets and their stern military countenances as they savour the verse. Walter Lloyd has one of his fellow magistrates translating as we proceed.

Next, Evan Evans, Ton-coch, Aberdare, delivers his *cywydd* calling on Satan to leave this world and retreat with all his minions back to the lower depths. This is not *Paradise Lost* but it uses Welsh of great beauty and has many touches of humour, including several references to the red-hot farts of the fallen angel. Some of the watchers laugh and there is much explanation. Walter Lloyd realises that a slackness has entered his ranks. He moves along the line restoring discipline, but in the absence of any galvanising action the morale stiffening does not last.

The hillside is our friend, as is the increasing heat of the day. I always choose remote places for *Gorsedd* meetings because I believe that in the open air the soul is freer to listen. Kings, judges and magistrates prefer palaces and courts built as theatre settings to demonstrate their importance. Out here, all the paraphernalia of uniform, ermine robes, and big hats appear pointless. In the presence of nature we are all as naked as children and as equal as one sparrow to another.

William Moses is next to recite. He offers a series of *englynion* teaching moral principles. Then we have an ode on great British victories. This last is loaded with ironies which fortunately do not translate. It is now my turn to mount the *Gorsedd* stone and deliver the promised ode. I could not have chosen a piece of verse more calculated to annoy Walter Lloyd: '*Breintiau Dyn*' or *Rights of Man*. Not for the first time I tease Walter Lloyd with a work that might be the famous seditious tract by the banned Thomas Paine – but is actually a deceptively gentle passage of my own devising.

O! Pam, frenhinoedd byd,
Ymelwch cwyn cyd
Mewn poethder gwŷn?
Clywch orfoleddus gainc!
Mae'r gwledydd oll fal Ffrainc
Yn rhoddi'r orsedd fainc
I freintiau dyn.

Gorfoledd! Cwyn dy lais!
Cwymp holl deyrnasoedd trais!
Maent ar eu crŷn.

Cawn deyrnas hardd ei gwedd,
Dan farn Tywysog Hedd,
Yn honno cwyn o'r bedd
Holl freintiau dyn.[49]

Walter and his magistrates are in conference again, simultaneously translating and dissecting the verse. I half expect them to ask me to repeat it in case they missed anything. What do they ask? Am I foreseeing the advent of the kingdom of heaven or inciting the destruction of the kingship of George III? Would what they think they heard stand up in court?

By now most of the watchers are seated on the grass. Jackets are unbuttoned. I see John Roberts, Millicent's boy. What does all of this mean to him? He's a big strong lad, although not the brightest. Not one to ask questions but usually content to go the way all the others go. He's drifted into the Volunteers because of the free beer and the easy camaraderie. Maybe he now has a choice.

Maybe now the Welsh have a choice as well, an alternative to the oppression of the Union Jack, a path that can lead instead to a nation at peace, valuing freedom, fraternity and the word of the Lord above all else.

I am content with my creation. My truth against the world. Let us see what the world will make of it.

---

49 Why, you kings who reign / Raise you such stir, / Such cries of pain? / Just listen to the voices blown / Across the sea from France, / Where planted on the highest throne / The rights of man.

Exultation fills the air / As tyrants fall / In grim despair. / Ours is a world of calm divine / Beneath the Prince of Peace / Whose resurrection will enshrine / All rights of man.

Historical note

I OLO MORGANWG LIVED for another twenty-eight years after the Glynogwr *Gorsedd* which ends this account. He devoted the remainder of his life to an inspired confusion of activities and causes. To avoid official harassment Iolo travelled to Dinorwig, north Wales, to stage his next *Gorsedd* in 1799. Continuing persecution explains a long respite before a revival of the tradition at the celebrated 'Rocking Stone' *Gorseddau* in Pontypridd in 1814. In 1819, in a ceremony at the Ivy Bush Hotel, Carmarthen, he succeeded in uniting the National Eisteddfod and the *Gorsedd*.

In the early years of the nineteenth century he devoted enormous energies to campaigning and organising on behalf of the Unitarians who, arguably, became the other cause which allowed him to spread radical political thought under the cloak of activities less open to official attack. Iolo's response to the imprisonment of Tomos Glyn Cothi spurred him on to establish a Unitarian association in south Wales. He worked tirelessly for this cause, writing pamphlets, letters and whole volumes of hymns, at one point adopting the title 'Bard to the Theo-Unitarian Society'.

He remained a campaigner, not only for the big causes he held dear, such as the abolition of slavery, but for individuals he believed had been wronged. He fought the cases of orphans whom the parish failed to support, labourers ill-treated by their employers, the underdogs and the downtrodden wherever he found them. He organised successful petitions to save the lives of men sentenced to death for minor crimes. He intervened with local magistrates on behalf of the poor and the oppressed.

Unsurprisingly, his shop in Cowbridge failed, as did all his previous business ventures. He was forced to return to life as an itinerant stonemason despite the increasing frailty of his body. He and Peggy were saved from total penury by the generosity of several local benefactors who joined together to provide him with a pension in later years. In his old age he became something of a celebrity as 'the venerable bard of Glamorgan'. His cottage received a stream of visitors; poets, antiquarians and researchers of all kinds, anxious to tap the apparently fathomless depths of his knowledge.

He continued to research and write on all sorts of topics; religion, agriculture, history, botany, architecture and, of course, Bardism. He filled the cottage in Flemingston with a vast archive of unsorted books and manuscripts. His son, Taliesin, became his father's loyal archivist. His daughters, Margaret and Ann, lived quiet lives, at one point jointly opening a milliner's shop in Cefn Cribwr which was no more successful than any of their father's business ventures.

Iolo died in December 1826, aged seventy-nine. He is buried beneath the floor of the church in Flemingston. The grave is unmarked but there is a fine monument to his memory on the church wall. Peggy died only weeks later. Their cottage in Flemingston does not survive but his papers were jealously protected by his son and are now preserved within an archive of great size and complexity at the National Library of Wales in Aberystwyth.

The tradition of the *Gorsedd* grew steadily during the nineteenth century. By the time of the Llangollen Eisteddfod of 1858, it had become a national pageant of epic proportions. It grew further in popularity to become a popular symbol of Welsh national identity, Welsh culture and Welsh language, reaching its apogee in the glorious festivals of the 1890s.

In the twentieth century Iolo's forgeries were gradually revealed through the forensic scholarship of G.J. Williams. A section of Welsh academia felt disgraced at having been unconscious collaborators in his fabrications for over a century.

Sir John Morris-Jones reacted with venom, 'It will probably be a long time before our literature and history will be cleansed of the stains of his soiled hands.'

The *Gorsedd* lost credibility and editions of Dafydd ap Gwilym's poetry shrank in size.

This partly explains why Iolo Morganwg became a name familiar to every Welsh person, but about whom little was taught or known. He remains to some a black sheep of the Welsh family; a topic best avoided in case of embarrassment.

A new generation of historians have painstakingly sorted, catalogued and ordered the vast archive he left and have reappraised his contribution. The seven-year project entitled 'Iolo Morganwg and the Romantic Tradition in Wales, 1740–1918' came to an end in 2008. All his surviving correspondence was published in a weighty three-volume edition. In a series of six more volumes the project sought to 'explain how this flawed genius constructed a complex historical and creative synthesis in his vision of the history and significance of Wales'. The general editor of the series and author of *Bard of Liberty* was Professor Geraint H. Jenkins.

Iolo's greatest legacy is certainly the *Gorsedd* of Bards which proclaims each National Eisteddfod and conducts its major ceremonies. To many, the *Gorsedd* is now little more than a picturesque ceremonial in which ordained ministers and TV personalities dress up and play pagan for the day. To others, it still enshrines values which remain fundamental to a distinctive Welsh identity: equality, pacifism, scholarship, democracy, religious tolerance, kinship with nature, and joy in the beauty of the Welsh language.

Bibliography

My grateful thanks to the Centre for Advanced Welsh and Celtic Studies, University of Wales, who, for seven years from 2001, undertook the gargantuan task of ordering and editing Iolo Morganwg's correspondence, bringing order to his enormous archive at the National Library of Wales and producing a series of scholarly re-evaluations of his role and historical significance. Geraint H. Jenkins and Mary-Ann Constantine directed the project under the banner, 'Iolo Morganwg and the Romantic Tradition in Wales, 1740–1918'. I have drawn liberally on their work through the volumes listed below. All are published by University of Wales Press, apart from *Iolo Morganwg y Gweriniaethwr* which is published by the Centre for Advanced Welsh and Celtic Studies at the National Library of Wales.

- *A Rattleskull Genius: The Many Faces of Iolo Morganwg*, edited by Geraint H. Jenkins (2005).
- 'A Very Horrid Affair: Sedition and Unitarianism in the Age of Revolutions', by Geraint H. Jenkins (2004).
- *Bard of Liberty: The Political Radicalisation of Iolo Morganwg*, by Geraint H. Jenkins (2012).
- *Bardic Circles: National, Regional and Personal Identity in the Bardic Vision of Iolo Morganwg*, by Cathryn A. Charnell-White (2007).
- *Iolo Morganwg y Gweriniaethwr*, by Geraint H. Jenkins. (2010).

- *The Correspondence of Iolo Morganwg*, edited by Geraint H. Jenkins, Ffion Mair Jones & David Ceri Jones (2007).
- *The Literary and Historical Legacy of Iolo Morganwg 1826–1926*, by Marion Löffler (2007).
- *The Truth against the World: Iolo Morganwg and Romantic Forgery*, by Mary-Ann Constantine (2007).

Other sources

- *Ackermann's Illustrated London*, by Fiona St Aubyn, Augustus Pugin, Thomas Rowlandson & Rudolph Ackermann (1985).
- *Bro Morgannwg*, by Aneirin Talfan Davies (1972 & 1976).
- *Cerddi Rhydd Iolo Morganwg*, edited by P.J. Donovan (1981).
- *Cowbridge Buildings and People*, edited by Jeffrey Alden (1999).
- *Diwylliant Gwerin Morgannwg*, by Allan James (2002).
- *Echoes of Old Cowbridge*, edited by Brian James (2011).
- 'Eighteenth-century literary forgeries with special reference to the work of Iolo Morganwg', by Gwyneth Lewis. Unpublished thesis, Bodleian Library, Oxford University (1991).
- *Hanes Gorsedd y Beirdd*, by Geraint & Sonia Bowen (1991).
- *Iolo Morganwg*, by Ceri W. Lewis (1995).
- *Iolo Morganwg: Bard of Liberty*, by Islwyn ap Nicholas (1945).
- *The Life of Samuel Johnson*, by James Boswell (1791).
- *London in the Eighteenth Century*, by Jerry White (2012).
- *Old Inns & Alehouses of Cowbridge*, edited by Jeffrey Alden (2003).
- *The Diary of William Thomas, 1762–1795*, edited by R.T.W. Denning (1995).

Thanks

My grateful thanks:

- To Eifion Jenkins for his creative insight and his faith in this project.
- to Lefi Gruffudd and the staff of Y Lolfa (Fflur Arwel, Carolyn Hodges, Meleri Wyn James, Alun Jones and Eirian Jones) for their skill and patience.
- to those who have read drafts and provided criticism: Mary-Ann Constantine, Emyr Edwards, Jon Gower, Brian James, Ann C. Jones, Shân Mererid, Stephen Sheedy, Guy Slater, John Stephens and Ewa Thomas.